Praise for

JACK CAMPBELL

and His Stunning Science Fiction Novels

"An excellent blend of real science and space action. I enjoyed myself thoroughly from first to last page."
—Brandon Sanderson, *New York Times* bestselling author of the Stormlight Archive

"Campbell builds compelling characters and surrounds them with authentic details of skirmishes in space, on the ground, and everywhere in between that make this adventure a page-turner of the first order." —Booklist

"Fans of David Weber, Ian Douglas, and John Scalzi should find plenty here to enjoy." —SFRevu

"Jack Campbell's *Vanguard* starts a new series with a bang. I can't wait to get my hands on the next installment!"
—Taylor Anderson, *New York Times* bestselling author of the Destroyermen series

"Strong characters, complex politics on multiple worlds, battles against impossible odds, this book has the whole package."
—Elizabeth Moon, Nebula Award–winning author of *Into the Fire*

"Combines the best parts of military SF and grand space opera." —*Publishers Weekly*

"Campbell's genius is action in space." —Tor.com

ASCENDANT

JACK CAMPBELL

ACE
New York

ACE
Published by Berkley
An imprint of Penguin Random House LLC
1745 Broadway, New York, NY 10019

ISBN: 9781101988398

Ace hardcover edition / May 2018
Ace mass-market edition / April 2019

Printed in the United States of America
1 3 5 7 9 10 8 6 4 2

Cover illustration by Jaime Jones
Cover design by Katie Anderson

ΛCKNOWLEDGMENTS

I remain indebted to my agent, Joshua Bilmes, for his ever-inspired suggestions and assistance, and to my editor, Anne Sowards, for her support and editing. Thanks also to Robert Chase, Kelly Dwyer, Carolyn Ives Gilman, J. G. (Huck) Huckenpohler, Simcha Kuritzky, Michael LaViolette, Aly Parsons, Bud Sparhawk, and Constance A. Warner for their suggestions, comments, and recommendations.

CHAPTER 1

Billions of years before, a star much like the one humans called Sol had formed, nuclear fires igniting to warm a bevy of planets, asteroids, and comets orbiting its mass. Millions of years ago, the star, its fuel dwindling, had gone nova, hurling its outer layers into space and ravaging the worlds that had once orbited it. No longer a nuclear furnace, the star still glowed with bright white light created by the heat of its collapse into a sphere the size of a world like Earth. Over the course of another billion years, the star would expend that heat and gradually cool.

Humanity arrived, in ships that needed the mass of stars to create jump points allowing those ships to cross light years of distance in a few weeks. The star was given a name, Jatayu, but with only a few battered rocks still circling it, humans went onward to other stars that still warmed worlds where men and women could find new homes. Jatayu was nothing but a waypoint, a place the ships of humans had to go through to get to places they wanted to go.

But one day some humans came to stay. They brought a small outpost that they placed in orbit about the white dwarf star and claimed ownership of Jatayu.

Billions of years after its birth, war followed humanity to the small, bright star.

"Leaving jump space at Jatayu in five . . . four . . . three . . ."

Commodore Erik Hopkins, formerly of Earth Fleet, braced himself for the familiar disorientation and dizziness that accompanied a drop out of jump space. He wasn't otherwise worried. Freedom of Space Navigation Operation. There was a checklist for that, and every item had been checked off. The destroyer *Claymore*, originally known as the *Garibaldi* when she was part of Earth Fleet, was at Standard Alert Condition Two, just as mandated by the checklist. The freighter they were escorting would come out of jump space behind *Claymore*, and they would proceed through Jatayu Star System, breaking the unofficial blockade of Glenlyon Star System. It had all been planned out.

Scatha Star System had claimed control of Jatayu, a claim without legal merit but one that Scatha might try to enforce against any unescorted freighter. With other star systems within reach of Glenlyon either claimed or controlled by Scatha, or by its partners in strong-arming their neighbors, Apulu Star System and Turan Star System, trade between Glenlyon and the rest of human space had been choked off. Glenlyon faced the alternatives of either fighting or submission, but, unwilling to make that stark choice, had instead decided on trying to call what it hoped was a bluff by Scatha.

Which was where *Claymore* and Commodore Hopkins came in. He wasn't worried about the outcome. Earth Fleet had had a checklist for everything, and checklists for the checklists. That was how Earth Fleet got things done, and Commodore Hopkins had risen to rank by making sure he adhered to those checklists. There wasn't much left of Earth Fleet anymore, mainly the men and women still tasked with decommissioning the last remaining warships, archiving the remaining data and records, and preparing to turn out the last lights and lock the last doors. Hopkins himself, along with the great majority of the crew and the *Claymore* herself, had been declared surplus years ago and been forced to find new employment out among the new worlds being rapidly settled far from Earth. Glenlyon had been a decent place to work with, but Hopkins and most of the crew still thought of themselves as being from Earth rather than their new home, and Hopkins still ran everything by the rules that Earth Fleet had once lived by.

As the destroyer left jump the formless, bland gray of jump space vanished from the displays on *Claymore*'s bridge, suddenly replaced by the familiar star-spangled black of normal space. One of those white dots was the star Jatayu itself, only a speck from the jump point five light hours away where *Claymore* had arrived. Velocity couldn't be measured in jump space, but back in normal space *Claymore* was only traveling at point zero two light speed, a crawl for a warship, because of the need to stay close to the plodding freighter she was escorting.

Dizzy from the drop out of jump space, Hopkins was still trying to focus on the display before his command seat when *Claymore* shuddered, then jolted as if a giant had slammed a hammer against her hull. Alarms blared throughout the ship.

"Situation!" ordered Captain Kanda Shade, commanding officer of the *Claymore*, as she also tried to shake off the disorientation.

"We're under attack!" the weapons watch officer reported. "Two opponents. Tentative ID—"

Claymore jerked again, hard. More alarms sounded.

"Shield failure amidships! Hull breaches in two compartments!"

Hopkins finally forced his eyes into focus, staring at his display. There were the two attackers, who must have been waiting at the jump exit for *Claymore*. And right behind *Claymore* was the freighter *Bruce Monroe*, having just left jump space as well.

"Attackers are a Sword Class destroyer and a Founders Class destroyer."

Hopkins opened his mouth to issue an order but hesitated.

The relevant checklists had automatically appeared on his display. When Attacked By Superior Numbers, the first item demanded "Accelerate at Full." But the list for Freedom of Navigation Operations had a block for "Maintain Close Escort of Freighter(s)." One list demanded that he order *Claymore* to accelerate at full, but the other demanded that he stay close to the *Bruce Monroe*.

Claymore jerked again.

"Another hit amidships! We've lost Particle Cannon One!"

"Shields at full!" Commander Shade ordered from her own checklist. "Main propulsion—" She paused, staring at her display where the other two checklists offered the same incompatible choices. "Commodore?"

Hopkins shook his head, wracked by indecision. "I don't— We can't—"

Two more jolts. "Main propulsion down by thirty percent! Shields have collapsed!"

The Commodore frowned at his display. Follow the checklists. He knew he had to follow the checklists. "We have to . . ." He looked helplessly at Shade. "Captain . . . ?"

Shade shook her head, baffled. "We're supposed to . . ."

Claymore groaned and shook as more blows landed. The lights went out, replaced by the dimmer glow of emergency lanterns. "Grapeshot launchers disabled. Particle Cannon Two destroyed! Serious structural damage amidships!"

"Orders, sir?" another watch stander pleaded.

Hopkins hesitated.

Shade tried to read through both checklists again.

A shudder ran through *Claymore*, followed by a deep boom that rattled through the ship as she broke in two.

Hopkins felt an overwhelming sense of relief as a new checklist appeared on the emergency display that had replaced his usual one. He knew what to do. It was right there, item one on the list. "Abandon ship!"

He was still running down Preparatory-to-Abandoning-Ship items on the list when a barrage of grapeshot struck and tore through the bridge of the wreck that had once been a destroyer.

Rob Geary, Senior Dock Officer for the orbital shipyard and station that was Glenlyon's main link with space, glared at the image of Council Member Leigh Camagan on his desk display. "The government really expects me to step up again?"

"Yes," she replied. "You came through for Glenlyon three years ago, Rob."

"What do they think I can do? *Claymore* was totally destroyed, I'm told, half her crew dead. I sent Hopkins a message before *Claymore* left, warning him that it had taken him so long to prepare for that mission that Scatha had to have plenty of advance warning. Everyone on this station seemed to know about it." Rob paused, miserable as he thought of the dead. "I wish either I'd been wrong, or Hopkins had listened. Why has *Saber* remained in orbit here?"

Camagan made a face. "Commander Teosig was ordered out but kept finding reasons to delay. He was fired this morning."

"He should have been fired at least a year ago! I had to work with that guy whenever *Saber* was in dock for refit. All he cared about was looking good to Commodore Hopkins, so he'd do his best to avoid actually doing anything that might mar his reputation. I told you all about that!"

"Yes, you did," Leigh Camagan agreed, exasperated. "And I told the rest of the council, who deferred to Commodore Hopkins, who as you say thought Commander Teosig was a perfect commanding officer. Why are you venting on me? Because I was chosen to ask you to return to service?"

Rob paused, angry with himself and with the universe. "I'm sorry. What is it the government wants me to do?" he asked again.

"Assume command of *Saber* and all fleet assets to defend Glenlyon."

"*Saber* is the only fleet asset left! Are they offering me a temporary, unofficial rank of lieutenant again?"

"Commander," Camagan replied. "Official rank of commander. And status as Commodore in charge of all fleet assets."

"They must really be scared."

"They are. Glenlyon is being choked to death by the grip that Scatha and Apulu and Turan have established over the trade routes out here. If we can't find a way to break through, Glenlyon will have no choice but to submit."

"Submit?"

Camagan's glare wasn't aimed at Rob this time. "What they did at Hesta. A so-called trade office that effectively ended up controlling not just trade but also the government."

"We came out here to be free," Rob said, feeling bleak.

"A lot of people did. But it has become obvious that others came out here to start building empires."

"What about Mele Darcy?" He owed Mele that concern after what she had done three years ago to defeat Scatha on the ground.

"We need her, too. I pushed through a vote to finally create a small Marine force to assist the fleet. Mele Darcy is being offered command of that force. It's only a Marine captain's rank, but it's official."

"Who will the Marines work for?" Rob asked, remembering some stories he had heard about the ground forces commander.

"They'll work for you. They'll be part of the fleet. You'll be in charge of Mele Darcy. I'm not sure anyone else would take that particular job."

"I need to talk to Ninja before I agree to anything."

"Of course." Leigh Camagan sighed. "Give your wife Lyn my best."

"You know Lyn is fine with you calling her Ninja. All of her friends call her that."

"I imagine that Ninja won't be feeling too friendly toward me because of this. I hope she doesn't decide to hack all of my personal data."

The walk through the orbital station to his home was short, one of the perks of being Senior Dock Officer. Usually he was happy about that, but today Rob wished he had more time to think before reaching the door to his quarters. In addition to his own name a small sign advertised *Ninja IT Consulting*.

Ninja, as usual, was seated before several displays as she worked. "Hey," Rob said, sitting down beside her.

"Hey, yourself." Ninja gave him a sharp look. "Don't bother summarizing your talk with Camagan."

"You listened in?"

"When the governing council makes a high priority call to my husband, I think I deserve to know what's going on."

"That call was secure. Triple encrypted," Rob pointed out.

"Oh, Rob, how many times have we gone over the secure thing? It's a myth." Ninja looked away, as if focusing on one of the displays to the other side of her. "So, you're going."

"I said I needed to talk to you before I decided."

"Nice words. You and I both know what you want to do."

"What I think I have to do," Rob said. He looked toward the door to the second bedroom. "Is Little Ninja asleep?" Even though their toddler daughter's name was Dani, she'd refused to answer to anything but Little Ninja ever since Mele Darcy had called her that about six months ago.

"Yeah. What, are you feeling a bit guilty for abandoning your family?"

"Ninja—"

"No!" She turned a furious gaze on him, a dark memory vivid in her eyes. "I've never been able to forget how I felt when everyone thought you'd died on *Squall*. Do you know how that felt, Rob?"

"No," he admitted, unable to meet her eyes.

"So who'd tell Little Ninja if her daddy never comes home, huh? And her Aunt Mele if something happens to her? You know how much Little Ninja loves her Aunt Mele. But that'd be my job, too, wouldn't it? And our next project?" She tapped her abdomen, where the two months of pregnancy barely showed. "Who tells that kid he'll never see his father? *Is that going to be my job, too?*"

He knew what was driving her anger. She was afraid for him, afraid for what might happen to him and to her and their children. She needed to vent that fear, to let him know how it was affecting her. And she was doubtless also angry that fate had once more put them in a position where she had to nurse such fears.

And having let him know, she'd probably never bring it up again. Because she knew the pressure he was under, that he'd need her support, and that arguing with fate was worse than useless.

What right did he have to put her through that? Rob bit his lip, trying to come up with words, and finally looked up at her again. "Ninja, I'd decided I should go because you, and those kids, deserved a free world to live in. I really don't want to leave. If it would hurt you that much—"

"Oh, shut up, Rob! You and I both know you have to go! Because that's the idealistic idiot that I was stupid enough to fall in love with and marry! And our kids will probably inherit your sense of duty and idealism so someday I'll have to see them off on some harebrained noble missions, too! And it'll be your fault! But you had better come back again, do you hear me? You come back, or I swear I will tell these kids that you were a fool and they should never be anything like you!"

He looked at her helplessly. "What is it you want?"

Ninja shook her head. "You figure that out for yourself."

"Do you think I want to do this?" Rob demanded. "Leave you and Little Ninja? Go out there and . . . watch men and women die because of orders I gave? Do you think I *want* to do that again?"

She looked at him without saying anything for a few moments. "You say their names sometimes when you're asleep. Did you know that? The names of the ones who didn't come back. I hear you say those names, and I don't know what to do." She reached out and embraced him, her arms gripping him tightly. "And then I think of Kosatka, and how many people would have died there if you weren't such an idiot. And how you got most of the crew of *Squall* home when it seemed hopeless. And here at Glenlyon, where Scatha would probably have been running everything by now. People like you and Mele go out and do things like this because you think you have to, and people like me and Little Ninja just hope and pray you come back each time."

"It really is about you," Rob whispered in her ear. "I can't let you down."

"I know." Ninja pulled back and looked in his eyes, smiling sadly at him. "The first time we met, you were the lieutenant in Alfar's fleet reviewing my case, and I was just some sailor who was being pushed out the door. And I realized you actually cared. I wasn't anybody to you, and the brass wanted me gone, but you wanted to be sure I got a fair shake. And I thought, if he's like that with someone he doesn't even know, what's he like with someone he cares about? I knew what I was getting. I wanted what I got. Usually that's great. Sometimes, like now, it hurts."

"I'll tell the council no if that's what you want."

She shook her head. "What I wanted was Rob Geary. I got Rob Geary. For better and for worse. I'm going to be mad, I'm going to be real unhappy, but I know why you're going. Do you know that guy Ferrer who works in station IT?"

"No," Rob said, puzzled by the apparent change in topic.

"His girl was on the *Claymore*. They were going to get married. Right now she's listed as missing." Ninja put her palms on either side of Rob's head, holding it so he had to look back at her. "Go out there and make sure there aren't a lot more people like Ferrer and his girl. You can do that.

Beat the scum who destroyed the *Claymore* and don't lose too many of our own doing it. Bring back alive as many of our own as you can. And remember that we need you. Make sure you come back."

"I will."

"And Mele. Bring her back, too. That girl is crazy."

"She's a Marine."

"That's what I said."

T he official workday on the orbital station had ended. Mele Darcy lounged back in one of the comfy chairs at her favorite bar, half-facing the floor-to-ceiling virtual window that offered a stunning view of the planet down below. As commander of the orbital station's security force Mele encouraged the members of the small police force to wear their uniforms when visiting places like bars. That way they could discourage troublemakers while enjoying themselves. Not being the type to ask one of her people to do something that she wouldn't do, Mele was both wearing her security captain uniform and enjoying herself.

Knocking back a shot, Mele nodded to Rob Geary as he walked up to her. "Have a seat, space squid. I hear you talked to Leigh Camagan, too. Are you a commander now?"

"It takes effect tomorrow," Rob said, sitting down and waving off an attentive server bot. "How about you?"

She paused to consider the question, remembering the events of three years before. Remembering the risks she had run and those who hadn't made it. "Still making up my mind."

"You'd get to be a Marine again."

Mele eyed him. "I never stopped being a Marine."

He looked properly abashed. But then Rob Geary was always so earnest. "Sorry."

"Yeah," Mele said, easing up on him, "it's like a perma-nent condition. No known cure." She examined the empty shot glass in her hand, then grinned at Rob, knowing that others found that expression on her both captivating and alarming. "I heard if I accepted the deal my new boss would be a real hard case."

"Yeah," Rob said. "He must be pretty dumb, too, to agree to be your boss."

"I'm not that bad. Unless people give me a reason to be." Unfortunately, that also conjured up memories of three years ago. Mele leaned forward, dropping her outward lack of concern, her expression suddenly intent. "I've done all right running the security force up here. Steady work, nobody looking over my shoulder as long as I do my job right, not too big a chance of getting killed."

"Me, too."

"How mad was Ninja?"

"Pretty mad."

"You and Ninja and your little girl are the closest thing I have to family out here," Mele told him. "Just in case you didn't realize that."

He looked away, obviously unhappy.

"You must have given Ninja a reason, Rob," Mele said. "Give me a reason."

He paused to think, looking out the virtual window that offered a view of night creeping steadily across the oceans and continents below. "They need us."

Mele snorted, letting her exasperation show. "Last time they needed us they got rid of us as soon as they didn't need us anymore."

"I don't mean the government. I mean Glenlyon. I mean people like Ninja and my little girl. Mele, you know what this place will be like if Scatha moves in and takes over."

"Yeah." Mele grimaced. "But I didn't like sticking my neck out, giving my all, then being kicked in the butt by the people whose butts I'd saved."

"I can't give you any other reasons," Rob said, his eyes on her.

"What, no appeals to my honor?" Mele asked, looking around for the drink bot. "No promises of fame and glory?"

"Sorry, no."

She sighed. "Fortunately for you, I gave up on fame and

glory during boot camp. There are only two reasons I'm considering taking their offer. One is because I don't want Ninja to be a widow, which means you need someone with restraint and common sense nearby when things get crazy."

"Are we talking about you?" Rob asked. "Because I thought you said restraint and common sense."

Mele grinned at him again. "That's the other reason. Because I know I'll be working for somebody who isn't an idiot."

"At the moment, Ninja might not agree with you on whether or not I'm an idiot," Rob admitted.

"It can't be easy on her." Mele shook her head, looking down toward the planet. "Do you really think you can bring around those Earth Fleet stiffs?"

"Danielle Martel told me that any Earth Fleet officers I encountered would be very skilled and good at what they do. She also told me they'd be unable to function without their checklists. She was right on both counts."

"What are you going to do?" Mele asked, finally tagging the serve bot. "You want anything?"

"I'm good," Rob said, as Mele dialed up another shot. "What am I going to do? First off, delete the checklists."

She couldn't help laughing. "Make them think? What kind of monster are you?"

"The kind that wants us to win and those Earth Fleet sailors to survive," Rob said.

Mele nodded, nursing her shot. "You'll still only have one ship. No way that'll be enough."

"We'll need friends," Rob agreed. "Hopefully we still have a few."

"Kosatka still owes you," Mele said, but couldn't resist adding more. "That's probably one of the reasons the government wanted you back so bad."

"Probably. I also need Marines."

"People in trouble often do." She smiled, toasting him with the shot. Mele downed it, sighing with satisfaction at the warm sensation of the liquor hitting her stomach.

Rob finally smiled back at her. "Do you think you can whip up a Marine force for me overnight?"

"Miracles usually take about a week," Mele replied, giving him a serious look. "It'll depend on what kind of warm bodies I get. According to Camagan, the government is ordering Colonel Menziwa to provide me with twenty volunteers from the ground forces regiment. Guess how Colonel Menziwa is going to feel about that?"

"Mad as hell?"

"Probably. I don't know if you've worked with Menziwa, but I've dealt with her a couple of times when her boys and girls got into trouble up here. She's not the warm and fuzzy type."

"So what are you going to do?" Rob asked. "I have no idea how much time we have before Scatha or their pals show up here."

Mele shook her head, trying to decide on a third shot or not. "We've got time. The wise general sees to it that his troops feed on the enemy."

"What?"

"That's a quote from an Old Earth guy named Sun Tzu," she explained. "He also said that the best policy in war is to take a state intact. That's what Scatha and their friends are doing. Like at Hesta. Take over without a fight so everything is undamaged." Mele jogged her head in the general direction of where *Saber* orbited. "They don't want to destroy *Saber*. They want her in one piece, ready to add to their own forces. All of which means Scatha won't be showing up with another invasion force. Not right away, anyhow. They want to see if we'll fold like Hesta did. That's why they let the *Bruce Monroe* bring back the survivors from the *Claymore*, to scare us into submission. Otherwise, why wasn't our first news about what happened at Jatayu the surprise arrival of an invasion force?"

"Damn," Rob said, nodding. "Maybe you should be the one in charge."

"I'm not stupid enough to want that job," Mele told him.

He paused, looking around the quiet bar where worried-looking men and women sat morosely facing each other. "But we may not have that much time. Scatha's plan may work. People are scared. We have to give them a reason to think this world can hold out." He paused again. "But the longer we do hold out, the higher the odds that Scatha and its friends will attack."

Mele, who had been looking about for the server bot again, focused back on Geary. "Because?"

"Because they don't want Glenlyon being a successful holdout, an example to every other star system that fighting back can work. At some point, they'll decide we need to be made into a different kind of example, a cautionary one of what happens to star systems that don't submit."

She nodded. "Good point. Yeah, if we inspire opposition, sooner or later Scatha and their pals will come in and start breaking things to cow anyone thinking about doing the same thing. So, we've got time, but maybe not a whole lot of time."

"We?" Rob asked. "Does that mean you're in?"

Mele frowned at her empty shot glass. "I need one more drink before I say yes. Don't go taking that the wrong way, squid."

"Ninja wouldn't like it if I did." Rob laughed. "We're both likely to get screwed anyway before this is over."

"But not in a good way." Mele sketched a salute toward Rob, wondering how much she'd end up regretting what she was about to say. "All right. You've got yourself a Marine. I'll call Camagan to tell her and go see Menziwa tomorrow about the warm bodies we've been promised."

"I'll need you in the morning if you can put off your visit to Menziwa until the afternoon. What are your plans if Colonel Menziwa won't deliver?" Rob asked.

"I'll tell her to talk to my boss."

He shook his head at her. "Thanks."

"But, seriously," Mele added, hoisting her third shot and looking through the amber liquid. "I don't think there's much chance Kosatka will come through for us because they're tied up with trouble at home. My old buddy from the Battle of Vestri, Lochan Nakamura, is still there, and the occasional messages I get from him say Kosatka's problems are getting worse. Who was that girl Lochan was hanging around with? The one who came out from Old Earth? Carmen . . . Ochoa." Mele downed the shot. "Tough girl, according to Lochan. I hope they're both okay."

Shadowy figures flitted along the edge of the spaceport terminal, some in battle armor and some only wearing chameleon camouflage fatigues but all bearing weapons.

Not wanting to be spotted by those others, Carmen Ochoa advanced cautiously through the layers of ornamental planters that offered the best cover along this part of the spaceport. Her own cammies helped conceal her, but Carmen had long ago learned to take nothing for granted. People who made assumptions like that didn't last long on Mars. Her rifle, a high-powered model with a large scope, wouldn't be much good in a close-in fight.

She'd made it off Mars and ended up on Kosatka. So far it hadn't exactly been a happily-ever-after thing.

Four years ago automated construction equipment had begun pouring the foundations and erecting the buildings that would someday be a city named Ani, the third city on the planet, preparing for an expected flow of new settlers. Three years ago she and Lochan Nakamura had reached Kosatka, he looking for a new start and she hoping to do something worthwhile in hopes that other worlds wouldn't end up like Mars had. He'd become a diplomat for the government. She had struggled to make a difference as a civilian, but eventually fell back on the skills learned while surviving Mars.

Those skills had been needed because two years ago the occasional acts of terrorism that were plaguing Kosatka had suddenly expanded into a low-level insurgency, and last year the low-level insurgency had become a small-scale war. Ani, its new downtown and spaceport gleaming with the sterile and pristine shine of structures awaiting their first use, had become a no-man's-land as the rebels declared it their capital and Kosatka fought to regain control.

Carmen paused, crouched behind a retaining wall, scanning the area ahead for the platoon commanded by Lieutenant Dominic Desjani. Three years ago, Desjani had been a public security officer, and Kosatka's army had consisted primarily of organizational charts prepared for a militia that few expected would ever have to be fleshed out. Today, he was out there somewhere in front of her, in charge of a group of hastily trained soldiers helping to defend the spaceport.

Carmen finally spotted him and his platoon, crouched behind one row of heavy planters. The contrast between the soaring, shining spires of the spaceport buildings and Desjani's dirty, battered group of soldiers felt unreal.

She called out. "Friendly!" Having announced her arrival to prevent any jittery soldiers from firing at her, Carmen, bent over to stay low so she wouldn't be visible to enemy soldiers, ran toward Dominic. She eased up close to him, carefully observing the advancing rebels through the scope of her rifle. "We need prisoners," Carmen whispered.

"Why are you on the front line again?" Desjani whispered back, anger in his voice.

"I wouldn't be anywhere near here if a certain cop hadn't decided he needed to be a hero," Carmen replied, feeling a rush of affection mixed with worry. "You could be fairly safe back in Drava, you know, maybe directing traffic in that city instead of being on the front here in Ani."

Her jab must have gone home because Dominic changed the subject. "Where's our aerospace support?"

"Ask your commander. I'm just a volunteer intelligence officer, remember?"

Desjani glanced at the weapon in Carmen's hands. "So that's an intelligence collection device?"

"Contrary to the old saying, dead men do tell tales," Carmen told him. "I'd prefer some live ones, though."

"You may get your wish very soon," Desjani said.

Carmen saw the figures of more so-called rebels appear, advancing in individual rushes among the waist-high barriers once intended to channel traffic approaching the spaceport terminal. Their chameleon camouflage was trying to match the metallic gleam of the road barriers, which made them stand out against the glass of the spaceport's main entry behind the rebels.

She waited as Dominic took aim, calling out to his soldiers in a low voice. "Steady, boys and girls. Pick your targets." He fired, the rest of his soldiers opening up, some of the rebels jerking at the impacts of hits and falling. Behind them, panels of glass hit by some of the shots shattered into shards that fell gleaming to the ground, the chiming of the broken glass lost amid the boom of gunfire.

Most of the rebels dropped behind the cover provided by the barriers, but one in battle armor stood, solid projectiles bouncing off, a hit from an energy weapon causing a section of armor surface to vaporize but not penetrating as the rebel fired back.

Carmen leveled her rifle, sighting carefully, the autosight zooming in on the face shield of the rebel in armor. Her rifle barked, and a moment later the face shield shattered.

As that rebel dropped, she heard Dominic Desjani calling out, "On the left! They're also coming up through that office access!"

Shots slammed into the heavy ornamental planters that Carmen, Dominic, and his soldiers were using as cover. Even though the flowers and bushes once intended for them had never been planted, the soil, once hopefully loaded into the planters, helped protect against enemy fire, while the weeds growing where carefully tended vegetation had been planned for helped mask sight of the defenders.

As the rebel force on the left pushed against Dominic's platoon, the whine of turbines announced the arrival of help. Carmen saw the manta shape of an aerospace craft glide overhead, pumping out shots that riddled and blew apart the road barriers where the first rebel force was taking cover. She sighted through her scope, recording the action for uploading to the intelligence office back at the capital city, Lodz.

Her elation was short-lived, as two missiles leapt up from different places along the rebel-held side of the spaceport. The aerospace craft began hurling out flares, chaff, and other countermeasures as the missiles each split into a dozen submunitions, all weaving through the air toward their target.

The countermeasures threw off most of the submunitions, but one got through, exploding and tearing a hole in one wing of the aerospace craft. "Cover him!" Dominic yelled to his platoon, firing to keep the rebels from targeting the wounded warbird as it staggered away, the pilot fighting to maintain control. Shots erupted all over the spaceport area as the rebels tried to down the fleeing aerospace craft and the defenders did their best to force the rebels to seek cover.

"When did the rebels get shoulder-fired Snipes?" Dominic shouted at Carmen. "That's the first time I've seen them used!"

"Me, too," she said, one eye on her scope as she continued recording the activity. "We didn't get any reports that the rebel forces had acquired those missiles. At least this will be proof the enemy has Snipes."

"They've got better, newer equipment than we do," Dominic complained as the warbird wobbled past overhead on its way back to the "temporary" forward air support base that had already been in use for five months. "What's it going to take to convince other star systems that these fake 'rebels' are an invasion being bankrolled by worlds like Apulu?"

"Those other star systems know what's happening," Carmen told him. "They're still too scared of becoming targets themselves. I hope Lochan Nakamura can talk some sense into them. I know he's trying."

Dominic shook his head. "What about Glenlyon? Weren't they going to send us something?"

Carmen shook her head slightly, her eye sighting through the scope toward the rebel positions. "If what I've heard is true, Glenlyon is going to have its hands full trying to defend itself. Star systems like Apulu, Scatha, and Turan are putting pressure on new human colonies all over this region of space. Damn," she added as a red warning symbol appeared on her scope. "The rebel jamming is too strong here. I need to get back so I can upload my scope video of those Snipes being used."

"It's funny how often your intelligence collection trips to the front happen to end up where I am."

"That is a strange coincidence, isn't it?" Carmen said, smiling at him for a moment.

His look back at her stayed serious. "You know, Carmen, you could always marry me and make the whole thing official."

"Why would a cop want to marry a Red?"

"He got to know her," Dominic said. "I know it's insane, but I don't want to give up hope that there's a good tomorrow for this world and this star system. And maybe even for you and me."

Carmen looked at him for a moment, her thoughts whirling inside her, before shrugging. "Hope got me off Mars when a good future seemed impossible for me. Maybe I'll take you up on that marriage thing."

"I hope you don't wait too much longer," Dominic said as a rebel shot rocked the planter they were hiding behind. "You never know what'll happen."

"I learned that when I was very young," Carmen said. Their conversation was interrupted as mortars thumped somewhere off to the left, hurling their deadly projectiles into the sky to bumble down onto defenders supposedly safe behind improvised barricades. "Indirect fire incoming," a voice warned over Carmen's headset.

Other mortars whomped well behind Carmen as her own side fired back at the rebel mortars. Hopefully the counter-battery fire would destroy the enemy artillery, but more likely the rebel mortars were already on vehicles, moving away from where they had launched their barrage. The duel might go on for hours, the rebels trying to wear down the defenders, and the defenders trying to knock out the rebel weapons.

Dominic looked to either side at his platoon. "Everyone shift positions one hundred meters to the right. They have too good an idea of where we are and might drop mortar rounds here. Stay under cover as you move."

Carmen stayed with him as they scuttled to new positions. She watched as he slid behind another planter, this one filled with weeds crowned by small, brilliant, orange blossoms, and leveled his rifle through the stalks of vegetation, being careful not to disturb the pretty flowers. Rebel snipers would be watching for that.

She reached out to squeeze his arm. "Be careful, Domi."

"You, too, Red."

What was normally an insult aimed at people from Mars had somehow become an affectionate nickname between them. Carmen grinned, but the smile quickly faded as she cast a cautious glance toward the rebel positions. With a nod to Dominic she turned and headed back, staying low again to avoid exposing herself to rebel snipers.

The so-called rebels were getting more help from off-world. If Kosatka was going to defeat them, it would need help as well. But Lochan had been keeping her up to date on his diplomatic efforts, and the ugly truth was that the rebels had a lot more "friends" in other star systems than Kosatka seemed to.

Far above the fighting in Ani, Lochan Nakamura, ambassador at large for the Kosatka Star System, walked slowly toward one of the bars on the facility orbiting the world also called Kosatka. A lot of businesses were struggling under the pressure of the conflict wearing away at Kosatka, but the bars were doing all right. Bars always thrived during uncertain times.

He paused at a single display panel showing the view of

the world below, where night covered most of the largest continent, home to most of Kosatka's settlers. Patches of light marked the cities of Lodz and Drava, but the place where Ani lay was as dark as the unpopulated regions. Lochan knew that if he zoomed in enough the sparkle of gunfire and explosions might be visible amid that darkness. But otherwise the combatants let the night shadow their movements and their actions. Small portions of Ani had once shone with light in the evenings, but those had been swallowed by the darkness over six months ago.

When it came to visualizing what was happening to Kosatka, and to Glenlyon, and what had already swallowed Hesta, spreading darkness was as good a way of seeing it as any. If only he could get other star systems to understand that before the darkness reached them.

"Lochan!"

Lochan looked down the bright, almost sterile corridor of the orbital station at the woman hastening his way. Even from a distance it was easy to see the emerald-green streaks in her hair that told Lochan who she was and where she was from.

He'd noticed that in a lot of the nationalities and ethnic groups who'd come directly from Old Earth. While finding homes for themselves on new worlds, they also displayed a tendency to be almost flamboyant about the symbols and other characteristics that helped define and identify them. "We can be ourselves out here," one had told him. "Take pride in who our ancestors were and who we are and make no apology for being that." Lochan could understand that feeling. Even on the Old Colony world of Franklin he had felt the pressure to conform, to minimize differences so as to supposedly minimize offending and maximize being able to live in mixed groups without friction. Intended to reduce chances of more conflicts like those that had battered Old Earth throughout human history, such policies had left many people feeling suffocated.

But now they were free thanks to the new jump drives that had allowed humanity to rapidly expand into new star systems, opening world after new world to whoever could raise the money and enough fellow settlers to stake claims to planets where humans had never before walked. Free to fulfill the age-old dream of futures without limits. It was a heady feeling, Lochan knew, like the buzz from a good, stiff drink. But just as too many drinks eventually turned that buzz into a painful headache, the fixations on differences and independence were keeping people apart who needed each other if they were going to stay free. *Leave me alone* was a fine enough sentiment when all was well, but it had its drawbacks when your house caught on fire and there wasn't anyone around to help put it out. If the likes of Scatha and Apulu continued to expand their control of space, this burst of freedom might turn into a brief blip in the long, troubled history of humanity.

Brigit Kelly reached him, breathing a little fast because of her quick walk, everything else about her face and voice telegraphing bad news. "I just got a dispatch from Eire that came in on the ship that jumped into the star system this morning. They're not ready to commit."

He nodded, trying not to let his full disappointment show. "For the same reason?"

"Yes. Lochan, my ancestors fought for freedom for their country. My people came out to Eire Star System to be free, not to be giving up our freedoms to others. It's hard to convince my people that we need to think of such a thing less than five years after landing on a new world."

"They wouldn't be giving up much! It's just a mutual defense agreement."

"With a star system like Kosatka that's already got internal fighting going on," Brigit said, her voice growing sharp. "I'm trying to convince my people, Lochan! But you could give me a better case of need to work with!"

"That's not internal fighting," Lochan explained, wondering how many times he had said that to how many different ambassadors and representatives of various star systems. "It's an invasion wrapped in a false flag of rebellion. If Eire won't help Kosatka, how about Glenlyon? Have you heard?"

"No. What's happened at Glenlyon?"

"We finally got news that one of their warships was destroyed at Jatayu trying to escort a freighter from Glenlyon through to Kosatka. The ships that did it were from Scatha."

"That's war. Scatha's claimed Jatayu, but that's not grounds for shooting."

"Then that should convince everyone of what we're facing and what we have to do!"

"It won't, which you know as well as I." Brigit looked around at the bare walls. "Remember back in the Old Colonies, and on Old Earth, where a corridor like this would be lined with virtual scenery?"

"Yeah," Lochan said. "What's your point?"

"We're not back on Old Earth, or in the Old Colonies anymore, Lochan, but too many people think we still are even though so much has changed. They think if things get bad enough, Earth will step in and fix it all, the mother looking after her children."

"Earth doesn't even have a space fleet anymore! The mother has sent her children to the stars and turned her back on them."

"Not quite. The mother's selling her babies guns and ships to kill each other with. There's money to be made, don't you know." Brigit sighed and nodded to Lochan. "There's another ship heading for Eire tomorrow. I'll try to convince my people to weigh in for Glenlyon."

"If they don't help Glenlyon," Lochan said, repeating another argument used many times without much success, "then Glenlyon won't be there to help them when they need it."

"We know the value of friends, Lochan. My people have to be convinced that those like Glenlyon are friends worth helping, friends who won't demand too much of us, and friends who could be counted on if we're in need."

Lochan nodded again, feeling tired.

How had he ended up with this apparently thankless and endlessly frustrating job after arriving at Kosatka? If he'd never met Mele Darcy on the way out from Franklin, hadn't let her convince him that maybe he could do something positive with his life, he might be running another failing business into the ground instead of beating his head against walls trying to convince people to do what any fool could see was in their own best interests.

Mele was probably still at Glenlyon, and if he knew anything about her it was that she'd be in the forefront of any effort to defend her new home against Scatha and the other New Tyrannies trying to create empires where others had seen opportunities for freedom. Warriors like Mele fought. Lochan knew that he'd be a lousy warrior. But he could do his best to help Mele by trying to get her the allies he was sure she needed.

"Let me know if there's anything I can do," Lochan told Brigit. "I hope you can convince them. Otherwise, there may not be any friends left by the time everyone makes up their minds that they need friends."

CH∧PTER 2

It felt oddly like entering hostile territory when Rob Geary walked off the shuttle, through the short boarding tube, and onto the closet-sized quarterdeck of the *Saber*, the flagship and only remaining ship in the Space Defense Forces of Glenlyon Star System.

Or perhaps not so odd, Rob thought as he watched a startled ensign snap to attention.

"I'm sorry, sir, but we weren't notified of your visit," the ensign stammered.

"My visit?" Rob wasn't happy to be here. Leaving Ninja this morning had been tough, even though she'd tried to hide her worries. The brand-new commander insignia he wore on a brand-new uniform felt uncomfortable. And the lack of notice to the quarterdeck that he was coming went beyond disrespect into a whole new problem area. "I want Commander Welk here. He has two minutes."

"Sir, the acting commanding officer is—"

"He now has one minute, fifty-five seconds."

Welk came out the hatch with ten seconds to spare, glaring at Rob. "What's the meaning of this?"

Rob held up his comm unit, his orders displayed on it. "I

hereby officially take command of this warship in the name of the government of Glenlyon. You were notified that I was on my way. Why wasn't the quarterdeck informed?" he asked Welk as the ensign tried to fade into the nearest bulkhead so he wouldn't be between Rob and Commander Welk.

Welk glowered at Rob. "We're in the process of renegotiating our contracts—"

"Wrong. You're in the process of trying to get out of your contracts. They remain fully in effect, and you are in violation of your obligations." Rob pointed back the way he'd come. "You're relieved of all duties and detached from this ship. The shuttle is still there. Get on it. Your personal effects will be packed up and sent down to the planet."

"I will not—!" Welk stopped speaking as Mele Darcy stepped onto the quarterdeck from the shuttle. Wearing a tough, black skin suit designed for use under battle armor, she didn't need to be physically large to instantly dominate the small compartment.

"Do you need me?" she asked Rob, eyeing Welk.

"Commander Welk needs an escort onto the shuttle," Rob said, glad that he had asked Mele to be along just in case things got difficult. "Commander Welk, I assume you've met Captain Darcy, the senior officer for Glenlyon's new Marine force."

Mele smiled at Welk, but it wasn't the sort of smile that anyone would want aimed at them. "Mind your step, Commander," she said, gesturing toward the shuttle.

Welk turned a furious gaze on Rob. "Good luck operating this ship without a crew!" Turning, he stalked off the ship and down the loading tube to the shuttle.

Composing his voice and his expression, Rob looked at the ensign, who gazed back, terrified. "You're . . . ?"

"Ensign Justin Torres, sir!"

"Thank you, Ensign Torres." Rob wondered briefly if he was any relation to the Corbin Torres who had offered as little support as possible to him three years before but decided that was unlikely. From his accent, Ensign Torres had come here directly from Earth. "Announce my arrival and call all officers to an immediate meeting in the wardroom."

"Yes, sir!" Torres tapped the ship's general announcing system panel, then rapped a small pad quickly two times, producing the "bong bong" sound of a bell ringing twice, then repeated it for two more bongs. "*Saber*, arriving," he announced. "All officers, your immediate presence is requested in the wardroom."

"Thank you. Can you monitor the wardroom from here, seeing and hearing what's going on?"

"Yes, sir. But I'm not supposed to do things like that which distract from my duties on the quarterdeck."

"You're authorized to do it this time. I want you to hear what I say to the other officers. Oh, and seal the outer hatch here to make sure Commander Welk does not come back on this ship before that shuttle departs."

"Yes, sir."

Rob went through the internal hatch leading aft into a narrow passageway that led to the wardroom, Mele following. As they entered the officers' wardroom, Mele stayed by the door while Rob went to stand at the front, fighting down nerves.

The small compartment with a rectangular dining table dominating it was large enough to hold all the officers with little room to spare. Rob waited as they came, casting wary eyes at him and especially wary looks at Mele Darcy. Five lieutenants, five ensigns, one warrant officer. They formed two lines facing him, lieutenants in front and ensigns and the warrant in the back.

"Good morning," Rob said. "I'm Commander Geary, your new commanding officer." He noticed most of the officers reacting with surprise, surreptitiously looking around for Commander Welk as if just realizing his absence. "Commander Welk has been relieved and has left the ship."

The surprise changed to shock. Rob watched the junior officers, knowing his next words would set the tone for his relationship with them. "I need to make a few things clear. The first, and most important to me, is that I had the honor and privilege of serving with a former Earth Fleet officer on the *Squall* three years ago. Before she died helping to lead a boarding operation of an enemy ship, Ensign Martell told me that any Earth Fleet officers I met would be the best at whatever they did. I consider it an honor and a privilege to serve with all of you."

Rob paused to let that sink in, knowing his next statement wouldn't be as well received. "You may or may not know that Commander Welk was attempting to break his contract with the government of Glenlyon, saying he was acting on behalf of the entire crew. Your contracts remain in effect. You are obligated to serve Glenlyon to the best of your ability and to follow lawful orders. Some of you, I know, have begun putting down roots here, becoming part of Glenlyon. You'll be defending the place you think of as home. Others of you have clung to your former identities in Earth Fleet. You may not think of Glenlyon as home, but some of those you stand with do. Your shipmates. They're counting on you. If you hesitate to give your all for the people on the world we're orbiting, give your all for your shipmates."

Another pause. "Over there by the hatch is Captain Mele Darcy, who will be in charge of Glenlyon's new Marine force. She's equivalent in rank to you lieutenants, but she works directly for me."

Rob ran his gaze over the officers before him, who looked back with a mixture of wariness and concern, as well as at least a little defiance aimed at him as an outsider among them. "And here's the last thing. I am the commanding officer of this ship, as well as the senior officer in Glenlyon's Space Defense Forces. I don't want any doubt regarding that. You'll be expected to follow orders. From this moment on, we're going to be focused on defending our home and avenging those who died on *Claymore*. The last time Scatha messed with Glenlyon, we kicked their butts out of this star system. We're going to do that again. We're going to make them pay for what they did to *Claymore*."

That seemed to go over well.

"I know some of you from working with you on shipyard issues in the past," Rob said. "I'm going to get on the general announcing system to tell the rest of the crew what I just told you, then I'm going to have meetings with each of you officers individually. Are there any questions?"

One lieutenant raised a hand. "Sir, has Earth been contacted about what's going on out here?"

Rob shook his head. "We can't contact them now, not until we figure out a way to get a message through the blockade of the star systems around us. We have to hope one of our friends like Kosatka hears and gets the word to the Old Colonies and Old Earth. If you're thinking that Earth will help us, though, you know better than I do that Earth has decided to get out of the business of rescuing worlds in distress. Any help is going to come from the new colonies out here."

He didn't say that such hope was not a given.

"Dismissed," Rob said, feeling relieved that things had gone much better than he had feared. The officers were still stunned, though, and hadn't had time to think about how to react to his assuming command. He'd have to stay on them, impress on them that he was in charge, before they had a chance to consider challenging his authority.

But for now, he was the boss. Rob nodded to Mele to let her know she could take off. She returned a quick salute and headed back to the shuttle for her own trip into a lion's den.

The flight down to the planet in the shuttle felt oddly routine to Mele Darcy, except for the outraged presence of Commander Welk in a seat at the front of the passenger compartment. Once the shuttle had set down, Welk bolted out. Her last sight of him showed Welk getting a ride toward the government buildings, where he doubtless planned to protest his sudden removal. Mele had a feeling that Welk would probably find that everyone he wanted to talk to was either in a meeting or out of the office for as long as he hung around.

For her part, Mele hopped on a bus toward the ground forces base that had grown up in the fields west of the city. She hadn't been back to the area for three years and couldn't help noticing the size of the new headquarters building.

Since the world of Glenlyon hadn't had a Marine force until this morning, Mele Darcy didn't have a Marine uniform. Figuring that showing up at Colonel Menziwa's office in a ground forces uniform would be a mistake, Mele wore the black skin suit.

It proved suspiciously easy to get in to see the colonel. Having spent years as an enlisted Marine on Franklin, Mele wasn't foolish enough to think her easy passage through layers of headquarters gatekeepers was for her convenience. Colonel Menziwa must want to see her. That very likely wasn't so the ground forces commander could congratulate her and offer her a drink.

She stood at attention before Menziwa's desk while the colonel leaned back in her chair and glowered at her. Menziwa had her black hair pulled back into a severely tight bun in which not a single hair dared to be out of place, her uniform showing the same strict and unforgiving approach to perfection. She studied Mele with a clear intention of finding some flaw in appearance to pounce on, but Mele had been careful not to leave any such openings for a dressing-down.

"Why aren't you in uniform?" Menziwa finally demanded.

Mele kept her voice professionally neutral. "This is an authorized working uniform, Colonel."

"Authorized by whom?"

Having been chewed on by sergeants as a private, Mele had the answer ready. "Glenlyon Defense Forces Uniform Regulations, Colonel. Section Two, paragraph five, subparagraph alpha."

That only fazed Menziwa for a moment. "And why do you think it is appropriate to report to me wearing a working uniform?"

"Marine service uniforms are in the process of being—"

"I didn't ask for excuses!"

Having confirmed that her expectations regarding Menziwa were true, and realizing that any further attempt to apologize or explain would result in more tongue-lashing, Mele stood silently, knowing that would force Menziwa to take the initiative in the conversation.

After waiting unsuccessfully for close to a minute for Mele to offer her another opening, Menziwa started in. "Let me make two things clear, Darcy. The first is that I consider the creation of a Marine force to be a mistake. I've advised against it from the beginning. Any fighting that needs to be done can be handled by my ground forces. There won't be any *Marine uniforms*. You will show up for duty tomorrow in a regulation ground forces service uniform."

Colonel Menziwa leaned forward, her eyes fixed on Darcy as if she were a target to be destroyed. "The second thing is that the only two words I ever want to hear from you are *yes* and *colonel*. Is that understood? Now, you will write up your proposal for standing up and training a small force for the purpose of being dedicated to fleet support. You will send that proposal up the chain of command to me, where it will be evaluated, and returned to you for further work as many times as necessary. Are there any questions?"

Mele managed to keep a straight face as she replied. "Yes, Colonel."

Menziwa had already been turning toward another task, but recentered her attention on Mele, her eyes narrowed with annoyance. "What is it?"

"Is the colonel under the impression that I am part of her forces and under her command?"

"You're skating close to insubordination, Darcy."

"I merely wish to ensure that the colonel understands that my chain of command runs through Commander Geary," Mele said. "I'm not part of the ground forces. The Marines, including me, are space fleet assets. Any requests from you regarding my tasking must be sent to Commander

Geary, who will also approve the design for the Marine working and dress uniforms."

Menziwa gave Mele a cold stare, then moved her fingers rapidly over her desk display, looking up documents, her expression growing unhappier with each search. Eventually, she returned her gaze to Mele. "That is your current status," the colonel said. "I'll be working to correct that. I want it clearly understood that Commander Geary's rank is lower than mine. You, and he, would be well advised to keep that in mind."

"With all due respect," Mele said, knowing that phrase would itself further annoy Menziwa. Everyone who had ever served knew that "with all due respect" was an outwardly respectful way for a junior to say "you're being an idiot" to a superior. "Commander Geary's status as Commodore in command of all of Glenlyon's space fleet assets is coequal with the colonel's." While Menziwa was trying to come up with a response, Mele pressed her advantage. "I was told the ground forces have already been tasked to provide volunteers for the Marines. When I requested the list of volunteers I was informed that I'd have to ask you personally."

The colonel glared at her, reaching to tap a command on her display. "The list of volunteers has been sent to Commander Geary. Now get out."

"Yes, Colonel." Mele brought her arm up in a rigorously regulation salute, holding it until Menziwa was forced to rise and return it.

Her walk out of the ground forces headquarters building felt like a withdrawal through hostile territory. Looking about her, Mele was surprised to see how large and elaborate the headquarters were given that Glenlyon only had a single regiment of ground troops. The headquarters alone seemed to employ almost a regiment's worth of men and women.

Menziwa and most of her soldiers had come from the Old Colony of Amaterasu, not Earth. Mele remembered bloated headquarters staffs on Franklin and wondered if that problem had spread like a plague virus from Old Earth to the Old Colonies and now was starting to infect the new colonies.

Glenlyon's main spaceport had expanded in the last three years, but there still wasn't anything like a military base there, just a small section of the main terminal building given over to supporting military personnel passing through. With an hour before the next shuttle lifted, Mele checked in at the automated support desk and took a seat in the waiting room, which was large enough to make her feel small but too small to handle large numbers of personnel. She was the only one using the room. The chairs were cheap, the sort of stackable metal and plastic contraptions that had been used for centuries where seating was needed but no one wanted to spend any unnecessary sums on making the seating comfortable. The walls were bare of anything except a single posted notice, neatly framed, warning that consumption of food and beverages in the room was Strictly Prohibited. Set directly beneath it, the room's trash receptacle held several used carry-out food containers and empty drink bulbs.

In its own way, that waiting room summed up many of Glenlyon's defense problems. Not enough resources and money given to the task, not enough people, spending just enough to get by, and settling for strong words without the means or will to back them up.

As she waited, a ground forces corporal came dashing in. "Excuse me, ma'am. You're Captain Darcy?"

"That's right," Mele said. "What's the problem?" Still wound up from the encounter with Menziwa, she took a moment to look over the corporal and size him up. Medium height, stocky, he had a reassuring stolidity about him.

"I'm one of your volunteers, Captain. Derek Moon."

"Are you?" Mele evaluated him again, wondering what was wrong with him. She fully expected Menziwa to try to off-load every problem child in her unit as "volunteers" for the Marines. "When are you being transferred?"

Moon held up his comm pad. "Transfer orders were

completed this afternoon so I tried to catch up with you. I'm yours, Captain."

"How long until you're ready to move up to the orbital station?"

"I'm ready now, Captain. My gear is already packed and tagged for pickup."

There had to be *something* wrong with him. "You seem to be really enthusiastic about volunteering," Mele said.

Corporal Moon grinned. "You'll have to forgive me, Captain. I never thought I'd have a chance to be a Marine again."

"Again?" Mele asked, her hopes rising. "What's your history, Corporal? How long have you been with Menziwa's unit?"

"About two years," Moon said. "They were at about half strength when they got hired from Amaterasu after the unit was downsized there."

"You're from Amaterasu?"

"No, Captain. I was only there a couple of months. Before that, Earth. Earth Fleet. Third Marines."

Mele felt her eyebrows go up as she looked at him. "Earth Fleet Marines? Service record," she ordered, holding her comm pad up.

Moon tapped his pad and Mele saw his service record appear on hers. As she quickly scanned the information, her eyes fixed on two words. "Gunnery Sergeant?"

"For about six hours," Corporal Moon said. "The promotion authorization came through in the morning, and that afternoon the latest downsizing orders canceling the promotions and identifying personnel and units considered surplus came in. I went from Gunnery Sergeant to surplus before the day was out."

"You're a gunny?" Mele wanted to pinch herself to be sure she wasn't dreaming.

"I . . . yes, Captain. If you need one."

"I don't think there's ever been any officer in the history of Marines who didn't need a good Gunnery Sergeant. Why'd Colonel Menziwa let you go?"

Moon shrugged. "Two reasons, I guess. One is that my company commander is more than decent. I told him I wanted to volunteer so he made it happen. The other is that a background as a Marine doesn't always impress ground forces."

"Tell me about it." Mele checked her comm pad, seeing that Rob Geary had already forwarded to her Menziwa's list of volunteers. One problem was immediately obvious. There were only sixteen names, not the promised twenty. One was indeed Corporal Moon. She wondered about the other fifteen. "Look at these names for me."

Moon read, a frown forming. "You've got . . . seven . . . no, eight dirtballs here."

"That's all?"

A knowing smile replaced Moon's frown. "The captain was thinking the colonel would unload every dirtball she had on you? This isn't all of them, but those eight are the worst."

"Are any of them salvageable?"

"No, ma'am. Not in my opinion. Of the remaining eight, one is me, and the other seven are decent. Not top grade, but you should be able to make Marines out of them."

"If you're a gunny," Mele said, "you're going to be the one making Marines out of them."

"I'm a corporal," Moon pointed out.

"You were. I need a gunny, and it looks like you'll do. Congratulations. Try to hang on to it for more than six hours this time."

"Yes, ma'am," Moon said, grinning like a kid who had just discovered that Santa was real.

"Here's your first job, Gunny," Mele said. "I need names. Good ground forces soldiers as replacements for the bad eight and four more capable, warm bodies to make up the twenty."

Moon nodded, his expression gone serious and professional. "I can get you those names. I talked to people yesterday when the word went around. I know easily a dozen good performers who said they were going to volunteer and aren't on this list. I'm guessing they were left off because Colonel Menziwa didn't want to part with them. I can call each of them and find out for sure."

"You do that, Gunny."

"But I have to warn you that Colonel Menziwa is not going to want to let any of them go."

"You let me worry about that," Mele said. "Just get me those names."

The captain's cabin on a destroyer was relatively spacious compared to those of the other officers, but that didn't mean there was much room to spare. Fortunately, Rob Geary didn't have much in the way of uniforms and other personal items to move into it. The most important thing, a holo of Ninja and Little Ninja, took up only a small corner of the pull-down desk.

"How bad is it?" she'd asked during a brief call.

"It's . . . different," Rob said. "On *Squall*, I had a bunch of people who were trying to learn their jobs as they did them but because of that were willing to try anything. On *Saber*, I've got a crew of extremely experienced people who are afraid to try anything."

Ninja shook her head. "You'd better tell your system security people to try something. Their firewalls have a few holes in them, and someone's been poking around trying to find their way in."

"Someone besides you, you mean."

"Yeah. I'll send you a file with some fixes that you can pass on to your extremely experienced people."

"Ninja—"

She'd smiled. "I know. Be careful. Talk to you later."

Rob had sent the firewall fixes on to Warrant Officer Kamaka, who like anyone else working IT at Glenlyon knew Ninja's reputation and didn't need to be told to take her fixes seriously. He needed to interview more officers, and he needed to talk to the senior enlisted leadership aboard *Saber*. He needed to do about a hundred more things. And Mele Darcy had just dropped another need-to-do on him.

Since that last was the need-to-do he wanted to do least, Rob figured he ought to get it over with.

With *Saber* in near orbit, there wasn't any noticeable delay in communications. His call went through swiftly, but then had to be shunted through several layers of head-quarters staff before Rob was finally connected to the ground forces commander.

He nodded toward the image of Colonel Menziwa. "Good afternoon, Colonel."

"What do you need?" Menziwa asked brusquely.

All right, then. "You were tasked by the government to provide twenty volunteers for a new Marine force. Only sixteen were provided."

"Only sixteen volunteered."

Three years of handling customers of the shipyard had taught Rob a little more about dealing with the difficult ones. He didn't reply to Menziwa's assertion, continuing his own statement. "I'm told that eight of the supposed volunteers are unsuitable and did not, in fact, put their own names forward. Fortunately, I have the names of twelve ground forces soldiers who did volunteer but through some oversight didn't get added to the list. That would bring the total up to the twenty required. You can see the list of names as an attachment to this call."

Menziwa's eyes shifted to one side, reading the names, then regarded Geary closely for a moment before replying. "Where did you get these names?"

"I know people. Can I assume you'll release those twelve to Captain Darcy?"

"The government asked for volunteers. That's not a blank check for you to cherry-pick men and women from my unit."

Rob shook his head, keeping his voice and expression calm but unyielding. "The government ordered the volunteers to be provided. And I'm informed that all twelve names on that list are indeed willing to volunteer."

"Are you accusing me of not following orders?"

That was an old trick, one to which Geary knew the right response. "Why would I do that, Colonel?"

Menziwa glared back at him, displaying no sign of giving in. "I don't like people accusing me and my officers of not correctly obeying orders, and I like even less people who try to raid my forces for their own needs."

There had been a time when someone like Colonel Menziwa would have caused Rob to second-guess himself. But he had seen some serious combat, had seen people die, and no longer saw any reason to give in to attempts to intimidate him. Especially since in this case he knew the government would support him. Menziwa must know that as well despite her attempt to bluff him into backing down. This might be how she always did business, or it might be a test to see if Rob would yield when pushed. "I don't like having to make this an issue, Colonel. We can do this easy, or we can do this hard. I can play as hard as I have to. Which way do you want it?"

Menziwa held her stare awhile longer before easing back. "Geary, I've looked into what actually happened three years ago, into what was left out of the official accounts. I know what you did, and you have my respect for that. But I'm commander of the ground forces for this star system."

"And you never liked having to provide soldiers to the space forces," Rob pointed out. "This is a win for you."

"Ground forces responsibilities should not be divided among multiple forces."

"Marine missions have not traditionally duplicated those of ground forces."

Menziwa tried another tack. "I've met people like Darcy before. She's a loose cannon. Loose cannons kill people."

"If you know what really happened three years ago, then you know what Mele Darcy accomplished."

"I know that you're friends with her. And that until yesterday the highest rank you'd ever held was lieutenant. If you think—"

"I was commanding officer of the *Squall*," Rob broke in, letting his tone grow noticeably colder. "I won my battles when it counted, Colonel. So did Mele Darcy."

Menziwa eyed Geary again before shrugging. "In the interest of establishing a working relationship, I will release those twelve individuals to you. Is that all?"

"Yes. Thank you."

After the call ended, Rob squeezed his eyes shut and tried to remember when he'd taken aspirin last. Maybe he should up that to a migraine dose.

He tapped his comm. "I'll see you now, Lieutenant Shen."

In Rob's admittedly limited experience, chief engineers on warships tended to fall into two types. Some resembled victims of trauma, like highly strung veterans of a battlefield littered with land mines who expected each step to bring another ordeal. They gulped coffee and yelled a lot, always struggling against the punishment that fate had assigned them. Others were almost the opposite, having adopted a Zen-like philosophy that the universe tended toward chaos, that the wheel of calamity would spin to bring new trials every day, but getting too upset would just feed the flames. They drank coffee slowly, smiling with the serenity of those who know that even the worst of things will someday pass.

Vicki Shen appeared to be mostly the second type, resigned to her fate.

Rob waved her to the other seat the captain's cabin boasted. "You've been chief engineer on *Saber* for four years."

"Yes, sir," Shen replied, "though *Saber* was the *Kamehameha* for the first year before Earth Fleet sold her to Glenlyon."

"Chief Engineer for four years," Rob repeated. "Did you commit some horrible crime in a past life that you're trying to make up for?"

His attempt at a joke apparently fell flat as Shen replied in an equally flat voice. "Commander Teosig didn't believe in rotating officers through jobs, sir. He wanted someone who knew the job to stay there."

Rob rubbed his chin as he studied her. "Just about every rank and position on this ship has been frozen because there isn't any other place for anyone to go. The ensigns have been ensigns for at least four years."

"We knew what we were getting into, Captain," Shen said, her attitude still guarded.

"It's going to be changing. I'm going to be direct with you, Lieutenant. The evaluations on file for you and every other officer on this ship tell me almost nothing. They say you're all very top-one-percent performers who deserve early promotion. The write-ups on those evaluations have obviously gone through customization apps to reuse the same words in slightly different ways. But I know you. I worked with you during periods this ship was docked at the shipyard. I noticed that while you paid close attention to checklists and operating rules for equipment and safety and maintenance, when it came to administrative and operational issues you were more concerned with getting the right outcome than you were with following the former Earth Fleet checklists."

Shen nodded as if she'd heard similar statements many times in the past, and not for the purpose of praise. "I am aware of my shortcomings in that regard, sir, and am attempting to place proper emphasis on all established guidelines and requirements in all areas."

Rob blinked at her, momentarily surprised by her apparently rote response until he remembered Earth Fleet's culture. "That wasn't a criticism, Lieutenant. I'm actually impressed by your ability to distinguish between those checklists that need to be followed and those checklists that are more of a hindrance to reaching a desired outcome."

"Sir, I . . ." Shen frowned in confusion. "Sir?"

"You impressed me," Rob repeated. "Both in your professional skills and your ability to get things done. How would you like to be executive officer for *Saber*? I need a good second-in-command. I think that's you."

Whatever Shen had been expecting from this meeting, it wasn't that. She stared at Rob, openly baffled. "Sir?"

"A promotion. To lieutenant commander. And assignment as XO of this ship," Rob said. "Can you handle it?"

That question produced an immediate and definite answer. "I can handle anything the universe throws at me, sir," Shen replied. She took a deep breath. "And I can handle being executive officer, Captain. Thank you for this . . . opportunity, and for your confidence in me."

"Good. Who should take your place as Chief Engineer?"

"I never thought I'd have to worry about that. Uh, Ensign Delgado, the Main Propulsion Assistant. He's got a feel for things, runs his division well, and he knows everything about the engineering systems on this ship."

"Have Ensign Delgado come up here so I can give him the bad news," Rob said. "You can tell him he's a lieutenant effectively immediately."

"Good news, bad news?" Shen said, finally smiling. "How quickly do you want me to turn over engineering to him?"

"As fast as you're comfortable with. I need a good exec backing me up, and I need her yesterday. I also need a recommendation for who to replace Delgado with when he moves up."

"Will do, Captain." Shen stood up to go, but paused. "Sir? Commander Welk wasn't . . . highly regarded. But he was one of us."

"I understand," Rob said. "But who is *us*? Is the crew of this ship going to gradually become part of this star system, or are you going to remain tied to Old Earth in your loyalties and your mind-sets?"

Shen pondered the question. "You've got it right that a lot of us have been thinking more and more of Glenlyon as home. But it's hard, Captain. Giving up what we were. We stayed with this ship because we wanted to remain what we were."

"You may be giving up something," Rob said, "but you'll be gaining a lot. You'll be building a real, long-term space force for this star system. We don't have much of a past, yet. But that gives us the freedom to focus on the future."

She nodded. "How much of a future have we got, sir? I come from a long line of people who kept fighting, no matter the odds, but this looks bad."

"It is," Rob said. "I won't lie to anyone about that. But it also looked bad three years ago."

He didn't add that he regarded his victory three years ago as something of a miracle and that depending on more miracles was a really bad way to plan. But at the moment it was all he had.

Rob waited until Shen had left before bringing up the star display, a three-dimensional projection in which names glowed next to stars and spiderweb-like lines leapt from star to star to show the jump points each star had and where those jump points led.

Either Commander Welk or Commander Teosig had tagged star systems claimed or controlled by Apulu, Scatha, and Turan. The resulting lopsided sphere of red-tinted stars didn't inspire confidence that Glenlyon, buried inside, would be able to hold out. Couldn't other star systems, farther off and still safe, see what was happening?

Glenlyon wasn't alone in its peril. The sphere of aggression was pushing up against Kosatka and had already apparently engulfed Catalan. He knew how badly Kosatka and Glenlyon were being pushed. What about Catalan? Did that star system have some breathing room while Glenlyon and Kosatka fought for their freedom?

And would Catalan's people have the foresight to do something before they, too, were forced into action?

"I heard from a friend back on Earth," Commander Dana Fuentes said as she sat down in the office of Catalan's Defense Minister. "The message was months old, of course, but it said Earth Fleet was preparing to dispose of their decommissioned light cruisers. You could get one for about what you paid for the *Bolivar*. Maybe less."

"And then we'd have to worry about paying to operate it," Minister Ross Chen replied. He had noticed that Fuentes didn't always take long-term expenses into account, which had created some short-term problems as the ministers balanced the many costs of settling a new world and creating the industry and farming it required for local needs. "Everything from fuel and food to pay for the crew, which is larger than that on the *Bolivar*, right?"

"You could get by with about the same size crew," Fuentes suggested. "But, a little larger, yes."

"We'll keep it in mind," Ross said, smiling politely.

Dana cocked her head at Ross. "Look, I know a lot of people in Catalan think the *Bolivar* is a waste of money that could be better spent on other things. And they're right that the money could be spent elsewhere. But you've seen the reports we're getting. My crew doesn't have happy feelings about things out here. I don't think I'm being alarmist. I just want to be sure you know that if the *Bolivar* faces an equal fight, we'll win. But if we're outnumbered two or three to one, I can't make any promises."

"No one has threatened Catalan," Ross said.

"Not directly," Dana agreed. "Did you see my report about those solicitations my crew has been receiving from Scatha? Scatha is trying to recruit my own crew out from under me. That's not exactly a sign of good intentions."

"No," Ross said. "But we should have plenty of warning if any other star system is planning to attack us." He didn't bother adding that the idea seemed ridiculous.

Dana Fuentes took on a questioning look. "How's the warning going to get here? We only know what reaches us."

"But . . ." Ross paused, thinking, and not liking where his thoughts were going. "We have a couple of trade delegations due to leave soon. I'll make sure they're told to also find out everything they can about what's going on in other star systems right now."

"That's a good idea." Commander Fuentes stood up, giving a casual salute. "Don't forget about the light cruiser idea, though. By the time you *know* you need one, it might be too late to get one."

"If it comes down to spending money on another ship of war or spending it for expanding agricultural resources on the planet," Ross said, "I'm going to need a lot stronger argument than maybe we'll need it someday."

Dana Fuentes nodded to acknowledge his words without either agreeing or disagreeing and left.

Ross Chen sighed and leaned back, gesturing so his display switched to show a low orbital view of the planet relayed from one of the satellites orbiting it.

Catalan. A world close enough to Old Earth's gravity and air and temperature to be welcoming to humans. Like all the other Earth-like worlds found so far, it had native life in a wide assortment of forms of animal and plant but nothing approaching the level of intelligence and self-awareness that marked humanity. It seemed insanely prideful to believe that humanity was unique in the galaxy, but no companions (or rivals) had yet been found.

There were those who argued that Others were indeed out there, though intelligence might be a far rarer occurrence than once thought. Others who were hiding their presence and deliberately avoiding humanity. In his darker thoughts, Ross had been able to understand why those Others might not want to reveal themselves to the trouble-prone and trouble-causing species of humanity.

Ross took a moment to relax, watching the slow movement of clouds above the planet, some of those clouds blocking the view from orbit of the city and building where he now sat. He could see portions of the two other cities, linked by a loose chain of farms, ranches, and heavy industrial areas. It was just a beginning, but anyone looking over it could see a wealth of promises for the future.

Anyone. He didn't want to believe that Dana Fuentes was right, that Catalan might in the future face threats serious enough that a single warship couldn't handle them.

But Ross Chen knew his history. The promise of wealth here could attract not only those seeking a new start but also the predators who had always plagued humanity.

Ross wondered how hard, or even whether, he should push Fuentes's suggestion to acquire another warship. Events a few years ago in other star systems had worried Catalan sufficiently that the government had scraped together enough extra funds to purchase a surplus warship from the rapidly dwindling Earth Fleet. Since the leaders of the new government had been unable to agree on another name, the destroyer had remained the *Simon Bolivar*. And so far, the *Bolivar* had kept trouble outside the bounds of Catalan's star system.

So far.

What *was* happening in other star systems at this moment? Ships could jump from star to star much faster than light, but it still took time to reach the jump points and to transit through jump space. News from even the closest star systems took weeks to reach Catalan.

Maybe he should—

An urgent tone sounded, warning of a high priority call. Ross tapped the receive command, seeing the image of the port director appear in place of the peaceful globe of Catalan.

"Have you heard?" the port director demanded.

That sort of opening usually meant bad news. "No. What is it?"

"Rates for shipping to and from Catalan are doubling. Effective immediately."

Ross stared at the port director. "Doubling?"

"Yes! And passenger fares will be going up at least as much. Supposedly because of increased costs, but that's nonsense. I warned the government about this! With the transit fees imposed by some star systems and the continuing problems with ships being waylaid, it's become more and more expensive to run shipping to new colonies like us. A lot of lines have stopped coming out this far. We're dependent now on two shipping lines, one that is owned by a state-corporation on Apulu and the other a supposedly private company from Hesta that was taken over by Scatha after they took control. I've told everyone what was likely to happen, and now it has!"

"Doubling," Ross repeated. "And we have no choice but to pay such a rate?"

"Not unless we can convince other companies to start coming out this way again or make it safe to operate our own lines."

"What about Vestral Shipping? They were still running ships here."

"They were, until that 'accident' happened to the *Morning Star.* Vestral got the message. They're cutting their losses."

"Can't we buy our own ships?" Ross asked.

The port director spread his hands in the age-old gesture of helplessness. "We could. But right now if we tried running freighters and passenger ships, they'd be either snapped up by piracy or charged huge transit fees to get through star systems controlled by people like Apulu. We'd lose ships and money faster than we could make up the losses. That's not a guess. It's a firm prediction."

"I'll call an emergency meeting of the ministers." Ross paused. Shipping costs like that would amount to a massive tax on everything, and everyone, coming into and leaving Catalan. And what would prevent those costs from being doubled again in a little while? It seemed all too likely that acquiring a light cruiser had suddenly become the less expensive option. "Commander Fuentes should be on her way to the port for a lift back to the *Bolivar.* Ask her to return here. I want the full council of ministers to hear her proposal."

He couldn't help wondering, though, whether it would stop with one light cruiser or if more warships would be required. Could Catalan afford that?

Why hadn't he heard of similar problems in other star systems?

Ross stared at his door as he remembered what Dana Fuentes had said. *"We only know what reaches us."*

And right now everything coming to Catalan had to come through ships controlled by two companies that in turn were controlled by Scatha and Apulu.

How bad was it out there?

Maybe whatever needed to be done would require someone with a different set of skills than the typical diplomatic or trade representative. Ross Chen tapped the link to his assistant. "Where's Freya Morgan?"

"She's handling the investigation of that incident on the orbital station."

"I need to talk to her. A much higher priority mission just came up."

Freya Morgan called in fewer than ten minutes, the background revealing she was in the high security office on the orbital facility. If she was concerned about the summons, nothing about her revealed that. But then, Freya Morgan never revealed anything she didn't want to let others see. "I assume a *call in immediately* meant you wanted a secure line."

"I do," Ross agreed. He explained the situation, trying to be as concise as possible without leaving out important details.

"You want me to find out what's going on?"

"And arrange help for Catalan if it's needed," Ross said.

"That's a pretty damned big *and*," Freya said.

"We're already in trouble," Ross said, "but we don't know how bad it is. You know people on Eire. They'll listen to you, and you'll know if you can trust what they tell you."

"This needs to be done yesterday?" she asked. "My only way out of this star system right now is a freighter due to leave in a few hours. They've only got room left for one passenger and . . . I just reserved that spot. But, if you're right, that freighter is controlled by people who don't want Catalan to know what's going on elsewhere."

Ross gave her what he hoped was an encouraging smile.

"Freya, Catalan spent good money to hire you away from Eire because you've got some hidden talents and because you don't look dangerous. You can get past any obstacles if anyone can."

"It's nice to be appreciated. But I still don't like going solo on this. There are times when backup can literally be a matter of life or death."

"I know," Ross said. "Catalan may be facing just such a time. I just had an epiphany hit me with a rock whose costs doubled overnight. See what kind of backup you can find for us. At the least, you're going to be empowered to acquire another warship. I'll get that authorization through on an emergency basis within the next hour and get it to you. Long term, we need to figure out how to make it safe for ships to go to and from Catalan at a cost we're able to live with."

"What about Kosatka?" Freya Morgan asked. "The freighter I'm hopping a ride on is stopping there on the way to Eire."

"Catalan's official position has been that we don't want any part of Kosatka's problems," Ross said. "But it looks like those problems may also be our problems whether we like it or not. See what you can find out."

"Does that mean Catalan might consider offering some of the aid that Kosatka's been asking for? I'm trying to find out the boundaries of my mission. How far am I supposed to go in terms of seeking assistance, knowing that whoever offers aid is going to want something in return?"

"I don't have an answer to that," Ross said. "Technically, you'll be labeled a trade negotiator. But the trades you'll be negotiating will be about protecting the people in this star system. If you see what you think is a good deal for Catalan, you'll have authority to explore that deal. But I can't guarantee that the government of Catalan will approve the deal. And ensure that anything that you do doesn't reflect badly on Catalan . . . or at least can't be traced back to the government."

Freya gave a short and sharp burst of laughter. "I think

I need to renegotiate my salary and job expectations. Just how much risk do you think is involved here?"

"I don't have an answer for that, either." Ross Chen gestured helplessly. "But if I thought it was safe, I wouldn't be asking you to do it."

"I won't be able to trust anyone else on that freighter," she told him. "That will complicate things if I run into trouble."

"You said they're stopping at Kosatka. Maybe there'll be someone at Kosatka."

"Maybe," Freya Morgan said. "I know someone there I can ask, anyway."

CHAPTER 3

Glenlyon Star System had won its last war on a shoe-string, which had convinced many that any lack of preparation for defense could be overcome by last-minute improvising. That was looking less and less like a viable way of doing business, but at the moment it was all Glenlyon had.

Which was why what amounted to a hastily organized council of war had gathered in the most secure room in the Glenlyon government office complex. Even Ninja had grudgingly admitted to Rob Geary that the room was "a little difficult" to penetrate with any possible surveillance method.

Rob sat next to Mele Darcy, she wearing the new scarlet Marine working outfit that contrasted sharply with the deep blue of Rob's fleet uniform and the dark green of Colonel Menziwa's ground forces garb. Glenlyon still had nothing in the way of aerospace forces for defense of her airspace and near orbital locations, so no one in the traditional light blue aerospace uniform was present. Despite the age-old rivalry for funding and missions between fleet warships and aerospace defenses, Rob wished Glenlyon had invested in at least a squadron of warbirds to back up *Saber*'s defense of the planet.

The three in uniform faced a long table where the Emergency Defense Committee sat. Rob had a sense of déjà vu as he looked at them. Council President Chisholm still led the government, having ridden to reelection on the popularity that had come with the successful repulse of Scatha's attacks three years ago. Council Member Kim beamed at the three officers with an outward show of support that Rob had learned the hard way didn't mean any personal concern for them. Council Member Odom still watched the others suspiciously, on constant guard against militarism. And Council Member Leigh Camagan eyed everyone else, alert, not betraying her thoughts, but also Rob knew his staunchest ally in the government.

President Chisholm looked around as if having to count the seven occupants of the room to ensure all were present. "This room is locked down. All security protocols in effect. Colonel Menziwa, please give us your assessment of the situation."

Menziwa pursed her lips as if still thinking through her statement, but when she began speaking her words were firm. "We cannot successfully defend this planet from invasion against the size of the forces arrayed against us. Our three options would be to either surrender before the enemy lands, engage the enemy as they land in a full-out battle that would result in my regiment being rapidly overwhelmed and forced to surrender, or disperse my forces into undeveloped areas and wage a protracted guerrilla war against the invaders in the hope of either other star systems eventually providing assistance or making the cost of the occupation too high for the invaders." Menziwa paused. "If the government is willing, I would recommend also dispersing forces through the cities to force the invaders to confront urban threats and the damage that would inflict upon facilities they want intact. But I have to warn the government that such a course of action would greatly increase the risk of injuries and death among the citizens."

The council members listened with grim expressions. "Which option do you think we should follow?" Chisholm asked in the manner of someone knowing she wouldn't like the answer no matter what it was.

"Protracted guerrilla warfare, in the countryside and the cities," Menziwa said as matter-of-factly as if proposing a parade.

Chisholm sighed. "Commander Geary?"

Rob tried to keep his own report just as professionally calm and detached. "If we are attacked with a force of two destroyers, there is a small but outside chance *Saber* might be able to repel the attack. If the enemy force includes three warships, which we believe is well within the capability of our opponents, our chances would be effectively zero. Against those kinds of odds we could harass the invaders or die trying to stop them, but we could not prevent an enemy force from bombarding this world and landing an invasion force."

"What could you do?" Leigh Camagan asked.

"Harass them, try to inflict losses as they approach the planet, continue to strike at any available targets as long as fuel permits," Rob said. "But we'd run low on fuel and face the choices of either surrender, of scuttling the ship to keep it out of enemy hands, or trying to fight our way through to a friendly or neutral star system where we could refuel."

"What would you recommend?" Chisholm said in the same reluctant manner.

"Harass the enemy and wait for an opening. If they did something really stupid, we could exploit that. But we'd eventually have to try fighting our way to another star system after the enemy establishes control of the orbital facility and the cities on this world. I would not consider our chances of making it to another friendly star system to be very high."

Odom shook his head. "You both say it's hopeless, but you both recommend fighting. That's irrational."

"War is irrational, sir," Colonel Menziwa replied. "I'm charged with defending this world, and I will do that to the best of my ability."

Rob's initial negative opinion of Menziwa improved considerably. "I concur," he said.

"Captain Darcy," Leigh Camagan said, "you're a strategic thinker as well as a tactician. What is your recommendation?"

Menziwa spoke sharply. "Council Member, with all due respect, Darcy is not an equal member of this group."

"She is the commander of our Marine forces," Camagan said, her voice mild but somehow still carrying force. "I want her opinion."

Rob's worries that Mele would take that as a chance to speak a little too freely weren't helped when Mele surreptitiously winked at him. But she kept her words as professionally cool as Rob had.

"I agree with Commander Geary and Colonel Menziwa," Mele said. "Scatha and Apulu and their friends know what our situation is. As I discussed with Commander Geary, they want us to surrender everything intact. If they know we're ready to fight, they'll wait to see if our resolve crumbles over time as the blockade remains in effect. We want to project an image of ready to defend but wavering on whether to give in. That's what will give us the most time to come up with better solutions than we now have available."

Menziwa looked as if she were tasting something bitter, but nodded. "I concur."

"How do we come up with better solutions?" Odom demanded.

"I can recruit more people into my ground forces," Menziwa said. "And industrial output can be shifted to produce more equipment and weapons. Given time, I can expand our ground forces and reserve forces to the level that could defeat an invasion outright. We have the means to construct antiorbital weapons, particle beams and missiles, which can defend this planet against any ship that comes close enough."

"Those weapons could be bombarded from outside orbit, though," Leigh Camagan noted. "We need warships in addition to the planetary defenses."

"Can we construct more warships?" Kim asked Rob.

Rob shook his head. "We don't have sufficient capacity. If we gave over the orbital shipyard to doing nothing else, it would take more than a year to turn out a couple more destroyers. But that kind of activity is easy to spot and keep track of. We've seen occasional visits from ships that pop out from a jump point, take a look around, and jump out again hours before we even know they've arrived. That sort of thing could easily tell when our ships were close to being ready and hit us then before we could actually use them. That would give the enemy two almost completed new warships."

"What can we do?" Chisholm asked.

"We need external assistance," Rob said. "Either forces from other star systems to come to our aid or else new units acquired from Old Earth or the Old Colonies. But both of those things require someone with sufficient authority getting through the blockade."

A long pause followed his statement, most of the council members looking at the desk as if answers lay scrawled on its surface.

"All right," Leigh Camagan finally said. "I'll go. As long as the council gives me the authority to reach temporary agreements with other star systems, and if necessary to purchase warships declared surplus by Old Earth or the Old Colonies. We still have the freighter *Bruce Monroe* in orbit. There are vital items we need from outside this star system. We can send the *Bruce Monroe* supposedly for that purpose, pay the extortionate demands to get through the blockade, and get the help we need."

"That'll be dangerous," Odom objected. "If you're identified, I can't imagine their letting you pass freely."

Leigh Camagan shrugged. "We're already asking many other men and women to risk their lives for Glenlyon."

"The council intends continuing to resist the demands on Glenlyon?" Colonel Menziwa asked. "Do I understand that correctly?"

Council President Chisholm nodded. "Our ancestors

fought many a battle against terrible odds, Colonel. I suppose we haven't learned much. We'll do the same."

"Our ancestors lost a lot of those battles," Odom pointed out.

"They were still worth fighting. We won't give up our freedom out of fear." Chisholm looked around the room again. "We're in agreement, then? Is there anything else?"

Rob nodded. "The *Bruce Monroe* brought back survivors from the *Claymore*. About half the crew, many of them injured. Their status has sort of been in limbo. I would like the council's assurance that all of those men and women are still under contract as part of the fleet's forces, and that the costs of their medical treatment will be covered. If we're going to get more ships, we're going to need good people to crew them. If we set a good example of looking out for our people with the survivors of the *Claymore*, it will establish an important precedent."

Kim frowned. "I regret having to bring this up, but all reports say that the *Claymore* was quickly destroyed without inflicting any damage on its attackers. Are those survivors really the sort of people we want crewing other ships?"

Rob made an effort to control his temper before replying. "The loss of *Claymore* was due to a senior leadership failure. There is *no* evidence that any of the crew failed in any aspect of their duties. Give them good leaders and they'll fight well to avenge the loss of their friends and shipmates and to defend this star system."

Menziwa shot Rob a sidelong glance as he waited for the council's reply. He wondered how the colonel felt about his clearly blaming *Claymore*'s loss on a failure by the senior leaders.

"I move we approve Commander Geary's proposal regarding the survivors of *Claymore*," Leigh Camagan said.

No one objected, leaving Chisholm free to declare the meeting over.

As Menziwa stood to leave, she walked closer to Geary, eyeing him. "I wasn't aware that the official investigation on the loss of *Claymore* had been completed," she said in a low voice. "You might want to be careful about too quickly assigning blame."

Rob nodded, but his words didn't reflect agreement. "I appreciate your concern. Both the Commodore and the Captain of the *Claymore* were probably once good officers, but they'd been subjected for too long to a training and evaluation system that robbed them of the ability to think and act when they needed to. I'm going to change that system."

"Are you? Take it all apart, discard tradition and the lessons of the past? You might want to be careful, Commander, when you start ripping out parts of a structure. Things you consider useless might turn out to be load-bearing walls, leading the ceiling to fall in and the floor to collapse, leaving you nothing to stand on." Menziwa nodded to him once in farewell before turning and walking over to speak with Council President Chisholm.

"I have to give her credit," Mele commented. "That was a pretty cool metaphor."

"Do you agree with the colonel?" Rob asked.

"Oh, hell, no. *This is the way it's always been done* is the stupidest reason possible for doing things a certain way." Mele stopped speaking as Leigh Camagan joined them.

"Thank you," Camagan said to them both. "Rob, I'm going to need some false travel identification documents so good that nothing and no one can see through them. Do you think Ninja would assist with that? Or is she still extremely angry with me?"

"Ninja wasn't that angry with you," Rob protested.

"I'm sure it's just a coincidence that my door access codes have been changing randomly for the last few days," Leigh Camagan said dryly. "No one can identify the problem."

"I'll talk to Ninja."

"Council Member?" Mele said. "Do I need the council's approval for the name of the Marine barracks?"

"There's a Marine barracks?" Leigh Camagan asked.

"That's what I'm calling the area in the orbital facility leased for my people's accommodations," Mele explained.

"I want to call it Duncan Barracks after Sergeant Grant Duncan."

"Who died while serving with *Squall*," Leigh Camagan said.

Rob couldn't help smiling at her. Three years had passed, but Camagan still remembered the names of those who had died in the battles then. His smile faded as he wondered if there would be so many dead in future battles that no one could recall all the names.

"I'm sure the council will approve," Camagan told Mele. "Go ahead. Take care of the star system while I'm gone, you two."

"How soon are you leaving?" Rob asked.

"As quickly as possible. I want to be on my way before any word of what's going on might be able to leak to our opponents."

"You'll be heading for Kosatka first?"

"Yes. It's along the way to almost every other place and the closest possible source of help for us."

"Do you think Kosatka will have anything to spare for us?" Mele asked. "They must have heard about what happened at Jatayu by now, but we haven't heard anything."

"I think," Leigh Camagan said, "that Kosatka and Glenlyon are both facing dangers that demand all we can manage. But even if we can't do anything else for each other, standing back-to-back together might help both star systems with the knowledge that we're not alone in our fight. And maybe seeing Kosatka and Glenlyon working together to defend each other will inspire others to come to our aid. I'm hoping that the pressure on us means that Kosatka is facing less trouble at the moment."

Rob saw Mele shake her head.

"If Scatha and its pals are smart," Mele said, "and they've been way too smart lately, they'll know we can't do much after losing *Claymore*. They might decide to hit Kosatka harder while we're unable to do anything."

"That makes way too much sense," Rob said, glancing toward the other council members as an idea came to him.

"Leigh, this might be the time to do something that could be either really smart or really stupid. I'll need council approval to do it, but it might help ensure you make it through to Kosatka. And if Kosatka is under more pressure, it might help them, too."

"I'm in," Mele announced. "You had me at *really smart or really stupid.*"

"Let's see if we can get President Chisholm to sign off on whatever your idea is, Rob," Leigh Camagan said. "For me, I trust your instincts. And Kosatka may need our help as badly as we need them."

Of the three cities so far constructed on Kosatka, Ani remained a shiny ghost town and battlefield, Drava had about two-thirds of its buildings occupied and the atmosphere of a place under siege, and the capital and original city Lodz was full of people, bustling with everyday life and commerce, only additional security checkpoints here and there hinting at the problems so far mostly kept far enough away to allow a feel of normality.

The intelligence offices occupied several rooms in a boxy structure once intended for record-keeping. Design features meant to keep out anything that might damage files also worked to keep in classified information. Those who came to Kosatka hadn't been eager to establish a formal means of spying on others, having seen too much of that sort of thing on Old Earth. Now that the need for that was as obvious as the fighting around Ani, Kosatka was still reluctant to create a permanent institution. So instead of a formal organization, the intelligence offices had been grouped under what someone had thought was the innocuous name Section Eight.

"Why does saying Section Eight always make you smile?" provisional intelligence chief Loren Yeresh asked Carmen Ochoa.

"It's just an old joke from Earth," Carmen told him.

"One of the largest militaries there also used the term. What is it you need?"

"One of our remote pickups in a rebel-held area intercepted this," Loren told her, bringing up an image on his display. Instead of words, stylized symbols appeared. "I assume it's a message, but it looks more like pictograms than words. None of our gear can make sense of it. Can you?"

She felt a shock of recognition that brought a lot of unpleasant memories with it. "Yes. This is an old gang code," Carmen said. "The Tharks. They control a lot of territory around Tharsis on Mars."

"Our enemies are still hiring Reds, then," Loren said.

"A lot of people will do almost anything to get off Mars," Carmen reminded her superior officer. "These Reds are being *paid* to get to go somewhere else. We could recruit our own," she added, not able to remember how many times she had made that recommendation.

And once again Loren Yeresh shook his head. "Carmen, no one trusts them. I agree that's stupid when we've got you as an example, but people don't look at you and see a Red."

"Maybe they should. We need fighters."

"I'll pass your recommendation up the chain again. What's the message say?"

"I don't know all the code," Carmen said, tapping a semicircular symbol with a short vertical line drawn inside. "That's a cent. It can mean one or one hundred. And this next one . . . that's like the beggar code symbol for full so I think it means the cent stands for one hundred. The mark is usually used for money but . . ."

"That next symbol looks like a gun. This is about an arms shipment?"

"No," Carmen said. "The gun represents a person. A man or a woman who is a gang fighter. That's how a lot of things are done on Mars. People are only worth what they can do or what their work is so they get represented by symbols showing whatever that is."

"Really?" Loren asked, studying the symbols. "What sort of symbol represented you on Mars?"

"None of your damned business." Carmen took a deep breath. "So, one hundred men and women, fighters. This here, that large, tall triangle with smaller triangles attached to the bottom on either side, represents a spaceship. But it's got a heavy line under it, so the ship is landed, which means a spaceport."

"What's the horse mean?" Loren asked.

It did look like a horse, the stick figure drawn with the legs straight up and down as if the animal were standing stock-still. Carmen didn't have to guess what that meant. "It means a trick. Like a Trojan Horse. That's where it comes from."

The pieces lined up in her head. "This says they're going to hit our main spaceport with a sneak attack."

Loren stared at her. "Are you sure?"

"That's what it looks like! Maybe some shipment along the rail line into the spaceport, maybe inside some trucks."

She waited as Loren Yeresh called up schedules, flipping rapidly through screens on his pad. "Because of the sabotage to the rail line from Drava, there aren't any freight trains due in today. But there's also the mass transit line that goes past the spaceport and has a stop there. I'll notify the security office—"

"Wait." Carmen pointed to another symbol she had recognized. "See that? A circle with short lines radiating out from it? That's a crater."

"A crater? How does that—"

"A crater represents a threat from above, because something falls and makes a crater. Maybe the threat is someone high-ranking who's out for you, or maybe it's a physical threat, like a bomb or an aerospace craft. But it means something dangerous coming from above."

"Coming from above. At the spaceport." Loren flipped through more screens. "There are the usual shuttle runs between here and the orbital facility. I'll notify security up there." He paused, thinking. "Trojan Horse. That literally was a big, fake horse, right? So nobody would expect it to hold people." Loren checked his pad again. "There are also a couple of cargo drops due in. One hundred people. Size . . . size . . . yeah, cargo containers that size could carry that many, and there's nothing unusual about cargo containers being pressurized to protect the contents. One of the drops is today."

"What freighter is dropping it?" Carmen asked as she tapped her pad to call up the data. "The *Terrance Griep.* Supposedly out of Brahma. Arrived here via the jump point from Kappa. Why would a freighter from Brahma have come here from Kappa?" Kappa was a red dwarf, smaller and dimmer and cooler than stars like Kosatka, with a bevy of cold, lifeless worlds circling it. With far better worlds available elsewhere, no one had settled at Kappa, but a few months ago Apulu had claimed ownership of it. Since there was no one with the means and the desire to dispute that claim, it hadn't yet been challenged.

Loren leaned over her shoulder to look. "He could have come to Kappa from Catalan. That's what he reported as his last stop."

"He also could have come from Hesta," Carmen pointed out.

Her boss pulled up more data. "*Shark* is handling patrol duties while *Piranha* is getting some repair work done. The *Terrance Griep* showed up while *Shark* was running down another freighter that had jumped in from Jatayu."

"That was convenient."

"Yeah. It kept *Shark* from doing any physical search of the *Griep* before the freighter reached this world. Maybe this job is making me paranoid, but right now I really wish I knew exactly what was in that cargo container that is due to drop in about an hour."

"I think we already know what's in it," Carmen said.

He hesitated. "If we're wrong . . . hell, I'll call in an alert," Loren decided. "That's what we're here for, right?"

"Supposedly. Look, we only learned of this because I was working here and I'm a Red," Carmen said. "We need to hire more. There are good people trapped on the hellhole called Mars. Give them an option to escape Mars and help ourselves at the same time."

Loren Yeresh paused long enough to nod to her, his expression serious. "I promise you that I will make that case in the strongest possible terms. You get to the main spaceport fast. I want you there when that drop comes down. Try to get us some live prisoners. The more proof we can get that these 'rebels' are being recruited by other star systems, the better our chances of getting help against them."

"I'm on my way." Carmen jumped up and ran out, pausing only to grab her rifle as she went.

It felt odd to hop into an automated public transit vehicle en route to a fight, but it was the quickest way to get there. The other passengers gave wary looks to Carmen, in her camos and resting the butt of her rifle on the floor of the vehicle. The main city still hadn't seen much violence from the "rebels," so Carmen seemed out of place.

By the time she reached the spaceport the scheduled cargo drop was only fifteen minutes away. Carmen saw soldiers and public security officers streaming toward the port as she dialed in access to the spaceport's official system to identify the drop pad the cargo would land at.

"Pad Six," a security officer called out as she raced by. Carmen joined her, another security officer dropping in alongside. Both carried sidearms in addition to the nonlethal shockers that used to be the sole armament of public security officers.

Carmen spotted a low shed that offered an overlook of Pad Six and veered off toward it as a squad of militia volunteers added their numbers to those of the public security officers. Hauling herself up on top of the shed, which proved to be a cover for equipment monitoring the cargo pads, Carmen lay down on the roof before looking upward.

There it was, a spark of light against the blue sky as thrusters fired to slow the descent of the cargo lifter and the container nestled under it.

Her comm beeped. "All personnel in the vicinity of the spaceport, switch to command frequency two."

Carmen made the switch as another announcement boomed across the spaceport's public announcing system. "All non–security personnel clear the spaceport immediately. Evacuate toward the terminal and out onto the plaza, then wait for instructions. Mass transit, road, and rail access to the spaceport has been temporarily suspended. Repeat, all non–security personnel must leave the spaceport immediately and gather on the plaza outside the entrance to the main terminal."

A lot of people were being inconvenienced, Carmen thought. If she'd made a mistake in interpreting that Thark gang code, those people were going to very unhappy with her.

She readied herself, staying prone as she loaded her rifle and sighted toward the pad, making sure the scope was set to start recording data and automatically relaying it back to where Loren Yeresh waited to forward the information to whoever needed it.

Another order came over the command circuit, the speaker sounding breathless with either excitement or worry. "All personnel hold fire until order is given. Repeat, do not shoot until order is given."

The cargo lifter came down in a flurry of dust devils, dropping nearly vertically on final to Pad Six. The last stage of the descent was slow, coming in gently. The cargo container, ten meters long, six meters wide, and three meters high, bore no external sign of being anything other than a routine drop.

It must be uncomfortable for those packed closely together inside, Carmen realized. But for a Red, brought up in the harsh living conditions that made Mars misery for all but the elite, it would be just one more thing to endure.

She really, really hoped none of the men and women inside that cargo container was anyone she had known back on Mars.

Maybe she was wrong. Maybe it would be the next drop. Or maybe she'd misread that gang code.

The lifter grounded.

Automated loading equipment began rolling toward the cargo container, the usual human supervisor nowhere to be seen. Would that tip off the possible occupants of the container?

The pressure seals popped, and the front of the cargo container dropped, not in the usual deliberate manner but in a sudden fall.

"Fire!" came across the command circuit.

Carmen's sights were on a man carrying a rifle who was in the front rank of those dashing out of the cargo container. He wore lightweight armor, the sort of thing more suited to police patrols than combat action.

She centered her sights on the man's chest and fired, deliberately avoiding looking at the man's face.

A barrage of fire erupted from a dozen points facing the cargo container, riddling the front ranks of the raiders. The falling bodies in front tripped up and hindered those behind, slowing them and making them easier targets for the defenders.

Carmen fired again, her scope recording the action. She could see the attackers shouting as they tried to get out of the container, struggling amid their fallen comrades blocking the way, screaming as they were hit, falling and bleeding.

She had to look away as the defenders' fire continued to rake the front of the container.

Cease fire. Please. Cease fire. They've been stopped. We're slaughtering them.

Realizing that she had to act, Carmen punched her comm. "Request cease-fire! I need prisoners! *Live* prisoners!"

Did her message jar someone out of a frenzy of killing? "Cease fire!" the command came.

How many were left? Carmen saw a dozen men and women stumbling out of the cargo container, their empty hands held up. Some of those lying in heaps near the front of the container were probably still alive. But at least half were surely dead.

"Thanks, Carmen," Yeresh said over her comm. "Great job. They could have done a lot of damage and killed a lot of people hitting the spaceport by surprise like that. Thanks to you, they never had a chance."

She looked at the bodies lying in front of the cargo container. "Yeah. Great job." Carmen dropped down off the shed and began walking toward the prisoners, her rifle held across her body. The prisoners were on their knees now, arms raised, nervous soldiers and public safety officers holding weapons still aimed at them.

Carmen paused to look at the tattoos on the arm of one of the male prisoners. "Tharks," she confirmed. "This one's a jed, a high-ranking member of the gang. Keep him separate."

The prisoners watched her, their eyes still stunned from the disaster that had befallen their planned attack. "Hey," one woman called out to Carmen. "You Hellas? ValMar? We deal."

Carmen shook her head. "Not Hellas or ValMar. If you talk, we'll deal. No talk, no deal."

"Wherefrom?"

"Shandakar."

"Shanda?" The survivors exchanged glances in which distress warred with the shock at the slaughter of their comrades.

"What's their problem?" a security officer asked Carmen.

"Shandakar is where the wimps on Mars supposedly come from," Carmen said. "They're embarrassed at losing to a Shanda."

"Reds are crazy," the officer said. "Except for you."

"No, I'm crazy, too," Carmen said. "Let's get all of these prisoners in restraints. I don't want to lose any more."

"What about the freighter that dropped them? They must have known about this. There's no way these people were hidden in that container all the way from Catalan."

"I doubt that freighter ever went to Catalan," Carmen said. "We'll see what his navigation files say when *Shark* intercepts him."

High above the planet, the destroyer *Shark* swooped down toward her prey, looking very much like her namesake on the prowl in the waters of the far-distant world of Earth. *Shark* had originally been built by the Old Colony of Franklin, using the same plans as those for the Founders Class destroyers of Earth Fleet, and spent over a decade as the *Bonhomme Richard*. Two and a half years ago, after being declared surplus, Franklin had sold her to Kosatka, which hadn't been sure who that guy Richard had been and decided that *Shark* made a better name. She wasn't the newest warship in space by any measure, but out here *Shark* was still a force to be reckoned with.

Especially when *Shark*'s target was a lumbering, boxy merchant freighter.

"Merchant ship *Terrance Griep*, your ship off-loaded a cargo container full of enemy combatants. Stand by to receive a boarding party," *Shark*'s commanding officer Commander Pyotr Derian broadcast. Trying to keep ships from smuggling combatants and weaponry down to the surface wasn't the most exciting job for a warship, but it beat boring holes through endless space while hoping for something interesting to happen. He turned his head to speak to the operations watch stander on the bridge. "Initiate final intercept maneuver."

"Initiating final intercept maneuver," the watch stander repeated before activating the command.

"How did they think they'd get away?" *Shark*'s weapons officer wondered.

"They probably hoped we'd be patrolling a long ways off," Derian guessed, "and that in the confusion after the attack on the spaceport they could get far enough to reach a jump point before we caught them."

The reply that came from the merchant ship was brief

and belligerent. "We have committed no crime. We will not permit an illegal search."

Shark's captain smiled, but his answer held no humor. "This is not a search. Your ship is being seized for aiding an attack on the people of Kosatka. I repeat, prepare to receive a boarding party."

Shark's main propulsion fired to brake the ship's velocity as the destroyer made its final approach on the freighter, her path curving inward to meet that of the other ship.

An urgent alert sounded, warnings appearing on the display before the captain. "He's shooting at us?" Derian asked in amazement.

"The freighter has a grapeshot launcher mounted," the weapons officer reported. "It was hidden, but we have the launcher site identified now. Our shields can take a lot more hits before they'd be in danger of failing."

Being shot at certainly justified the use of force. "Use the pulse particle beams. I want that launcher fried."

Pinpoint targeting in combat situations often wasn't possible, but with the two ships so close and moving slowly relative to each other it was a simple task for the fire control systems. *Shark* trembled slightly as the streams of charged particles tore through space before slashing through part of the freighter and the grapeshot launcher.

"Launcher out of commission, Captain," the weapons officer reported. "We've rescanned the freighter, looking for anomalies that might indicate other hidden weapons, and found nothing else. Which part of the freighter should we target next?"

Commander Derian frowned as he considered the question. Taking out the freighter's propulsion would prevent it from accelerating any more but would force *Shark* to put across a towline and go through a long, tedious process of using her own propulsion to get the freighter to Kosatka's orbital facility. There was also a real chance those shots could cause serious structural damage. On the other hand, destroying the control deck and other living areas would only require *Shark*'s engineers to install temporary controls to replace any destroyed. And the threat of shooting up the areas where the crew was located would more likely cause the freighter's crew to back down.

Decided, Derian tapped his comm controls again. "*Terrance Griep*, cease maneuvering and stand by for a boarding party. If you do not comply, my next shots will be into your control deck and crew compartment." He looked over at the weapons station. "Did you copy that?"

"Yes, sir. Targeting control deck and crew compartment."

"Captain? The boarding party commander wants to know whether nonlethal shockers or lethal weaponry should be employed in case resistance is encountered?"

Derian almost tossed off a casual command to use lethal weaponry, pausing as he realized how easily that decision had come to him. Lethal weaponry. Just like that. A few years spent fighting an unpredictable and ruthless enemy had resulted in some uncomfortable changes in perspective. Adding nonlethal shockers to the boarding party armament wouldn't add a significant burden, and would give them alternatives to killing. "Carry both," the captain finally ordered. "Their orders are to employ shockers first. But lethal force is authorized if required by circumstances or if the freighter crew employs lethal weapons."

Shark glided right next to the freighter, which was now behaving itself. Derian eyed the other ship with suspicion, though. "Make sure our maneuvering systems are set for automatic collision avoidance. If he tries to use his thrusters to bump us, I want us out of the way before he gets there." On automatic, *Shark*'s thrusters should easily get the far more agile destroyer clear before the freighter could collide with her.

A secondary display lit up next to the captain's seat, showing the boarding party in survival suits preparing to leap across the gap between ships toward the access hatch for the freighter crew compartment. Both ships were moving through space, but with their vectors matched it felt as if they were sitting absolutely still next to each other.

"They're getting awfully bold, aren't they?" the operations officer said, her voice worried. "What kind of idiot uses a single grapeshot launcher to attack a destroyer?"

"Yeah. Crazy for them to do that when it's just them and us." Derian paused, thinking. "I wonder what kind of backing they're expecting to show up? Maybe that was part of their plan for getting away. Comms, get a message off to *Piranha* and the defense office. Tell them we might have some dangerous company coming."

"Nothing specific, sir?" the comms watch asked. "Just a concern about dangerous company?"

Another alarm sounded on the captain's display, this time accompanied by two red markers four light hours away at the jump point from Jatayu. Four hours ago, a pair of destroyers had jumped into this star system, the light from that event only now reaching ships near the inhabited world.

Neither destroyer was broadcasting any identification. That was both odd and threatening.

"Both new contacts are traveling at point zero four light speed," operations reported. "It will take them one hundred hours to get here at that velocity."

That changed things. Derian grimaced, unhappy at having his guess proven accurate so quickly. "Tell *Piranha* and the defense office that unknown destroyers have entered the star system and at current velocity will reach our position in a little more than four days. Request orders."

This day had just gotten far too interesting.

He felt *Shark*'s thrusters fire before seeing the alert on his display.

"The freighter is firing full thrusters in an attempt to collide with us," the operations officer reported. "We're evading."

"What's the status of the boarding party?" Derian demanded.

"All still aboard. They were lining up to jump when the freighter started moving."

"He jumped the gun," the weapons officer remarked. "If

that freighter had waited until our boarding party was moving, we'd have had to figure out how to recover them. What the hell is he trying to do?"

"Disable us with a low speed collision so we'd be easy pickings for those two destroyers, maybe. He's not going to get a second chance," Derian said. "Open fire on the freighter's control deck and crew compartment. We'll see how they like playing tag with particle beams and grapeshot."

He'd tried to be humanitarian, and they'd forced him into killing all or most of them anyway.

"If those two destroyers are commanded by officers as zealous as whoever captained that freighter," the operations officer said, "we're going to have a nasty fight on our hands."

"I was just thinking the same thing," Derian said as he watched the freighter's bridge and crew compartment dissolve under the fire from *Shark*. Fortunately, *Piranha* was not far off, docked at the orbital facility for some minor repair work. She could rejoin *Shark* in plenty of time to face those two newcomers at equal odds.

"Sir, we've got some odd readings from the freighter's power core," the engineering watch reported.

"He's launched an escape pod," the operations officer called out a moment later as the alert appeared on Derian's display. "They must have been in it before the freighter began that last maneuver. It was all on automatic."

The *Terrance Griep*, still sliding toward *Shark*, was now angling beneath the destroyer as *Shark* continued to climb to avoid a collision.

"They launched that escape pod at maximum boost, but they can't outrun us even with that," Derian said. "What the hell are they trying?"

"Captain, the readings from the freighter's power core indicate it's becoming unstable!"

He got it then. He understood the entire plan. The only question left was whether he still had a chance to frustrate it.

Derian had spent years learning to follow proper procedures, but had also served under a commanding officer who had introduced him to the dangerous idea that sometimes proper procedures weren't the answer.

Instead of following proper procedures now, calling out a propulsion order for the watch stander to confirm and carry out, Derian hit the command on his display for propulsion, running the power level up to full.

Shark jerked as her main propulsion cut in at full power, shoving the ship ahead and away from the freighter. Members of the crew grabbed for handholds, crying out in surprise, as Derian punched the control for the ship's general announcing system. "All hands in survival suits! Brace for—!"

The *Terrance Griep* exploded as its power core overloaded. This close, *Shark*'s sensors only had time to begin sounding an alarm before the shock wave of gases, heat, radiation, and debris hit the fleeing destroyer.

Hit from behind and below, *Shark*'s stern pitched up, her maneuvering systems firing to try to prevent the ship from going into an end-over-end tumble through space.

"Main propulsion is off-line," the engineering watch stander on the bridge reported in a shaky voice. "Serious damage aft. Engineering is not responding to requests for their status."

"How's the power core?" Derian asked, before getting a partial answer as the lighting went off, replaced with the dimmer glow of emergency lanterns.

"Checking, sir . . . our power core just carried out an automated emergency shutdown due to damage."

He couldn't afford to let anger overwhelm him, Derian told himself. "Do we still have comms?"

"Yes, sir. Primary comm system is rebooting, but the secondary is online and running on backup power."

"Send a message that we've lost main propulsion and sustained other damage to engineering. Casualty count unknown. A full update will follow as we assess damage and get more details. Ensure that *Piranha* knows about the escape pod that left the freighter. Maybe they can catch it."

"They set us up," the operations officer said, angry and

ashamed in equal measures. "The raid on the spaceport, the freighter that was intended to take us out, and those two destroyers arriving from Jatayu."

A backup display appeared next to Derian's seat. He saw the red markers on it showing where *Shark* had taken damage. It could have been worse. If he hadn't ordered full acceleration, *Shark* would have taken the full force of the freighter's death throes.

But that was small comfort at the moment. The enemy had been two steps ahead of them at every point.

"The orbital facility reports that it's sending a tug to intercept us and help us get back for repairs," the comm watch said. "The escape pod from the freighter is heading down toward the planet. Best estimate is a landing site near Ani."

"Can *Piranha* handle those two destroyers alone?" the operations officer wondered.

"I hope so," Derian said, bitterness filling him. He'd saved his ship but otherwise failed.

It would be up to others to save Kosatka.

CHAPTER 4

The *Bruce Monroe* had left orbit about Glenlyon's primary world, making a freighter's slow, lumbering path to the jump point for Jatayu. *Saber* had escorted the *Bruce Monroe* all the way to the jump point. According to the plans briefed to everyone, the destroyer would leave the freighter there, *Saber* remaining at Glenlyon to protect the star system.

Leigh Camagan, traveling on the *Bruce Monroe* under a false identity, had chafed at being unable to talk with Rob Geary during the journey to the jump point. She hoped he was both asserting himself as commanding officer and beginning to make changes to the way the former Earth Fleet crew reacted to the challenges of combat. *Saber* had carried out every maneuver with precision and skill, but then the Earth Fleet–trained crews had always displayed that.

Right up until *Claymore* had been destroyed at Jatayu. What would be waiting at Jatayu this time when the *Bruce Monroe* arrived on its own?

At least the freighter's trip through jump space was exactly the same length as it would be for a far more maneuverable ship like *Saber*. Jump space didn't care how fast a ship could accelerate in normal space. No matter what their velocity when they entered jump (and at the moment the jump drives only worked if ships were traveling at point zero six speed or less) everything in jump space moved at the same pace from jump point to jump point, for reasons that remained unexplained by science. And everyone in jump space experienced the same feelings of discomfort that got worse as the period in jump space went on. Itches that weren't itches, and a growing sensation that your own skin no longer fit right. There were horrible stories about what had happened to the crews of ships that had spent too long in jump space. Most of them were probably made up, but whenever Leigh was in jump space she found herself believing all of them.

All of which was why it was both a relief and a tense moment as, after days of travel, the *Bruce Monroe* left jump space at Jatayu again.

This time no warships awaited the arrival of the freighter. But one was patrolling several light minutes away, and soon altered vector to intercept the *Bruce Monroe*.

"He's a Buccaneer Class cutter," the *Bruce Monroe*'s captain announced to the dozen passengers. The captain didn't look happy, but he kept his voice and his body language calm and firm to avoid feeding any fears. "We can't outrun him. We'll comply with their orders, pay their 'transit fees,' and hopefully get cleared to continue on to Kosatka."

Soon enough a message arrived from the warship. Maintain your current vector, await the cutter's arrival, and be prepared to be boarded by an inspection team. Also be prepared to pay a transit fee to Scatha, a fee whose cost had tripled since the last attempt to pass through Jatayu.

The inspection team that boarded the freighter was armed with both hand weapons and swaggering attitudes that practically begged for someone among the freighter's crew or passengers to give them an excuse for using those weapons.

But the crew of the *Bruce Monroe* and the passengers were all too smart or too scared to give the inspectors an opportunity for violence. When told to line up for screening, Leigh Camagan joined the others meekly enough. She watched the freighter's small supply of alcoholic beverages being carried off. "Taxes were not paid on that liquor, so it's contraband and is being confiscated," the officer in charge of the inspection announced as if hoping that someone would object. When no one did, he started going down the line of passengers, checking their travel documents as well as the contents of their personal comm pads and universal wallets.

He reached Leigh and looked her up and down, leaning close to physically intimidate her. She thought the officer from Scatha had the attitude of a school bully who has achieved a lifelong dream of being able to apply those talents in his job. "Identification!"

Leigh Camagan tried to project nervousness underlain by fright, just the sort of reaction a bully would glory in, as she handed him her identification.

He squinted at the results that popped up on his pad. "Alice Mary Norton. Librarian." The officer seemed to find that highly amusing. "Hey, she's a librarian!"

"She knows what sort of trash you've been reading," one of the other members of Scatha's boarding party warned with a mocking grin.

"Yeah. You chasing down some overdue hardcopy books, Mary Alice?"

"I'm going back to Earth. I'm going to look at the wildflowers when I get there," Leigh Camagan said. "I miss them." Every word of which was true. Her decade of political experience had taught Leigh that telling a misleading truth instead of lying about the real reason for something always came across as much more sincere.

It also helped fool interrogation apps.

The officer glanced at his pad, apparently saw nothing to concern him, then stuck out his hand again. "Universal wallet."

"Yes, sir," Leigh Camagan said like the meek librarian she was supposed to be. She brought out the small, slim rectangular box and held it before her.

"Access code!" the Scathan bully demanded.

Letting her hand shake a bit with a show of fear, Leigh punched in the code that would let the officer's pad read her wallet.

"They don't pay librarians much, huh? There's an individual transit fee, too. Authorize it!"

The "transit fee" charge that popped up on Leigh Camagan's wallet amounted to nearly half of the unimpressive sum available. "Sir, please—"

"Are you resisting?" the officer asked as two of the other inspectors stepped forward eagerly.

"No, sir." Leigh tapped the approval.

The officer moved on to the next passenger. She closed the wallet access and waited, guessing that the inspection team was waiting for someone to ask if they could sit down or leave and thereby make themselves a target for more harassment.

She'd have to thank Ninja for doing such an excellent job on her identification documents and her wallet. "They'll ask for your passwords and codes," Ninja had explained. "This pad isn't your pad, but it's loaded with lots of stuff that makes it look appropriate for your fake identity. Enter this code in your wallet and all they'll see is a shell with not much money in it. Enter this *other* code and you'll have access to the actual wallet with the Glenlyon government account that'll pay for new ships."

And then Ninja had refused payment. "Get through the blockade, get help for us, and save Rob's butt. That's what I want out of this."

"If it can be done," Leigh had promised, "I will."

The officer from the Scathan cutter was shaking down the last passenger when his comm pad beeped and someone began talking loudly enough for Leigh to hear. "A destroyer just arrived in system! Get back here now!"

Annoyed, the officer tapped the pad. "That'll be one of ours. What's his ID?"

"He came in at the jump point from Glenlyon, and he's broadcasting a Glenlyon ID!"

Cursing, the officer and his team raced off the freighter's crew deck and through the access tube to the cutter.

Leigh and everyone else waited, unmoving, until the air lock cycled closed.

The moment that happened the captain of the *Bruce Monroe* ran to the freighter's control deck, Leigh close behind. "Is that *Saber*?" the captain gasped.

She looked at the information displayed below the contact. "This says she's *Saber*."

"What are they doing here?"

Leigh felt a smile on her lips. "Surprising a lot of people, it seems."

Morale aboard *Saber* was shaky at best. Everyone followed orders, every task got done, but Rob could tell that the officers and crew lacked confidence. The shock of *Claymore*'s loss had hit them hard. The inactivity as Commander Teosig kept the ship in orbit afterward had let the shock settle in. "They're ready to lose," Mele had told him. "One hit and they'll fold."

"What do you recommend?"

"Do something," Mele said. "Anything."

He'd come up with something, an action that had led Mele to comment that she hadn't meant doing *anything really stupid*.

He didn't think this was really stupid. Hopefully, he was right about that.

The reaction of the crew of *Saber* as Rob ordered the ship to the jump point hours after the *Bruce Monroe* had departed both worried him and convinced him that he was doing the right thing. Shock vied with what looked too much like fear even though the crew carried out their orders with the usual practiced skill.

Rob had made sure that Lieutenant Commander Vicki Shen was on the bridge when he gave the order. If someone was going to challenge his authority and his orders, he wanted it done to his face. But even though Shen looked as surprised as the others, she said nothing.

He activated the ship's general announcing system. "This is the captain." That still felt weird to say, bringing back both fond and disturbing memories of his time on *Squall*. "We're going to jump, arriving long enough after the arrival of the *Bruce Monroe* to surprise anyone waiting at Jatayu. If the odds are bad, we'll distract the enemy forces enough to help the *Bruce Monroe* get through the star system before we jump back here. If the odds are good, we're going to start making them pay for *Claymore*. Regardless of exactly what happens, we'll disrupt the enemy's plans."

Rob paused, trying to remember the rest of the speech he had carefully rehearsed in his mind. "No matter what we find at Jatayu, I know *Saber* and her crew will be able to handle it. Before this is over, Scatha is going to find out the hard way not to mess with the kind of crew *Saber* is fortunate enough to have, and your friends on *Claymore* are going to be avenged."

Ending the speech, Rob turned to look at Shen. "I'm sorry I couldn't brief you on this beforehand. Let's go talk."

Once in his stateroom, Shen declined his offer to take a seat, her expression as stiff as her words. "Since the captain lacks confidence in me—"

"Let's not finish that," Rob said. "I do have confidence in you. I'm sorry I couldn't brief you beforehand, but only two other people in Glenlyon knew we were going to Jatayu. One of them was Council President Chisholm, who ordered me not to tell anyone else until we headed for the jump point."

Shen frowned, but her posture relaxed a bit. "What's our objective, sir? We're supposed to defend this star system."

"Defense doesn't have to be a passive thing. Hitting enemy warships at Jatayu without warning will disrupt whatever they're planning."

"What if they're waiting for us?"

The unspoken part being *like they were for* Claymore.

Rob grimaced, trying to figure out how to say it nicely and finally deciding to be blunt. "Commodore Hopkins practically told Scatha exactly when *Claymore* would arrive at Jatayu. He took weeks to prepare and let detailed information about his plans be known."

"There was a reason for that!" Shen protested. "To ensure that Scatha knew we were coming so they'd back down. The Commodore wanted to ensure there wouldn't be any accidental exchange of fire."

"Really?" Rob shook his head. "I guess that might have worked if Scatha hadn't chosen to start shooting again. Why was the Commodore so certain that Scatha would back down?"

"Deconfliction, sir. It's a necessary element . . . it *was* a necessary element for offensive operations in a situation short of war, giving the opponent a chance to back down before fire is exchanged."

It made sense, in a way, if you assumed that your opponent was as interested in avoiding hostilities as you were. Or if avoiding hostilities was a high enough priority to sacrifice ships and people for if the assumptions were wrong. And Commodore Hopkins's assumptions had been badly wrong.

Emphasizing that now to Vicki Shen would serve no purpose, Rob knew. "Here's what's important this time. Scatha won't have time to learn we jumped and get word to Jatayu before we arrive. It's physically impossible. We're going to be the ones pulling a surprise. Here's what I need from you. Confidence. Let everyone else aboard see that you're concerned about what might be at Jatayu but certain that we can handle it. The officers and crew don't entirely trust me yet. But you're one of them."

Shen nodded slowly, her expression worried. "I'll have to fake the confidence."

Rob smiled. "I was an ensign once. Just like you were. And every ensign has to learn how to look confident even when they have no idea how things are going to work out. Right?"

She smiled back at him. "I won't have to fake confidence in the crew. They'll do what we ask of them."

"I have no doubt of that," Rob said. He didn't have to fake that statement, either.

Which is why *Saber* arrived at Jatayu, the entire crew at full alert, shields at maximum strength and weapons prepared, Mele Darcy and her five-Marine detachment also at ready. After the initial shock at Rob's ordering them to the jump point, morale had noticeably improved aboard *Saber*. But if two destroyers were waiting anywhere near the jump exit, it would take a lot more than morale to inflict any damage on the enemy and still get away without taking hits.

"Leaving jump space."

He felt the familiar shock of returning to normal space, the confusion and blurry vision that always accompanied the drop out of jump space, the moments of fearing that *Saber* was about to suffer the same fate as *Claymore*.

An alert sounded, but it wasn't the urgent shrill warning of imminent danger.

"Only one warship is in Jatayu Star System," Lieutenant Cameron reported. "A Buccaneer Class cutter currently alongside the freighter *Bruce Monroe*. Cutter is broadcasting Scatha registry. Distance two light minutes."

"Get me an intercept vector," Rob ordered, feeling a leap of elation that the odds had turned out to be very much in *Saber*'s favor.

"We're going for him, sir?" Cameron asked.

"Hell, yes, we're going for him. Comms, give me a link to send him a message."

"Aye, sir. Ready, sir."

Rob took a couple of slow breaths, wanting his voice to sound not just steady but also full of confidence. "Scathan cutter, this is the Glenlyon warship *Saber*. You will lower your shields, power down all weapons, and prepare to be boarded. Failure to surrender will result in our use of all necessary force. Commander Geary, out."

"Here's the intercept, sir," Cameron said.

The curving path through space arced from where *Saber* was, slightly above and to port of the cutter's current location, to where the cutter would be when *Saber* got there. "Execute intercept course," Rob ordered. "Come starboard zero zero three degrees, down zero one degrees. Accelerate to point zero eight light speed." That would be pushing even a destroyer like *Saber* but would achieve an intercept in about thirty minutes, well worth it to give the cutter the least possible time to run.

Saber trembled as her main propulsion cut in at full power and maneuvering thrusters pushed her around slightly to aim for the intercept.

"It's been two minutes. He should be seeing us now, Captain," Ensign Reichert reported from the weapons station, her eyes fixed on her displays.

It would be at least two more minutes before Geary would see the cutter's reaction. Maybe longer if the cutter's crew dithered before deciding what to do.

"Sir?" Lieutenant Cameron asked. "That's the same class ship as your former command, *Squall*, right?"

"That's right," Rob said. "I know everything that ship can do. And everything it can't do." But thinking of *Squall* made him recall his last fight, and Danielle Martel, who had died defending a world that still shied away from acknowledging her contribution to the victory.

To distract himself from those thoughts, Rob called back to where Mele waited with her newly minted Marines. "Captain Darcy, we're facing a Buccaneer Class cutter. Standard crew size twenty-four. The one we captured from Scatha three years ago only had about twenty in the crew."

Mele's voice, usually cheerful, sounded deadly calm as she replied. "Understand we'll probably face approximately twenty hostiles if we conduct a boarding operation. Do you have any estimate as to the likelihood we'll be needed?"

"We should know in a couple of minutes," Rob replied.

"The cutter was alongside the *Bruce Monroe* when we arrived."

"They might turn it into a hostage situation," Mele warned. "If they think of that."

Rob hadn't considered that possibility. What if the cutter's crew took hostage the passengers and crew of the freighter? How much could he risk the lives of those men and women in the pursuit of that cutter? "Let's hope they don't think of that," Rob finally said.

Rob finally saw signs that the cutter was reacting more than five minutes after *Saber* had arrived at Jatayu. "Is he pulling in his boarding tube?"

"Yes, sir," Ensign Reichert confirmed.

"Contact the *Bruce Monroe*. I want to know if they're all right and if the cutter took any hostages with them."

A minute and a half ago, the cutter had begun pulling away from the freighter, lighting off its main propulsion to accelerate on a course away from *Saber*.

"Captain, it looks like he's heading for the jump point for Kosatka," Lieutenant Cameron said.

"Give me an updated intercept vector," Rob ordered.

Catching a ship or planet or satellite on a fixed vector or orbit through space was a little complicated but about as simple as anything in space could be. The math got more complex when what you wanted to catch was accelerating.

"Captain? Can we assume standard acceleration profiles for the cutter?"

"Standard or worse than that," Rob said. "After we captured *Squall*, she needed a lot of work to get her equipment in shape."

"Revised intercept ready, Captain."

Rob checked it out. "Very well. Execute revised intercept."

"Captain," Ensign Reichert said, "request targeting priority."

"Propulsion and weaponry if fire control can hit them. But just about any hit on that cutter will strike something important," Rob said.

He had a strange sensation as *Saber* swooped toward her fleeing prey. Something like this had happened three years ago at Glenlyon. Only he had been commanding the cutter, trying to figure out how to both survive and defeat a destroyer that outmaneuvered and outgunned his own ship. Now he was on the superior warship, and it was the other crew that was trying to figure out how to survive.

Rob wondered why that moment of empathy didn't bother him, then he remembered how many aboard the *Squall* had died because of Scatha, and that recently half the crew of *Claymore* had also been killed. Glenlyon didn't want to fight. Scatha did, and the people Scatha had hired to crew its warships weren't worried about whether or not they were aggressors. Crews who hadn't worried about opening fire on *Claymore* without warning. Instead of sympathy for their plight, Rob felt a grim satisfaction in knowing that this time it was Scatha's people who were in trouble.

Saber's automated systems took that moment to pop up a checklist on Rob's display. Engaging Lesser Warship In Overtaking Maneuver. "I thought we cleaned these checklists out of the systems." He searched in vain for a "close" command. "How do I get rid of it?"

Lieutenant Cameron sounded apologetic. "You can't, sir. It stays up until every item is checked."

"Can't I just check everything now?"

"No, sir. It's tied in to the ship's systems so it knows if you've done something or not."

"How did you guys ever get anything done?" Rob complained as he moved the checklist as far to one side of the display as it would go.

"Getting things done wasn't the point, sir," Cameron said. "Filling out the checklist right was what counted."

Lieutenant Commander Shen called up from engineering. "Captain Geary, the cutter is only putting out about seventy-five percent of what should be his maximum acceleration. It looks like that's the best he can do."

Rob smiled at hearing that the already sluggish Buccaneer was further handicapped by main propulsion that wasn't able to operate at full strength. "Thank you," Rob said. "Lieutenant Cameron, update the intercept using seventy-five percent maximum for the cutter."

"Fifteen minutes to intercept on revised vector," Ensign Reichert reported, an undercurrent of excitement in her voice.

"Captain," the comms watch said, "the *Bruce Monroe* reports all crew and passengers are safe aboard her. The boarding party from the cutter left in a panic when they saw our arrival."

"Has there been any response from the cutter?"

"No, Captain."

Rob touched his comm link command. "Scathan warship, this is the Glenlyon destroyer *Saber* demanding that you surrender. Cease accelerating, drop your shields, and power down all weapons. If you do not comply immediately, we will use all necessary force. Acknowledge this message. Commander Geary, over."

Five more minutes passed, *Saber* racing past and slightly above the *Bruce Monroe* as the freighter plodded along toward the jump point for Kosatka.

"What is that cutter doing?" Cameron wondered. "The Scathans know we'll catch them."

"They might be hoping that help will show up from the Kosatka jump point," Rob said. "Or they might be planning to wait until we make one firing run and go on past them, before they turn and try to make the jump point for Glenlyon."

"But we're faster and more maneuverable. We'll catch them again before they can do that."

Rob nodded, feeling a tightness inside born of tension and the knowledge that his orders would soon result in more deaths. "Right. They don't have any good options except surrender, and they're not doing that."

Another five minutes.

"Target is changing aspect," Ensign Reichert reported. "He's cut his main propulsion."

That was expected. Standard tactics in space as the moment of combat approached was to swing the ship around so the bow, with the strongest armor and shields, was facing the enemy. With the main propulsion off, the cutter would continue moving backward at an extremely high rate of speed while also turned toward the oncoming threat of *Saber*. But something didn't look quite right.

"He made that move a little early," Rob said. "How's his bow lined up? Is he going to face us straight on at intercept?"

A moment passed while Lieutenant Cameron checked on his own and consulted with some enlisted specialists. "No, sir. Not straight on. He'll be several degrees off."

"What vector is he pointing toward?"

Another pause. "The jump point to Glenlyon."

"Three minutes to intercept," Reichert warned.

"Put the maneuvering systems on automatic adjustment for the intercept," Rob ordered. "Bias them toward assuming the cutter will begin braking velocity just before we reach him."

The former Earth Fleet officers might not be used to improvising in response to events, but they were very good at what they did. Rob saw control screens flashing past before his watch standers as they entered the changes. "Weapons are ready as ordered, Captain," Ensign Reichert reported.

"Confirm that weapons are set to fire on automatic," Rob said.

"Confirmed," Ensign Reichert replied. "All weapons on automatic. One minute to intercept."

"He's lit off his main propulsion again!" Cameron warned a moment later.

The cutter, its propulsion facing in the direction the ship was going, was now using it to brake its velocity, suddenly altering the point of intercept. Humans would have had trouble calculating the changes and making the necessary inputs to *Saber*'s own maneuvering systems, but with everything on automatic the destroyer changed her own course swiftly enough to counter the enemy move.

The moment of combat came and went in a tiny fraction of a second, *Saber*'s two grapeshot launchers and three pulse particle cannons firing at a target that was there and gone far too swiftly for human reflexes to have reacted in time. Rob glared at the checklist that had placed itself in the center of his display again, shoving the checklist to one side a second time so he could see what was going on. "Give me another vector to intercept," he ordered while waiting for *Saber*'s sensors to report on the outcome of the exchange of fire.

"Two hits on our forward shields," Reichert said. "No penetration, no damage. We knocked down his forward shields and got some hits, damage unknown."

"Change course up two six zero degrees," Rob ordered. "Port zero two degrees."

Saber began a long, wide curve upward through space to reverse course and come back at the cutter.

Cameron shook his head. "The cutter is still killing velocity before it'll be able to accelerate toward the jump point. When we hit him again he'll be almost at a dead stop. His forward shields aren't rebuilding. We might have knocked them out."

Rob tapped his comm controls again. "Scathan warship, your situation is hopeless. Broadcast your surrender, drop your remaining shields, and power down your weapons."

No response came.

"Listen up, everyone," Rob told the bridge crew. "I was in a hopeless situation commanding a ship like that and managed to cripple my opponent. Don't ease up, don't get overconfident, don't give him a chance to surprise us. Let's see how much damage we can do this time." He called back to Mele again. "If we can do enough damage on this run, I might try a boarding operation so we can capture it. That cutter isn't much, but he is a warship."

Twenty minutes later *Saber* tore past the cutter again, which this time didn't maneuver to face the attack with its unshielded bow. Instead, *Saber* was able to target the weaker shields at the stern of the cutter.

"*Yes!*" Ensign Reichert cried, immediately flinching apologetically as she realized she'd shouted. "His aft shields collapsed," she continued in calmer tones. "We scored several hits. Estimate he is now at less than twenty-five percent propulsion. Correction, his main propulsion has just failed."

"Any damage to us?" Rob asked.

"No, sir! He only scored one hit on our shields."

Unable to maneuver, his shields down, the cutter was helpless. Rob called the enemy warship a third time. "Scathan warship, broadcast your surrender immediately or we will continue our attack."

What if the cutter didn't surrender? Rob wondered as he waited for a reply. Order Mele to try to capture the cutter? Or continue to pound the cutter until it either surrendered or was destroyed? With its propulsion badly damaged, getting that cutter back to Glenlyon after it was captured might be very difficult.

His thoughts were interrupted by a report from his engineering watch stander. "Captain, we're getting fluctuating readings from the cutter's power core."

"Is he doing a shutdown?" Rob asked.

"No, sir. It's jumping up and down as if . . . sir, I know how crazy this sounds but it's as if someone was trying to control the power core manually rather than using automated systems, overcorrecting each time."

"The Buccaneer cutters use an obsolete, bug-prone operating system. Scatha was using manual controls on *Squall*'s power core before we captured her," Rob said.

"*Sir?* If that's what's going on, they're losing control and that power core is going to blow real soon!"

"He's launched his lifeboat!" Cameron called out.

"He's approaching overload, Captain!"

The image of the Scathan warship on Rob's display disappeared, replaced by an expanding ball of dust and debris that had once been a human warship. The wave of death engulfed the fleeing lifeboat, tearing it apart, just as if the cutter had been a ship on an ocean dragging its crew down with it as it sank.

A moment of stunned silence on *Saber* shattered as cheers resounded through the ship.

Rob let them cheer. He'd given the cutter's crew every chance he could.

And *Claymore* had been partially avenged.

Close to a day later, *Saber* slid close to the small facility that Scatha had left orbiting Jatayu as a sign of Scatha's claim to the star. Scatha hadn't wasted any money on the structure, which consisted of a bunch of various-sized drum-shaped cylinders with rounded edges linked together, the largest big enough to serve as a small warehouse for parts and supplies and the smaller ones plainly intended to serve as living quarters for a small crew.

Mele Darcy stood in the open air lock hatch as *Saber* came to a halt relative to the facility. The outfit she wore was a toughened survival suit rather than a set of armor designed for use on ships, but in her hands was a pulse rifle as good as anything she'd carried in Franklin's Marines. With her stood the five newly minted Marines who had seemed best able to handle things after the short period of training so far.

Mele wished she could have had Gunny Moon with her, but he had been needed far more to stay at Glenlyon training the other new Marines.

"Let's go," Mele broadcast to her Marines, leaping outward first. The universe spun about her, an infinity of dark with endless stars and galaxies, but her eyes stayed locked on the hatch to the facility. There hadn't been any replies to demands that the facility surrender, so there was no telling what kind of reception was waiting on the other side of that hatch.

She flew through emptiness, a weapon in her hands, her heart pounding with anticipation and excitement, feeling for those seconds as if she had bought a ticket on the best, scariest ride humanity had ever built.

Mele cushioned her landing with her arms, coming to a

gentle halt against the facility. To her left the other five Marines landed, two hard enough that they almost bounced back off into space despite the cling of their gecko gloves.

"Get it open, Giddings," Mele ordered her one-man hack-and-crack team. As Corporal V. T. "Glitch" Giddings moved next to the hatch's exterior controls, Mele pushed herself out to arm's length from the side of the facility, holding on with one hand while her other aimed her rifle at the air lock hatch. That let her both guard against anyone waiting in the air lock and watch the progress of breaking in. This was her first chance to see how Giddings did in an operational setting and to be certain that his nickname referred to the things he could do on purpose to the enemy and not to things he could inadvertently cause in friendly software systems.

Giddings bent to work but almost immediately paused. "Captain, it's not locked." He reached for the controls.

"Wait!" Mele ordered. "That's either very good or very bad. Get to one side of the hatch before you hit the enter command, out of the line of fire from it just in case there's a booby trap inside. The rest of you brace yourselves." She pulled herself next to the facility, waiting anxiously as Giddings pressed the enter control.

The hatch swung open with the silent grace of objects moving in the void of space. No explosion followed, but that didn't mean someone or something might not be waiting. Mele unsnapped a carryall bag from her waist and tossed it into the hatch so it would bounce around and set off any motion-activated traps.

Still nothing. Bracing herself, Mele swung inside.

The air lock was bare of anything except the two control pads. The inner hatch and the small display on it to allow an interior view showed no sign of tampering or sabotage. Mele scanned the inner walls, ceiling, and deck of the air lock carefully, finding nothing. The control for the inner door also wasn't locked.

She was either dealing with a very good trap or opponents so confident they'd grown careless.

"I'm going through first with Yoshida," Mele told the others. "If nothing explodes, the rest of you follow."

"What if something does explode?" Giddings asked.

"Once it stops exploding, follow me anyway. And kill whoever set the explosive as a favor to me." Mele waved Yoshida into the air lock, knowing that she should send someone else in first, that as senior officer she should sit back and supervise the actions of the others. But this was the first combat action of Glenlyon's Marines, and she was determined not to establish a precedent of officers holding back while they sent others to do the dirty work.

She held her breath as she hit the cycle command, but nothing happened that wasn't supposed to. The outer hatch closed, air pressure equalized with the interior, and a green light glowed reassuringly above the inner hatch.

Mele popped the inner hatch, paused to see if anything happened, then leapt out of the air lock, planting herself against the far side of the interior passageway, her rifle held ready as she swung it from side to side, seeking targets. Yoshida jumped out as well, his weapon covering one way down the passage so Mele could keep her weapon pointed in the other.

The external mics on her suit picked up the sigh of air as vent fans circulated atmosphere in this part of the facility but no other noises. Was everyone here asleep? That should be impossible. They would have seen the destruction of the cutter and *Saber*'s approach afterward.

The air lock finished cycling a second time, and her other four Marines came through. "Yoshida, Lamar, come with me. Gamba, take Giddings and Buckland that way. No shooting unless necessary. Commodore Geary wants some live prisoners."

The rudimentary heads-up display on her modified armor didn't show much except the relative positions of her group and the other Marines as they moved in opposite directions down the passageway, weapons at ready. They had no information on the layout of this facility, but in one corner of her helmet display a map filled in as they walked, showing where they'd been.

"Dead end, Captain," Corporal Gamba called over the comm circuit. "Some kind of office with three desks. No one here. None of the desks are powered up."

"Got it," Mele replied. "We're coming up on something." She swung the muzzle of her rifle ahead of her as she came around a corner into a small rec room. Off to one side was an even smaller kitchen. Spaced around the walls were three closed doors. "The one on the left is yours, Yoshida. Lamar, take the right one. I'll handle the middle. All at once on three. One, two, three."

Three doors slammed open under the force of kicks, and three rifles led the way into three rooms.

Three empty rooms.

"Could they be in the nonpressurized sections?" Lamar asked, her voice puzzled.

"We'll find out," Mele said. "Giddings, start breaking into the systems here and find out how many people are on this station. *Saber* is also going to want to know what parts and supplies are stored here for emergency use."

A quick check found a secondary air lock, which was locked. As Mele was preparing to head into the nonpressurized sections to search them Giddings called her. "Captain Darcy, there's nobody here."

"They abandoned it?"

"No, ma'am. There's a note, I mean, a physical note, stuck on one of the desks saying the facility caretakers were hauled off to help fill out the crew on one of Scatha's warships." Giddings sounded like he was having trouble not laughing. "The note has all the log-on codes written on it for whoever showed up next. I *think* I'm going to be able to get into their files pretty easily."

"Congratulations," Mele said, feeling both foolish at assaulting an abandoned facility and relieved that things had gone so well.

Rob Geary sounded happy at the news. "Scatha had to

strip the people out of here so they could fill out the crew on one of their ships? That sounds like they're overextending themselves."

"As long as they outnumber us," Mele pointed out, "that's not much comfort. But, yeah, if we can knock them onto their heels, they'll have trouble recovering. Corporal Giddings should be sending you files listing what's on this station."

"We're already receiving them. We'll take off most of the fuel cells and all of the emergency spares stockpiled here. What was that quote about feeding off the enemy?"

"I'm glad you were paying attention, sir. Speaking of feeding off the enemy, we'll empty out the pantry here, too, and the stocks of emergency rations," Mele said. "They don't have anything fancy, though. Just a bunch of past-their-expiration-date Earth Fleet rations. Scatha isn't wasting money on tasty treats for the troops."

"I'll have some sailors over there in a few minutes to start hauling stuff off. You can bring your Marines back as soon as you're done."

"Yes, sir." Mele headed for the other side of the facility, where Giddings was seated at one of the workstations as he downloaded every file in the system. Corporal Gamba and Private Buckland were busy searching every drawer and cabinet and nook in the room for anything else of interest. "Any surprises?"

"No, Captain," Giddings said. "No secret war plans or anything like that. I did find the records of traffic through the system. There were a couple of other warships here, but they jumped out before we arrived."

"Jumped for *where*?" Mele demanded, suddenly tense at the thought that the enemy might have launched an attack on Glenlyon at the same time as *Saber* was heading for Jatayu.

"Way over there," Giddings said, worried by the tone of her voice. "Not anywhere close to where we came in."

Mele squinted at the display. "I think that's the jump

point to Kosatka. We'll let the space squids confirm that. What else is in there?"

"Operating procedures. Maintenance requirements. Communications logs. Not much personal stuff like music or vids or books, though. That's kind of strange."

"Scatha doesn't like its people using official equipment for personal entertainment," Mele said. "We learned that from the stuff we captured a few years ago. What's this file?"

"Pictures. Not too many. I guess having a few pictures was okay with Scatha." Giddings brought up a series of photos. A young man in a chair. An older woman standing by a wall. A child playing outside. The sort of pictures that could have been taken anywhere humanity had settled so far. "Do you think the crew from this facility were on that ship that blew up?" he asked.

"Maybe," Mele said.

"Why the hell did they do it, Captain?" Buckland asked. "Why start a war?"

"Because someone wanted something that other people had, and people like the crew on this facility were willing to do anything they were told to do." Mele shook her head at the pictures of people who might never know what had happened to whoever had once valued those photos. "If I buy a one-way ticket into the dark, it's going to be while I'm fighting to protect people and things I care about. It's not going to be because some powerful scumbag wants more power and people to push around. How about you guys?"

"It's been a job," Corporal Gamba admitted. "Jobs could be hard to come by where I came from. But after a while it became . . . what's that word? A profession. Like, a special job. I stuck with the unit when we came out here because Glenlyon looked like a place that just wanted to defend itself. And I can do something to help. There're worse ways to buy that ticket, I guess."

"A lot worse ways," Mele said. "We're going to focus on buying tickets for Scatha's people, though. While you guys finish up here, I'm going to lead the other three in a careful sweep of the rest of the place for anything that might be hidden. Let me know when you're done."

None of them found anything else worth taking. The only other real trace of any of the former occupants was some obscene graffiti scratched by a tool in an unobtrusive spot. "Nice," Lamar commented in a flat voice.

"Captain?" Yoshida said. "What do we do when those space squids give us a hard time about capturing an empty facility?"

Mele's answering smile was thin and hard. "Tell them we led the way inside, and we'll do the same when there are a hundred weapons pointed at us."

Rob Geary wondered why he felt a little guilty to be plundering the Scathan facility's small store of emergency supplies. One of the advantages of everybody's using surplus warships from the same sources was that for the moment everyone was able to use the same fuel cells and spares. But he still felt better when *Saber*'s supply officer reported with a straight face that the enemy supplies had been "requisitioned in accordance with applicable regulations and procedures." That sounded a lot better than "looting."

He knew that his concerns were particularly absurd given what was about to happen to the Scathan orbital facility.

"Senior Chief Daniello requests permission to send the detonation command," Vicki Shen told Rob.

"Are we outside the blast radius?"

"Yes, sir."

"Just where did Senior Chief Daniello acquire the knowledge of how to rig fuel cells to detonate?"

"I didn't ask, Captain," Shen replied.

"That's probably wise. Permission granted to detonate," Rob said.

A few seconds later the remaining fuel cells at the Scathan orbital facility expended all of their energy at once, blowing the facility into dust and fragments that would continue to orbit the star named Jatayu for ages to come.

"I need a meeting with you and Captain Darcy," Rob told Shen, his eyes on his display where the jump point back to Glenlyon beckoned.

But another jump point kept drawing his attention as well.

He was supposed to take *Saber* home now.

Doing what he was thinking instead would be insanely risky.

Or would it?

CHAPTER 5

A ship the size of *Saber* didn't have conference rooms. Rob's cabin felt a little crowded with only two people in it. Three people didn't leave much room for moving around.

Rob sat at his desk, Lieutenant Commander Shen sat in the other chair, and Captain Mele Darcy leaned against the door. "The plan up to this point was to head back to Glenlyon now," Rob told the other two. "I'd like your input on another option, going ahead of the *Bruce Monroe*, jumping to Kosatka to make sure everything is clear there, then jumping back to Jatayu and home to Glenlyon."

Shen looked startled. "That's a long side trip, sir."

"How long would it be?" Mele asked.

"I'm guessing three weeks if we don't linger at Kosatka. If we spend any time there, it'll be longer."

"That's a while," Mele agreed. "What's your thinking?" she asked Rob.

"I'm thinking," Rob said slowly, "that the surveillance records on Scatha's facility showed the two destroyers that were here jumped for Kosatka about a week before we arrived. Kosatka might really need some help."

"It'll take us a while to get to Kosatka," Shen pointed out. "By the time we arrive, things might already be decided. And the last we heard, Kosatka has two destroyers. They'd face even odds."

"Unless," Mele said, "they've already lost some of their ships, or unless other enemy forces jumped to Kosatka from other star systems."

"We can't know that," Shen said. "We have no way of knowing that or anything else about what's happening at Kosatka until we actually got there. This would be a leap into the dark."

"You think we shouldn't go to Kosatka," Rob said.

"That's right, sir. We'd be leaving Glenlyon without any warship protection for more than twice as long as anticipated. We don't know what might be waiting at Kosatka. If those two destroyers return to Jatayu, we could run into them close to the jump point and at best face a running fight back to the jump point for Glenlyon."

"Those are all good reasons for not going," Rob said. "Captain Darcy?"

Mele grimaced. "Commander Shen is right on all counts. But . . . if Kosatka needs us to defeat an attack by Scatha . . . it would be very much in our interest to go there and help. If we caught those two destroyers while they were tied up fighting Kosatka's ships, we could ensure they were destroyed."

"*If*," Vicki Shen repeated.

"Granted," Mele said. "Those are just the two possibilities that would benefit us the most. As you said, there are others that wouldn't be so great."

Rob nodded, rubbing the back of his neck with one hand. "At best, it'd be a risk. I know that. I know all the reasons I shouldn't even be considering it. I *want* to go back to Glenlyon. So why do I keep having a feeling we should jump to Kosatka?"

"Is there something else you know that we haven't been told?" Mele asked.

"No," Rob said. "You two know everything that I know. And your advice is good. I know that."

Shen frowned at him. "But you still feel we should go to Kosatka?"

"Can either of you see anything in this situation that might be leading me to feel that way?"

"No, sir."

Mele Darcy paused before replying, then spoke reluctantly. "It's usually a good idea to follow up on success. Keep hitting the enemy while they're off-balance instead of giving them time to recover. Is that what you're thinking?"

"Maybe," Rob said.

"But," she added, "you have to balance that against the fact that when it comes to warships, *Saber* is all Glenlyon has. Can you afford to risk *Saber* or leave Glenlyon unprotected for that much longer?"

Shen sighed like someone who had just come to an unhappy conclusion. "Those two Scathan destroyers jumped for Kosatka. The enemy's eyes are clearly focused there, not on Glenlyon."

"You think Glenlyon will be okay if we jump for Kosatka?" Mele Darcy asked her, surprised.

"I think, from what we know, Scatha and its allies are aiming to knock out Kosatka," Vicki Shen said. "It makes sense strategically if they want Glenlyon to surrender without a fight. Taking out Kosatka would leave us even more isolated, without any friendly star system within two jumps of Glenlyon. Our situation really would be hopeless then." She focused on Rob. "Captain, you said you *want* to go back to Glenlyon?"

Rob didn't have to think about the answer. "Yes! I want to be where Ninja and my little girl are so I can be there to protect them."

"But?"

"But every time I look toward Glenlyon I get a sense of the jump point to Kosatka pulling at me."

Vicki Shen startled him again by nodding. "Sometimes we know things. Maybe we don't understand them, but we know them. Somehow. If you've got something pulling at you that strongly, maybe you should listen to it."

"I didn't expect to hear that from you," Rob said.

"I didn't expect to say it. But I've learned to listen to my gut. And we do know that the enemy is currently hitting Kosatka." She paused, inhaling deeply before nodding to herself. "My advice has changed. Let's go to Kosatka."

Mele Darcy stared at her, then at Rob, then back at Shen. "*I'm* supposed to be the voice of reason?"

"Give it your best shot," Rob told her.

"Fine. The government is likely to freak if you take *Saber* to Kosatka. They'll have no way of knowing what happened here. And you know they wouldn't approve of your going to Kosatka. You might lose your command, Captain Geary."

For some reason he found that funny. "The last time I lost my command it was because I'd won."

"You and me both," Mele agreed. "And you didn't leave me hanging that time, so I won't leave you hanging now. I'll make it unanimous. Let's go."

Rob shook his head at them. "You two were supposed to talk me out of the idea of going to Kosatka."

"Sorry about that."

He looked at Shen. "How do you think the crew would take it?"

She gave him a crooked half smile. "Blowing up that facility wasn't exactly a second victory, but the crew is feeling it that way. Two wins. They're going to be worried about what's waiting at Kosatka, but they're not going to expect defeat."

Mele Darcy nodded. "You've got a bunch of happy space squids. They always had mad skills when it came to their jobs. Now they've got confidence, too."

"Overconfidence can also be a problem," Rob said. He realized that he actually had been hoping the other two would convince him to forget about Kosatka and head back to Glenlyon immediately. That left the decision once more in his lap.

What would Ninja tell him to do?

She'd tell him to make up his mind and do what he already knew he should.

"All right," Rob said. "We're going to Kosatka. Our best chance to take out those two Scathan warships is if we're fighting alongside Kosatka's forces instead of facing the enemy alone."

He made the announcement from the bridge, reassured by the grim enthusiasm with which the crew reacted. After setting *Saber* on course for the jump point for Kosatka, Rob walked through the ship, talking to the officers and crew.

The wariness and caution he had felt in his interactions with most of the officers and crew were no longer apparent, and the aura of doom that had haunted the ship had dissipated. Apparently he'd done mostly the right things since taking over command.

But he knew others might not react as positively to his move. As soon as he got back to his cabin, Rob called the *Bruce Monroe* and asked to speak with "Mary Alice Norton."

Leigh Camagan heard him out before shaking her head. "You're going to catch hell when you get back. The council is going to be furious that you left Glenlyon undefended for more than twice as long as expected. Be prepared for the worst."

"I know. But I'm certain we can't just sit and wait for whatever Scatha and its friends are planning next," Rob said. "Everyone's been playing that game, sitting back and leaving the initiative to the people who want to cause trouble for others. Unless we start hitting them when they don't expect it, they'll keep taking down star systems one by one."

Leigh Camagan shrugged. "I won't argue that. And I admit that I'm grateful that *Saber* will be going through ahead of this freighter. With two of Scatha's warships already at Kosatka we might have run into serious trouble there. But I won't be at Glenlyon when you get back, Rob. That may be a rougher fight for you than whatever waits at Kosatka."

"I'm not in this to build a career," Rob said. "There's a job that needs doing, and I'm doing it."

"Rob, do you want to establish a precedent of officers

disregarding their orders from the government? Even for what they think are the best of reasons?"

He shook his head. "No. I don't want that. And I'm not doing that. President Chisholm told me to do whatever seemed best while I was at Jatayu. Those were her words. Those are my orders."

"You know that she didn't mean going on to Kosatka."

"She gave me discretion to act," Rob said. "I know this is risky, and I'm willing to accept the consequences if it turns out to be a mistake."

"Rob," Leigh said with a sigh, "what about the others who will also bear the consequences if this is a mistake?"

He paused, anger at the question warring with the realization that it was a fair thing to ask. "Those others include my family. Don't think I don't realize that. If my daughter is going to grow up free, I think I need to take this chance. And afterward I'll face the council. If they don't like what I've done, they can go ahead and replace me. I'll know that I've done what I can to protect Glenlyon."

After thinking for a moment, Leigh Camagan nodded. "Rob, tell me this. What if the president's orders to you had been to return to Glenlyon as soon as you dealt with whatever was at Jatayu?"

He didn't have to hesitate, having already asked himself the same question and remembering Danielle Martel's warning that everything he did would serve as an example to everyone who came after. "I'd be heading back to Glenlyon."

"Thank you. I needed to hear that. So will the council. Never forget that one of our greatest fears is that we'll become too much like our enemies because of what we'd do to win. The history of Old Earth is full of bad examples. We want Glenlyon to be an example of how to win while holding to our principles."

"I understand," Rob said. "That's one reason I want to go to Kosatka. If they need our help, we need to help. Because we don't leave friends hanging."

"That'll be a good precedent to set," Leigh Camagan

said. "Good luck. And don't linger at Kosatka any longer than you have to."

It wasn't until the call had ended that Rob realized Camagan's last words were something like an order. And that as a member of the government's defense council she could have ordered Rob to immediately return to Glenlyon. Whether she had the authority to unilaterally issue such orders wasn't clear, but she could have tried to prevent him from going to Kosatka. And she hadn't.

He had to make sure she didn't regret that.

Rob called Vicki Shen into his cabin again and replayed the entire message. "I wanted you to see that," Rob said, "because of the possibility that the council will relieve me of command when we return to Glenlyon."

She frowned. "I understand that the council might not be happy. It also has the right to make that decision."

"Yes. I wanted you to know that I wouldn't contest the council's right to relieve me," Rob said. "That would set a very bad precedent. If they do relieve me, you'll be the senior officer left aboard, and you'll probably get offered command."

"I hope you don't think I'm maneuvering for that!"

"Not at all. I want you to know I'm going into this with my eyes open and that I think you can do a good job if it comes to that. Don't let things revert to how they were. Don't reinstall the checklists for anything that doesn't absolutely require a checklist. Otherwise, follow your instincts and lead the crew."

She paused, looking away as if searching for words. "Were you thinking of this when you made me XO?"

"Yes."

"Thank you. I honestly never thought of that."

Rob nodded to her. "That's one of the things that I thought qualified you. When I was a junior officer in Alfar's fleet I met far too many people who only cared about getting promotions and getting the right tickets punched. You did your job as if *that* was what counted. And I think it is what counts."

Shen raised an eyebrow at him. "What about Darcy?"

"You mean if you get my job? I guess you'd be the one in charge of her."

"Tell me that wouldn't be as bad as everyone says."

He laughed. "It wouldn't. She knows her job, and she does it. Mele Darcy just doesn't suffer fools very well. She's not bad."

Shen shrugged. "For a Marine."

"You can't ask for a better ally at your back. If it comes to that."

"Thank you for taking me into your confidence, sir," Shen said, her tone formal as she got up from her chair. "You do realize that you've given me a weapon to use against you?"

"Yeah," Rob said. "But if I can't trust my XO, I'm toast anyway."

Shen paused before opening the door. "Sir? There's one thing that's confused us. I mean, those of us from Earth Fleet. We were taught to prize experience. You don't have that much experience as an officer or a commanding officer. But . . . you seem to be doing things right."

He smiled slightly at the question, knowing his expression reflected not humor but both regret and melancholy. "I didn't have a very long period in command of *Squall*, I guess, but that included some very intense experiences. *Squall* was a small ship. Just a cutter, with a crew of amateurs. There was a lot packed into a short period of time. And then I had three years to think about it, remember everything I did wrong, and try to figure out how to do it better if I ever had to."

"I see. You got your experience in sort of a burst mode, a lot compressed into a short signal. Then you had a long time to analyze the meaning of it."

Rob nodded to her. "That's a good way of summing it up. Does that make sense to an Earth-Fleet-trained officer?"

"It does." Shen gave Rob a salute as she left.

A couple of hours later *Saber* raced past the *Bruce Monroe* on her way to the jump point.

———————

"Get out while you can."

Lochan Nakamura stared at the image of Carmen Ochoa. She was calling from the planet below, from what he could see of her surroundings just outside the building where she worked as part of Kosatka's budding intelligence service. "You think it's that bad, Carmen?"

"*Shark* is out of commission for a while. The work on *Piranha* is being rushed so she can get under way, but she'll face two-to-one odds." Carmen paused, her expression worried. "Those two destroyers who jumped in aren't heading for this planet, Lochan. They're heading for the jump point from Kappa. That looks a whole lot like they're planning to meet somebody there."

"An invasion force?" Lochan blinked in disbelief, trying to get his head around the idea and failing. "An actual attack? They've been wearing us down by feeding the so-called rebels. Why would they openly invade? And who is this attacking us? I thought those destroyers looked like they were from Scatha."

Carmen answered the last question first. "As far as we can tell they match warships bought by Scatha. But if an invasion force is on the way through Kappa, it's likely to be coming from Apulu, maybe reinforced by troops from Turan."

"So it's all going to be in the open." Lochan slammed his palm against the surface of the desk. "Why?"

"Maybe they're worried that you're doing too good a job," Carmen said. "Maybe their sources in other star systems are saying that people are beginning to think they need to stand by Kosatka before it's too late."

"So they'll make it too late, right now," Lochan said. "And do it in a way that makes it clear the same thing can happen to anyone else who puts up a fight. Carmen, you and I both decided to make Kosatka our home. How can I run away when it's going to need everyone who can fight?"

She gazed back at him with a sort of fond sadness that made Lochan remember his once-upon-a-time dreams in a failed marriage to another woman back on Franklin. He'd wanted that sort of look from a woman, and thanks to the universe's sense of irony, he'd finally found it in one who was "only" a close friend. "Lochan, you're not a fighter. What you can do is talk and convince people. Get out of Kosatka. Go where you can find help for us. We'll hold out until you get back."

"I don't want to leave you here," Lochan said.

"Domi is going to be in the thick of any fighting. I can't leave him."

"Then marry the guy before it's too late!"

She shook her head, looking down. "Being married to a Red would ruin Domi's career and probably his life."

"Oh, hell, Carmen! Why don't you stop thinking about what you think is best for him and start thinking about what he thinks is best for him? Which is you if that wasn't clear."

Carmen looked him in the eye, clearly aggravated. "When did this conversation become about me? Lochan, I know the freighter docked up there is going to pull out as soon as it can get clearance from the government, and that will be pretty soon. Get aboard. Get help."

"I also need clearance from the government! I'm an official, remember?"

"Then get it!" she almost shouted. "What other hope do we have?"

"Glenlyon—"

"If they have any sense, Glenlyon's forces are huddled close to their primary world waiting for the hammer to fall on it! We need whatever you can get us, Lochan!"

He nodded in reluctant agreement. "All right. I'll try. Do your best to stay alive until I get back. Say hi to Dominic for me."

She gazed back at him, some unreadable feeling in her eyes. "May . . . your ancestors guide you safely home again. Take care, Lochan."

"You, too. And I still think you should marry that guy

because you want that as much as he does but won't admit it to yourself." He ended the call, wondering how he'd ended up with someone who had come to feel more like a daughter than a friend.

And wondering if he'd ever see her again.

The captain of the freighter *Oarai Miho* openly glared at Lochan as the ship finally broke free of the orbital station and began its lumbering escape from what looked more and more like an impending war zone. "I don't appreciate having my ship's departure time held up for the benefit of someone with special connections. If my ship doesn't make it to its next stop on schedule, we'll have to pay the penalty, not the government of Kosatka!"

"The warships don't seem to care about this ship," Lochan pointed out, thinking that threat must be what had the captain in such a bad mood. "They're, what, about three and a half light hours from us? And heading for the jump point from Kappa."

That statement earned him another glare from the captain. She swung one hand up to the control deck display and touched a command. Long, long lines speared forward from the two enemy destroyers. A much, much smaller line appeared from the front of the *Oarai Miho*. "Those are vector markers, their length matching the velocity of the ship. Notice any difference?"

"Yes," Lochan admitted.

"They're fast hunters, we're slow prey. Don't you decide for me what to worry about!"

"I didn't mean—"

"I work for a shipping line that expects me to make my schedules! You'd better not expect any special treatment on this ship!"

"I wouldn't dream of it," Lochan said. "I guess you're not planning on returning to Kosatka?"

"Of course I am," the captain told him scornfully. "We're

merchants, not fighters. We'll do business with whoever is in charge at Kosatka when we come back."

She turned away, the glares from other crew members on the command deck making it clear that Lochan wasn't welcome there. Since he wasn't interested in staying, Lochan went back to the closet-sized cabin assigned to him, one of a dozen identical cabin doors in a passageway running down one side of the crew area on the ship. The walls of his cabin were unadorned metal and composites, the ceiling not much more than two meters high, the bathroom a toilet built into one wall with a tiny sink set above it. A battered sign above the sink warned that all water use was metered and would be cut off if the allowed daily amount was exceeded. Freighters didn't waste much space or money on passenger accommodations.

The scramble to get approval to leave, get a room on the freighter, and get necessities packed had left Lochan physically worn-out on top of the emotional stress of leaving. Sitting down tiredly on the bench that would become a narrow bed, he saw the message light blinking on the pulldown desk. Hoping it was from Carmen, Lochan tapped receive.

Instead, Brigit Kelly looked out at him, her eyes shadowed by worry, even the normally brilliant green streaks in her hair seeming subdued. "Lochan, I'm sorry I couldn't catch you before you left. I'm staying here as my duty requires. I'm a neutral party, so whatever happens, I should be all right. I'm going to try to get reports back to Eire. The ship you're on is carrying a report from me of what has happened so far and what's expected to happen next. I've attached a copy to this message. Please download it and if . . . something happens . . . make sure the message gets to Eire. It's not proper diplomatic protocol to entrust a message like that to a third party, but I know you can be trusted.

"This is as bad as we'd feared it could be. Hopefully, it will spur worlds to action rather than scaring them into submission. My own people don't scare very well. They're going to want to fight when they see what's coming. That may be small comfort to Kosatka if it's already fallen by then, though."

She paused, her eyes looking outward as if searching for him. "You're a good man, Lochan. I've been meaning to tell you that. I hope to see you again. Try not to get your fool self killed before then."

Lochan replayed the message before tapping the reply command. The freighter was still within a few light seconds of Kosatka's orbital facility, but he was still surprised when the reply went live and he saw Brigit looking at him from the screen. "Lochan? You got my message?"

"I did," he said. "I'll make sure your other message gets to Eire. I'm really sorry I didn't have a chance to say good-bye in person."

"Don't be thinking you'd have gotten anything special out of a good-bye," Brigit warned him with a slight smile. "But I will miss you and worry about you."

"Same here. You're going down to the planet, right? Staying in orbit could be dangerous if the facility is attacked."

Her eyes lit with defiance at the idea of running. "I'm neutral. They have to respect that."

"*Shark* is being towed to the facility," Lochan warned. "If the facility is attacked before *Shark*'s main propulsion can be repaired, my understanding is the government intends having *Shark* act as part of the facility, using her weapons to defend it."

"She'd be a sitting duck," Brigit objected. "Unable to maneuver out of a fixed orbit."

"*Shark* will fight as long as she can. Which means anyone in the facility could be in danger when the attackers shoot back. Particle beams don't care about the diplomatic status of any person who happens to be in their path."

"True enough," Brigit admitted with obvious reluctance. "I'll consider moving down to the planet, though if they decide to bombard, that won't be any safer."

"They wouldn't—" He stopped, thinking that maybe they would. The exact identity of the old Warrior Class destroyer that had bombarded Lares three years ago, and apparently sought to bombard Kosatka as well, had never been discovered. Rumors of those responsible had ranged from plausible accusations against Turan, Apulu, or Scatha, to the extreme of claims that it was a ghost ship whose crew had been driven insane by prolonged exposure in jump space.

How had it come to this? The slow buildup of the insurgency had suddenly exploded into war in space and the threat of planetary invasion. Perhaps historians, looking back, would trace a clear pathway of steps that had led to this point. But at the time it had always seemed under control. Worrisome, problems to be dealt with, but not a full-scale war in which Kosatka seemed to be standing alone.

"I'm sorry," Lochan finally said, unable to think of anything else.

"It's my job," she reminded him. "And you're doing your job."

"If you run into any problems, you know Carmen Ochoa can help."

"The lass who works for your intelligence people? And how would it look if a diplomat was spending time with someone like that?"

Lochan laughed briefly, surprised that Brigit could joke at a time like this. "Carmen is pretty resourceful. She's a good friend to have."

"She's a Red," Brigit pointed out, then paused, waiting for Lochan's reaction.

He shrugged, having heard variations on that statement many times in the last few years. "Carmen came from Mars originally. That's what she was. It's not who she is."

"So I've heard. And the quality of her own friends speaks to her quality. I'll look her up, Lochan. And you be careful. If Scatha and its friends have set things up this well here, they might have agents elsewhere whose duties could include making certain that someone like you doesn't succeed."

Those last words chilled him inside. And yet it made a lot of sense.

He'd felt guilty to be leaving others to face any upcoming fighting, but maybe he wasn't going to be all that safe himself. "Thanks for the warning. I hadn't thought of that. Are you . . . concerned about this ship?"

Brigit Kelly made a noncommittal gesture. "Why would I worry about that ship? It's owned and operated by a reputable company based on Hesta."

That was a double-edged statement if ever there was one, Lochan thought, since Hesta was firmly under Scatha's control. Was that why, despite her words, the ship's captain had seemed more worried about her schedule than about those Scathan warships here at Kosatka? "I'll keep that in mind," he said.

"And you won't be alone. Maybe you and one of the other passengers will hit it off if you find yourself in need of company," Brigit said with a slight smile.

"I don't usually make friends that easily." Lochan hesitated, wondering again about Brigit's other words, what they meant as far as he was concerned. "I . . . I'll look you up when I get back."

Brigit smiled politely and nodded. "You do that. I'll look forward to it."

Afterward, he sat for a while staring at the blank display. Him leaving just as Brigit showed possible interest in him probably wasn't a matter of bad timing. More likely she, and he, were reacting to the rush of events, which made it clear that everyone's time was limited. That sort of thing tended to focus people on what they really wanted.

Lochan finally checked the relayed data from the control deck, seeing how far it still was to the jump point that the *Oarai Miho* was heading toward. He lay down on the chair/bed, gazing up at the metal forming a ceiling for his room. He had a suspicion that by the time the freighter reached its destination he'd know every imperfection in that surface and would have rehearsed in his mind a few hundred times every conversation he'd ever had with Brigit Kelly.

He'd thought he was safe once this freighter had left the orbital facility. But apparently he'd have to worry until he reached Eire.

No matter what, at least he'd have time to catch up on his reading.

Carmen woke up with a headache and a brief sense of confusion. It took her a moment to realize she was on the cot in the back room at work.

She sat up, rubbing her eyes and feeling achy. Too many hours spent in this building, too many attempts to figure out what would happen next, too many dangers to even know what to focus on. She had once imagined that intelligence offices were like they were shown on vids, all-seeing centers where quirky individuals discovered important insights from the smallest possible clue picked up by the most amazing possible sources. The reality was more like this back room: dark, dingy, smelling of old coffee and too many people who hadn't had time to get clean for too long, and a perpetual headache as analysts often unsuccessfully tried to fit too few bits of information into some sort of useful picture.

Carmen gradually realized that the outer room was very quiet. Much more quiet than it should be with everyone working.

She went to the door and looked out, seeing several men and women standing, silent, their backs to her.

Walking up to them, Carmen saw what they were looking at. The big display had an image of Kosatka's star system on it. A large symbol marked the orbital location of the crippled *Shark*. Another marked where *Piranha* was, only half a light hour from this planet, holding orbit while waiting to see what happened next. Farther out was a symbol for the freighter *Oarai Miho* still on its slow, steady way to the jump point that would allow it, and Lochan Nakamura, to escape this star system.

All of that was as it had been for days. But something else was new. Nearly four light hours from this planet, the two destroyers, which had still refused to identify themselves, had reached the jump point from Kappa. As had been feared, other ships had arrived, jumping in from Kappa and heading to rendezvous with the destroyers that would protect them as the entire force headed for the planet.

She spotted the somber face of her boss, Loren Yeresh, and pushed through the group to him. "How bad is it?"

Loren shrugged as if no longer able to care. "Bad enough. Some sort of cutter along with several freighters and a big passenger ship that probably isn't bringing tourists."

"How many soldiers do you think are aboard?"

"It depends on a lot of factors, but our best guess is anywhere from several thousand to ten thousand." Loren's grimace held a mix of despair and grief. "That doesn't sound like much to invade a world with, but they've also got however many troops the rebels can field. Given the size of our current population, it ought to be enough to take over."

"We've only got a thousand regular troops," Carmen said, staring at the symbols on the display. "And, what, three thousand militia?"

"That might be enough to stop them," one of the other analysts commented. "Except that they'll also have control of space around the planet. They'll be able to bombard from orbit any place where we try to make a stand."

"Can *Piranha*—" Carmen began.

"*Piranha* is outnumbered three to one," Loren said. "If they hadn't taken out *Shark*, we'd have a chance. But not at these odds."

"What's the government going to do?"

Another shrug. "As I understand, at the moment they're debating whether we surrender outright to avoid tremendous destruction and loss of life or whether we put up the toughest fight we can to make their conquest of Kosatka as costly for them as possible."

Carmen had been sensing an odd feeling of familiarity as she stood among the others. As she spoke to Loren, she finally realized what it was. That old sense of helplessness and hopelessness that she had known on Mars, which had filled the atmosphere of Mars like a toxic perfume that never went away. Carmen had grown up among people who never spoke of success, or of winning, but only of what had to be done to survive. "No!"

It wasn't until everyone turned to look that Carmen realized she had said that.

But it didn't matter. Her anger flared as she looked at those dull, defeated expressions. "This is our home! And you're all giving up? You're not even thinking about how to win?"

"It's impossible to win," Loren said in the tone of someone speaking to a child who couldn't grasp a hard truth.

"It's not impossible until you give up!" Carmen shot angry looks at them. "I made it here! I survived! I won! And I will not give that up to anyone! If they want my home, they'll have to fight for it. I don't care what the government decides. I will fight!"

Some of the others were videoing her with pads they weren't supposed to use inside this building, but Carmen wasn't worried about that. She shoved Loren, seeing fire in his eyes as he staggered back. "Are you giving up? Are you ready to surrender your freedom and this world's future?"

"Why fight if you can't win?" he demanded.

"I saw this on Mars! Don't you understand? No one wanted to fight battles they thought were hopeless, and every battle that could make things better seemed hopeless."

"This isn't Mars," someone else said.

"It can become Mars," Carmen said. "A place where every dream is dead and force is the only law. Mars became like that because everyone there gave up. I gave up, too. That's why I left. I'm not going to leave Kosatka." Carmen paused to breathe, looking at those around her. "I'm not going to leave this new home, and I'm not going to surrender. I'm going to fight for it, no matter what anyone else decides."

Loren Yeresh shook his head, unhappy. "Carmen, you're talking about dying in a fight you can't win."

"No! Mars was too far gone. Kosatka still believes in freedom. We *can* win! Or we can go down fighting, and make Scatha and Apulu pay such a price that they will never dare attack another star system. That's what I'm going to do," Carmen said. "I'm not running away from another world. I'm going to stand here. When people remember me, it will be as someone who died on her feet. I won't kneel! I'll stand. Will you stand with me?"

Loren Yeresh frowned at her a moment longer before nodding. "I sure as hell will. Yuri? Did you get all that? Send it to the legislative chambers right now. I want our representatives debating what to do to see what this woman said."

"It's only two-to-one odds," one of the others said as Yuri sent the vid. "And destroyers don't have much in the way of bombardment capability."

"If we hit them coming down, we could inflict serious losses," a third added.

"Figure out how to do that!" Loren ordered. "I want everything we've got on how our enemies might be planning to land ground forces on this planet. Once we have that we'll start figuring out recommendations for how to hit those forces on the way down. Move it!" He bent a sharp eye on Carmen. "Well? Didn't you hear me? We've got work to do."

She grinned at him. "Yes, sir. I'm on it."

As she dropped into the seat at one of the desks and started searching for data, Carmen felt a momentary qualm, imagining people watching that vid of her.

But what the hell. She had far worse things in her past.

Loren Yeresh bent down next to her as she worked. "Carmen? Where did that come from? I knew you were tough, but . . . man, that was something."

She paused, thinking about the question. "I spent my earliest years fearing that I'd die on Mars, a victim of the red planet like so many others. If I hadn't fought back against those fears, I'd still be there. Then I spent years trying to become someone else, someone educated, someone who wouldn't scare people the way a Red would. All that time I was afraid that someone would find out, would tell others. I had to overcome those fears. Now I tell people

I'm a Red. Now I have a home where . . . I'm accepted as who I am. I won't let fear stop me now."

Loren nodded slowly as he straightened up. "That Dominic Desjani is one lucky guy."

She smiled, embarrassed. "I'll tell him you said so."

But her smile faded as she thought about the thousands of invading soldiers on those newly arrived ships. Soldiers who might all be wearing battle armor and carrying military weapons. Domi would be in the front ranks of those fighting to stop them, with a mix of old and improvised equipment, against bad odds, and with death looming from orbital bombardment. What were the chances that he'd survive? How much longer would she have with him?

And what did she want of what might be only a couple more weeks with the man who had asked her to marry him?

Carmen paused her work long enough to tap out a quick message to Dominic, hesitating only for a moment before sending it. *Yes. Let's do it.*

CHAPTER 6

"Twenty minutes until arrival at Kosatka."

Rob Geary waved one hand to acknowledge the report. He was doing his best to appear confident and relaxed, when in truth his stomach was clenched into a tight knot and his mind was filled with endless variations on possible disasters that *Saber* might encounter after leaving jump space.

It didn't help that jump space itself was acting odd.

"There's another one," Lieutenant Cameron said.

"What the hell are they?" Ensign Reichert asked.

Rob watched the mysterious light bloom on his display where only the drab gray of jump space should be visible. Like the one seen the day before, the light flared in a sudden burst of brightness before quickly fading and disappearing.

"Nothing on it from our sensors, Captain," Reichert reported. "Just the light itself. No heat, no other radiation, no indication of how close or far away it was. No detectable source."

"Very well," Rob said, which was what someone in charge on a ship said when they couldn't think of anything else to say. He'd heard a few stories about inexplicable lights in jump space but had never seen any himself before this jump.

"After the one we saw yesterday, I checked the ship's records on human experience in jump space," Lieutenant Cameron offered. "The first jumps never encountered any lights. The initial reports of them later on were discounted as hallucinations or equipment malfunctions. But the number of sightings may be increasing. We don't have enough data aboard to know whether that's true."

"Is it some kind of reaction to us?" Reichert wondered as she studied her display. "Jump space itself, I mean. Maybe when human ships pass through we cause something or trigger something. The more ships, the more it happens."

"There's nothing in jump space that could be reacting," Cameron said. "Not as far as we can tell."

Chief Petty Officer Quinton on the engineering watch station spoke up. "There are stories going around that the lights are something watching us. Or something that signifies good luck. Nobody seems to think the lights are dangerous or malevolent."

"They don't look or feel dangerous," Reichert agreed.

"Let's take it as a sign of good luck," Rob said, aggravated by the conversation when he was worried about what would happen when they left jump space. "There's nothing we can do about them. Everybody focus on their tasks. We don't know what'll be waiting for us at Kosatka."

Silence fell on the bridge. Rob stared at his display, angry at himself. Great. He'd turned into THAT kind of commanding officer. Chewing out his crew for being human, and in this case for discussing matters that arguably were of professional importance. He could let it rest at that. Or not. The last thing he wanted was for his crew to be focusing their attention on the captain's moods instead of on their jobs.

"By the way," Rob added, trying to sound professionally casual and certain that wasn't going over right, "that was an interesting discussion. I'd like to follow up on those lights when things settle down. Maybe on the way back to Glenlyon we'll see more and get some better data."

The bridge stayed quiet, but Rob could feel that the tension was once again aimed at what might await them rather than on him.

"Five minutes to Kosatka."

Rob nodded toward his display. "Confirm status of weapons and shields."

"Weapons are active, particle beam projectors powered, shields at maximum," Ensign Reichert said.

"Captain, should we set weapons to engage targets upon exit from jump space?" Lieutenant Cameron asked.

"No," Rob said. "The first ship we encounter might be one of Kosatka's. We can't risk firing on them. If we come under fire after exit, we'll accelerate away from the engagement and figure out who we want to shoot at before we open fire."

The timer on his display counted down the remaining time. At one minute, Rob used the ship's general announcing system to speak to the crew. "We're about to arrive at Kosatka. All hands brace for action."

A brief alarm tone sounded as *Saber* dropped out of jump space and into normal space. Stars once more blazed amid infinite blackness outside the ship as Rob fought to regain his mental sharpness and clear the blurring in his eyes that kept him from reading what was on his display. At the moment, he'd much rather humans figured out how to avoid jump exit mental fog than whatever those lights were.

But the lack of alarms sounding was a good sign. As Rob finally blinked his eyes back into focus he saw ship markers updating as *Saber*'s systems automatically took in everything visible in the star system. The data was in some cases hours old, because light took that long to cross so much distance, but at least it told him where those ships had been. And those other vessels wouldn't see the light announcing *Saber*'s arrival for hours, giving Rob a chance to decide what to do before acting.

At first glance, the picture was puzzling. One of Kosatka's ships, *Piranha*, was broadcasting her identity from where she orbited about half a light hour out from the primary inhabited world. But the other destroyer that Kosatka had, *Shark*, was apparently docked with the planet's sole orbital facility. Why, when a flotilla of ships not broadcasting any identifying data was heading toward that world after apparently having arrived at the jump point from Kappa?

"Why's *Shark* sitting there close to their primary world?" Rob called out. "Have our sensors focus on it and give me a detailed image."

That world, and *Shark* orbiting it, was about four light hours, or roughly four billion kilometers, from where *Saber* was. But space offered few obstacles to clear views of objects even many billions of kilometers distant. With the right multispectrum sensors picking up even the faintest images impinging on them, a fairly sharp image could be obtained. A four-hour-old sharp image, a picture of how things had been in that other place in the recent past, but still clear enough to see details.

"There's work going on," Lieutenant Cameron reported. "And damage visible on *Shark*. Most of it aft."

"Main propulsion damage," Chief Quinton said. "See that gear? They're trying a full rebuild. Something trashed *Shark*'s main propulsion."

"How long would that kind of repair take, Chief?" Rob asked.

"Depends on a lot of things, sir, but it couldn't be anything less than a couple of weeks even with people working around the clock."

"That's why *Piranha*'s on her own facing those others. Who are they?" Rob asked of the watch standers.

"We're not seeing anything to indicate where they're from," Lieutenant Cameron said.

"Our systems are showing visual identification of one Sword Class destroyer, one Founders Class destroyer, and one Adventurer Class cutter," Ensign Reichert said. "They're escorting several freighters and a Fellowship type passenger ship." She paused, peering intently at her display. "The freighters have heat radiating from many of their cargo areas. They must be pressurized and at livable temperatures. They're carrying people. A lot of them."

"A Sword Class and a Founders Class ship," Rob said. "The same types that station's records showed leaving Jatayu for here. And the same types that destroyed *Claymore*."

"The time line fits," Lieutenant Cameron confirmed. "They got here long ago enough to have gone to the Kappa jump point to meet up with those other ships. What are we going to do, Captain?"

Rob looked over his display again before answering even though he already knew the answer. Saying it still felt a bit like stepping off a cliff, though. "The enemy is obviously concentrating efforts against Kosatka. We're going to give Kosatka all the help we can. If we can defeat these guys here, they won't be able to hit Glenlyon later. Comms, I need a transmission lined up on the inhabited world."

"It's ready, sir. Tab Two."

The signal wasn't aimed at where that planet appeared to be, which was already four hours ago. By the time the signal got there, the planet would be four more hours along its orbit from where it really was now. Worlds orbiting nearer their star, the ones that were most likely to be livable for humans, tended to move faster than planets farther out. In this planet's case, that meant twenty-six kilometers per second. By the time the message Rob was sending got there, the planet would be about seven hundred fifty thousand kilometers from where it now appeared to be. In space, comms had to lead their targets by some pretty large amounts.

He took a deep breath, sat up straight, and touched the control. "To the government of Kosatka, this is Commodore Geary aboard the Glenlyon destroyer *Saber*. We intend assisting you in defending your star system. *Saber* will proceed in-system on a course to intercept the force approaching your world from the Kappa jump point. Request advise . . ."

Advise what? Kosatka couldn't give orders to him, and if they tried, he shouldn't obey them. Big details like who would be in charge if the two star systems ever cooperated in defense had helped hold up for years the formal signing of a mutual defense agreement.

But if he operated *Saber* independently of *Piranha*, each ship doing its own thing, they'd lose the advantages gained by cooperating in planning their actions. With the odds still against them, they'd need every advantage they could get.

"Request advise your desires for employment of *Saber*," Rob finished, hoping that was sufficiently vague to fend off a court-martial when he got back to Glenlyon. "Geary, out."

He gestured to the comm watch. "Give me a signal to *Piranha*."

"Yes, sir. Ready, sir. The beam will be a little wide to include all the places she might be by the time the signal reaches her. Tab Three."

"*Piranha*, this is Commodore Geary aboard the Glenlyon destroyer *Saber*. You look like you could use a little help. We're on our way. It's my intention to . . . cooperate with you in your defense of this star system. Please advise me of your intentions. Geary, out."

"Intercept course on your display, Captain," Cameron said. "Three and a half light hours distance. At point zero eight light speed estimated time to intercept is forty-three point seven hours."

Almost two full days, Rob thought. They'd jumped into the middle of an invasion, and it would be almost two days before they got close to the action. "All hands stand down from general quarters. Reduce shield strength to standard. We expect to reset battle conditions in approximately forty-two hours."

He took a moment to study the maneuvering solution that Lieutenant Cameron had worked up with the help of the ship's systems. Space had no up or down, but every star system had a plane that its worlds orbited in. Humans just had to arbitrarily label one side of that plane *up* and the other *down*. Right and left were also meaningless outside of any given ship so those were set in terms of the direction toward or away from the star. Given those human rules, nearly four hours ago *Piranha* had been slightly above where *Saber* now was, off to one side of the star that *Saber* was nearly pointed at. The intercept vector aimed at meeting the invasion force, a long curve through billions of kilometers, required *Saber* to go a little up, and turn a ways *port*, or away from the star. "That looks good given what we know. We'll adjust it when we get data that's not as time late and when *Piranha* lets us know what she's planning to do. Come up zero four degrees, turn zero one six degrees to port, accelerate to point zero eight light speed."

"Understand come up zero four degrees, turn zero one six degrees to port, accelerate to point zero eight light speed," Cameron repeated. It was an old ritual, arguably very redundant with modern maneuvering systems, but it ensured that everyone heard and understood orders correctly before beginning to carry them out.

As far as Rob was concerned, that particular tradition was a good thing.

As *Saber* strained to accelerate to a small but decent fraction of the speed of light, Mele Darcy came up on the bridge. She stopped by Rob's command seat, gazing at his display. "I understand there're a few thousand ground forces potentially on those ships. We might need more than a half dozen Marines to handle that."

Trust Mele to find a way to lighten the mood. He gave her an amused smile. "Too bad we couldn't have brought all twenty-one Marines."

"Is one of those destroyers an internal match for this one? I see one is labeled Sword Class."

"Yes," Rob said, "but that's not the one that's a sister ship to *Saber*. That would be the one labeled Founders Class."

Mele shook her head. "This isn't a Sword Class ship, so it got named *Saber*."

"Military logic," Rob said. "Though in this case it was the logic of the government of Glenlyon. Maybe someday they'll name a ship after you."

"No thanks. The only people who get ships named after them are dead heroes and living politicians, and I have no desire to be either. Is it okay if my grunts do some drills on this ship to get familiar with fighting through it?"

"Sure. But coordinate with every department head whose compartments and passageways you're going to be using so nobody gets shot or gets scared." Rob gestured around to encompass the entire ship. "How's the boarding training for the crew going?"

Mele shrugged. "They're squids. I'm doing what I can. If somebody boards us, they'll face a tough fight. If we board someone else, it could be ugly. Being on the attack is tougher." She paused, her eyes on him growing somber. "I'm sorry. You already knew that."

"Yeah," Rob said, remembering those chaotic moments during the boarding of a Scathan warship three years ago. For some reason the instant had always stayed particularly sharp in his mind when the shot that killed her had knocked Danielle Martel across a passageway. "That's okay. Mele, do you think we'd have a shot at taking one of those warships?"

She shrugged. "Maybe. Depends what they've got. Depends on a lot of things."

Including what he did, Rob knew. And whether he made any big mistakes.

Hopefully, he had enough work to keep him busy for the next two days. Otherwise, he'd spend all of that time worrying.

Messages began arriving for *Saber* about eight hours after Rob had sent his own messages out. Because of the closer orbit of *Piranha*, her reply came in first.

Piranha's captain was an older woman whom Rob found oddly familiar at first glance. He found out why when she began talking. "Commodore Geary, this is Captain Tecla Salomon. Welcome. I understand you also used to serve in Alfar's fleet. I haven't received any instructions from Kosatka yet on how to deal with you, so let's just say I'm grateful for your support in a very difficult situation and hope we can figure out how to work together to defeat this threat. I'll contact you again after I hear from Kosatka. Salomon, out."

Soon after that, an unexpected message arrived from the invasion force. A man wearing an attitude as big as the shoulders on his uniform bore a stern, intimidating look as he spoke. "You've been identified as a warship belonging to the neutral star Glenlyon. This star system is a war zone. Apulu has chosen to intervene for humanitarian reasons in the cruel war raging in Kosatka and causing numerous civilian casualties. They will bring a halt to hostilities and allow the people of Kosatka to vote for new leaders under the protection offered by Apulu's volunteers.

"Scatha and Turan have chosen to assist Apulu in this humanitarian operation. Any attempt to hinder our compassionate mission will require us to use all available force and will result in Glenlyon's being identified as an enemy of peace and security. Change your vector immediately and leave this star system as soon as possible. Failure to do so risks sharing the unfortunate fate of Glenlyon's only other warship, leaving your home defenseless. Out."

The commander of Scatha's ships hadn't even had the courtesy to identify himself, perhaps thinking that would further frighten the crew of *Saber*.

"Let the crew see this," Vicki Shen advised, her words coming out fast and clipped with anger. "It'll make them even madder, even more determined to kick that guy's teeth in. Humanitarian! How long have wolves been wrapping themselves in that form of sheep's clothing?"

"And an election under the *protection* of soldiers from Apulu," Rob said. "I'm sure Apulu's puppets would win a huge majority. Go ahead and release the message to the crew so they can see who and what we're dealing with."

Lieutenant Commander Shen shook her head, looking angry. "The same sort of lies they fed Commodore Hopkins. I've been remembering the things he said before *Claymore* left. Someone was feeding him information that led him to believe Scatha didn't want a fight. The Commodore didn't want a war. He believed what he was being told."

"I don't want a war, either," Rob said. "Unfortunately, that scum and the people he works for do want a war."

Finally, the first reply came in from Kosatka. First Minister Hofer looked considerably older than Rob remembered, but given how things had been the last few years that was understandable. "Captain—Commodore! Once again you arrive when Kosatka needs you. We'd already resolved to fight rather than surrender, but with your ship our chances will be much improved. I don't know what your instructions are, and I can't issue orders to you, but I will instruct Captain Salomon of the *Piranha* to work with you to the best of her ability."

Hofer hesitated, his smile wavering. "Unfortunately, I cannot yet allow *Piranha* to be placed under your command. My government is still . . . debating that issue. If you've been instructed to place your ship under our command, that will simplify things greatly. Please let us know so we can proceed. Hofer, out."

Vicki Shen shook her head in disbelief after she'd seen that message. "They've got an invasion fleet on their doorstep and they're still playing politics? Does our side deserve to win? Because from where I sit, we look too stupid to win."

Rob nodded, his mouth twisted unhappily. "We seem to be doing our best to lose, don't we? We have something going for us, though. I know Tecla Salomon. I finally remembered why. She was an officer on a ship I spent time on while I was training."

"And that's good?"

"I think so. My memories of her are that she was good at what she did and didn't seem interested in playing political games. It's not too surprising that she ended up out here. Politics was the way to get ahead in Alfar's fleet."

"Politics is the way to get ahead in every fleet," Shen said. "Are you considering placing *Saber* under Salomon's overall command?" she added in a cautious voice.

Rob couldn't help a bitter laugh at the question. "I can't

do that. You know I can't. I have no authority to surrender control of this ship to someone from another star system. And while our goals match, the means we'll be willing to employ won't be the same. Salomon and I both want to defeat that invasion force, but she can afford to have *Piranha* beat to a wreck doing that and be hailed as a big hero on Kosatka. But if I don't keep *Saber* in good enough shape to get back to Glenlyon and defend it, I'll be labeled a failure and probably deservedly so."

"They'll never agree to putting *Piranha* under your command," she added.

"No, they won't."

"Because they're going to be worried that you'd sacrifice *Piranha* to advance Glenlyon's interests. How are we going to win this under those conditions?" Vicki Shen asked.

"Hopefully, one of us will come up with a brilliant plan," Rob said. "Let me know if you do. Fortunately, we still have almost a day and a half before we get near that invasion force. As we get closer to it, and *Piranha*, I'll be more easily able to exchange ideas with Commander Salomon."

The next eight hours brought them steadily closer toward a meeting with the invasion force, the long arc of *Saber*'s path angling upward and to one side to meet with the sweeping curve of the invaders' vector through space.

Rob spent some of that time walking through the narrow passageways of *Saber*, talking to the crew, and looking over the equipment. *Saber*'s most powerful weapons, her pulse particle beam projectors ranged around the bow, hunched like gleaming monsters of metal and composites. In Alfar's fleet, similar weapons were sometimes emblazoned with small images of deadly real or mythical beasts, or at least had names stenciled onto them, as if the weapons were indeed some kind of ogre or other creature. Either Earth Fleet or Commodore Hopkins hadn't tolerated such frivolities so the only markings on these weapons were their numbers: 1, 2, and 3.

But Rob took the time to give each one a pat as the weapon crew looked on, happy to see their captain treating the device with respect. "Get us some good hits," he told the beam projectors before nodding to the gun crews to show he respected them as well.

From inside the ship the grapeshot launchers actually looked a bit like guns. Big-Ass Shotguns, Mele Darcy called them. Firing patterns made up of solid metal ball bearings about five centimeters in diameter, the grapeshot had to score multiple hits to take down shields or inflict enough damage, making them short-range weapons just like their namesake in the days when warships had used sails on the waters of far-distant Old Earth.

He stopped by the small medical compartment, barely large enough for a desk, a single bunk, and a variety of trauma care devices whose glowing status lights provided both comfort and apprehension. "How's it going, Doc?"

Chief Petty Officer "Doc" Austin stood respectfully and gestured to his equipment. "Ready and waiting, sir."

When Rob had first come aboard he'd been surprised to see that the "ship's corpsman" on *Saber* had completed requirements to be a fully qualified doctor but had remained a chief instead of being promoted to officer rank. "It's simple, Captain," Doc Austin had explained. "Regulations call for the medical support on a destroyer to be a Petty Officer First Class or a Chief. If I were to be promoted to officer rank, I'd have to be transferred to a larger ship."

"There is no larger ship in Glenlyon's fleet," Rob had pointed out.

"Exactly, sir. If I was promoted to officer rank, I couldn't stay aboard this ship, but I couldn't go anywhere else. Rather than risk creating a paradox that might rend space and time, I decided to decline a promotion. Though," Chief Austin had added, "I do get more respect from the crew as a chief than I would as an ensign, and the food in the chief's mess is better than they serve the officers, so there are some benefits."

Now Rob looked over the trauma equipment again, trying not to dwell on the fractured memories of the time when such gear had saved his life. "I'll try not to give you any extra work, Doc."

Austin shrugged. "Sir, back in Earth Fleet I was told that when destroyers go into a fight they either come out pretty much untouched or they get blown to hell. There aren't a lot of minor damage situations for a combatant this size. You know how that works."

"Yeah, I do."

He also stopped by the mess decks, pretending to share a meal with the off-going watch even though he didn't have much of an appetite.

"Are we going to get those bastards, sir?" one of the sailors asked. "I had friends on *Claymore*."

"Yes," Rob said. "We're going to make them pay for that."

Eventually, he found himself back in his stateroom, looking at the small display built into his desk, which was focused on a magnified image of the enemy force. The large passenger ship, carrying the bulk of the invasion troops, sat at the center of a hollow cylinder shape formed by the eight large freighters carrying supplies and more soldiers. The two enemy destroyers and their cutter were arrayed in a vertical triangle in front of and slightly below the cylinder, facing the approaches of both *Saber* and *Piranha*. The most powerful enemy destroyer, the Founders Class ship, was positioned at the lower corner where *Saber* would come in, the Sword Class warship was at the apex of the triangle facing *Piranha*, and the cutter sat at the third corner. The Adventurer Class cutter was still no match for either *Saber* or *Piranha*, but newer and better than the older Buccaneer Class cutter that *Saber* had destroyed at Jatayu.

The Scathan commander could easily shift his forces to concentrate all three ships against either *Saber* or *Piranha* as they attacked. Even if the warships from Glenlyon and Kosatka managed to work out a coordinated attack, they'd still face a slightly superior enemy force blocking their path to the freighters and passenger ship.

"What's Earth Fleet doctrine in a case like this?" Rob asked Vicki Shen.

She shrugged unhappily. "Earth Fleet doctrine assumed

that both friendly ships would be under Earth Fleet command. Beyond that, we'd either be told to concentrate on the warships, or on the freighters, and try to wear them down by repeated passes."

Rob gave her a sidelong glance. "No offense, but that doesn't seem very imaginative."

Another shrug. "Space limits your options," Vicki Shen said. "The enemy is going to see you coming from a long, long ways off. They can easily adjust their formation to meet you."

"We can make last-moment adjustments," Rob said.

"So can they. And if the adjustments mean we miss the intercept, passing outside effective weapons range, that's a win for them. We have to hurt them. All they have to do is keep us from hurting them."

Rob frowned before nodding in reluctant agreement. "What's your advice?"

"Hit the freighters. There's a limit to how much damage we can do on each pass, but that's our best bet for inflicting significant damage before they reach the planet. Just doing some damage to the escorting warships won't stop the invasion and won't help Kosatka."

"Do you see any way we can stop them from reaching the planet?"

"With two destroyers?" Shen shook her head.

He stood up, frustrated, and hit the nearest bulkhead. "Earth Fleet could do anything. That's what I was told growing up, and in training. Where's my miracle, Commander Shen?"

"Earth Fleet was better at building its reputation than it was at doing things," Vicki Shen replied, both her voice and expression somber. "Like, here? This situation? There were checklists. And if we did everything on those checklists, it would be an official victory. It wouldn't have mattered if the planet fell to invasion. We'd completed the checklists, and that was the only win or loss criterion that counted."

Rob dropped back into his seat as something finally went home inside his head. "I've always thought in terms of us building on what Earth Fleet did, of using their methods as the foundation for our own ways of winning. But there wasn't any real foundation, was there? Great technical skills, highly trained individuals, but no real ideas how to translate those things into victories that mattered."

"That's a fair assessment."

He could see how much that admission hurt her. "Lieutenant Commander Shen, what we do is going to matter. Others are going to build on what we do even if they don't remember we're the ones who did it."

She managed a tight, ironic smile in response. "Or they're going to remember us as the examples of how not to do it."

Ten hours later, nineteen hours until intercept with the enemy. Both sleep and inspiration remained elusive. A message arriving from *Piranha* proved a welcome distraction.

Captain Salomon had the look of someone who hadn't slept well. Rob understood that and imagined he looked the same. "My guidance is unchanged. Work with you to defend Kosatka. Do not agree to any relationship subordinate to *Saber*. We're still stuck being on the same side but unable to work as one.

"As I see it," Salomon continued, "we have three basic options. One is to jointly but separately engage and try to defeat the escorting warships, then go after the troop transports. The second option would be to jointly but separately try to avoid the escorts and hit the transports. And the third would have us agreeing that one of us would engage and try to draw off the escorts while the other attacked the transports."

Salomon paused to take a drink of coffee. "Acting jointly but separately in a tactical situation would put us at a serious disadvantage against the unified command on the enemy side. But acting singly raises the risk that one of us will be defeated, allowing the other to be the sole target of the enemy. That might still be our best option, though.

"It's my job to stop the enemy. Therefore, I propose that *Piranha* engage the escorts, keeping them busy, while *Saber* hits the transports. If you can do enough damage to those troop ships, the invaders will have to withdraw. Even if all you do is damage some of those ships so they require a longer time to slow down when approaching the planet, it might give us enough time to get *Shark* operational again."

Piranha was still far enough away that a real-time conversation was impossible, giving Rob time to think about Salomon's proposal. "What do you guys think?" he asked Vicki Shen and Mele Darcy after replaying the message for them.

"She's offering to do the heavy lifting," Vicki Shen said. "Keeping those escorts busy would mean giving them decent shots at *Piranha*."

"Yeah, I give her full credit for that. *Piranha* could get badly beat-up fighting single-handed against three opponents."

Mele shook her head. "I'm guessing *Piranha* wouldn't last long doing that. You know my usual advice, which actually comes from that Sun Tzu guy. Figure out what the enemy is going to expect you to do, then do something different. So, what are they going to expect? Are they going to be thinking that we'll act as one with *Piranha*?"

"No," Rob said. "Nobody out here has acted together except the bad guys. The good guys have been too busy clinging to their virtue to consider compromising enough to work together."

"You sound a little bitter about that, sir," Mele observed.

"I am. A lot of people have insisted on everything being just as they want, and other people end up paying the price for that purity. Including people like us and the ones we command." Rob waved one hand toward them. "Not that either of you are to repeat a word of that to anyone. To answer your question directly, what the enemy will expect is that *Piranha* and *Saber* will operate independently, each refusing to surrender any degree of control to the other."

"That means we know what'll surprise them."

It was Vicki Shen's turn to shake her head. "That's nice in theory, but how can we operate jointly with *Piranha*? There *can't* be a single commander. We're not permitted to yield command, and neither is *Piranha*'s commander."

Mele looked at Rob. "You're willing to listen to suggestions. Maybe Salomon is, too."

"Suggestions?" Rob asked. "How can you run a battle on the basis of suggestions?"

"It's not about me. It's about you. Can you and *Piranha*'s commander agree on a specific course of action? And then agree on what to do next?"

Shen sighed. "Captain Darcy, you know what combat is like. There's not much time for trading suggestions and negotiating a mutually agreeable middle ground."

"You space squids have a lot more time between shots than we Marines and ground apes do," Mele pointed out. "Commander Geary," she added in formal tones, "can you check your ego at the air lock and find a way to dance with *Piranha* as your partner? Neither one of you leading, but both of you knowing what step the other one is going to take next."

Rob gazed at Mele, thinking over her words. "Dancing. That's an interesting way of putting it."

"You know how renowned Marines are for our verbal skills. Show the enemy what they expect to see. They'll believe it because they expect it. And then do a switch up at the last possible moment that would only be possible if you and *Piranha* were working as one."

"That's good," Vicki Shen said, eyeing Mele with surprise. "If we can hit them hard enough on the first go-round, it might give us the advantage we need."

Rob checked his desk display. The distance between *Saber* and *Piranha* was down to one and a half light hours. Which still meant a three-hour time delay to send a message and get a reply. "I'm going to have to get a lot done with a few messages. Let me think over what to try and get back to Commander Salomon. She can't agree to do whatever I say, but maybe she'll accept an invitation to dance."

Aboard the *Oarai Miho*, Lochan Nakamura morosely
eyed the tiny display image offered by the panel in his
room. The jump point that offered escape toward areas as
yet free of conflict was close as such things were measured
in space. Several light hours away on the other side of the
star system, warships were moving toward each other.

The display in his room offered minimal useful features
beyond a no-frills depiction of space outside the freighter,
and showing or playing books or vids. It had been ridicu-
lously difficult to figure out how to use the "intuitive inter-
face" to calculate movements ahead. But Lochan had finally
managed to figure out that the warships would meet about
five hours before the *Oarai Miho* jumped out of the star
system. Which meant the light showing what happened
would still be hours away when the freighter left. He
wouldn't even see the results of the first clash.

It didn't look hopeful in any event. Two defenders against
that big group of invading ships.

Carmen had sent another update, which had arrived an
hour ago. Kosatka's two occupied cities were emptying out,
the citizens spreading through the vast as yet unsettled
countryside to prevent their being targets for orbital bombardment. Not that anyone expected indiscriminate bombardment, but someone had done it before at Lares, and
that someone might have been tied to Scatha or Apulu or
Turan.

Kosatka's militia was being rapidly expanded as volunteers flocked in. There weren't enough weapons to arm
everyone who wanted to fight. Dominic Desjani had been
promoted to captain and placed in command of a company
of soldiers. Carmen had admitted, with a wry look that
warned him against any future "I told you so," that she and
Dominic had quickly married, so at least she'd taken his
advice on that.

Lochan sat, his head in his hands, thinking of war rolling across the world he'd come to care for deeply. A world

that held both Carmen and Brigit, and now Carmen's husband as well.

At least Mele Darcy was probably safe back at Glenlyon. As safe as anyone could be these days, anyway.

But he was leaving. Leaving them all. And no matter how Lochan tried to tell himself that he was doing something critically important, that victory might ultimately rest on whether he could gain Kosatka the help it needed, he thought of others fighting and his leaving them and felt a deep emptiness inside.

Humans feared death. Lochan knew he did. All of science's advances over the centuries had served to keep people healthier and stronger for longer, but the total life span had not budged much in millennia. As ever, humanity's means of killing advanced more rapidly than its means of sustaining life.

And he, not a hero, not a fighter at all, wished that he was holding a rifle and standing with Carmen and risking death doing that rather than leaving her to her fate while he rode a freighter fleeing to safety.

CHAPTER 7

Two individual ships and one group of ships were all moving through space at very high speeds, but because they were all heading for pretty much the same point in space where their paths would intersect, they grew closer and closer but maintained the same relative bearings to each other. From *Saber*, the group of invaders was slightly above and a bit to the right, while *Piranha* was also slightly above but farther to the left. As the distances between them dwindled from light hours down to light minutes, everyone seemed eerily suspended in space, only visible because of the magnification offered by *Saber*'s sensors.

Rob and Commander Salomon had exchanged a few more messages, setting up a dance that would hopefully surprise the invaders. Salomon had been cautious, but once she understood the idea had seen its potential.

Saber's vector had been adjusted so she was heading for an intercept not just of the invading force but aimed precisely at the enemy Founders Class destroyer. To the invaders, it must look like a reckless charge against the primary villain in the destruction of *Claymore*, with *Saber* on a mission of revenge regardless of all other factors.

Piranha had also adjusted her vector, aiming to bypass the escorts and hit the freighters. *Piranha* had also braked her velocity to point zero five light speed, an obvious attempt to ensure her weapons could score as many hits as possible on the troop carriers. But that change in velocity also meant that *Piranha* would come in behind *Saber*, striking brief minutes later.

"It looks exactly like *Piranha* is going to let us take the brunt of enemy fire so she can get to the freighters with minimal risk," Vicki Shen commented.

"The Scathan commander ought to believe that's what's intended," Rob said.

"*I* believe it! Are we sure *Piranha* won't let that happen instead of doing as you and Salomon agreed?"

"I'm certain," Rob said. As certain as he could be, anyway. If he'd badly misjudged Salomon, *Saber* might end up paying a heavy price. "We're going to act as Salomon and I agreed. If this fails, it won't be because *Saber* failed to live up to her commitments or I failed to live up to my word."

Shen studied the depiction of the enemy warships. "Do you think they'll be suspicious at how easy it will be to counter *Saber*, then *Piranha*? All they have to do is collapse down that triangle at the right time so they can hit *Saber* with all three ships at once, then pivot up and to the side a little to catch *Piranha* as she comes through."

"I'm hoping that tempts the enemy commander enough that he doesn't question his good fortune," Rob said. "He has a chance to knock out both of us on our first firing runs. Is he going to question that? Because if he doesn't react with the textbook solution you described, he'll miss that chance. And if he does react that way, we'll have him." Rob checked the time. "One hour left to intercept. It's still a little early to set battle stations."

Vicki Shen smiled. "I'll bet you that everyone in the crew is already at their battle stations. They know who we're going after this time, the ships that destroyed *Claymore*. They want blood, Captain. But I suggest waiting until forty-five minutes prior to estimated contact to go to full combat readiness."

"Why?"

"Because that's when the Earth Fleet checklists call for going to full combat readiness. When we do that, increasing our shields to maximum and powering up the pulse particle projectors, the enemy will be able to see it. If those enemy ships see us acting as if we're still using the checklists, it will help convince them they have nothing to worry about."

Rob grinned. "That's an excellent suggestion. Thank you."

"But we're still coming in at point zero eight light," Shen noted. "Deke, what velocity would the old checklists require?"

Lieutenant Cameron paused, frowning in thought. "They mandated a combined speed at contact of point zero six light speed or less to maximize hit potential. The velocity adjustments are to be completed ten minutes prior to contact."

"Ten minutes?" Rob said. "That gives the other guy plenty of warning, doesn't it? All right, work up when we need to start braking." He called *Piranha*. "Commander Salomon, we're going to act as if we're following Earth Fleet checklists on this engagement. That means braking down to just under point zero six light speed by ten minutes prior to contact. I'll send you the exact planned maneuver prior to that. If you wait until you've seen us start braking to begin slowing down yourself, it'll support the image that we're not coordinating actions. Geary, over."

"Coordinate." That was a great word. One of its definitions was, literally, "equal in rank, degree, or importance." He and Salomon could coordinate back and forth all they wanted without either accepting subordinate status.

Another definition of "coordinate" was "actions or processes properly combined for the production of one result."

Yes. "Coordinate" was definitely Rob's favorite word at the moment.

With one hour left to contact, the ships were much closer. Only about five light minutes separated them so Rob got a reply in ten minutes.

"I understand that you'll begin braking down to point six light speed," Salomon said, looking far more relaxed than Rob thought he appeared. "We'll act as if we had no advance knowledge and react after sighting your maneuver to apparently brake down our own velocity to maintain the same distance behind you at contact. By the time the enemy realizes that we're not braking velocity as much as we ought to, it should be too late for them to figure out what we're doing. Let me know of any other changes. Salomon, out."

At forty-five minutes to contact Rob ordered full combat readiness aboard *Saber*, everything happening right on schedule as mandated by the old checklists.

Be complacent, Rob wished at the enemy commander. *Assume you've got this nailed. Assume we're dumb enough to charge right in.*

"Three light minutes to intercept point," Lieutenant Cameron reported.

Three light minutes. The distance light traveled in three minutes. About fifty-four million kilometers. An impossibly huge distance in human terms because human senses thought in planetary concepts where fifty kilometers was a long ways to go on foot or even by ground vehicle. But traveling at point zero eight light speed meant *Saber* would cover that remaining distance in a little less than forty minutes. They'd slow down some before then, to just point zero six light speed, so the actual time left was a bit more than that.

The apparent position of the enemy hadn't changed, slightly above and to the right as *Saber* saw it. *Saber*'s path wasn't aimed at the enemy ships but at where those ships would be when *Saber* got to the same place.

"No reaction by the enemy yet," Vicki Shen commented. "Everything looks good. With your permission, Captain, I'll head back to engineering."

"Permission granted," Rob said. Aside from the benefits

of having Shen's experience in the engineering compartment, that also physically separated the ship's second-in-command from where he, the captain, was located. Any damage to the bridge that claimed the captain should leave the executive officer alive and able to assume command. It felt odd, Rob realized, that the arrangement *didn't* feel odd, that it was simply something to be accepted, an acknowledgment of the dangers that *Saber* and her crew were about to confront.

That despite all of their planning, things might go wrong, and he might soon be dead.

Rob did his best to banish that thought. He couldn't let it affect his decisions and couldn't let it show in his voice or his expression or his body language. The crew would pick up on that. Fear was contagious, racing from person to person at a rate no other malady could come close to matching. And fear of impending danger carried its own risk of creating the conditions under which that imagined danger became real.

So Rob relaxed a bit in his command seat, breathing in deeply and letting it out slowly. To keep himself occupied as the minutes crawled by he tried replaying the projected course of events.

Physics made doing things hard but made predicting them easy. If *Saber* held her current vector aiming at the Founders Class destroyer, the most effective move for the Scathan warships would be *that*, with the Sword Class destroyer moving *there*, and the Adventurer Class cutter moving *there*. In order for those two ships to get to those positions, they'd have to move *this* way at *that* time. If the Scathans did as expected, then Rob could predict exactly where all three warships would be at a certain point in time.

And he had done all he could to ensure the Scathans did do as he hoped, offering them an apparently perfect target. Just as *Claymore* had done. Militaries were notoriously slow to learn lessons inflicted by opponents in battle, clinging to doctrine as long as possible, sometimes past the point where that refusal to change made it impossible to win. Rob had done something unexpected three years before to defeat a Scathan ship, but the details of that action had been fogged by time and official accounts, and in any case the enemies here in Kosatka Star System probably didn't even know yet that Rob was now in command of *Saber*. The commander of Scatha's warships had every reason to expect his foes to be blindly predictable, ignoring what the enemy might do in favor of their own preconceptions.

"Captain, the braking maneuver should begin in five minutes. Request permission to set maneuvering system to automatic for that maneuver."

"Permission granted," Rob said.

Ensign Reichert spoke up next from the weapons watch station. "Request permission to lock weapons systems on enemy Founders Class destroyer."

"Permission granted," Rob said. "But be prepared to shift targets immediately when I give the order."

"Shift targets, sir? What's the secondary? I can set that up so all I have to do is tap it and redirect all weapons systems."

"Good. Secondary target is enemy Sword Class destroyer."

He had to admire the calmness with which the bridge crew were going about their tasks. They didn't know in any detail what was intended, but even if they were diving straight into the teeth of the worst Scatha could throw at them they'd do it without flinching. "You're all exceptionally fine sailors," Rob said out loud. "Everyone on this ship. I'm proud to be leading you into battle again."

No one said anything in reply. What could they say? But their smiles told him that his words had gone home.

"Braking maneuver initiating," Lieutenant Cameron reported.

Thrusters fired, pitching *Saber*'s bow up and around so it was facing toward the rear, the main propulsion aft now forward as the ship raced backward through space. As the ship's aspect reached the proper position the main propulsion lit off, its force now directed toward slowing down

Saber to just under point zero six light speed. *Saber* shuddered under the stress, her hull groaning, the whine of the inertial dampers rising to audible levels as they worked to keep the strain from tearing the ship apart and crushing the human crew.

As the stress levels shown on Rob's display climbed into the yellow caution zone, he saw a message appear and called Vicki Shen in engineering. "Is this right? The system will automatically ease off if we go into red?"

"That's right," she said. "It's built into the software to prevent overstress."

"What if we need to go into the red?"

She took a moment to reply. "We're not supposed to."

"What if we need to?" Rob repeated.

"Right now, we can't."

"Can we fix that? So I can override if necessary?"

Another pause before the reply came. "It'll take a while, but I'm sure we can go through the system and create an override. However, I'm not sure how good an idea that would be, Captain," Shen added in a diplomatic tone of voice.

"Understood. Remind me to talk about it once this is over."

Lieutenant Cameron called out as the main propulsion shut off and thrusters fired again. "We're at point zero five seven light speed. Bringing bow around to face the enemy. Ten minutes to contact."

"*Piranha* is braking velocity," Ensign Reichert added. "It looks like she's still planning on passing the enemy escorts a few minutes after we go through."

Rob felt tension knotting his stomach as he gazed at his display. The maneuver he had to order was there, constantly updating as the time ran down to contact. *Saber* would reach a point where he could no longer make the necessary corrections in time, but that was still several minutes away. "Very well. I'm entering a last-moment maneuver into the system. I'll execute that maneuver from my command display at the right moment."

Scatha's commander would also be waiting to give maneuvering orders, waiting until it seemed *Saber* and *Piranha* were committed to their own paths. Waiting until it would be too late for *Saber* and *Piranha* to realize what he was doing and adjust their vectors. Even with the distance separating the different warships down to light seconds there would still be a slight delay in seeing what the other side was doing.

With ten light seconds separating the warships from intercept, less than two minutes to contact at their current velocity, Rob called the maneuver out loud at the same time as he pushed the command to carry it out. "Up point zero one five degrees, come starboard zero zero one degrees." Immediately afterward he called out again. "Switch weapons systems to secondary target, Sword Class destroyer. That is now primary target."

"Understood switch all weapons to target Sword Class destroyer," Ensign Reichert responded, her words as rushed and sure as her movements as she tapped the commands. "Sword Class destroyer is now the primary target."

"The enemy is maneuvering!" Lieutenant Cameron said.

Rob waited, tense, to see whether the enemy was doing as he and Commander Salomon had hoped.

"Sir, *Piranha* ceased braking early! She's going to intercept within seconds of our own attack and . . . she's shifting vector!"

Rob grinned. "Very well."

It would be a few seconds before the enemy could see that *Saber* and *Piranha* weren't doing what they were supposed to do. How much longer before the commander realized the implications? He wouldn't know for certain until *Saber* and *Piranha* steadied out. Would he flinch? Or would he try to bull through?

At *Saber*'s velocity she was covering about seventeen thousand kilometers per second. One moment the enemy was very far away as humans thought of such things, but very close in terms of space. The next moment *Saber* had passed close to the Sword Class destroyer and was still shuddering from the impacts of hits on her and the jolt of firing her own weapons.

The Sword Class destroyer was a bit smaller than Founders Class ships like *Saber* and *Piranha*, and carried fewer weapons as well as shields that weren't as strong. Against only *Saber*, the enemy ship could have gotten off with only minor damage from the exchange of fire.

But Commander Salomon had made the last-moment changes necessary to also bring *Piranha* close to where that enemy destroyer would be, at almost the same moment as *Saber* engaged. Grapeshot from both warships hit the Scathan vessel's forward shields, knocking them down so that every pulse particle beam projector on *Saber* and *Piranha* had clear paths into and through the enemy ship.

"Bring us up and over to intercept that cutter," Rob ordered while *Saber*'s systems were still trying to assess the damage done to the enemy destroyer.

Saber went into a wide, wide turn, climbing up and over to swing back at the Adventurer Class cutter.

"*Piranha* is diving down," Lieutenant Cameron reported.

"She's going to come back at the Sword Class destroyer," Rob told him. "How's *Saber*?"

"Our forward shields held, Captain. Spot failures, but nothing got through."

"Outstanding. Ensign Reichert, what did we do to that Sword?"

"Still evaluating, Captain," Reichert said, speaking quickly but clearly. "His forward shields are not recovering. Unknown amount of damage to weapons, but at least one of his particle beams is assessed destroyed. Maneuvering capability appears to be compromised."

"You set him up," Lieutenant Cameron said, his voice reflecting admiration and surprise. "You and *Piranha*."

"That's right," Rob said. "We coordinated our actions. Our best chance was to take out the Sword Class ship by surprise. With that one badly hurt, we'll have a chance to beat the remaining enemy warships." He had been watching the movements of the enemy warships, seeing the Founder Class ship and the cutter moving close to the Sword Class ship to protect it. "Shift our vector. We're going to hit the freighters." He tabbed the comm channel. "*Piranha*, this is *Saber*. If the enemy continues to protect their damaged ship, I intend striking at the freighters. Either that will draw them away from the Sword Class ship so you can hit it again, or leave me free to hit their troop ships if they stay close to their damaged companion. Geary, over."

The two warships were still close enough together that the reply came in less than a minute. "*Saber*, this is *Piranha*. I will continue my attack run on the damaged ship but break off if I face all three combatants at once and join you in a strike at the troop carriers. Salomon, out."

Coordinating didn't seem all that difficult, Rob thought. Perhaps he and Salomon weren't doing it "right."

"You've got him stuck," Ensign Reichert said with sudden comprehension. "He either protects that warship we've already damaged, or he protects the freighters. He can't do both."

"He'll have to leave the destroyer, won't he?" Cameron said. "His job is to protect the troop ships."

"You're right," Rob said. "I expect he'll try to intercept us before we can hit those freighters. We'll let *Piranha* try to finish the Sword Class ship."

"We helped take that ship down," Ensign Reichert insisted.

He knew why she felt the need to say that. *Claymore* wouldn't be properly avenged if someone else struck the death blows to one of the warships that had destroyed her. "That's right," Rob said. "It'll be a joint kill in which *Saber* played an equal role."

Saber was at the top of her loop and *Piranha* just beginning to turn up from the bottom of her curve when the enemy ships made the move that Rob was expecting.

"Enemy Founders Class destroyer and cutter are breaking away from the Sword Class ship," Cameron reported. "They're coming back and up."

"They're going to try to hit us," Rob said, "or make us turn away. For now, keep us on a vector to pass through the enemy formation, targeting the passenger ship. We'll shift vectors on final approach to avoid giving him a shot at us and try to hit one of the freighters."

An internal comm alert came on as Mele Darcy called. "He's going to be mad," she said, obviously speaking about the enemy commander.

"I know," Rob said. "Mad enough to make mistakes."

"Maybe. Also mad enough that if you give him an opening he'll go for your throat. You're feeling pretty confident right now. Don't."

He hesitated, recognizing that Mele was right, that without realizing it he was feeling almost giddy with assurance after the success of the first maneuver. So confident that he might have given the enemy commander just such a shot at him. "Thanks. I needed to hear that."

"That's why I'm here," Mele said. "That, and to break things that need breaking."

"Captain!" Ensign Reichert said. "Warrant Officer Kamaka reports that we're getting some very aggressive attacks on our system firewalls. The transmissions carrying the attacks appear to be originating from the enemy passenger ship. So far nothing has gotten through, but he's monitoring the situation closely and wanted you to be informed."

"Thank you," Rob said. "Mele, if your code monkey isn't busy maybe he can help Kamaka."

"Will do. I'll have Corporal Giddings get in touch with Warrant Kamaka. Sir," Mele added, "if those software attacks are coming from the passenger ship, that means their offensive hackers are aboard it, and most ground forces I know of keep their hackers close to the headquarters unit."

"Understood," Rob said, his eyes on the display where the arc of *Saber*'s path through space was projected to meet with the near-future position of that passenger ship. *Pira-*

nha was still coming around as well, her vector aimed at hitting the crippled Sword Class destroyer. And the remaining enemy destroyer and cutter were curving up and back to hit *Saber* just before she reached the passenger ship. He was still twenty minutes out from encountering those enemy warships.

Rob tapped his comm control again. "*Piranha*, this is *Saber*. We're under software attack from the passenger ship and assess that the enemy ground forces command structure is probably aboard it. Recommend we concentrate attacks on that ship. I'll try to draw off the enemy combatants. Geary, over."

The reply took about a minute to show up. "*Saber*, this is *Piranha*. I may not be able to finish off the damaged enemy warship on this firing pass. It'd be helpful if you could make another run on it after mine. I agree with trying to cripple and destroy the passenger ship. That's their highest value target. Salomon, over."

Rob checked his display, realizing that personally running the options would be too distracting. "Lieutenant Cameron, have someone work up some options for hitting that Sword Class destroyer again if *Piranha* doesn't finish him."

"Yes, sir!"

"*Piranha*, this is *Saber*. Understood. Will attempt to hit the damaged enemy ship again if necessary. Geary, out."

That left the question of whom to try to hit on this pass. Ensign Reichert took that moment to complicate the answer. "Captain, the enemy warships are going to intercept us at a point close enough to the other enemy ships that if we engage them our weapons won't be able to reload or recharge before we're past the passenger ship or freighters."

He took a closer look, realizing that not only was Reichert right, but that the intercept point was perfectly positioned to catch *Saber* if she continued a firing run on the freighters or passenger ship. The enemy warships would catch *Saber* no matter which ship Rob tried to target with a last-moment course adjustment. "He's good," Rob muttered in reluctant appreciation of how well the enemy commander had planned his intercept maneuver. "Ensign Reichert, what's our worst case if we take the maximum number of possible hits from both of those remaining warships?"

"Wait, sir," Reichert replied as she ran a simulation. "There's a better than even chance of spot failures in our shields and hits on *Saber*. Our combat systems are estimating anywhere from one to three hits on this ship."

He didn't bother asking where those hits would fall. There were too many variables to offer any meaningful prediction. The hits could pass through nonessential areas, or through some of the crew, or strike critical systems and knock them out. There wasn't any way of knowing in advance.

Rob took another long look at the aspects of the two oncoming enemy warships. They were close enough to each other that he couldn't hit the cutter without the destroyer also hitting back at *Saber*.

None of his options were looking good. But if he didn't press the attack, *Piranha* might feel that *Saber* was failing to live up to its part of the bargain. Could he risk that?

A red marker abruptly appeared on Rob's display.

"We've lost primary controls for thruster group two," Chief Petty Officer Quinton called out from the engineering watch station. "Cause unknown. Auxiliary controls . . . Captain, the auxiliary controls are having trouble taking over."

Rob took only a couple of seconds to confirm where maneuvering thruster group two was located on the hull of *Saber* before realizing that he couldn't continue this attack run. With one of the three primary maneuver thruster groups out, the loss of a second could render *Saber* a sitting duck. Coming right or up was already hindered, so he ran a hasty vector change to the left and down. Even if the enemy warships pursued, that would give at least half an hour to get those thrusters back online. "Come port five zero degrees, down zero three zero degrees."

"Understand come port five zero degrees, down zero three zero degrees," Lieutenant Cameron replied. *Saber* rolled to the left and dipped her bow as the remaining thrusters fired.

"Let me know if they come around to intercept us," Rob ordered, worried that the enemy would spot *Saber*'s problem and attempt to attack while the ship couldn't maneuver well in all directions."

"There's no sign they're following," Ensign Reichert said. "Holding position near the passenger ship. They probably think we're pulling an injured bird."

Rob twisted in his seat to look at her, puzzled. "An injured bird?"

Reichert in turn appeared startled that he didn't know the term. "It's a deception maneuver to try to draw off escorts or attackers by feigning damage and apparent vulnerability, sir."

"It's on the checklists," Lieutenant Cameron said.

"Right. So the enemy would have known we might try that if we were paying attention to the checklists and probably assumes that's what we're doing."

"Thank you," Rob said, surprised that something from the Earth Fleet checklists had proven so useful in confusing the enemy about the real problem that *Saber* was experiencing.

An internal call from Vicki Dorset came in as Rob settled in his seat again. "Sir, I'm on-site where the failure occurred. It's a relay junction."

"Can you identify the cause of the failure?" Rob asked, thinking of hacking messing up a critical part's functions.

"It looks like a normal failure," she replied. "Relay junctions on Founder Class ships are notorious for sudden no-apparent-reason RJ fails. That's why we carry several spares. I've sent a team to pull a spare so we can do a replace. If nothing else complicates things we should have the junction up, synced, and working in ten minutes."

"Thank you," Rob said, grateful that he had people with so much experience working for him. With the enemy not in pursuit of *Saber*, and now sure of the problem, he called

Salomon. "*Piranha*, this is *Saber*. I suffered the temporary loss of a thruster group due to part failure and broke off my attack run. *Saber* should be fully combat ready again in ten minutes and will reengage at that time. Geary, out."

He refocused on his display in time to see as *Piranha* raced past the injured Sword Class destroyer. The battered enemy ship had tried to shift his bow away, but Salomon had correctly anticipated the maneuver so that *Piranha* crossed the enemy bow. With the enemy's forward shields still down, *Piranha* was able to fire her pulse particle beams down the length of the Scathan warship. Rob flinched, thinking about those streams of highly charged particles tearing through everything in their path, whether equipment or members of the enemy crew.

A moment after the particle beams hit, *Piranha*'s grapeshot struck the enemy's bow. The grapeshot, nothing but metal ball bearings depending on their mass and velocity to do damage, hit with enough energy to vaporize the front of the Scathan destroyer.

That was one ship that wasn't going to be worth salvaging after this was over.

Piranha continued up and around, aiming for the Scathan troop carriers as a reply came in from Salomon. "*Saber* this is *Piranha*. I think your guess regarding the value of the passenger ship is right. I'm going to try to draw off the remaining escorts by hitting the freighters farthest from them. If they go after me, that should give you a shot at the passenger ship. Salomon, out."

"Lieutenant Cameron," Rob said, "as soon as we get all thrusters online again I'll want an intercept trajectory on the passenger ship, timed to get there right after *Piranha* makes her run on the enemy freighters."

"I'll have it ready, sir."

"Ensign Reichert, how badly hurt is that Sword Class destroyer?"

Reichert shook her head as she studied her display. "He's either completely dead or very good at playing dead. His power core has shut down, and we're seeing no signs of any systems still working."

Something about that didn't fit. "Why haven't the surviving crew abandoned ship?" Rob wondered.

"I have no idea, sir."

Out of commission as it apparently was, the Sword Class destroyer continued moving with the enemy formation since the passenger ship and freighters hadn't maneuvered. But the hits on the destroyer had slowed it a little and knocked it onto a slightly converging vector, so the Sword Class ship was slowly drifting higher and closer to the rest of the ships. If none of the freighters or the passenger ships changed their own vectors, the badly damaged warship would drift through them and out the upper edge of their formation. "Maybe they're waiting to abandon ship until they're in among the other ships friendly to them," Rob said. "How are the repairs on thruster group two going?" he added, realizing that ten minutes had come and gone.

Chief Petty Officer Quinton relayed the question, remaining impassive as he heard the reply. "Lieutenant Commander Shen says the junction repair is complete but something else is causing problems. She's got specialists trying to run down the problem."

"Any new estimate of repair time?" Rob asked, trying not to snap the question in frustration and afraid that he already knew the answer.

"No, Captain. Until they find what's wrong they can't say how long it'll take to fix. Whatever this problem is isn't showing up on remote diagnostics so they're having to do physical checks."

Rob rubbed one side of his face, thinking, as *Saber* continued to arc past the enemy formation. *Maybe if we . . .*

"Captain?" Lieutenant Cameron said. "I don't know how much experience you have with our systems. They will automatically analyze and report any unusual behaviors in another ship."

Rob looked back at Cameron, trying not to glare. "And?"

"Sir, the enemy destroyer came from the same source and has the same analysis systems as we do. If we maneuver without using thruster group two, the systems automatically will spot that and notify the enemy commander."

Damn. "Thank you, Lieutenant," Rob said. "I didn't know they'd do that. There's no way we can maneuver without giving it away?"

"No, sir," Cameron said.

"Then we'll have to do the best we can without those thrusters and make sure we don't give the enemy warships a chance to intercept us while we've got limited maneuvering capability. Work me up an intercept on one of the freighters."

What to tell Salomon? Regardless of her wishes, he couldn't hazard *Saber* in an attack in the ship's current condition. Coordination could only go so far, and his primary duty remained to Glenlyon.

Unhappy but determined, Rob tapped his comms again. "*Piranha*, this is *Saber*. My number two thruster group is down for an undetermined period. I'll attempt to continue attacks on enemy shipping but cannot risk an engagement with the enemy warships while my maneuvering is compromised. Geary, out."

Salomon didn't respond as *Piranha* swept around to hit one of the freighters at the end of the enemy formation. Rob watched, frustrated by *Saber*'s inability to match the maneuvers, as *Piranha*'s weapons tore up one side of the freighter. "Give me an intercept for that trailing freighter," he ordered. As soon as the solution came in, he approved it, *Saber*'s remaining thrusters firing to bring her around in the long sweep to the left that should end at where the freighter would be.

"Sir!" Ensign Reichert called out. "*Piranha*'s trying something else!"

Rob took another look at *Piranha*'s vector. The enemy warships protecting the passenger ship had lunged back and up in an attempt to catch *Piranha* as she pulled away for another firing run. *Piranha* had seen, too, and was rolling down and over to strike at the momentarily unguarded passenger ship.

Had the enemy lunge always been intended as a feint, or had the enemy commander lost his nerve and aborted the attack run? *Piranha* and the enemy ships were close, very close, and moving very fast as *Piranha* dove at the passenger ship and the enemy destroyer and cutter abruptly altered their own vectors.

At the velocities such ships were moving, any misjudgment could be catastrophic. Cruel momentum held them in its grip and would not yield easily to even the power of thrusters.

Rob felt a reflexive yell of caution stick in his throat, too late even as it formed. By the time anyone on the other three warships could see what might happen, by the time even the automated maneuvering systems could spot the danger and make the necessary changes, the enemy cutter and *Piranha* had momentarily touched hulls as both crafts raced past each other moving at thousands of kilometers per second.

At that velocity, the energy of the impact was enough to vaporize most of the cutter and at least a third of *Piranha*. The cutter and its crew simply vanished, turned into dust and tiny fragments. *Piranha*, slammed off vector by the collision, with all propulsion and maneuvering knocked out, tumbled away from the enemy formation, pieces of the stricken warship breaking off as the wreck spun wildly through space.

Rob stared at his display, momentarily shocked into inaction. Salomon might have survived, since the bridge was located in one of the best protected places inside *Piranha*'s hull, but even if she and some of her crew were still alive, they and their ship were out of this fight.

"Captain?"

Lieutenant Cameron's stunned question brought Rob out of his paralysis. "Continue attack run on the last freighter," Rob ordered as he tried to grasp what had just happened.

The enemy cutter was gone, but so was *Piranha*. That left *Saber* against the enemy Founder Class destroyer. Even odds, or it would be if *Saber* didn't have one-third of her maneuvering thrusters down.

Lieutenant Commander Shen took that moment to call the bridge again. "When the junction failed so did protective breakers along control lines. We've got burned-out lines to most of the thrusters."

"Can we replace them?" Rob asked, his mind mechanically seizing on something he could still control.

"Yes, sir. But I'm estimating at least ten hours for the job."

Rob inhaled slowly before replying. "Make it as much shorter as you can. We just lost *Piranha*. *Saber* is all that's left to stop that invasion force." The words felt hollow as he gazed at the surviving enemy destroyer and the freighters and passenger ship. *Saber* couldn't handle that all on her own.

He might be able to inflict some more damage, but barring the miracle that had yet to appear this invasion wasn't going to be stopped short of the planet it was aiming for.

CHAPTER 8

Long ago, on Old Earth, people must have only looked to the sky with fear during those times when thunder rumbled and lightning flashed. But humans had first learned how to fly, then how to enter space. It hadn't taken them long to realize that weapons and soldiers could be dropped from above. Ever since, the sky and the stars had just been one more battlefield for humans to cross and contest, one more source of danger for those on the surface of a planet.

On Kosatka, the intelligence offices had been watching space, using the latest sensors available, but were as impotent to do anything about the threat as primitive humans fearing the strike of lightning.

"Everybody out," Loren Yeresh announced. "The invasion fleet will reach orbit soon. You have thirty minutes to copy any files, collect gear, and leave the building. After that a special team is going to wipe every file from the gear we have to leave, then start planting physical booby traps where they can and malware booby traps in the equipment."

Carmen Ochoa had already prepared for what had increasingly seemed an inevitable step. She did a final update on the data coin holding the backed-up files she wanted to save. Popping the data coin out of its slot, she sealed it into one of her jacket pockets, then picked up her bag as she stood.

The situation display looked depressingly similar. The invasion fleet getting ever closer, while *Saber* and the remaining enemy destroyer tangled repeatedly as Glenlyon's warship tried to stop that invasion force. But with the enemy ship able to concentrate on one opponent *Saber*'s efforts had mostly been frustrated.

Loren paused beside her to look at the display, his face haggard with weariness and worry. "We actually got a question from someone in the government demanding to know why Glenlyon's ship hadn't stopped the invasion fleet."

"You're kidding." Carmen shook her head. "They don't have any obligation to do what they're doing. But they're still fighting to defend us. And people are complaining about that?"

"Sure. The same people who kept finding reasons for the last few years not to sign a formal defense agreement with Glenlyon," Loren said, his voice derisive. "I hear Glenlyon's ship has been asked to help defend our orbital facility once the invasion gets here. *Shark* would be a sitting duck at the facility if she was alone, but if Glenlyon's ship stays to help, that last enemy warship won't be able to face both of them at once."

"But we don't know if Glenlyon will do that?"

"They've already done far more than we had any right to expect. I hope they will. Otherwise, we'll lose *Shark* for certain, along with the orbital facility."

"What do you need me to do?" Carmen asked.

"I want you to link up with one of the defensive ground units and assist them in any way you can. There'll still be intelligence sections active with the ground forces command, and I'll be with the high command staff, so feed those sections and me anything important you run across," Loren said.

"One of the ground units?" Carmen asked, not believing her ears.

"Yeah." Loren gave her a look that felt far too much like a final good-bye. "You pick the unit. I can't officially assign you to the same place as Dominic because of the rules. Something about married people in the same combat unit. But I can leave it up to you. Try to get through this in one piece, Carmen."

"You, too," she said. "I'd hate to have to train another boss."

"Don't forget your rifle."

"I won't."

Carmen said a few more good-byes and left, her rifle in one hand, a pack with all of her personal gear and as much extra ammunition as she'd been able to acquire on her back. The campaign to hold Ani against the "rebels" had been abandoned, the entirety of Kosatka's ground forces and militia volunteers supporting them concentrating around Drava and Lodz where the enemy invasion forces were expected to land. Dominic Desjani's company had taken up positions a few kilometers from the spaceport, hiding amid office buildings and stores that were now deserted except for the too-few defenders.

Mass transit in the city had already shut down, the controllers for the buses and trains wiped and locked to prevent the enemy from quickly making use of them. But Carmen was able to hop a ride on a military vehicle heading in the same direction that she needed to go. She sat in the back, along with a few others whose expressions were as numb as hers probably was, while the lightly armored vehicle rumbled through the nearly deserted streets of Lodz.

If the dreams of those who had built this city were to survive, many of those same dreamers might have to die. Carmen looked upward to where the invasion fleet was steadily drawing closer and thought curses at whoever had sent them here.

"Thruster group two is fully operational!"

Rob swung his gaze across his display, his mind running through a series of lightning estimates. *Saber* was making another attempt to get at the invasion fleet, climbing upward from the front of the enemy formation and below to hit the passenger ship. But the enemy destroyer was already coming in on a vector from one side to hit *Saber*'s vulnerable rear shields. It was a well-planned defensive move, taking advantage of *Saber*'s by-now-obvious thruster problem.

But Rob saw another chance that had suddenly appeared as thruster group two came back online. "Come down zero one degrees, come left zero zero three degrees," he ordered. "Lieutenant Cameron, give me a refined intercept solution on that trailing freighter!"

Saber's sudden move, impossible before all of her thrusters came back into use, threw off the enemy destroyer's counterattack. The enemy shot past, out of range of *Saber*, as Rob's warship aimed for the freighter that had already taken damage earlier from both *Saber* and *Piranha*. "Ensign Reichert, I want maximum hits on that freighter. We may not get another intercept like this."

"Weapons targeted," Reichert said. Like the others on the bridge, she had been up for too long, still going thanks to Up drugs that could keep people awake and mentally sharp for days on end. Afterward, those drugs exacted a price when the metabolism of those people crashed, but in the short term they could mean the difference between survival and death.

Saber whipped past the lagging freighter, whose hull already bore scars from previous hits. With a perfect, clean shot at vital areas, the destroyer pumped particle beams and grapeshot into the freighter's bridge and engineering areas.

Cheers erupted on *Saber* as the freighter's power core blew up, taking with it everything and everyone the freighter had been carrying.

"We got one," Lieutenant Cameron said, grinning.

"Let's hope it was carrying a lot of important stuff," Rob said. "Give me a vector back to hit the invasion fleet again. Best target given our current vector."

"Yes, sir. Sir, we're about to hit fifty percent on our fuel cell reserves."

"Very well." Rob sat back, rubbing his eyes and hoping that the Up drugs weren't impairing his thinking. If he let fuel get too low, he wouldn't be able to get *Saber* back to Glenlyon. And there wasn't anywhere in Kosatka that he could refuel while that enemy destroyer was still on the prowl.

"Sir, we've got an incoming call from Kosatka."

The distance to the planet was only measured in a few light minutes now, making a conversation possible but also emphasizing how little time was left for *Saber* to stop the invasion.

First Minister Hofer of Kosatka stood in his office, his attitude that of someone about to depart. "Commodore Geary, I'm not certain if I'll be able to speak with you again. I've been advised to evacuate along with what is left of the government here in the city. I . . . wanted our gratitude for your assistance to be on the official record."

Hofer paused, a shadowy thought darkening his features. "And yet I ask one more thing of you. *Shark* is still helpless at our orbital facility. The invasion force hasn't attempted to destroy our facility or damage *Shark*. They obviously plan on capturing both. Kosatka urgently asks if you can remain in the vicinity of our facility to help *Shark*. Emergency repairs are still under way. If you can hold off an attack on the facility for long enough, *Shark* can join you. If not . . ."

The leader of Kosatka shook his head helplessly. "Please do what you can. And when you return to Glenlyon, let them know Glenlyon will never stand alone while Kosatka remains free. May our ancestors bless your efforts. Hofer, First Minister, out."

Rob rubbed his eyes again as the message ended, wondering what he should do.

"I hear we're at fifty percent fuel reserves," Vicki Shen said in a low voice nearby.

Absorbed in the message, he hadn't heard the executive officer come onto the bridge. Rob lowered his hand and nodded to her. If anything, Shen looked a lot worse than the rest of the crew after her nonstop efforts to get the thrusters working. "How is the rest of your repair team?"

She shrugged. "Still able to work. What are you going to do?"

"What would the checklists say?" Rob wondered.

"At fifty percent? Request permission before continuing mission, and if that's not possible break off and return to the closest refueling location."

"Is that what you recommend?"

"No, sir. That guy," Shen said, pointing to the symbol representing the enemy destroyer on Rob's display, "has to be lower on fuel than we are. On the way up here, I asked our sensors for an analysis on *Shark*'s status, which I confirmed by some one-on-one coordination with *Shark*'s executive officer. If repairs continue at their current rate, and if we can buy them three more days, they should be able to get under way."

"And then we'll have the enemy destroyer outnumbered two to one while he's really low on fuel," Rob said. "It's still a helluva risk."

"Yes, sir."

"Can they land anybody on that facility if we're helping *Shark*? If they can do that, they could capture *Shark* by storm along with the facility."

"You're asking the wrong person, sir," Shen said.

"Yeah." He tapped one of the internal comm circuits. "Mele, I need you on the bridge. We need some Marine input." Rob looked at Vicki Shen again. "Before Captain Darcy gets here, I'd like to know your recommendation."

The hesitation he saw in Vicki Shen didn't have anything to do with her tiredness, Rob knew. This was the sort of tough decision that Earth Fleet had long ago outsourced to automated checklists. The kind of decision that Shen and the other Earth Fleet veterans aboard had been trained to avoid making.

"In your gut," Rob asked softly, "what do you want to do?"

Shen stared at the display. "Win. Beat these guys. Avenge *Claymore*."

"Then—"

"Captain, if I'm thinking with my gut, if I go with what I *want* to do, I may not be thinking about what I *should* do."

"Fair point," Rob said. He lowered his voice even more to ensure they weren't overheard. "My gut keeps telling me to get back to Glenlyon, where my wife and girl are. I know why that is. I'm afraid for them. So your gut is telling you to stay and fight, and mine is telling me we've done all we can and should get back to the place we're obligated to defend."

A long moment of silence stretched between them as Rob thought through his options. "Three days. You think they can get *Shark* under way in three days?"

"Yes, sir," Vicki Shen said.

"But can we be sure of holding that facility even if we stay those extra days?" Rob asked himself as much as her. "And by then our fuel reserves will certainly be less than forty percent. Can they hold that facility if we stay?"

Mele Darcy came onto the bridge, still in the lightweight battle armor she'd been wearing since before the engagement began. Even though she had surely napped at times, she couldn't be feeling good after being inside the armor so long. "Does somebody need a Marine?" she asked Rob.

He stared at her, suddenly realizing that she could not only help answer his question but that he had a weapon he'd forgotten about. "Yeah. I need Marines. Lieutenant Cameron, how long until the next intercept?"

"Thirty-five minutes, sir. But the enemy destroyer is coming around and will meet us in thirty-three minutes."

"Good." Rob stood up, surprised at how unsteady he felt on his feet and wondering how long he'd been sitting. "I'm going to hold a conference with Commander Shen and Captain Darcy in my stateroom. I'll be back in fifteen minutes."

It only took a couple of those minutes to explain his idea. Mele Darcy frowned, looking toward one corner of Rob's stateroom as she thought it through before replying.

Vicki Shen spoke carefully, each word precise and well thought out. "We have time to set up the necessary maneuvers, Captain. We should be able to do what you ask."

Mele glanced at her, then at Rob. "We can count on *Shark*?"

"I'll get a commitment from them before we launch you," Rob promised.

"Are there any soldiers already on the facility?"

"I'll find that out, too."

"But you know already that you can limit how many enemy shuttles reach that facility?" Mele pressed.

"Yes," Rob said. "The enemy will be able to tie us up for a short period by threatening an attack run on *Shark*. But that will only give them a narrow window to get shuttles through, and only by angles of approach that are masked from us by the bulk of the facility structure."

"Are we expected to hold the whole facility for the necessary length of time?"

"No," Rob said. "Your job will be to keep the enemy from capturing *Shark*."

Mele nodded, her eyes thoughtful. "We can trade space for time. That's the Marine version of Relativity. Time equals space multiplied by effort. Yes, sir. We'll keep them from getting *Shark*. I'm going to need schematics of that orbital facility and as much as we can find out about what's stored up there and how many people are left on it."

"Thank you, Captain Darcy. You may need to get most of that after you arrive at the facility." Rob turned to Vicki Shen. "Start working out how *Saber* is going to handle the delivery while I call *Shark*'s commanding officer. We can't stop the invasion fleet from reaching Kosatka, but this battle isn't over yet."

"Captain . . ." Lieutenant Commander Shen hesitated, then spoke with unnatural calm. "There's one other thing we can do to help *Shark* and Kosatka. *Shark*'s chief engineer was killed in the ambush attack on their ship. *Shark* is also a Founders Class destroyer. If we provided them with a skilled, experienced chief engineer, it might make all the difference in their getting those repairs done."

He stared at her. "You're volunteering to transfer to *Shark*? Knowing that the ship might be captured?"

Shen smiled slightly. "I have confidence in Captain Darcy, sir."

What else did he need to ask? Rob wondered. "The remaining officers aboard can handle all possible engineering situations that might occur on *Saber*?"

"Yes, sir. I trained them, sir."

Rob nodded, reluctant, unsure what else to say. "Your offer to volunteer is accepted, Lieutenant Commander Shen. We'll send you over along with Captain Darcy's Marines."

"Thank you, sir." Shen pointed to Rob's desk display. "We're also still on an intercept run," she reminded him.

"Yeah. I need to handle that, too." Rob dashed back onto the bridge, reacquainting himself with the current situation with a glance at his display as he dropped into the command seat. "I want an estimate of our odds of inflicting critical damage on another freighter or the passenger ship before the invasion fleet reaches the planet."

"We already ran it, sir," Lieutenant Cameron said, sounding not proud of having anticipated the need for the estimate but unhappy at the results. "The odds are effectively zero. We don't have enough time left, or enough firepower, given that the enemy destroyer is still a threat. If we persist in attacks on the invasion fleet, there's at least an even chance that *Saber* will receive disabling damage."

Rob knew he could dispute those estimates, which after all were only the result of imperfect attempts to quantify things that couldn't really be quantified. But, after two days of trying to stop the invasion fleet single-handedly, he felt the truth of these estimates. It was only because *Piranha* had helped damage that one freighter, and because *Saber*'s sudden return to full maneuverability allowed a move the enemy hadn't anticipated, that a single freighter had been destroyed. Other ships had taken damage, but not nearly enough to stop them. And *Saber* herself had narrowly avoided receiving serious damage on some of those attack runs.

Moreover, he could easily see that the current firing run would result in the enemy destroyer getting far too good a shot at *Saber* on the way.

"Break off this attack," Rob ordered, feeling a burst of anger at the necessity.

"Yes, sir," Lieutenant Cameron responded. "Breaking off attack. Request new vector guidance." He sounded unhappy, resigned to the inevitable.

Everyone on the bridge looked like they felt the same way, Rob saw. He tried to inject more confidence into his voice as he gave the next command. "I want a vector to Kosatka's orbital facility. Work up what we need to do to slow enough to drop off our six Marines, then stay close enough to the facility to protect *Shark* against attack and the facility itself from enemy shuttles dropping off an attack force."

Used to having the well-trained veterans of Earth Fleet respond smoothly to orders, Rob was startled when they reacted by staring at him.

"We're not giving up?" Ensign Reichert asked, grinning in disbelief.

"Hell, no, we're not giving up," Rob said. "We're attacking along a different vector. This battle is not yet lost, and I intend to continue doing whatever we can to win it."

Half a day later, Mele Darcy paused in one of *Saber*'s air locks as the destroyer continued braking, matching vectors to soon and momentarily match the orbit of Kosatka's orbital facility. Gazing across the gap between *Saber* and the open construction area around *Shark*, the facility glowing beyond in the light of Kosatka's star and the planet below dappled with a living world's heraldry of white and blue and green and tan, Mele couldn't help wondering why she'd been stupid enough to volunteer for the job of leading Glenlyon's Marines. "I just had an epiphany," she said to Rob Geary over the command circuit in her armor.

"How beautiful the universe is even when people are trying their best to kill each other?" he asked. "One minute to when you jump, by the way."

"Thank you, sir. No, I realized that success in most things depends on finding people stupid enough to volunteer to try doing them but smart enough to have a chance of succeeding."

"That's very profound," Rob Geary said dryly. "Hopefully, we all still occupy that sweet spot with just enough stupid and smarts. Thirty seconds."

"Thirty seconds," Mele called over another circuit to her five other Marines before switching back to the private one between her and Rob Geary. "My hope is to survive long enough to be promoted so I'll be able to send other people to do jobs that I'm stupid enough to volunteer for."

"There you go," Rob Geary agreed. "You just have to hold off any attackers for two and a half days, Mele. Keep the invaders off *Shark* until then and you'll have a safe ride off that facility."

"Piece of cake," she replied, trying to sound a lot more confident than she felt.

"Commander Derian is the captain of *Shark*. He can't give you orders," Rob Geary emphasized. "If Derian or someone else tries to tell you what to do, you have to refuse. And you can't give them orders. But, as a certain Marine told me, that doesn't prevent you from dancing together. *Saber* will give you all the support we can. Vicki, do your best," Rob continued to Commander Shen. "Mele's Marines will watch your back."

"Piece of cake," Vicki Shen said, echoing Mele.

"Five seconds."

"Five seconds," Mele repeated to her Marines, bracing herself preparatory to the leap across space. Vicki Shen braced herself at the other side of the air lock, the remaining five Marines lined up behind Mele and Commander Shen.

"Go."

"Go!" Mele lined herself up on a relatively open area around the construction and pushed off as *Saber* came to a momentary complete stop relative to the orbiting facility. Both ship and facility were still moving at about seven kilometers per second as they orbited the planet, but with their motions perfectly matched they might as well have been motionless as Mele flew across the gap between them. Behind her and Shen the other Marines literally ran off the air lock, jumping into space.

Mele looked down at the planet during the brief moments between leaving *Saber* and reaching the facility, seeing its surface rolling past beneath her. Some people had trouble with looking outward while free flying through space, but it'd never bothered Mele. She gazed at the surface of an ocean over one thousand kilometers below her and imagined diving all that way down until the waters closed over her.

Of course, if she really did that, falling all the way unchecked and somehow avoiding being fried by the heat of moving so quickly through atmosphere, she'd hit the water so fast that it would be like striking a steel wall. The only things left to rest in the water would be tiny pieces of her.

Mele laughed at the universe that she knew wanted to kill her and everyone else in any way that it could. Because that was what the universe did. And she would fight to keep herself and others alive because that was what she did. And when the universe eventually won, because in the end it always did, she'd take a break until whatever came after, if anything. Because, whatever came after, they'd probably need Marines there.

She rolled her body to check on Lieutenant Commander Shen and the Marines, seeing Shen flying not far from her and the five Marines spaced out behind in fairly good alignment. *Saber* had begun accelerating again as soon as the last Marine cleared the air lock, already vanishing into the distance as the ship leapt away to become one more speck of light in a darkness filled with infinite lights.

Rolling to face forward again, Mele brought her feet to the fore and down as she reached the facility, dropping onto the platform she'd aimed for and grabbing a brace to check her motion. She used her free hand to grasp Shen's arm and help her land as the other Marines went past, grabbing at objects, doing a decent if not great job of also landing on the facility.

"Thanks," Vickie Shen said, her voice shaky.

"This wasn't your first space jump, was it?" Mele asked.

"As a matter of fact, it was the second. The first and only other was during my officer training," Shen replied, her breathing slowing to a calmer pace.

"You did pretty good," Mele told her. "Pretty good for a space squid, that is."

"I'll try not to let that praise go to my head," Shen said.

Mele straightened to look around, one hand still holding securely to the brace as Shen steadied herself and the other Marines moved closer. A couple of people in standard shipboard survival suits were headed her way. The flurry of activity around *Shark*'s main propulsion units had paused as *Saber* came by but almost immediately resumed. Despite the frantic work in that part of the dock area, the orbital facility already had an empty, abandoned feel.

"Captain Darcy?" one of the approaching sailors called over the common use circuit. "Commander Derian would like to speak with you and, um, Lieutenant Commander Ivanova."

"I'm Darcy," Mele replied, "but this is—"

"Ivanova," Shen broke in. "I'll explain."

Since the talk with Derian had been phrased as a request rather than an order, Mele waved to her Marines to stay with her and followed the two sailors. Switching to a private command circuit, she called Shen. "Ivanova?"

"Politics," Vickie Shen explained, sounding completely calm again. "Commander Derian can't give an officer from Glenlyon a command authority position on *Shark*. But if a former Earth Fleet officer calling herself Ivanova happens to show up, he can appoint her chief engineer. Derian pretends he doesn't know I'm Commander Shen from Glenlyon, and I pretend I'm Commander Ivanova who's not working for anyone else at the moment so I can give real orders aboard *Shark*."

"I didn't realize Earth Fleet officers could be that devious," Mele said admiringly.

She could hear the smile in Shen's reply. "When you operate in a highly political environment, you learn how to get things done despite the political obstacles."

Shark lay oddly canted in the space dock. Mele wondered at the reason for that. The forward air lock, the entire forward part of the destroyer, looked to be in great shape. The only clue as to the desperate situation lay in the frantic work aft and the grim attitudes of the sailors Mele saw.

Mele left the other Marines in the ship's passageway as she and Shen crowded into the captain's stateroom. Commander Derian's quarters were identical to Rob Geary's on *Saber* except for the few personal items. Derian himself had a haunted look as he welcomed them. "Captain Darcy. Thank you for, uh, assisting us. Commander . . . Ivanova. I've already informed the crew that you're the new chief engineer."

"Then I'd better get to work," Vickie Shen said.

"You had four years as chief engineer on your ship?"

"Yes, sir. I could take every engineering system on *Shark* apart and put it back together with my eyes closed." She nodded a farewell to Mele. "I know that Captain Darcy will ensure we have the time we need."

"Thank you," Mele said, for once not entirely comfortable with that degree of confidence in her capabilities.

"By your leave, sir," Vickie Shen told Derian. The moment *Shark*'s captain nodded, Shen was out the hatch and headed aft.

Derian sighed heavily, sitting down with the weariness of someone who had been going all out for too long. "Major Brazos is in command of the forces defending inside the facility," Derian said. "I've asked him to join us so you two can, uh, talk."

She sized up Derian and felt sympathy. "It must be hard sitting here in dock."

Derian gazed unhappily into space as if recent, unwelcome events were replaying before him. "Hard. Yes. Watching the others fight on their own. Captain Salomon . . . apparently *Piranha*'s bridge was destroyed. The survivors who've gotten off don't think anyone in that section of the ship survived. Captain Darcy, our best-case estimate is that we can get *Shark* under way, patched but ready to fight, in two and a half days. With the help of Commander . . . Ivanova, I think we can meet that. But we need two and a half days."

"We can do our best to keep the enemy from reaching this dock through the inside of the facility," Mele warned, "but we can't cover the outside if they attack the dock that way. It's too much area to cover."

Derian smiled, his lips pulled back tightly over his teeth. "Did you notice how we're positioned in the dock? *Shark* can't move right now, but our weapons work and our fire control is fine. If anyone comes over or under or around the facility toward this dock, we'll spot them silhouetted against space and they'll get a particle beam through them. Those beams move at nearly the speed of light. This close we don't have to lead the target or worry about it dodging."

Mele raised her eyebrows in admiration. "Nice. I understand your weapons are designed for bursts of fire, though, not sustained fire. How many enemy soldiers can you take out before the pulse particle beam generators overheat?"

"A lot. We can use a low power setting that can keep shooting rapid bursts for a long time," Derian said. "Low power would be useless against the shields on a warship,

but against an individual in a suit it'll be more than enough."
He looked unhappy again, waving toward the facility. "But
we can't use that against people coming at us *through* the
facility. Too hard to spot until they were right on top of us,
then too close to be able to bring our beams to bear. If they
get to this dock through the inside of the facility, we'll face
a boarding situation and my crew will have to fight them off
hand to hand. We'd prefer that not happen because we lost
some people in the sneak attack that damaged our propulsion. We're already short on personnel. That's where you
and Major Brazos come in."

"Is he a professional or one of Kosatka's militia?" Mele
asked.

"Brazos? Militia. Police experience. That's it."

As if summoned by the third mention of his name, Major Brazos entered the stateroom, saluting Derian before
turning a wary gaze on Mele. "You're a real Marine, huh?"

"As real as they come," she replied, thinking that Brazos
didn't seem particularly welcoming.

His next words confirmed her assessment. "Kosatka can
defend her own world," Brazos said, as if daring her to
challenge the statement.

"We were asked to help," Mele said, trying to be diplomatic.

"Not by me. I hope you're not planning on calling the
shots here. You're not needed."

So much for diplomacy. Mele nodded and smiled tightly.
"I'll just ask Commodore Geary to bring *Saber* back to
pick us up, then."

"That won't be necessary," Derian interrupted, glaring
at Brazos. "As senior officer on this orbital facility, I'm
grateful for the assistance that Commodore Geary and his
crew have provided to Kosatka. I want it clearly understood
that the presence of these Marines from Glenlyon to assist
our defense here is welcome. The goal for all of us is to
ensure that the work on *Shark* is completed so we can join
Saber in defeating our common enemies."

Mele hadn't been sure what to think of Derian, who after all had let his ship get crippled and as a result sat out the fight where *Piranha* had been destroyed. But Derian hadn't hesitated to assert his authority over Brazos and had made it clear he was itching to get into the fight.

"Yes, sir," Major Brazos said, little about him indicating the agreement expressed by the words. "We don't know how much time we have left before the enemy attacks. With your permission, I'll get back to preparing the defense of the facility."

Derian didn't let him go that easily. "I expect you to cooperate with Captain Darcy. I suggest that you listen to her advice. Marines are trained specifically for missions such as this involving ships and orbiting facilities. And Glenlyon beat back the attack on them three years ago. They must know what they're doing."

"Yes, sir," Brazos repeated. "I'm not aware of whether this individual had any role in the action three years ago."

Mele wasn't the sort to brag on herself, but given that sort of passive-aggressive put-down she couldn't avoid taking the shot. "I trained, organized, and commanded Glenlyon's ground forces in the field three years ago," she said.

Commander Derian looked visibly impressed, but Brazos didn't do a good job of hiding his skepticism. "Sir," he said to Derian, "if there's nothing else . . ."

"You have your orders," Derian said, with a look at Mele that told her clearly to let him know if she needed to have Brazos kicked in the butt.

"We'll do what we can," Mele said as Brazos left. "After all, you guys are our ride out of here."

"Thank you." Derian gestured aft. "The workers trying to get our main propulsion online again are all volunteers. They could have taken shuttles down to the comparative safety of the planet, but they chose to stay here and work. Look out for them as well, Captain Darcy. Please," he added after a pause.

"I will," she promised, rendering Derian a salute. "I need to look out for Commander Ivanova, too."

Mele and her Marines caught up with Brazos as he was

entering one of the air locks that gave access from the open-to-space dock area to the pressurized interior of the facility. "My biggest worry is friendly fire," Mele said without any sort of polite preamble. "I need links into your command net so my Marines show up as friendlies and I can see where all of your people are."

Brazos made a face, his eyes shifting toward where *Shark* and Commander Derian sat before he nodded. "All right."

"Listen," Mele added, "you don't have to like that we're here. But we're on the same side."

"Is that supposed to make me happy?" Brazos snorted in derision. "I worked law enforcement on Brahma before I came out to Kosatka. Trying to keep law and order. We had a base not far off, and I had to deal with Marines more than I ever wanted to."

"Marines on liberty can be challenging," Mele admitted, thinking of some of the things that she'd done as a private after having a few too many drinks. "But this is different. We're on the job."

"I don't see any difference."

"Know what?" Mele asked, her patience at an end. "I don't care. We're going to do our job. You do yours. How do we get access to your command net?"

Brazos glared at her as the air lock finished cycling and he pulled off his survival suit helmet. "Have your IT specialist request access from OrbitFacDefCom." The inner hatch opened, and he stomped away without another word.

"You get that, Giddings?" Mele asked.

"Yes, Captain." Corporal Giddings paused as he worked through the request. "Got a link. They say they need approval."

"Tell them Major Brazos approved it."

"Done . . . I've got a wait status, Captain."

"Fine. Let's walk around and see how things look." Orbital facilities tended to grow over time, adding on structures and manufacturing sites and living areas and even recreational locations. Compared to the many facilities orbiting Old Colonies like Franklin, this structure at Kosatka hadn't yet grown into a city. But it was already much bigger than a destroyer such as *Saber* or *Shark*, more like a really large factory building complex, add-ons and new structures grafted onto the original like a three-dimensional sculpture constructed of blocks sticking out and up and down. Also unlike the warships, the facility didn't have a sleek exterior or a well-defined center of mass. As one of Mele's training instructors back on Franklin had put it, orbital facilities were all about function. "Ugly as a junkyard dog because looks don't matter when all you need is something that can do a job."

Inside, the absence of its normal occupants made the emptiness feel huge, every shadow suspicious and every corner or closed door a potential hiding place for something or someone.

Mele led the way through the nearly deserted facility, their movements sounding unnaturally loud amid the silence that reigned in most parts of the station. The basic life support functions were still working, but nonessential services had already been shut down. Scattered display screens that normally would have shown art or information instead revealed only the dead black of no input. They passed bare bulkheads and ceilings, empty rooms and offices, most showing signs of hasty departure.

They reached a food court, where minor efforts had been made to dress up the functional needs of a food court to make it look slightly special rather than the same as every other food court from here back to Old Earth. A dozen men and women in a mix of industrial and survival space suits, and carrying a mix of hand weapons, were sitting at a few tables that had been pulled together. They started to rise in alarm at the arrival of the newcomers, but relaxed when Mele waved at them with an open hand. "Captain Darcy, Glenlyon Marines. We're here to help."

Relieved smiles replaced anxious looks as one of the men walked over to Mele. "Damn! Marines! That's great!"

"You guys all militia?" Mele asked.

"Every defender on the station is militia," he replied. "I mean, except you guys."

That explained their happiness at seeing regular military personnel. Mele gestured around. "Are any of the food stands working?"

"Anything with lights on. Help yourselves if you need anything. It's on the house."

Grateful for the chance at food better than that served on a warship, the Marines all grabbed meals and sat down around one of the larger tables. As they did so, another group of militia came in, calling out greetings to the first group.

"How's that access coming?" Mele asked Giddings as she eyed her pack of fries. They looked entirely too "healthy" to taste good.

"Just got in now," he reported. "We're getting a real basic data feed. It's letting us ID ourselves as friendly, and showing up IDs of nearby militia like these guys. Nothing else."

"There has to be more to their command net than that," Mele said.

"There is," Corporal Giddings confirmed, his eyes shifting back and forth as he scrolled through data on his pad. "I'm seeing virtual walls blocking us from other parts of their command net. They look makeshift, though. That's probably why it took so long to get us access. They were throwing together these walls to limit what we could see."

"Huh," Mele said, not wanting to openly disparage Major Brazos in front of the enlisted. "Can you get through those walls, Glitch?"

"What do we need to see, Captain?"

"Where every friendly soldier is located," Mele said. "Any detections they have of the enemy. Any fights going on. Any orders being issued by Major Brazos or anyone else."

Corporal Cassie Gamba gave a sidelong look at the militia. "How many have they got, Captain?"

"I don't know."

Giddings spoke up. "Eighty. Eighty-one counting Major Brazos. I just got into that part of the command net. All militia, like that guy said."

"Eighty." Gamba grimaced as if she were tasting the number and not liking it. "How many hostiles?"

"It depends," Mele said. "*Saber* is going to try to keep shuttles from reaching this facility to drop off troops, and *Shark* can hit any that come within its line of sight. But any shuttle coming in with the facility between it and *Shark* will be safe from that. And if the enemy warship makes a run on *Shark*, *Saber* is going to have to move to support *Shark*. We're expecting that to happen. That'll give the enemy a narrow corridor to run a few shuttles through."

"A few shuttles?" Private Yoshida said. "They could have, what, three hundred on those?"

"Depending on the shuttle type and what kind of armor they're wearing," Private Lamar said. "If four shuttles make it through, the numbers they carry could range from, um, two hundred eighty to three hundred fifty."

Mele gave Penny Lamar a questioning glance. "You're a shuttle expert?"

"It's a hobby, Captain," she admitted.

"She builds shuttle models from scratch," Private Buckland added, laughing.

"Do you have any other interests I should know about?" Lamar paused. "No others you should know about, Captain."

"So," Corporal Gamba continued, "we're talking at least a few hundred hostiles, eighty friendly militia, and us. How good are the hostiles?"

"We don't know," Mele said. "The ones I fought three years ago from Scatha were mercenaries hired as a unit from one of the Old Colonies. Kind of like you guys but not as professional. But we've had word that Scatha and Apulu, and Turan, have been hiring anyone willing to carry a gun. If we're lucky, that's who we'll be facing."

"Reds," Yoshida offered. "I heard a lot of them are from Mars. Somebody told me there's like hundreds of thousands of Reds who'll do anything for a job, and they're cheap hires."

"Reds can be bad news if they're gang fighters or warlord troops," Gamba said. "Not as good as professional ground forces, but tough."

"Got it!" Giddings announced. "We're in the command net. No restrictions. I gave you a ghost ID so even if their system watchdogs notice you they'll think you're okay, Captain."

"You're a credit to the Marines of Glenlyon," Mele said, running through the data now available on her pad. "Oh, yeah. And here's the Major's plan. Look." She titled the pad so the others could see it. "He's breaking his forces into squads and posting them at major intersections to stop any advance."

"What about the ways past those intersections?" Lamar asked, eyeing the plan.

"That's thinking like a Marine," Mele said, nodding in approval. "The militia is trying to seal off routes, but they can't seal off every possible path. Once aboard this facility the attackers can go up, down, right, left, and everywhere in between. They'll either try to overrun the individual squads of defenders, which will be fast but expensive in terms of casualties, or bypass the defenders using other routes, which will take longer."

"So what are we going to do, Captain?" Gamba asked.

"Reaction force," Mele said. "Or fire brigade, as they used to call it, because we're going to be putting out fires. As the enemy hits these militia forces, or bypasses them, we'll hit the enemy. If there's a breakthrough likely, we reinforce the militia if we can get there in time. If a breakthrough occurs, we stop it."

"Six of us?" Buckland asked.

"That's right," Mele said, trying to sound confident but not insanely confident. "I'm going to personally command Team One. That's me, Corporal Giddings, and Private Lamar. Corporal Gamba, you command Team Two, with you, Yoshida, and Buckland."

"Major Brazos has a reaction force designated," Gamba pointed out.

"Yeah, but that reaction force is also assigned defense of a critical intersection just short of the space dock. That's a mistake, people. He's going to be afraid to move that reaction force because its other job is so important."

Buckland looked around as a burst of laughter came from one of the militia squads, the sound a little too high-pitched and forced, like people trying to appear unworried rather than people who weren't worried. "Can they do this, Captain?"

Mele knew what the question meant. It was as simple as the way the different groups appeared to an outside observer. The militia members looked dangerous in a haphazard, chaotic way, whereas her Marines appeared dangerous in a very controlled and capable way. "They can," Mele said, "if we show them how."

"Captain," Gamba said, "with all due respect—"

"I know what that really means, Corporal."

"Uh . . . my apologies, Captain. How can we show them how to fight in the middle of a fight?"

Mele nodded to show her understanding of the reasons for that question. "I've done this, led volunteers against regular troops. Because that was all I had. Give them good leaders, good examples, and they can do a lot. Respect them, boys and girls," she told her Marines. "They know they're not good at this, but they're facing death anyway because there's no one else to handle the job. That takes guts. Lets help them ensure their deaths make a difference.

"Because plenty of them are going to die trying their best."

CHAPTER 9

None of them disputed her statement. Mele hadn't expected any of them to do that, but she had wanted to see how they reacted. To see if any of her new Marines suggested abandoning the militia to their fate. Anyone who would do that might later decide to abandon their fellow Marines.

But they just sat, quietly absorbing her words or looking toward the militia.

"We can try teaching them a few things," Yoshida finally suggested. "How long do we have?"

Mele nodded approvingly before checking the time on her pad. "We've got two hours left before the estimated time the invasion fleet gets close enough to the planet to start dropping shuttles."

"When will they try to send shuttles here, Captain?" Buckland asked.

"You know, I may look like I know everything, but I don't." Mele tried looking for information in some other parts of Major Brazos's command net. "Ah, this will help. It's a look at the outside, where the ships are operating. There's the enemy destroyer. If Commodore Geary is right, when that destroyer lines up to hit *Shark*, it will be our warning that the enemy is about to send shuttles here."

Corporal Giddings looked up from his own pad and around at the food stalls. "Excuse me, Captain," he said as he got up.

"What's he up to?" Mele asked Corporal Gamba as they watched Giddings walk quickly to an unobtrusive stall whose lack of decoration implied either a bare-bones operation or one so well-off that it could ignore the need to try to impress potential customers.

After a couple of minutes, Giddings walked back, unsuccessfully trying to look casual despite the bulging bag he was now carrying.

"Open up," Mele ordered. Inside the bag was . . .

"Chocolate," Lamar whispered.

Mele pulled out one of the bars and examined it. "Old-Earth-origin chocolate. Do you rob banks on the side, too? How much do these things cost?"

"They told us everything was on the house," Giddings said defensively.

"These are all the bars they had?"

"Yes, Captain. I was able to remotely pop the lock on their storage."

Corporal Gamba spoke up. "We shouldn't leave them for the enemy, Captain. That would be wrong." The other enlisted Marines nodded in solemn agreement.

"It would be," Mele agreed. She looked around the food court, counting the militia members present. "Giddings, you and Gamba divide up those bars into enough pieces for everyone in this area."

"Everyone?" Lamar asked plaintively.

"Yeah, everyone." Mele stood up to attract attention. "Hey! Kosatka militia! Come on over. We got something special here."

As the militia and the Marines shared the unexpected feast, Mele was able to speak to Kosatka's defenders. She knew people like them. She'd led people like them. The similarities with the eager and naïve enthusiasm and the worries and barely hidden fears of those Mele had trained and commanded three years before were painful, calling up memories of the ones who hadn't survived. She wondered how well she was hiding the reactions those memories were creating in her.

Like other newly settled worlds out here, the first set of colonists had come mostly from one region or state or area, with subsequent waves including people from a broader part of the vast variety of human cultures and places. Mele couldn't help noticing that nearly all of the militia up here seemed to be from one of those subsequent waves, and that all the ones she was speaking with were lower-level techs and assistants. Worker bees. Hardworking. Essential. And replaceable.

And only eighty of them. It wasn't hard to factor that equation.

Did Commander Derian on the *Shark* know? Had First Minister Hofer of Kosatka's government known when he asked for help from Rob Geary? Probably not, Mele thought. More likely, the highest levels of Kosatka's military command had run their simulations using the parameters they thought were right and made their decisions to leave the defense of this facility to what was poetically called a *forlorn hope*. Because *forlorn hope* sounded a lot better than *human sacrifices*.

More time had passed than she realized, or the invaders had moved faster than expected. The facility's public announcing system suddenly boomed to life. "The invasion fleet has begun launching its attack! All personnel to defense positions!"

The militia members waved hasty farewells and dashed off. Mele stood, waiting, until they were gone, then checked her information again. "All they've launched so far are warbirds," she told her Marines. "They're still a little ways out from the planet."

Lamar spoke up. "That's probably so they can get the warbirds in position to screen the shuttle launches from *Saber*. Just in case our ship makes an attack run on them."

"Right," Mele agreed, pleased that Lamar had also been studying up on landing procedures. "Standard tactics for a landing operation. We've still got some time. Giddings, I want to know the location and type of everything left on this station that can explode."

"Captain, I've got an Improvised Explosives certification," Yoshida reminded her.

"So you do," Mele said, berating herself for not remembering that. "Work with Giddings. This is a nice, central location," she told the other Marines. "We wait here until we see what else is happening."

Gamba came close to Mele, speaking in a very low voice. "Captain, talking to those guys, this looks worse than I thought. All militia up here, no regular ground forces. Not very many militia. And no one they can't afford to lose. I know what that means."

Mele nodded, impressed that Gamba had also put together all the pieces of the picture. "I came to the same conclusion. Kosatka's high command must have written off this facility. They left just enough defenders to put up an inspiring fight before losing because they figure it's sure to fall."

Corporal Gamba seemed momentarily surprised by how calmly Mele agreed with the assessment. But after a second, Gamba smiled. "We're gonna prove 'em wrong?"

"Damn right we are."

"Captain?" Yoshida called. "They've got some grain storage compartments on this facility."

"And?"

"They've got fans to suck up any grain dust and filters to collect it, because fine particles of grain dust can be explosive in the right concentrations."

Mele raised her eyebrows in surprise. "Grain can explode?"

"Grain dust, Captain. If it's fine enough and there's enough of it." Yoshida pointed to a portion of the facility shown on Giddings's pad. "That's why they've got the fans and filters. Those grain storage compartments are almost empty, but nobody bothered emptying the dust collection bins. If we disable the filters, open the collection bins, and reverse the fans, we'll get a real nice concentration of dust in those compartments."

Mele nodded as she studied the image. "All we need is a spark?"

"That's all we need," Yoshida agreed. "We've got access to some maintenance shops and spare parts lockers on this facility. I can rig up something using stuff in those."

"You do that. These grain compartments are located under two of the main approach routes the enemy might use trying to get to *Shark*. How long will this take to set up?"

"Half an hour."

"Get it done." She thought about whether to tell Brazos, who'd probably find some reason to object to the plan, but decided that keeping him in the dark wouldn't do anyone any favors.

Mele went a few steps away to call the major, waiting impatiently for him to reply.

Brazos finally came on. "What is it?"

To hell with you, too, Mele thought. But she kept her voice professional. "I need to inform you of two things—"

"We're busy here."

Narrowly avoiding spitting out a nasty comeback, Mele kept speaking. "We're rigging the grain compartments to blow if the enemy penetrates that section of the facility—"

"No!"

"Excuse me?" Mele said, surprised that she didn't sound angrier.

"You're not authorized to plant any of your explosives anywhere on this facility!"

"Any of *my* explosives? You mean any explosives we brought with us?"

"That's right! Am I clear?"

"Absolutely," Mele said, having decided that if Brazos wanted to dance on his own he was more than welcome to it. "Thank you." She ended the call and went back to her Marines.

"Any problems, Captain?" Gamba asked.

"Nah."

"Yoshida and Lamar went to set up the grain compartments to blow. They'll have to break a few physical safety interlocks and plant the spark generators."

"Good. I'm going to make some calls to individual militia squad commanders so they know who we are, and so I can get a feel for who they are."

She was well along in that process when Yoshida and Lamar returned, the former grinning and giving her a thumbs-up.

Soon after, a call came in from Commander Derian. "Yes, sir," Mele responded immediately.

"The enemy destroyer is clearly setting himself up for an attack," Derian began without any unnecessary greetings. "And several enemy shuttles are positioning themselves in orbit where they're screened from fire from *Shark*. *Saber* can't move to engage them without exposing *Shark* to attack. We estimate you've got roughly one hour before enemy shuttles will begin reaching the facility and dropping off soldiers. Thanks to the expert knowledge of Commander Ivanova, our new repair estimate is one and a half days from now to get under way. Please give me that time, Captain Darcy."

"We will," she replied, her conscience nagging at her. "Sir, we've found a way to weaponize some of the materials on the facility, which would mean destroying part of it. I don't see any alternative, though."

"Why are you—? Oh. Captain Darcy, I think that Major Brazos is too concerned with balancing multiple responsibilities," Derian continued. "Brazos has been ordered to both defend the facility and prevent it from being too badly damaged."

"I'd gained that impression," Mele said.

"I can't override Brazos's orders from the government, contradictory as they are. But I also can't give orders to *you*. Your orders are from Commodore Geary. If he ordered you to do what was necessary to hold this facility long enough to allow the repairs on *Shark* to be completed, then I'm in no position to tell you to disobey those orders."

"Thank you, sir. I understand." That was as close to a go-ahead as Derian could give her. "We'll get you that day and a half."

The call ended, Mele turned to her Marines. "It's down to a day and a half. That's how long we've got to keep the enemy from reaching *Shark* on the dock. Estimates are the enemy will land in about an hour. That gives you all thirty minutes of leisure. Half an hour from now we go on full combat readiness. Expect to stay that way until *Shark* pulls out of here."

They'd all been in long enough to know how to make the most of thirty minutes. Bathroom break, raid the snack dispensers, catch a brief nap, write a message that might never make it to the intended recipient, or whatever else served to prepare for the worst.

Mele did some of that, too. But mostly she sat a little apart from the others as she obsessively studied the layout of the orbital facility and tried to work out plans that might keep *Shark* safe and her Marines alive.

At the thirty-minute point, Mele stood up, adjusting her armor and checking her weapons. The other Marines did the same without being told.

The estimate proved to be fairly accurate. "They're on their way," Mele said as alerts showed up on her pad. "Twenty minutes until estimated arrival. Six shuttles and an aerospace warbird."

The Marines nodded and stood before her, outwardly casual but inwardly tense, she knew. Just like her.

She ought to say something. Mele hesitated, looking them over. "All right, you apes. This'll be the first real fight for the Marines of Glenlyon. Centuries from now, I want people to be looking back on this fight with awe and toasting us with the best booze money can buy. Make me proud. And let's all make a memory that no one will ever forget. Any questions? No? Seal armor. Keep it sharp from this moment on."

As her helmet display activated, Mele checked it against the pad she still carried. There was a lot going on in orbit. The enemy must have launched every shuttle they had. The many shuttles not heading for this facility were dropping down toward the planet, escorted by warbirds. *Saber*, tied down protecting *Shark* from the enemy destroyer, could do nothing.

For how many thousands of years had humanity waged wars, developing better and better weapons? And how many times during those thousands of years had someone proclaimed that some latest weapon had made foot soldiers obsolete? But here, on and above Kosatka, the fight would once again be decided by grunts, fighting face-to-face and maybe hand to hand. Because that was what grunts did, and that's why, in the end, they were always needed no matter how many other fancy toys people came up with to wage war.

She hoped the grunts on the ground were better prepared than Major Brazos and his militia up here.

"Here they come," Dominic Desjani said, gazing upward.

Carmen Ochoa looked up as well, seeing the glint of sunlight on dozens of shuttles as they dropped from orbit toward the surface of Kosatka like sparks from a fire falling to earth. She couldn't help smiling at the memories the vision brought. "A dream come true," she said, the words dripping with sarcasm.

Domi gave her a glance. "A dream?"

"When I was a little girl on Mars, after my parents were killed, I had to spend a lot of time hiding," Carmen said, her eyes still on those shuttles high above this world. "I spent some of that time daydreaming, imagining a day when shuttles would fill the Martian sky, dropping down from space like a shower of leaves from a tree killed by a flash freeze. Fire from the sky would strike the dictators and oligarchs and gangs who made life on Mars a living hell for most of us, then the peacekeepers would leap out of the shuttles. Their armor would be gold and silver, and their weapons would shine as they killed every single one of those who had spent their lives making others fear them. And then the peacekeepers would wave me aboard and take me with them when the shuttles lifted. I'd sit in a safe and comfortable seat, with as much food and water as I wanted, and watch the surface of Mars dwindle behind us as we rose, and when we reached Rhiannon Station in high orbit my parents would be there, not dead after all, but waiting for me. And we'd get on a ship and leave Mars and never look back."

Domi's gaze on her grew anxious and sad. "That's one hell of a daydream for a little girl. I'm sorry, Red. No one should have to live a life that spawns those sorts of dreams."

"People still are living such lives," Carmen said with a sigh. "When I finally really got on a ship and left, still alone and years later, I didn't look back. Because I didn't have to. I couldn't leave Mars. It's still there," she said, tapping her head as she looked back at Dominic. "And now people like the rulers of Mars are trying to come here and make life hell for other little girls and boys," Carmen added, her voice going from softly contemplative to hard as steel in the space of a few words. "Not while I'm alive to fight them, Domi. Not while I can fight them."

"Not while *we* can fight them," Dominic said, reaching to grasp her hand with his. "Did you ever daydream a honeymoon like this?"

"No," Carmen admitted. She smiled again, a hard, relentless smile, as manta shapes bolted skyward, heading toward those points of light far above the planet.

"Let's hope our own ships can keep the enemy warships busy," Dominic said, also watching Kosatka's counterattack zoom upward. "Even those aerospace craft have a hard time dodging particle beams fired from low orbit."

"Warship," Carmen corrected. "The enemy only has one left, thanks to *Piranha* and *Saber*. But we also have only one left, and that's not even ours. If *Saber* leaves . . ." She shook her head. "If only we had enough warbirds to hit that enemy warship if it came down to low orbit."

"We don't even have nearly enough to stop those shuttles," Dominic said.

The sky filled with far-distant blossoms of smoke that glittered with embedded chaff and flares as the landing shuttles threw out countermeasures to hide themselves from the weapons on Kosatka's aerospace craft.

High above Carmen, where the sky turned black and the world formed a blue-white-green-brown curve beneath, where the thin atmosphere glittered with ice crystals and humans had once believed angels and gods dwelt, death now danced on thrusters, hurling charged particles and missiles and projectiles of metal. Unarmed shuttles dodged and dropped in erratic movements designed to throw off enemy predictions of where they'd be and when. Warbirds from Apulu, dropping with the shuttles, engaged Kosatka's warbirds, while Kosatka's aerospace craft tried to shoot down anything they could. Badly outnumbered, Kosatka's warbirds had the advantage of knowing just about everything else in the atmosphere was enemy, while the enemy had to take more time to identify targets to avoid hitting their own birds.

Little could be seen with the naked eye from ground level but occasional flashes of light amid the clouds of countermeasures covering the sky and the broken shapes of stricken craft spinning downward out of those clouds. Carmen raised her rifle and sighted through the scope, but even with maximum magnification not much was visible unless she happened to be viewing just the right spot at just the right time. "That's a shuttle. Falling fast and on fire, but still under some control," she told Dominic. Carmen felt a weird simultaneous mix of sympathy for those trapped inside the burning shuttle and satisfaction that they were unlikely to survive to reach the surface. "A warbird. *Half* a warbird. I can't tell whether it was ours or theirs. Oh, hell. Something just blew up inside the chaff clouds. Bigger than a shuttle or warbird."

"Maybe a couple collided," Dominic suggested.

"If so, I hope it was two of theirs." She saw light reflecting off many shuttles dropping out of the chaff, heading for their landing points. "A lot of them made it through."

Three warbirds came into sight, twisting around each other in wild gyrations. Carmen had no way of telling who was who, whether it was two invaders versus a single defender or if two of Kosatka's warbirds were trying to take out a single one of Apulu's.

One of the three warbirds exploded, while a second whirled away with a broken wing spinning off. The pilot of the stricken craft ejected, a dot falling through the sky until a parachute bloomed. The third warbird zoomed back up into the chaff, vanishing from her sight.

Who had won? Carmen stared at the falling pilot, wondering whether she should be hoping he or she made it down safely, or if they were an enemy and hoping the chute would fail so one more foe would be out of the fight for good.

"Our systems are starting to project landing sites," Domi said beside her. "No surprises. Looks like they're going to land around the main spaceport here, power generation centers, ground transportation hubs, and industrial areas. Here and in Drava. They've already got everything in Ani since we had to abandon it."

"There are small special forces units that are going to keep hitting the 'rebels' in Ani so they can't help attack Lodz or Drava," Carmen told him. "But if the invaders gain control of all those critical areas they'll eliminate our ability to sustain a fight over time."

"I've got a big knife that doesn't need ammunition or power," he replied.

"Domi . . ." Carmen squeezed her eyes shut, struggling against a wave of despair. "Damn. I don't want you to die."

"I'll make you a deal," he said, his voice soft. She wondered how his face looked, but wouldn't open her eyes to find out. "I'll keep you alive," Dominic continued, "and you keep me alive."

She inhaled deeply before she could reply. "Deal."

He paused as a call came in. "We've got orders to move to a projected landing site in the warehouse area just west of here. You coming, Red?"

"Sure." Carmen lowered her rifle, waiting as Dominic roused his soldiers and gave them orders. The unit broke into small groups, all of them scuttling through alleys and next to buildings, trying to remain as much under cover as possible to avoid being tracked from above.

The city they moved through was still unnaturally quiet. An occasional stray animal or rodent, some native to this world and some brought by humans, dashed into hiding as the defenders ran past. Otherwise, the streets and buildings felt empty, the normal noises of people and their devices gone, only the faint sigh of the wind audible between the sounds of boots striking the still-new pavement.

The block of warehouses they'd been sent to defend was centered around a large, open loading area that made a perfect landing site. Carmen frowned as Dominic began dispersing his soldiers to cover the loading area. "Domi, if these guys use Red tactics they'll land a diversion force in the obvious place but also drop forces on the streets around it, behind wherever anyone targeting that landing spot would be positioned."

Dominic paused, his eyes shifting around the area as he thought. "What's the best move for us if they do that? We don't have enough people to cover the loading area and all the streets around these warehouses."

"Cover part of it. Have soldiers targeting the loading area from one or two sides, but also have people covering the streets behind them so you can ensure an escape corridor for those in the warehouses."

He nodded, looked around again, then started giving orders to his company. "Platoon One, occupy the warehouses on the west side and cover the loading area; Platoon Two, cover the street behind them. Platoon Three, take the warehouses to the south, and Platoon Four, cover the street to the south. Questions? Go!"

Dominic watched his soldiers move but took a moment to give Carmen a questioning look. "Just what was it you did on Mars, Red?"

She shook her head. "You agreed never to ask about that."

"Sorry. It's just . . . you know a lot about certain things."

"I survived, Domi. By doing a lot of different things. That's what you need to know." Carmen took up position inside one of the warehouses to the south, kneeling next to a partly opened door she could fire through. With the power to this part of the city shut down, and even the emergency lights inside the warehouse turned off, the brightness of the day outside formed a stark contrast to the interior dimness. Carmen blinked against the brilliant light, her body turned mostly away from Dominic, signaling that particular conversation was over.

The only person she'd ever unburdened herself to, spilling out many of her secrets and the hidden past, had been Lochan Nakamura. And he had, as promised, never spoken of any of it afterward.

She'd slowly come to realize that Lochan was like the man she'd hoped her father would have been if her father had lived long enough for her to really know him. Lochan was the sort of guy you could count on. So was Dominic, but in a different way.

Carmen heard the roar of the descending shuttles before she saw one coming into view as it settled toward the center of the loading zone.

"Fire!" Dominic ordered.

She didn't think she had much chance of hurting the shuttle with her rifle, but Carmen aimed at what should be vital spots and fired, making sure each shot was centered. She couldn't afford to waste ammunition, which would now be even harder to come by than before.

Someone else among the defenders had a "dumb" shoulder-fired rocket, though. Unaffected by the countermeasures thrown out by the descending shuttle, the rocket zoomed straight into the craft and tore a hole in the underside near the middle. The blow must have crippled the shuttle's maneuvering systems. The smooth descent changed to an abrupt leap sideways, the shuttle twisting under the push of thrusters venting out of control.

Carmen flinched back behind the door as the shuttle slammed into a warehouse along the north side of the loading area. Shuttle, warehouse, and the contents of both exploded, rocking the building that Carmen was in.

As the echoes of the blast faded, Carmen heard more shuttles coming in to land on the streets on all sides. Sounds of battle erupted to the south and west as the screening platoons opened fire to keep the escape routes clear.

"First Platoon, Third Platoon! Fall back!" Dominic ordered.

Carmen joined the others in her building as they hurled themselves across a street that had suddenly become a free-fire zone, solid slugs and energy pulses flying in seemingly every direction, the shapes of shuttles rising skyward again after dropping off their first load of attacking soldiers, the crash of grenades punctuating the other noises, and under it all the cries of pain and shock as some of the shots and flying shrapnel struck and tore human bodies.

She lunged into the nearest doorway, gasping for breath, her heart pounding, as the fight continued to rage just outside.

"Pull back! Come on!" Dominic was yelling, gesturing to his soldiers still on the street, exposing himself to enemy fire to help cover their retreat.

Carmen shook her head to clear it as a string of projectiles traced a line of holes along the wall above her with a close-set series of bangs and crashes. *Don't lie there. Don't panic. Paralysis and panic mean death. You learned that as a little girl. Don't forget it now.* Getting her feet under her, she moved next to Dominic and yanked at him. "Get down, you fool!"

He glared at her, resisting her pull. "I have to lead my unit!"

"Which you can't do if you're dead!" she yelled back.

"Right now you're not only exposing yourself to fire, you're also clearly giving orders! Why not hang a big sign on yourself saying *I'm in charge, kill me now*?"

Dominic's glare changed to reluctant understanding as he dropped back a little inside the building and began calling orders on the command circuit. "First and Third Platoons, confirm you've pulled back. Second and Fourth Platoons, withdraw through the First and the Third. We're going to pull back three streets to the office complex at the corner of Zavadska and Petrikower. All units acknowledge!"

He gave Carmen a desperate glance. "Red, cover me while I make sure everyone heard. There's a lot of jamming."

Carmen checked her own gear, seeing the enemy jamming also interfering with her scope's ability to transmit video to whatever was left of Kosatka's command structure. She knelt by the nearest window, rifle leveled but ensuring the barrel didn't stick out to be seen by enemies, controlling her breathing and focusing on the sounds of battle nearby.

She heard racing footsteps coming along the street from her left as the fire from Dominic's unit faltered while the defenders fell back. The footfalls were heavy, reflecting the weight of someone in battle armor.

The invader came into sight with shocking suddenness, running toward the door protecting Dominic. Carmen's finger twitched without conscious thought, firing at the right moment for a high-powered shot to smash into the side of the enemy's battle armor.

Even at point-blank range the round might not have penetrated the front or back armor, but the sides of battle armor, where the protective layers thinned to ease arm movement, were more vulnerable. The impact of the shot knocked the enemy soldier sideways, falling onto the street. He rolled to a halt, using one arm to raise a weapon toward the window where Carmen was still aiming from.

She put a second shot into his faceplate.

Carmen heard shouts outside, but as she strained to understand the words over the sound of battle someone yanked her back away from the window.

She spun with a snarl of defiance fed by fear to see Dominic still pulling at her. "They know you fired from there! We have to get clear!"

Part of learning to survive was learning to listen to good advice. Carmen yielded to his pull, following Dominic as they ran into the next room just before the window she had been crouching at exploded under the impact of at least two grenades. Debris rattled against the interior wall they ducked behind and in some cases punched through.

Carmen rolled back to her knees and covered the door while Dominic tried to get through to his unit. "All platoons report. Are you clear?"

She spotted movement near the exterior door and fired. "We can't stay!"

"Got it. Give me one more minute, Red. All platoons, report!"

"Anyone who isn't already out of these buildings is probably dead," Carmen snapped at him.

"They're *my* people!" he shouted back, anguished.

"So are the ones still alive, and they need a leader. Come on, Domi!"

Under her urging he followed as Carmen ran through the building and out the other side to a street that felt bizarrely untouched by the violence raging just a street away. She dashed across the street while Dominic covered her, then rested against a pillar supporting an overhang, her rifle aimed at the building they had just left, as Dominic sprinted to join her.

They fell back through another street, finally slowing a little as they jogged toward the meet-up point. She kept an eye out for trouble as Dominic concentrated on trying to get his unit re-formed and assessing their losses.

The office complex had provided high-value financial services, so the ground floor offices had substantial walls for security. Carmen sat in a high-backed leather chair once used by a senior executive, her rifle resting between her knees, trying to rest. She watched the men and women of Dominic's unit meet up with cries of relief as they discovered friends who had made it here, or suppressed cries of pain at realizing other friends were missing.

"How bad is it?" she asked Dominic as he walked past.

"It could have been worse," he muttered. "We've got twenty unaccounted for. Some of them may still be trying to get here."

Twenty out of about a hundred. Carmen nodded in understanding. "Get something to eat. What can I do?"

"Help watch the streets. We need as much warning as possible if any of the enemy show up around here."

"Got it. Eat something," she repeated.

Carmen found the lobby security desk and activated the exterior cameras using the building's backup-power batteries. She sat watching, but no enemies appeared. The exterior mics did pick up noise, though. The sounds of fighting elsewhere in the city, the roar of warbirds or shuttles passing overhead, and sometimes between those noises the deceptive quiet that made the empty streets seem peaceful.

Dominic found her still there. "We've got orders to head for the park in front of the opera house."

"A park? Out in the open?"

"It's full of trees and low stone walls. Sort of a maze with overhead cover. I don't know how long we'll be there."

The unit moved through the streets in quick rushes, watching for trouble but encountering none until they reached the safety of the park's cover. "Post guards," Dominic told his platoon leaders. "Four per platoon, rotate them every two hours. Make sure everybody else gets as much rest as they can. I was told we might try to retake part of the east warehouse district."

"How are things going?" Dominic asked Carmen as they sat down in the grass next to one of the low walls. "How much of the city is under enemy control?"

She shook her head. "It's hard to tell. Everything's confused. Both sides are jamming every signal they can, every one of our satellites has been knocked down, and we can't risk our remaining warbirds on reconnaissance missions. We can still use landlines as long as the enemy hasn't cut them or tapped in to them. From what remains of our intelligence capability, about all I've seen for certain is that there's still fighting going on around the government complex."

As she talked, Dominic had been chewing mechanically on the food bar she had given him. "Why?" he asked after swallowing. "There's no government there. They evacuated days ago."

"It's the symbolism," Carmen explained. "Strange thing to die for, huh? The symbolism of buildings that no longer contain anything. I saw that on Mars. Certain old buildings, old sites that had held government functions in the old days, were fought over all the time. Some of them were just piles of rubble. But lives were still sacrificed over being able to claim control of that rubble. Domi, the situation is confused as all hell, but I think we're holding our own. We might be winning."

"Winning." Dominic sat back against the wall, gazing up at the stars beginning to appear between the leaves of the trees as the sky darkened into night. "Winning here won't be enough, will it? A few years back Scatha tried to invade Glenlyon, and got kicked out of the star system. I was like most people, I guess, thinking, good, they learned their lesson. They won't try that again."

"Wishful thinking," Carmen murmured.

"Yeah," he said. "Scatha just got some friends and built up their forces and came at us and Glenlyon in a different way. If we beat them here, no matter how badly we beat them, they'll just come back again someday, won't they? It's not enough to stop their attacks. We're going to have to take the fight to them. Show them they can't keep attacking others while they and their own star systems stay safe."

She nodded slowly, looking at the pain and weariness graven on his face like some ancient statue bearing the marks of time. "It's looking like that, isn't it? We can't stay on defense." Carmen followed Dominic's gaze upward to the stars multiplying in number and growing more brilliant in the darkening skies. "Their plan here should have worked. Wear us down, isolate us, make sure Glenlyon had nothing to spare for us, take out *Shark*, then come in with three-to-one superiority against our one remaining warship. They should have succeeded, Domi. This invasion should have been covered by three warships in low orbit. Scatha, Apulu, and Turan had it all figured out because we gave them the time and the opportunity to do that. If Glenlyon's ship hadn't shown up and helped, we'd be halfway to defeated on this planet already. And there was no reason to expect Glenlyon to send that ship."

Dominic nodded as well. "We got lucky, or someone on Glenlyon got smarter than any of us deserve. Did you say you know that guy? The commander of Glenlyon's ship?"

"Rob Geary. Sort of. I know a friend of his, Mele Darcy, and I only know her because Lochan met her on their way down and out and they got to be friends."

"The people you know are good to have as friends," Dominic said, smiling slightly. "Lochan made it out okay? I never got a chance to ask."

"Yes. The ship he was on jumped safely for Tantalus. If anyone can get help for us from other star systems, he will."

"I hope you're right, Red." Dominic finally looked at her, his smile growing affectionate. "Thanks. I'm pretty sure you saved my life at least once today. I'm glad Lochan is out of this."

Carmen nodded, smiling back at him. "Lochan was worried about Mele, but she's probably the safest of us all right now. I'll bet she's in a bar somewhere having a good time."

Mele ducked as a burst of solid slugs tore along a shelf near her, shattering heavy glassware and hurling shards in all directions. A rain made up of droplets of expensive booze splattered her, Giddings, and Lamar.

"Monsters!" Giddings complained. "Who does that to good scotch?"

"Just get me a clean signal!" Mele ordered, trying to sort out where the enemy forces were. The attackers were trying to jam the defenders' links but with only partial success.

"I've almost—There! Got a strong link, Captain."

Mele's display steadied out, displaying red markers where enemy movement had been detected. There were a lot of red markers in the two corridors she could see, and more were joining them as continuing fire raked the bar.

The oddly named Buffalo Grass Bar sat at an intersection of two main routes through the facility, opening out into both before they diverged again beyond the bar. That made it a good spot from which to cover both routes. It also made it a really good target once the attackers figured out Mele and her fellow Marines were holed up there, trying to buy time for the militia who had survived earlier attacks to re-form and set up new defensive positions.

The assault had been by the book, the enemy shuttles coming in screened by the bulk of the facility from fire by either *Shark* or *Saber*. But Rob Geary had managed to get *Saber* into position to nail one of the shuttles despite the efforts by the remaining enemy destroyer to keep *Saber* tied down protecting *Shark*.

Before the shuttles had dropped off their occupants, the single aerospace warbird escorting them had torn up the areas of the facility facing them to take out any defenders there. Fortunately, Brazos had paid attention to that part of the book as well and kept his forward militia forces far enough back to be safe as the warbird fired everything it had.

The by-the-book attackers had come swarming down the primary routes into the station, aiming to overrun the defenders fast, and ran into the by-the-book defenses set up by Brazos. Mele had watched the first engagement play out on her display, trying to remain dispassionate as friendly markers winked out and the forward militia platoons fell apart under the attack by greatly superior numbers with better weapons and equipment.

She'd already chosen this bar as the point where her part of the Marine force would halt the enemy advance. Corporal Gamba had been sent with the remaining two Marines to block a third corridor.

Watching the movement of the red markers on her display, Mele sensed the next assault building. "Grenades," she told Giddings and Lamar. "Prime 'em."

The incoming fire abruptly grew in volume as the attackers charged.

"Let them have it!" Mele ordered, pitching her grenade into the corridor nearest her as the other two tossed theirs down the other. The roar of the resulting explosions hadn't faded when Mele reared up from behind the barricade formed by the bar and began firing. Her mind stayed cold and sharp as she centered her sights on an enemy, fired, and shifted to a new target. "Lamar! They're trying to get past on my left!"

"On it!"

Mele heard Lamar scrambling past behind her, but stayed focused on her front, firing with enough speed and precision to throw back an attack already disrupted by the grenades.

She knelt behind cover and recharged her weapon as the attackers fell back. "Report."

"Good on this side," Giddings called in, sounding breathless but fine. "They're pushing hard, Captain."

"Yeah. Lamar?"

"Um . . ." Lamar's voice came across the circuit, high-pitched with pain. "I stopped two of them trying to get past, but also stopped something with my leg. Oh, man. Hurt."

"Giddings, get over to Lamar. I'll watch our front." Mele waited, tense, for Giddings to report in again. "Gamba, how are things where you are?"

"We held them," Gamba said, sounding unnaturally calm. "But I don't think we can hold them much longer."

"Understood," Mele said, peering through the murk of chaff grenades in search of more enemies. On her display, she could see that the militia's retreat had halted at the next set of defenses.

She could also see the location of the booby-trapped grain compartments, between her Marines and where the militia now was. "Yoshida, are those compartments ready to blow?"

"Yes, Captain. Just give the word."

"You're going to have a very short count," Mele warned. "When we pull back they're going to be right on our heels."

"Captain?" Giddings said. "I got a big battle patch on Lamar, but she's not doing any walking or running. Her left leg's a mess."

"Can you carry her?"

"Sure."

"Get going. Take her back to the next militia position."

"But—"

"Go!" Mele paused to fire into the cloud of countermeasures slowly drifting across the corridors in front of the bar. "Gamba—"

"I got movement! They're coming again, Captain!"

"Expend all your remaining grenades and get back as far as the closest militia position! Yoshida! Stand by to blow those compartments!" Mele primed her last two remaining grenades, waiting as sudden motion appeared in the murk before her. She tossed both, crouching as they detonated with blasts that shook the corridor. The moment the explosions ebbed she leapt up and ran, chasing after Giddings and Lamar.

Shots rang out behind her, solid slugs and energy bursts whipping past as Mele crouched and dodged and ran.

But she kept her eyes on the building schematic on her display, measuring her distance to the grain compartments. She was above them, then just past them, the enemy fire growing heavier and more accurate by the moment. Red threat markers filled the corridor behind her. "Now, Yo-shida!"

"You're too close, Captain!"

"I said *now*!"

A shot skipped off the upper edge of her shoulder armor, staggering Mele, just before the world behind her blew up.

CHAPTER 10

The overpressure from the exploding grain dust burst the compartments and tore through surrounding areas in a wave of destruction, ripping apart floors, walls, and ceilings and turning their fragments into deadly projectiles.

The shock wave hit Mele in the back, hurling her forward. She went into a tumble to break her fall, trying to stay low so none of the shrapnel bouncing off the surviving nearby structure would hit her.

She paused, trying to catch her breath, her arms shaking, trying to figure out if any parts of her had been hit. Air was rushing past as the atmosphere left in this part of the facility vented through the holes torn by the blasts, making it harder to focus her impact-rattled brain. But aside from an ache in her back where the shock wave had probably planted a massive bruise she seemed to be intact.

The buzzing in her ears resolved into frantic calls. "Captain? Captain!"

"Here," Mele said. She got to her feet, grimacing at the effort, and looked back at the mass of wreckage behind her. "I'm okay. You guys?"

"We're all with militia units, Captain."

It was Giddings calling, Mele realized. "I'll be with you soon."

She started moving down the corridor, wincing, picking up speed as she moved. By the time she reached a wide-open area where three corridors met Mele thought she was moving almost normally.

Hands waved her toward an improvised barricade at the far side of the area. There she found more than a dozen militia, as well as Giddings and Lamar. The militia were posted along the barricade, while Giddings was a short distance behind, kneeling beside Lamar as he checked her injury.

"What was that?" someone asked Mele.

She turned to see a man with lieutenant insignia and anxious eyes. "The compartments for grain storage blew. I, um, guess that's what happened."

"How did they—? Never mind. They took maybe thirty or forty of the enemy with them," the lieutenant said. "And stopped their attack cold."

"Good," Mele said, trying to decide whether to sit down or not. Uncertain whether she'd be able to stand up quickly again, she elected to remain standing. "What are your orders?"

The lieutenant gazed back at her, his distress growing.

"Your orders," Mele prompted. "What has Major Brazos told you to do now?"

"Major Brazos . . ." The lieutenant gestured back toward the areas now held by the enemy. "He was up front, at the forward defensive positions. We haven't heard . . . he told the people with him to fall back, and he'd cover them. We think . . . we think he's dead. Holding off the enemy."

Mele barely held back uttering one of her most vicious curses. "Dead?"

"We think . . ."

"Who's in command now?" The militia officer gazed back at her blankly. "Lieutenant! Who is in command of Kosatka's militia forces on this facility?"

"We don't know," he replied, sounding helpless.

"How can you not know?" Mele demanded, making an effort to calm herself. "Who's the senior surviving officer?"

"All of us! There're three lieutenants, and we all got our militia appointments at the same time."

Mele slumped back against the nearest wall. "Call Commander Derian on the *Shark*. Ask him to designate one of you as the militia commander."

"Yeah! Good idea!" Happy to be given clear instructions on what to do, the lieutenant hunched over, speaking rapidly into a comm link, but after a few moments turned to Mele again. "Commander Derian wants to talk to you privately, Captain."

"Me?" Mele exhaled heavily in frustration before clicking on the proper circuit. "Captain Darcy here, sir."

Derian replied in tones so heavy that each word seemed to have extra weight. "Captain, we have a problem."

"We do?" Mele couldn't help replying.

"Major Brazos died valiantly—"

"Major Brazos chickened out," Mele replied, her anger boiling over. "He knew he wasn't suited to command this defense. That's why he gave me so much trouble. And that's why, when the fight began, he went to the farthest forward position he could so he could do what he knew how to do, die valiantly! And leave his soldiers without a commander!"

Derian paused before replying. "I understand."

"He'll be remembered as a hero but he left his people in the lurch," Mele finished bitterly. "Now that I've vented I won't say that again. Please excuse my candor, sir."

"I understand," Derian repeated. "Here's the problem. I've got three lieutenants who could command the militia. None of them are suited for it."

"Sir—"

"Listen to me, Captain Darcy! I can tell when someone lacks confidence in themselves. Those three lieutenants got rank pinned on them along with a lot of responsibility, but they don't have the training or experience to command combat troops. They know it, and the rest of the militia knows it."

Mele did her best to rein in her temper again. "Commander, with all due respect, those three lieutenants are all you've got."

"No. I've also got you."

"I can't be placed in command of Kosatka forces!" Mele almost yelled in reply. "I have no legal basis to give them orders!"

"I'm the senior surviving officer of Kosatka's forces on this facility!" Derian yelled back. "As such, I invoke emergency powers and place the remaining Kosatka militia aboard this facility under your command, Captain! And if the government of Kosatka disagrees with my decision, assuming a government of Kosatka still exists, and assuming that government continues to exist, they can take it up with me after this is over! I *will* save my ship and crew, Captain! And that means I need *you* to hold off those attackers!"

Mele stared at nothing as she thought.

Derian spoke again, his voice calmer, but insistent. "And if you need a personal incentive to take command, Captain Darcy, I think you'll agree with me that unless you do so, the odds of you and your Marines surviving this engagement are too small to measure."

Still slumped against the wall, Mele looked over the militia, reading their body language. It wasn't only the lieutenants who lacked confidence in themselves. "They have to accept me," Mele said, knowing that was a weak comeback. "They have to be willing to take orders from me."

"Ask them," Derian said. "Thank you, Captain."

"Just get that damned ship of yours fixed!" Mele snapped in reply. "Sir!"

She ended the call and turned to the lieutenant, who was waiting with obvious concern. "Commander Derian has appointed me your commander," Mele said.

The reaction startled her. The lieutenant's eyes lit with hope, and he straightened as if given renewed strength. "You're in command? Can I—? May I inform the troops, Captain?"

"Yeah," Mele said, calling up all the information her

display had on the militia positions. "Gamba, how are the militia where you are?"

"Shaky," Corporal Gamba replied. "Hold on. Something's happening. They're showing a lot more confidence. Buckland, ask them— What? Captain Darcy? You're in overall command now?"

"I guess so." Mele forced herself out of her slump, seeing the militia near her looking far more ready to fight. Intangibles. You could calculate weapons and numbers and supplies and distances, but those didn't always win battles. "Fighting spirit" didn't always win battles, either, though coupled with poor leadership it could produce massive friendly losses. But soldiers without confidence in those leading them didn't win many fights, and these militia seemed to have confidence in her. Like that Old Earth guy Sun Tzu had said: *"Because such a general regards his men as infants they will march with him into the deepest valleys. He treats them as his own beloved sons . . .*

. . . and they will die with him."

"Listen up!" Mele said over the command circuit. "We've been hurt, but we've hurt them worse. We stopped them once, and we can stop them again. As we get closer to the dock area, the available approach routes for the enemy are going to neck down so we have to defend fewer spots. Give me all you've got and we'll kick these scum all the way back to Apulu!"

Switching to another part of the circuit, she spoke to the three lieutenants in charge of what were now the farthest forward militia positions. "Send out scouts to see how many routes are blocked by damage from those blasts. We need to know which routes are still open because the enemy is looking for those as well. If you've got any portable surveillance devices, plant them in the open routes and link them to the command net."

Mele spent another moment looking over the situation on her display, her eyes lingering on the final defensive positions just short of the dock area. If the enemy got that far, those militia would have to hold no matter how many losses

Mele, her Marines, and the other militia had already suffered.

There was something she could do about that.

Walking back to where Giddings was still fussing over Lamar, Mele gestured toward the lieutenant. "Get with him and make sure I have full access to what's left of the command net. Then see if you can break into the enemy net."

Giddings straightened up, saluting quickly. "I've done everything I can for Private Lamar, Captain."

"Thanks, Glitch," Lamar called up to him.

As Giddings hastened over to the lieutenant, Mele knelt by Lamar, studying the wounded private. Her left leg was sealed into a full-limb battle bandage that had hardened into a cast. There was still atmosphere here, so Lamar's faceplate hung open, revealing her strained face with beads of sweat spotting it. "How you doing, Marine?"

"Okay," Lamar said, the gasp in the single word robbing it of its intended meaning. "I just got some more pain meds. Be ready for action in a minute."

"Good. I've got a job for you," Mele said. "Back toward the dock."

Lamar shook her head stubbornly. "Captain, I can still fight. I should stay up here with the rest of you."

"You can still fight," Mele agreed. "What you can't do is run. Which makes you perfect for this job. I'm going to have a couple of the militia get you back—"

"Captain—!"

"Shut up. Back to this final defensive position. See? A squad of militia holding the area just short of the dock where that broke-butt warship is sitting. You're going there. If the fight reaches you, and I'm not there and Gamba and Giddings and Yoshida and Buckland aren't there, it's going to be up to you to stiffen the spines of those militia and make sure that position holds until the *Shark* gets away."

Lamar blinked at Mele, confused, then with growing understanding. "You mean if I'm the last Marine left, I need to make sure those militia hold?"

"Yeah. Show 'em how it's done."

"But . . . Captain, I'm just a private."

"You're a *Marine*. Which means you get the job done and done right." Mele studied Lamar, wondering if she'd be up to the task. "Understand?"

A pause, then Lamar nodded. "Yes, Captain. I understand."

"You'll show those militia how to hold their ground."

"I'll show them."

"Good." Mele stood up. "And you get to be carried there, so that's a bonus."

"I always like to arrive in style," Lamar said, grinning. The expression was too anxious, too tight with worry and the pain getting past the meds, but also laced with determination. "I won't let you down. Not any of the others, either."

Mele waited impatiently, not knowing how much time she had before the enemy regrouped, while a couple of militia members ran up with a mobile med bed and hoisted Lamar onto it. She gave Lamar an encouraging wave as the private was taken back toward the dock area.

The rest of the Marines took the news of Lamar's new assignment stoically. All except for Yoshida, whose grumble carried easily across the comm circuit. "She owes me a twenty I lent her until next payday."

"Maybe she'll survive and be able to pay you back," Giddings said.

"Yeah," Yoshida said, cheering up.

"Yoshida," Mele said, "have you found anything else in this facility that will blow up on command?"

"No, Captain," Yoshida said, sounding annoyed this time. "They seem to have off-loaded everything useful over the last week."

"That's bad," Gamba commented. "The grain dust explosions saved us back there."

"There's a good part," Mele reminded them. "The enemy doesn't know we don't have any more big explosions ready and waiting for them. They lost a good number of people when the grain compartments blew. They'll be worried that more traps like that have been set up."

"Which means they'll advance more cautiously," Giddings said. "Right?"

"Right. They're going to be more cautious, slower to follow up when we pull back, and spend more time checking out areas before they enter them. That's all good for us."

"Captain?" Yoshida said, sounding worried. "You meant anything that could blow up except the fuel cells, right?"

"The fuel cells?" Mele asked.

"There's a bunch located in secure storage near the dock. To refuel ships."

"Those make a really big bang when they blow, right? Why did you think I wouldn't want to know about those?"

"Because," Yoshida explained, "if we blow the fuel cells, they'll take this whole facility with them. They'd blow it all into really little pieces. And everyone on it would be blown into little pieces, too."

"Like us?" Giddings asked.

"We can't control it?" Mele said. "Like, blow one cell or part of one fuel cell?"

"No, Captain," Yoshida said. "If you disrupt a fuel cell, the whole thing goes. And if we set off one, it'd probably cause the others nearby to blow as well."

Gamba's words came out with careful precision, as if she wanted to ensure there was no chance of anything being misheard. "So blowing fuel cells would be a very bad idea."

"Here it would be, yes," Yoshida agreed. "It would also be the last very bad idea of whoever did it. Guaranteed."

"Okay," Mele said. "Understood. We don't blow the fuel cells." But inside she was wondering what to do if defeat was inevitable, if the enemy was about to seize the facility and *Shark*. Wouldn't it make sense then to trigger a detonation of those cells as a last dying gesture to ensure that the enemy didn't profit from their triumph? Should she . . . ?

Was that the sort of legacy she'd want to leave her Marines who were still at Glenlyon? Not just giving their all to win but accepting certain death if they lost? Did she want Marines following that example in the future, committing grand suicidal gestures rather than surrender?

Hell, she *already* didn't like the idea. Suppose she went through with it and people decided to do the same thing because she'd established that precedent? How many would refuse surrender and fight to the death, senselessly, because Mele Darcy had done the same thing even though she hadn't really?

Mele looked around at those with her, realizing that it was one thing to demand their best of people, because that would not only give the best chance of success but also the best chance of them living through the fight. But it was a very different thing to demand their deaths. That was a step she wouldn't take. None of that victory or death garbage. The dead couldn't win the next fight. What had that Clause-witz guy called it? *Husbanding resources.* As in *don't waste the lives of your own troops.*

"Captain?"

Mele realized that she'd been lost in thought for long enough to worry her Marines. "Sorry. I was thinking. Listen up. My reaction force plan didn't work. There aren't enough of us. We need to disperse among the militia to stiffen them. I'm staying with this bunch along with Giddings. Gamba, you take that group on the far right of our positions. Buckland and Yoshida, I want you to stay with the group you're in."

Mele paused, knowing her next words had to be phrased right. "All of the militia are going to be looking to you. The officers, too. Yeah, you're corporals and privates, but you're all veterans of years of service. You're used to someone else telling you what to do when the bubble breaks, but now you have to be that someone and let the militia know what you think should be done. I'm going to be monitoring as much as I can, and giving you orders when necessary, but if I'm out of loop because of jamming, you make the calls for what to do. Use your heads, remember your training, and remember that these people are looking to you for examples and hope. Gamba, if I'm cut off and you're still linked in, give the orders you think are right. If Gamba is cut off, Giddings takes over. Any questions?"

"Why did I volunteer for this?" Giddings asked, causing laughter from the others.

"Find out what the scouts are reporting back to the militia lieutenants with you," Mele ordered. "Giddings, get me into the enemy net. I want to know what they're doing and where they are."

"Captain?" Mele turned as the lieutenant approached her. "I've got something that's probably important."

"What is it?" Mele asked. "What's your name?"

"Freeman. Lieutenant John Freeman, Kosatka Defense Militia," he replied. "Um, we've got some good code monkeys in this group, and they were looking at what we were picking up of the enemy signals before the explosions." Freeman pointed to data on his pad. "See here? They're thinking this node indicates the enemy commander was there, and this other one maybe the second-in-command since it seemed to be mirroring the commander's signals."

Mele studied the images with growing hope. "Those were both inside the blast zones. They were leading from the front."

"We're thinking maybe one of them, maybe both, got killed."

"You might be right. That'd explain why they're taking a while to resume the attack. Whoever is third in line is trying to figure out what happened and trying to assume command." Mele paused as her helmet display updated, the schematics of the station taking on numerous damage markers. "I'm getting some of the reports the scouts are sending back. Good."

"Captain, do you think we can do this?"

Mele focused on Freeman, knowing her next words would be important. "Hell, yes, we can do this. You and your soldiers are equal to this challenge."

"Thank you." Freeman smiled, saluted, and went off to talk to his fellow militia.

Damn, I'm a good liar, Mele thought to herself, as Giddings called in.

"Captain, I got a few snapshots of the enemy net before they closed me out. Here they are."

Mele examined them, unhappy with the number of remaining enemy soldiers shown. But the casualty count was gratifyingly high and might limit the enthusiasm of the enemy to keep pushing the attack. And the enemy force was still clearly disorganized and trying to re-form after the grain compartment blasts that had torn up both the leading elements of the enemy force and substantial parts of the facility they now occupied.

Unfortunately, there didn't seem a lot else she could do at this point but try to spot new attacks developing and try to stop them, or at least hold them up as long as possible. "Lieutenant Freeman, can you give me a comm link to the *Saber*? I ought to report in while I have a chance."

"Oh, sure, Captain. We should be able to run a link through *Shark*. Hold on. Yeah. Circuit six."

"Thanks." Mele switched over to six. "*Saber*, this is Captain Darcy. Is Commodore Geary available?"

Geary himself responded. "I'm glad to hear from you. How are you doing, Mele?"

"I'm not dead yet."

"We worried when we saw a big chunk of that facility blow out. Was that your work?"

"Maybe. It slowed down the bad guys pretty good. How's life in the fleet?"

Rob Geary sounded frustrated. "The good news is that the *Bruce Monroe* made it to the jump point for Tantalus and is on her way to find help for us. Otherwise, we're stuck here keeping that enemy destroyer off *Shark*. The only good part of that is the enemy warship is tied up tying us up, so they can't support any other part of the invasion. From what we could see, the initial invasion drop lost a lot of shuttles to the defenders. Those losses wouldn't have been nearly as bad if enemy warships had been covering the invasion force from low orbit."

"So you are accomplishing something."

"Yeah. But I wish we could do a lot more. *Shark* will be

ready in only another twenty-three hours, but that's a very long time under current circumstances. How are you and Commander Derian getting along?"

"We may get married when this is over," Mele said, unable to resist.

"What?"

"Kidding. He's in charge. He put me in charge of the militia."

"Kosatka's militia? He can do that?" Rob asked.

"He says he can, and he made some compelling arguments for why I should agree," Mele said. "Once I did, he gave me an impossible job to do. Sort of a pattern for me. I need to change how I look for bosses."

"Sorry about that," Rob said. "Why do you keep looking for that kind of boss?"

"I don't know. Maybe there's a reason why Marine and masochist both start with *m*."

"Good luck, Mele."

"Same. Out." She took a moment to mentally regroup, then turned to Lieutenant Freeman. "All right. The scouts are spotting the routes the enemy will have to use to move forward. Let's set up some forward firing positions to hit them as soon as they stick their noses out. It'll take them a while to realize we're not holding any spot near the wreckage in strength."

"Should we move everyone forward?" Freeman asked, gazing at the schematic of damage to the facility.

"No," Mele said. "Look at the possible routes and what's around them. We'd also be limited in our routes, so if the enemy breaks through at any one point everyone else would be trapped, unable to withdraw to good positions in time."

"Oh. Yeah. So, two-person teams for the forward positions?"

"Right," Mele said, pleased that Freeman was listening and learning. "Let me get the other two lieutenants going on this as well. Send some of your people to cover these three spots."

"How will they know when to fall back?" Freeman

asked, anxious again at the thought of some of his militia being trapped.

"I'll make that call," Mele said.

"Then I know they'll be okay," Freeman said, turning to get his teams sent forward, pausing to turn back and salute before rushing off.

Wondering how long it would take messy reality to tarnish Freeman's total confidence in her, Mele talked to the other militia commanders and got things moving. It would have been nice to sit down and rest after that, but her bruised back was threatening to stiffen up so Mele had to keep walking and stretching.

"We're getting an increase in enemy net traffic," Freeman called to her.

"They're getting ready to move," Mele told him, alerting the other lieutenants.

She checked the time. Twenty-two and a half hours left. Less than a day. But it looked like it was going to be a very long less than a day.

Carmen was roused before dawn by one of the soldiers who was going from person to person waking them. The stars above the darkened city were still clearly visible in the small patches of sky that could be seen between the branches and leaves of the trees in the park. She caught a glimpse of a small, oddly regular constellation of unfamiliar stars and realized it must be the enemy ships in orbit about this planet, illuminated by the sun that hadn't risen for those on the surface.

"We're moving out in half an hour," Dominic told her when she joined him. "Headquarters is trying to set up a counterattack in the government district."

"Why?" she asked before stifling a yawn. "Didn't we talk about that yesterday? The government completely evacuated that area. There's no there there."

"Which is why the enemy left a relatively small force to hold it. We think we might be able to overrun them."

"I'll see what I can find out," Carmen said, trying to link to one of the surviving intelligence coordination nets.

She finally linked up using a buried landline that the enemy apparently hadn't discovered yet. The official picture offered was fragmentary, dismaying, and hopeful all at once. Lodz was no longer a single city but a collection of areas, some controlled by the invaders and some still in the hands of Kosatka's defenders. The edges of the areas weren't clean lines but blurs where one side's control faded and eventually yielded at vague boundaries to the presence of the other side. Humans liked clearly defined boundaries, and given enough time would end up with them, where a single street would mark the border between one side and the other as it did in most places on Mars. But Carmen could see Loren Yeresh's quantum mechanics background in these assessments. Given how little was known and how fluid the situation was, enemy positions and strengths and areas of control were defined as much by uncertainties as they were by precise information.

"Here's what we've got," she told Dominic.

He squinted at the image. "It's too bad we don't have more soldiers. The enemy hasn't linked up the places they've captured. We could hit them while they're still isolated from each other."

"That's probably why we're aiming to recapture the government complex," Carmen said. "See? It's between this industrial area that's been captured and the spaceport. If we retake the government area, we'll be between those two areas so they can't link up."

A moment later the full implications of that hit her. "We'll be between two strong enemy forces."

"Yeah," Dominic agreed. "A number of other units are going in with us. But it will feel like being in a nutcracker, won't it?" He hesitated. "Red, why don't you—"

"I'm staying with you."

"The attack is going to be hazardous, and afterward the enemy is going to be hitting us hard from at least two sides," Dominic argued.

"It sounds like you'll need me there," Carmen said.

"Red, please . . ."

"Domi, I spent my childhood fighting my battles alone. And I promised myself then that if I ever found someone I could count on, no matter what, that I would never let them fight alone."

He gazed back at her silently for a long moment before sighing and nodding. "All right. I can tell you're not going to give in."

"Smart man." Carmen smiled in what she hoped was a reassuring way. "Get back to leading your unit. I'll see if I can find out anything else before we move away from here and I'm dependent on wireless again."

"All right," Dominic said again. "I wish you'd never left Albuquerque. You'd be safe there."

"Safe? You obviously don't know much about Albuquerque. This sort of thing is just a typical quiet Saturday night in Albuquerque."

They set off before sunrise, the men and women of Dominic's unit moving in small groups from cover to cover, keeping careful watch on the silent buildings around them and the sky above where newly placed enemy satellites might already be watching these streets. Carmen took a look back at the park, wondering how much longer those trees would stand. If the fight went on for long inside the city, the enemy would realize those leaves offered too much concealment. A single overpressure munition would strip the trees of leaves and bark and smaller branches, leaving bare trunks where a small, cultivated forest had once stood.

Somehow the thought of that bothered her more than the craters in the streets and the holes in some of the buildings.

They'd been warned to avoid the subway tunnels and the other underground passages. Those were such obvious means to sneak through the city that the invaders had quickly laced them with sensors and automated sentries. "Why don't they use those automated sentry robots aboveground?" one of those with Carmen and Dominic asked. "Why didn't we ever use them against the rebels?"

"I read up on them," Dominic replied, his eye never halting in their search of their surroundings. "Even after all the work on artificial intelligence those things still end up targeting the wrong people and getting jammed. As panicky and confused as humans with weapons can get, they're still a lot more reliable when it comes to choosing the right targets. But down in the subway and maintenance tunnels the only people they should encounter right now are defenders like you and me."

"There's another reason they don't get used," Carmen said. "Hacking."

"They can get taken over by the other side?"

"Any AI can get taken over. Rewritten. Modified. Earth and the other places in Sol Star System try new ones out sometimes on Mars to see how long it takes the Reds to hack them." Carmen smiled, baring her teeth. "It usually doesn't take long."

Dominic eyed her. "Do we have people working on that? Against these guys?"

"Maybe," Carmen said. "If I knew, I couldn't talk about it."

"Sure."

A warning alert pulsed through their headsets and everyone froze, gazing about cautiously. "All units," the report came through bursts of static caused by enemy jamming, "shuttles on their way to the surface."

Crouched against the nearest building, Carmen gazed upward, seeing the just-risen sun illuminating a wave of specks growing in size rapidly as they dropped toward the city. There weren't nearly as many as yesterday. The enemy must have lost a lot of shuttles during the initial invasion.

"They're still coming down in waves," Dominic said beside her. "Escorted by their own warbirds. That means they're still worried about our warbirds. We must have a few left."

As the shuttles neared the surface they broke into smaller groups, heading for parts of the city already held by the invaders. The enemy warbirds escorting them stayed higher, circling protectively.

"I wonder if we're going to hit them?" Carmen asked Dominic.

Her answer came in the form of a sudden high-pitched whine growing rapidly in volume. A warbird tore past just overhead, jinking between higher buildings at the lowest altitude it could manage at that speed, aiming for the enemy shuttles on their final landing approach.

The roar of weaponry sounded, followed by one of the shuttles exploding. A second shuttle tried to reverse its drop and climb, but hits ripped holes in it. Out of control, the shuttle nosed over and dove into the ground, vanishing from Carmen's sight. The blast from its impact could be seen, heard, and felt even from this far off.

A barely audible cheer sounded from Dominic's soldiers as the warbird dashed away to avoid enemy warbirds diving toward it. Carmen watched the warbirds for only a few seconds before the running fight was blocked from her view by intervening buildings.

"Pilots," Dominic remarked. "They're all crazy."

"Whatever was in that one shuttle made a big explosion," Carmen said. "Maybe power cell replacements for their battle armor?"

"It was something important to them," Dominic said. "And it's gone. So that's good. I hope that crazy pilot got away."

Carmen focused on her pad as an alert appeared. "I've got a feed from one of our drones! It's . . . gone."

"Jamming?"

"Looked more like a swat." Drones had combat life spans so short that they made mayflies look long-lived by comparison. Once people had figured out that even little drones moving through the air made fairly easy targets for the right sensors to spot, sensors modeled on the ways that creatures like frogs detected and tracked the movement of small flying insects, drones became the pawns of battles, quickly sacrificed in the opening moves. Any that survived the initial engagement, or new ones constructed afterward, had to face an array of antidrone systems collectively known as flyswatters, as well as the same sort of jamming that every other system had to deal with.

Which meant that Carmen was happy to get even one useful image from a friendly drone before it was swatted. "It's the Central Coordination Building." An unpoetic name for the large structure built to house the offices of a lot of people doing unpoetic but necessary government work. "There aren't defenses visible on the outside. Something must have taken down that drone, though, so they must have sensors and some weapons hidden on the exterior."

Dominic studied the picture before nodding. "What we heard is right, then. They're forted up inside the buildings."

"And those shuttles that were shot down were trying to land in the central courtyard on the other side of this building. See the smoke rising from behind it?"

"Some of their reinforcements didn't make it." Dominic smiled. "Come on, everyone. Move it. We need to get into position to hit them before they get any more help sent their way."

But when they had finally made their way cautiously to buildings on the street facing the government complex, the order came to wait. Everyone sat or lay down among the abandoned, everyday trappings of the buildings they were hiding in. Work desks piled with once-urgent tasks, displays without power, shelves of clothing or other goods that had been too bulky or heavy to haul out of the city before the invaders landed. Carmen lay flat on a carpet in a comfortable office area, occasionally gazing up at a bare ceiling whose lights were as dead as the rest of the city. The rest of the time she worked at trying to pick up anything she could of friendly net traffic or enemy activity. "There's something going on," she told Dominic. "All kinds of activity nearby on just about every frequency."

"Any idea what—?" Dominic paused as the muffled sound of weapons suddenly came from outside. "How far off is that?"

"Not far at all," Carmen said, staring at her screen. "It's underground."

"In the subway and maintenance tunnels?" Dominic hesitated, listening to something on his command circuit. "You called it, Red." Switching circuits, he transmitted to his unit. "Most of the automated sentry bots the enemy placed in the underground approaches have been turned by our hackers. They've been ordered to assault the enemy forces they were guarding. We're going to give the enemy five more minutes to send their troops down to fight their own bots, then we're going in on the surface. We're promised a chaff cloud cover for the assault. Everyone be ready to assault the Central Coord Building when I give the command."

Carmen sat up, readying herself and wishing she had a sidearm. Her rifle wasn't well suited for the sort of close-in work that would soon be necessary.

Concealed inside the buildings facing their objective, Carmen and the others didn't hear the incoming chaff rounds. Enemy counterfire aimed at the rounds missed as the chaff detonated short of the enemy positions. Clouds of smoke filled with glittering metallic strands and glowing "fireflies" that created heat decoys filled the street as if a sudden, mystical fog had been summoned by magical means. The sunlight, striving to pass through chaff designed to scatter and confuse any radiation, could create only a dim glow in the street like a suddenly fallen night.

"Go! Everyone go!" Dominic called into his command circuit as he bolted for the nearest door onto the street.

He'd probably hoped to lose her in the fog, Carmen thought. Lose her so she'd lag behind looking for him and not be in as much danger. But she stayed right next to him as they ran. The chaff clouds blocked everything so their own command circuits and pads and all else went dead, leaving them isolated in the glowing cloud.

An enemy shot tore through the cloud, passing uncomfortably close to Carmen, as the invaders fired blindly into the chaff in hopes of hitting someone or at least slowing down the attack. The curb on the other side of the street suddenly appeared underfoot, nearly tripping her, then the sidewalk and just beyond that the Central Coordination Building, constructed of sturdy materials using the latest architectural techniques. The latest techniques available here in the down and out, anyway. A strong building, meant to stand for a long time, but not designed to serve as a fort.

Wide, low windows on the ground floor, their polymer glass already blown out in many cases by earlier fighting, gave easy access to the soldiers of Dominic's unit and the other Kosatka defenders. The chaff filling the street had drifted in through the openings, blinding defenders of Kosatka and invaders alike. Carmen flinched as she came through one of the windows in the face of a storm of un-aimed enemy fire, but her luck held and nothing hit her.

Several steps into the large ground floor reception area, the chaff thinning around her, Carmen saw figures crouched behind a row of desks that had been turned into a barricade. She and Dominic dove for the floor to avoid the invaders' fire as some of Dominic's soldiers tossed grenades. Smart rounds would have been confused by the drifts of chaff, but simple, dumb grenades went where they were thrown, be-hind the desks to ravage the ranks of the invading troops.

She came over the tops of the desks, seeing a wounded enemy soldier trying to bring his weapon around to shoot at her. By chance her rifle was nearly pointed at him already, so Carmen was able to aim and shoot before the soldier could. He fell back, the weapon dropping from his hands.

There were other wounded behind the desks, along with several dead. Carmen covered them as the wounded who could raise their hands in surrender did so. She risked a few glances around, realizing that she'd lost Dominic. The sound of fighting was receding through the building as the fight went deeper inside, up to higher floors and down to-ward where the rattle of bot sentry weapons could still be occasionally heard.

Carmen realized that she was shaking with reaction and sudden weariness after the assault. She sat down on an un-damaged section on the top of one of the desks, keeping her rifle canted toward the wounded invaders who'd surrendered. "When the medics get here they'll take a look at you," she told them. "Try any funny, you dead," Carmen added, deliberately reverting to Red street speech.

None of them appeared to question her willingness to carry out her threat. That didn't surprise her. She'd learned as a girl back in Shandakar that threats had to be delivered in ways that left no doubt about their sincerity.

Running her gaze across the prisoners as the remnants of the chaff drifted past in thin wisps and the racket of battle continued elsewhere in the building, Carmen couldn't tell where they were from in their mix of armor and equipment. Two had reacted to her Red talk with recognition, though.

"Wherefrom?" she asked the nearest of those two.

Might as well do her job of collecting intelligence while Dominic and his soldiers did theirs. Carmen wondered how many of those soldiers had already been lost trying to capture this building and how many more of Kosatka's defenders would die holding off the inevitable counterattacks by the invaders.

"Benway," the invader she'd asked spat in reply.

Carmen gave the woman her coldest smile. Benway. A simple way of saying the acronym BNW. Brave New World. The unofficial, ironic, all-purpose, angry motto of Mars, also employed as an obscenity. "Not this world," she told her prisoner. "You won't bring that here."

Brave words. But the scars of battle around her and the continuing sound of fighting told Carmen that the doom of Mars had already been brought to Kosatka. The question was whether it would stay here, or be stopped dead.

"I've lost contact with forward post seven!"

Mele Darcy checked the position of the two militia soldiers who had either just died or been captured. "Get everybody else back!" she ordered all three militia lieutenants. "Withdraw them to the main defensive positions."

Lieutenant Freeman, with her, immediately began transmitting the orders to his forward posts. "But the rest are still holding," one of the other lieutenants protested.

"They'll get cut off! Bring them back now and make it quick." Mele watched movement popping up in a dozen places on disposable sensors seeded in corridors and tunnels. Whoever was in charge on the other side now had been smart enough to set up and launch a broad front attack. She wouldn't be able to concentrate her forces against a single enemy thrust. But there was still a bright side to that.

"They're spread out," Mele transmitted to her Marines and the militia. "They won't be able to hit any point of ours with overwhelming strength. We can hold them, and the longer we hold them here, the more time *Shark*'ll have to get going."

"Here they come!" Corporal Gamba called.

Mele spotted motion in the corridor leading toward the improvised defensive position where she waited with Lieutenant Freeman's militia. She leveled her weapon, aiming carefully.

Suddenly there were enemies everywhere to the front, enemy fire slamming into the mix of desks and chairs and cabinets that formed a bulwark for the defenders. Mele fired. A moment later the militia around her also opened up.

CHAPTER 11

Six hours. Three assaults.

The militia soldier closest to Mele on her right fell backward, already limp from the shot that had killed him. Mele aimed and fired, taking down the attacker who had fired that shot. As she sought another target, Mele realized that the invaders had fallen back again to regroup for a fourth assault.

"How do we look?" she asked Lieutenant Freeman.

Freeman had so far beaten the odds that said lieutenants had short life spans in combat. But he'd seen a lot of his militia hurt or killed, and sometimes seemed in as much pain as if he'd suffered physical wounds. "We're down by about a third," he said, his voice ragged with weariness and grief.

But they were still holding. Mele looked about at the grim-faced militia behind the barricade, impressed. "A lot of professional military forces would break with those kind of losses," she told Freeman. "You've got some damned good soldiers."

He nodded wordlessly in reply but then turned to pass on Mele's praise to his people.

"How are things where you are?" she sent over the circuit dedicated to her Marines.

Corporal Gamba called in from her position with another militia unit. "Estimate twenty percent casualties with this bunch, Captain. And they're pretty worn-out. They can't take much more."

"Understood. Yoshida?" No reply. "Yoshida? Buckland? Answer up."

Yoshida finally replied, his voice thin with stress. "Buckland's dead, Captain. I've got . . . ummm . . . I got hit. Can't use my right arm or shoulder."

Damn. Mele called her next words like a command, trying to snap Yoshida out of his shock. "What's the status of the militia you're with?"

"Ummm . . ."

"Answer up, Marine!"

"I, uh, twenty or thirty percent casualties, Captain."

Mele wished she could pull up her faceplate and rub her eyes, but this part of the facility was in vacuum, the atmosphere having vented through the many holes created by active combat. "Giddings, I need you—Giddings?"

She realized that she hadn't seen or heard from him since the last attack had ended.

And was relieved a moment later when Giddings came toward her at a crouch to stay beneath the top of the barricade. Giddings tapped the side of his helmet.

Mele looked and saw damage along the right side, where an energy pulse had slagged that part of Giddings's helmet. The self-repair material in the helmet looked like it had expanded to fill the gap. "Have you got any leaks?"

He shook his head and made the hand sign for "say again."

She made the hand signs for "leak" and "interrogative."

Giddings shook his head again before signing more. "Comms. Negative."

His communications capability had been knocked out, perhaps literally fried by that hit. So much for the idea of sending Giddings to help Yoshida.

Mele turned back to Lieutenant Freeman. "Has there been any more activity in the maintenance access shafts?"

"They made one more try," Freeman said. "We tossed a grenade down that shaft and sealed it. Captain . . ."

"I think we should pull back," Mele said.

He nodded again, not hiding his relief. "Yes. I was about to ask that. My guys are hurting. They need a little time to recover."

Mele grasped his shoulder reassuringly before calling out commands. "We're going to fall back to the next set of positions. Lieutenant Veren, Lieutenant Danzig, Lieutenant Freeman, designate five people from your units to take up hidden positions where they can cover the back side of our current locations. When the enemy forces make their next rush and get over the barricades, they'll pause to regroup. The five-person rear guards will open fire on them while the enemy is exposed there so the attackers will drop back to use our own barricades as cover from the rear guard. That'll slow them down. Make sure the rear guards know their job is not to hold their positions. They're to hit the enemy, force the enemy to take cover, then drop back to join the rest of us."

She switched to the Marine circuit again. "Yoshida? Can you fall back with your militia?"

"Yes, Captain," Yoshida said, his voice steadier. "I'll stay with them. Just fighting one-handed now."

Mele recognized the false confidence of antishock drugs, but there wasn't anything she could do about that. "Good. Stay with them. Keep them steady when they fall back. Corporal Gamba, do the same with your militia."

"Keep them steady," Gamba replied. "Will do."

"Giddings has lost comms, but he's not hurt. He's staying with me."

Anything else she might have said was forestalled by more movement in front.

It was the worst possible time for another enemy attack, while the militia was falling back and another push might drive them into a panicked retreat. With more than half the surviving militia here already having left the barricade to withdraw, those remaining couldn't hold. "Everybody back now!" Mele ordered. "Make sure those rear guards take their positions. Everybody else back!"

She'd half risen to join the retreat when Giddings jerked and fell. Mele caught his arm, seeing a hole in the chest armor, Giddings's eyes wide through his face shield.

Mele knew she had less than a second to decide what to do.

"Lieutenant Freeman! Carry Giddings!"

"But—"

"I'll only stay here a second! Get away!" Mele grabbed the weapon Giddings had dropped. A Springfield Armory Model Seven Pulse Rifle. Designed to be safe from any attempts by soldiers or Marines to mess with its controls and do something crazy like increase the power of each pulse shot to dangerous levels, or, even worse, set the power supply to release all of its energy at once and turn the rifle into a sort of super grenade.

Mele had been a private when those rifles began being manufactured on Franklin. It had taken the enlisted Marines less than a week before they'd figured out how to bypass all the safety protocols on the controls.

And how to enter the right commands in the wrong ways to make the rifle explode.

Her hands flew over the rifle's controls, making the necessary inputs. "One thousand. Two thousand." Mele rose up, Giddings's rifle in one hand and her own weapon in the other. "Three thousand." She aimed at the attackers who were very close to the barricade, "four thousand," firing twice at the two closest, "five thousand," not pausing as her two targets jerked from impacts and stumbled, raising Giddings's rifle, "six thousand," and hurling it one-handed into the center of the corridor, the attack was coming down, "seven thousand," spinning on one heel and running all out to catch up with Freeman as he ran carrying Giddings.

"Eight thousand." A shot clipped her side, glancing off

the armor. "Nine thousand." More shots came after her as the enemy reached the barricade.

"Ten—"

Giddings's rifle exploded, tearing apart the corridor and the enemy soldiers packed near the barricade.

The shock hit Mele in the back, but she managed to keep her feet under her this time as she staggered from the blow. A piece of shrapnel wedged into the armor covering her upper left arm but didn't completely penetrate.

She, Freeman, and Giddings reached the next set of defensive positions, where the squads left holding those locations stared anxiously at their battered comrades dropping down behind the safety of another set of improvised barricades. Mele paused long enough to give them a confident thumbs-up before leaning heavily on the top of the barricade, gazing back the way she'd come. "Gamba, Yoshida, talk to me."

"We're in place," Gamba said, sounding comfortingly assured. "The rear guard has already engaged and is falling back to join us."

"Yoshida?" Mele pressed.

"Here, Captain. Everybody's back at the new position. The rear guard is just rejoining us."

"How are you doing?"

"I'm feeling frosty, Captain," Yoshida said. "One thousand percent."

"You're doped," Mele said. "Don't let the meds make you too frosty. How are the militia with you? How steady are they?"

"Okay, I guess. Still ready to fight, but they're tired."

"So are the attackers," Mele said. "Gamba?"

"I think my guys would have kept going when they reached the fallback position, but I stopped there right in the middle of it all so they stopped, too. Agree with Yoshi, Captain. The militia who haven't been in the fight yet are rattled and those who have been fighting are worn-out."

"Is the enemy pressing you?" Mele asked. "I'm not seeing anything on my net."

"No, Captain. When the rear guard opened up on the enemy they took cover and haven't come out again."

"Good. Make sure the militia you're with have forward scouts or disposable sensors to spot anyone coming. Rest while you can, and remember to look confident for the militia with you." Mele switched circuits to speak to the militia lieutenants, who all sounded tired as well. Veren and Danzig both also sounded rattled by events and their responsibilities, but it wasn't like Mele could relieve either one. She gave both brief pep talks and hoped that would be enough.

After that she sat down, wincing as her back protested. Lieutenant Freeman sat down next to her, calling on a private circuit so that even though their suits were sealed it was like having a conversation with the person beside you. "We evacuated your guy Giddings to the sick bay on *Shark*."

"He was still alive?"

"Yes," Freeman said. "That's good news, right? I heard that if they're alive when they make it to a medical facility, they'll survive."

"Not always, but usually," Mele said, feeling relieved.

Freeman turned his head to look back toward the enemy. "If I ask how we're doing, will you be honest with me?"

"Maybe."

"How are we doing?"

Mele looked at the time on her faceplate display. "Sixteen hours to go."

"We've lost about two-thirds of the facility," Freeman said, sounding despairing.

"That's okay," Mele told him. "I mean it. When they first hit us we had a lot of territory to defend, and they were fresh and at their best strength. Yeah, they've pushed us back, but it's cost them. They've lost more than we have, and being on the attack is physically tougher than defending. We're tired. They're more tired than we are."

"If they hit us again soon . . ."

"Then we'll face a tough situation," Mele said, leaning

her head back and looking up at a ceiling that seemed oddly clean and pristine after the fighting the rest of the facility had seen. "It depends if the enemy has reserves to throw into the fight. If they've been throwing everything they've got at us, and don't have any rested troops to order in now, any attacks are going to be by exhausted soldiers at the end of their strength."

"You think we'll have time to rest some, then?" Freeman asked, sounding hopeful.

"I'm hoping we do. I think we do," Mele amended her words. "If fresh troops had hit us when we were starting to fall back they would have overrun us. But the enemy soldiers who took that last position were worn-out, and no one has pushed on to hit us before we got settled in these new positions. So I'm thinking the enemy has been hitting us with everything he has, hoping it'll break us, but we've held, and now he can't keep hitting us."

"What if he does?" Freeman asked.

"I keep forgetting you haven't done this," Mele said. "Put it this way. Suppose I ordered your militia into an attack now. Right this moment. How fast would they move?"

"Not very. They might have a burst of energy, but then they'd be burnt-out."

"Yeah. And the enemy is more tired than your guys. If their commander throws them at us now, we'll be able to knock them over with harsh words."

"Really?"

"Lieutenant," Mele said, "I have my faults, but I wouldn't lie about something like that. If we talk tactics and the situation, I'm telling you what I really think."

"Thanks. That's okay to share with my guys?"

"Yeah. Sure."

Mele closed her eyes, trying to relax, but that effort lasted only a few seconds before the nagging tug of duty caused her to call up the other two militia lieutenants and give them the same updates as well as another round of quick encouragement. Afterward, she looked around at Lieutenant Freeman's troops. The unit was a mix of those few who had

made it out when the forwardmost defenses were overrun
and Major Brazos killed, Freeman's own personnel, the soldiers who'd been posted here to hold this place until the
fight reached it, and several militia from the other units who
had been cut off from their own people during the most recent retreat and instead found refuge with Freeman's.

She studied the men and women she could see, trying to
make out expressions through helmet face shields and otherwise trying to judge how much their drooping demeanor
was the result of tiredness and how much it might indicate
dwindling hope. Either way, if the enemy had been able to
mount another attack right away with rested troops, Mele
didn't think these militia would have held.

But they'd done all right when properly led. Give them
a few hours to rest, and maybe they (and she and her Marines) would get out of this alive.

The moment of cautious optimism shattered as Corporal
Gamba called in. "We've got movement to the front of us!
They're coming again!"

Carmen flinched as the building trembled, a long, slow
shaking that told of some portion of the structure collapsing. Probably the far end of the eastern wing, she
guessed from the direction of the vibrations and sound.

The rumble only momentarily eclipsed the sounds of
battle as invader forces pressed at the northeastern and
southern sides of the government building that Carmen had
helped recapture that morning. Night had long since fallen
outside, but the conflict raged on regardless. She wondered
how many defenders had already been lost in what increasingly felt like a losing battle.

But that concern was almost immediately replaced by
worries about a very specific defender. Carmen moved cautiously down a darkened hallway, seeing a few defenders
huddled over pads. That was surely a command group.

She recognized one of Dominic's officers in the glow of
the pads. "Where's Captain Desjani?"

The officer, face lined with worry and weariness, blinked at her as if trying to grasp the question. "Captain Desjani? I . . . he got hit."

"Hit?" Carmen said, hearing the way her voice choked off. The darkness of the hallway seemed to press in on her.

"He's down at the medical station. In the basement."

Dominic wasn't dead, then. Or hadn't been dead when he'd been sent to medical. Her own fatigue forgotten, Carmen turned and ran until she reached stairs and rattled down them so fast she nearly fell.

The building's power had gone out long ago, even the emergency systems fed by solar cells and batteries lost when damage caused the circuits to trip. The belowground portions of the building were pitch-dark except where stickup lights had been slapped into place at wide intervals. Carmen hastened through the darkness, the sounds of battle muffled down here, dust filtering down from the ceiling as the building shook from nearby explosions and impacts on it.

She found the reinforced vault intended to protect vital documents but now pressed into service as a medical station. Carmen paused in the entrance, seeing the injured laid out side by side on the floor as medics triaged and treated them. Several maintenance carts with solid tops had been fastened together to serve as an operating table. A single trauma bed, probably an emergency unit normally kept in the building, sat in the corner with its lone, lucky occupant unmoving as the bed tried to save her life.

Carmen knelt by one of the medics. "Captain Desjani. Where is he?"

The medic barely spared her a glance. "Uh . . . over there. Are you next of kin?"

"What?" Carmen stared at the medic, paralyzed at what the question might mean.

"If you're not, you can't be in here unless you're his commander."

"Oh." Carmen exhaled, realizing that she'd briefly ceased breathing. "We're married."

"That counts." The medic bent back to work, eyes intent, expression numb as if all feeling had been momentarily buried to allow total focus on his task.

She made her way in the direction indicated, moving carefully among the injured, the smells of spilled blood and antiseptics and skin seal bandages mingling to make Carmen dizzy.

Dominic rested next to one wall, his eyes closed. She went to one knee beside him, watching his deep, slow breaths and knowing they meant he'd been sedated.

The reason why was clear enough, a tourniquet on Dominic's left leg above where the knee and the rest of his leg had once been.

Carmen had enough first-aid training to read the status patch stuck onto Dominic's forehead, the figures and codes flickering as they updated. Stable. That was the critical part. He was stable.

She fought off tears that threatened, looking around her. "Are any of the wounded being evacuated?" she asked the nearest medic.

The woman, looking too old to be working in a combat environment, shook her head. "Too much fighting outside, and the subway tunnels are blocked. They're all stuck here with whatever we can do for them until either they die or our side breaks the siege of this building or the invaders come down here and shoot us all."

Carmen looked down at Dominic. She'd almost forgotten that she was still carrying her rifle. "Hold on," she whispered, leaning close to his ear. "I have to go and help fight. We have to win so we can get you to a hospital. I have to go," Carmen repeated. "I love you, Domi."

She picked her way carefully out of the medical station, staying out of the way of the medics and doctors and not jostling any of those hurt. Once in the gloomy hallway again Carmen ran for the stairs leading up, through the stretches of darkness punctuated by small lighted areas, gripping her rifle tightly.

The stakes of this fight had changed. It was no longer

about freedom or peace or anything but one truth that filled Carmen. They had to hold this building, had to push back the attacks, or Dominic would die.

Tantalus was a red dwarf star, not far from Kosatka as interstellar distances go. Which meant it was roughly twenty trillion kilometers, or two light years, from one star to the other. Just a hop, skip, and a jump in a galaxy like the Milky Way, which was about one hundred thousand light years across. Even the time spent in jump space had been relatively short, just three days.

There were a lot of red dwarf stars in the Milky Way; which, now that Lochan Nakamura really thought about it, was an odd name for a galaxy. Red dwarfs were small, relatively dim, and relatively cool, burning their limited supplies of hydrogen at a rate that would keep them going for billions of years longer than hotter, flashier stars like Sol that warmed Old Earth. "Why did they name it Tantalus?" Lochan asked the captain of the *Oarai Miho*, who only shrugged in reply.

Relieved that they'd made it safely here, and with little else to do but worry about whether Carmen was all right while the freighter chugged across the expanse of Tantalus's star system, Lochan looked up the name. Tantalus had been a greedy individual in old myths. Tantalus the star had a lot of objects orbiting it, and a lot of those objects were pretty close in, as if the star was worried about any of them wandering off. None of the orbiting objects were particularly impressive, rocks ranging from minor planets to belts of asteroids, but there were significantly more of them than usual for a star system. There were several theories about how and why Tantalus had acquired its hoard of useless rocks, but Lochan had to admit that the name of the star seemed appropriate. As to the strangeness and uniqueness of the star system's configuration, humanity had spent millennia learning that the galaxy was full of things and places that deviated from any norm that existed. Given enough stars (and there were hundreds of billions of stars in the Milky Way alone), just about anything could end up happening somewhere.

But what should have been a curiosity, another strange thing in a galaxy filled with strange things that humans were often still trying to figure out, became something else when one of the objects orbiting Tantalus began accelerating.

"What is it?" one of the other passengers asked the captain.

"A ship," she snapped in reply. "What else could it be?"

"Why didn't we notice it before it started accelerating?" another passenger demanded.

"This is a freighter. We have sufficient instruments and sensors to run cargo and passengers between planets and stars. We don't invest money in warship-grade sensors that would have scanned all those rocks in search of something that didn't belong!"

Lochan spoke up as the captain tried to stomp away. "What sort of course is it on? That other ship?"

The captain paused, glaring at all of the passengers. "It appears to be accelerating on a vector to intercept us."

"It's not a warship, though? It's not accelerating like a warship."

"No. It looks like a freighter. Calls itself the *Brian Smith*. But it wasn't going anywhere. It was lurking in rocks, and now it's aiming to intercept us. What does that sound like?"

"A pirate," one of the other passengers said with a gasp.

"That's ridiculous," another protested. Tall and thin, he had struck Lochan as the sort of man who was so sure of his own facts that no actual events would convince him otherwise. His next words confirmed Lochan's assessment. "Piracy can't work under these circumstances! It's economically unfeasible."

Lochan replied before the increasingly irate captain could. "The *Brian Smith* was taken by supposed pirates about three years ago. At Vestri. I know because I was on the

Smith. They're not really pirates. They're privateers. They pretend to be pirates operating on their own, but they're working for stars like Scatha and Apulu."

"Oh, yes, another claim of interstellar conspiracy and aggression by someone from Kosatka!" the man scoffed.

"You saw what was happening at Kosatka before we jumped out of that star system," Lochan said, surprised that he could speak so calmly. But people didn't listen when voices were raised and anger or fear was obvious so he found the strength to sound composed despite the emotions tugging at him. "Didn't that look like aggression to you?"

"I heard them announce that they were peacekeepers, there to oversee free and fair elections."

"You believed that?" another passenger asked with open incredulity.

"It's not a matter that concerns me," the tall man replied. "Nor is this so-called pirate. I'll need a lot more proof than the claims of Kosatka's partisans before I believe that other ship is any danger to me."

The captain surprised Lochan with a harsh laugh. "Proof? You'll get proof. They've got augmented propulsion, better than ours. We can't outrun them, and we're not going to waste fuel cells trying. And you can bet they mount some weapons. When they intercept us, you'll get so much proof it just might be the death of you."

With that cheery last statement the captain physically shoved one of the passengers out of the way and walked off toward the freighter's control deck.

"We should have expected this," a woman passenger murmured to Lochan as the small group of passengers broke up and headed back to their rooms. "They planned everything else."

"What do you mean?" Lochan asked.

The woman looked around to see if anyone else was close before replying. "They must have realized that any ships at Kosatka would flee when the invasion fleet showed up and that those ships might carry people trying to get away as well as valuable cargo being shipped out before the invasion force could reach the planet."

Lochan nodded in understanding. "So they made sure there was a 'pirate' waiting here at Tantalus to catch any freighters fleeing Kosatka."

"Backup plans," the woman said in a very low voice. "Have *you* got one?"

"What do you mean?"

"You've encountered pirates before?"

"Yeah. At Vestri, like I said."

She looked him over, then nodded. "Okay."

Lochan watched her go back to her cabin, wondering what all that had meant.

"Captain Geary!"

Rob struggled back to awareness. Having finally forced himself to get some rest in his stateroom, it had probably been inevitable that something demanding that he be awake would happen. "Here," he said, fumbling for the response tab on his stateroom's display. "What's up?"

"The enemy destroyer is accelerating toward us, Captain," Lieutenant Cameron said, speaking with exaggerated clarity "It looks like an attack run. Estimated time to intercept forty-five seconds."

"I'm on my way to the bridge. Lock all weapons on the enemy ship."

It only took a few seconds to reach the bridge, drop into his command seat, and take in the sweep of the enemy destroyer's projected path on the display before the seat. Hanging in orbit near the facility, *Saber* was hardly moving through space. Rob knew he needed more velocity to deal with an attack. "Accelerate to point zero one light speed."

"Accelerate to point zero one light speed, aye. Taking into account our acceleration, we're now twelve seconds from intercept."

Rob ran his eyes across his display, confirming that *Sa-*

ber's shields were at maximum strength and all of her weapons were ready.

"He's been sitting there in orbit just watching us for hours. Why now?" Ensign Reichert wondered in a low voice.

"We know his fuel cells are low," Rob said. "He can't refuel as long as we're a threat. He needs to try to take us out."

Only a few seconds left as Rob's thoughts raced. Should he evade the enemy attack, frustrate the attempt to disable *Saber*? But that would leave Kosatka's orbiting facility past *Saber*, and *Shark* still in the dock there, wide open to attack by an untouched enemy warship.

Too late anyway. In one second they'd be—

Saber shuddered from a series of shocks as the two warships tore past each other and exchanged fire.

"Bring us around on an intercept," Rob ordered. "Assume the enemy will continue on to hit *Shark*."

"*Shark*'s shields are at maximum and all weapons ready," Ensign Reichert reported.

Red symbols had appeared on Rob's display to show damage to *Saber* from the encounter. *Saber*'s shields had held, mostly, but the hull had been penetrated in two places, and one of the grapeshot launchers was out of commission.

It felt weird to be maneuvering this close to a planet, to have that huge mass and the threat of its atmosphere hanging nearby, eager to clutch at and claw the little toys of humanity. All it would take was a miscalculation, a slight error, or damage that sent a ship plowing at extremely high velocity through rapidly thickening air until the friction vaporized the hull in a matter of seconds.

Saber whipped up and around, coming back to hit the enemy destroyer again.

But he could only watch as the enemy tore past *Shark*, space lighting up with the energy released as particle beams and grapeshot contended with shields and hulls.

"Captain, he only used one pulse particle beam on that attack," Lieutenant Cameron said. "We must have taken out the other."

"How's *Shark*?" Rob demanded. "It looked like he was trying to hit *Shark*'s propulsion."

"Her shields suffered some spot failures, Captain," Cameron said. "*Shark* swung something between her and the attack that absorbed anything that got through."

"Big plates of material from the dockyard," Chief Quinton said. "They pushed them into place as sort of standoff armor."

"Smart," Rob approved. He realized he wouldn't have thought of that because normally the idea could never work. Ships moved too fast. Any protection moving in a fixed orbit or trajectory would be very quickly left behind, useless. But not if the ship was itself stuck in a fixed orbit while being repaired. "Did *Shark* do any damage to the enemy?"

"He's lost some thrusters," Cameron said, grinning. "His shields didn't have time to rebuild after the encounter with us before they engaged with *Shark*. He's also lost at least one grapeshot launcher, and his amidships shields are rebuilding slowly."

"Captain, our fuel cells are at thirty-eight percent," Quinton warned.

"Adjust intercept," Rob ordered as *Saber* finished the long loop above the planet and aimed to hit the enemy destroyer again. "He's got less fuel than we do."

Projected paths on Rob's display shifted, the arcs altering their curves.

"He's coming around to meet us head-on," Reichert said.

"Make this one count, Ensign," Rob said.

"Yes, sir," she replied, smiling slightly, her eyes fixed on her controls.

Another flash-quick moment of intercept, the two ships racing past each other, *Saber* shaking from more hits as the two ships exchanged fire.

"No damage to *Saber*," Chief Quinton said. "All shields held. He's lost enough weapons that he can't hurt us on one pass."

"His amidships shields are gone," Lieutenant Cameron said, sounding remarkably calm. "He's definitely lost an entire thruster group. Possibly two thruster groups."

"Let's get him again," Rob ordered. "New intercept."

"Sir, he's not coming back around. He's diving toward the enemy freighters and passenger ships."

Why? They couldn't offer any protection to the stricken enemy ship. "See if we can catch him."

"Captain, we're receiving a high priority call from *Shark*."

That was a distraction he didn't need. Rob almost told the comms watch to tell *Shark* to call back before realizing that Commander Derian must know how busy Rob was at the moment. If he felt the need to send a high priority call anyway, he might have something very important to say. "Link me."

Derian's image popped into view before Rob. *Shark*'s captain appeared to be simultaneously worried and elated. "Be careful! The freighter that we encountered had a hidden grapeshot launcher. Those ships might also have some armament that they've kept concealed until now. And don't forget that they sacrificed a ship to try to destroy *Shark*. If any of the freighters are empty . . ."

"Damn." Rob realized that he had said that out loud. "Thank you, Commander."

Maybe those other freighters and the passenger ship weren't armed. They hadn't fired earlier when *Piranha* and *Saber* were attacking. But if *Saber* came close now, concentrating on the enemy destroyer, and got hit by grapeshot from several launchers, it could do a lot of damage.

And if one of the freighters overloaded its power core at the right moment to catch *Saber* with the shock wave, it could even the odds, or worse, again.

The enemy destroyer was braking velocity to match orbit with the invasion fleet. He'd be an easy target for an attack run by *Saber*.

Too easy a target.

"It's another setup," Rob told his bridge team. "They

want us to dive into the middle of their formation to hit that destroyer again as soon as possible. Give me a vector change at the last possible moment to bring us along the outside of their formation instead of going straight through it."

"Are we targeting one of the freighters, Captain?" Ensign Reichert asked.

"If we can swing a vector past one of them that wouldn't have expected us to come close to it," Rob said. He saw their reactions, trying to hide their puzzlement. "Remember what happened to *Shark*. These guys will sacrifice a freighter to take us out *if* they know what our trajectory is going to be."

"We have a recommended vector change, Captain," Cameron said. "In one minute, thirty seconds. We'll be able to hit one of the freighters with particle beams as we pass the enemy formation."

"Target that freighter and enter the maneuver in the system. I want it to occur automatically at the right moment."

"Yes, sir. Maneuver entered. Request confirm."

The confirmation command appeared on Rob's display. He tapped it, uncertain if he was being spooked by fears of what the enemy could do. Was he passing up a chance to finish off that destroyer for no better reason than what the enemy might do?

"Freighter targeted," Reichert said.

"How're repairs coming on number two grapeshot launcher?" Rob asked.

"Under way, Captain. No estimated time to repair as of yet."

He focused on his display, watching *Saber*'s shields rebuilding.

Out in space, up and down were concepts that existed only because humans defined them in terms of the plane within which a star system's planets orbited. But, close to a planet, down was always toward it, and up was always away. *Saber* was diving toward the enemy formation, angling down, the bulk of the planet offering an odd background to the space engagement.

The seconds counted down. *Saber* jerked as her thrusters fired, pushing her onto the new vector that would skim the outside of the enemy formation instead of diving through it. But the move had come so late that the enemy would have already had to react as if *Saber* were coming through. Any trap would've had to have been put into motion already, impossible to stop by the time the enemy realized that *Saber* was taking another path.

"Something's launching from two of the freighters!" Lieutenant Cameron yelled as new threat symbols appeared on Rob's display. "One . . . three . . . six . . . eight. Eight aerospace craft!"

Eight warbirds. Rob did some quick mental estimates, realizing that if *Saber* had held her course those warbirds would have popped out right on top of the destroyer as it plunged into the enemy formation.

Why hadn't he expected that? How had he forgotten such a threat when *Saber* was close to the mother ships the enemy warbirds were using? The warbird activity had been screened from *Saber*'s view for the last couple of days by the bulk of enemy shipping, and in any event aside from one warbird that had covered the landing on the orbital facility, all other aerospace craft activity had been inside the planet's atmosphere, and his attention had been focused on both the enemy destroyer and the fighting aboard the orbital facility, but none of those things were an excuse for his not remembering that the additional threat existed.

Though from the expressions on the rest of the bridge crew he wasn't the only one who'd forgotten about those warbirds.

"Sir," Cameron said in a calmer but worried voice, "eight warbirds exceed safe engagement parameters for a single Founders Class destroyer."

"I'd already guessed that," Rob said. Warbirds were useless in deep space, carrying too little fuel to go far or outaccelerate warships. But this close to a planet, with *Saber* at a relatively slow velocity, the conditions for aerospace craft to engage a warship were nearly ideal.

"Earth Fleet guidance in such a situation," Cameron continued, "is to avoid engagement."

"Run away?" Rob asked. "What will they do if we run? They were desperate enough to attack us with their sole destroyer. If we run, and leave that orbital facility unprotected, will they go after *Shark*?"

Ensign Reichert was already running the simulation but didn't wait for it to finish. "Estimate they'd lose about half of their warbirds, but with *Shark* a sitting duck they'd inflict critical damage on her."

Which meant *Saber* would have to fight, Rob realized. The enemy warbirds were already adjusting vector, angling up and out to intercept *Saber*'s new path through space. "Get me an optimum engagement vector. We need to keep those warbirds busy and take out as many as we can."

"Sir," Lieutenant Cameron said, visibly worried. "Yes, sir. But I feel obligated to warn the Captain that our chances in an engagement against eight warbirds are less than fifty percent."

"Forty-two percent," Ensign Reichert said. "If we get number two grapeshot launcher back online. If we don't, the odds are—"

"I understand," Rob snapped at them. Had he pushed this as far as he should? *Saber* had to survive, had to get back to Glenlyon. *That* was his duty. He had no obligation to sacrifice his ship and crew in defense of Kosatka, especially after doing so much to aid this star system. Had he come to the point where further sacrifice was senseless at worst and unwise at best?

Not that he could completely avoid the warbirds. They had a better mass-to-thrust ratio than even a destroyer, allowing them to outaccelerate and outmaneuver the warship for a short period before their fuel levels went too low. The warbirds would catch *Saber* at least once no matter what Rob did.

His eyes went to the image of the orbital facility and *Shark* on his display. Commander Derian would understand. Even Lieutenant Commander Shen would understand. She wouldn't want *Saber* sacrificed in a battle facing such odds.

His responsibility felt all too clear: to run, having done all he could, and . . .

Mele Darcy.

"Marines and the Fleet have to depend on each other," he'd argued with her during one conversation. *"They have to know they can count on each other no matter what."*

"Sure," Mele had said with a sardonic laugh, *"right up to the point where* other requirements *enter the picture. Then the Marines get left holding the bag."*

"That won't happen when I'm in command," Rob had told her.

She'd been nice enough not to laugh again, but he'd seen the skepticism in her.

He'd sent those Marines to that facility.

If he abandoned them there . . .

Was this about Mele Darcy being his friend? Or about the need to set that precedent? That the Fleet didn't run and leave the Marines in the lurch?

Rob realized that he didn't really care which reason was motivating him and that his internal debate had taken less than two seconds. "We're going to see how much damage we can do," he told the bridge crew. "We have people on *Shark* and on the orbital facility. We won't abandon them without a fight."

"Five minutes to intercept," Lieutenant Cameron warned. "Sir, if all eight hit us in a short interval—"

"I understand," Rob said. "We can't avoid this encounter."

"Captain," Ensign Reichert said, "they've started evasive jinking to confuse our fire control systems."

"How effective will that be against our fire control systems? I haven't dealt with that problem except for some drills in Alfar's fleet."

"It will complicate achieving hits," Reichert said. "The small, random changes to their vectors are just large enough to ensure that *Saber*'s fire control systems can't predict exactly where the targets will be when a weapon reaches them. If we pulse a particle beam at them at the right time, it'll travel so fast that we can score a hit anyway, but if the targeted aerospace craft jinks just as we fire, we'll miss. They're too small for us to have any real margin of error in targeting."

That left the grapeshot launchers. Or launcher, since number one was still out of commission. He remembered that grapeshot was his best weapon against the warbirds since it fired a shotgun-like pattern that would have a high chance of getting hits close in no matter how the birds jinked. And if the birds didn't get close enough for grapeshot to have a hit chance, they wouldn't be close enough to do much damage to *Saber*.

"Ensign Reichert, I want the pulse particle beams set to fire as soon as the fire control system gives a better than fifty percent kill probability."

"Yes, sir," Reichert said. "Sir, that kill probability will be based on some unknown variables, so it won't be reliable."

"It's all we've got. Make sure the grapeshot launcher targets a different warbird than the particle beams."

"Yes, sir."

"Three minutes to intercept," Cameron reported. "Recommend shutting off main propulsion and bringing our bow around to face the oncoming aerospace craft."

That was doctrine. Warships had their strongest shields facing forward and could employ the most weapons against anything coming toward their bow. But Rob hesitated. "Lieutenant Cameron, can our bow shields hold against eight warbirds?"

"No, sir," Cameron said. "There's a one hundred percent probability the bow shield will collapse and incoming fire will impact the hull."

Warbirds didn't have the armament of warships and had no shields to speak of, but eight-to-one odds put *Saber* at a disadvantage.

Rob sat back, thinking, knowing he had two and a half minutes to decide what to do. *Saber* was standing on her stern, accelerating straight "up" away from the planet. The warbirds were coming in from *Saber*'s aft quarter, angling in to catch her as *Saber* climbed. If he did nothing, the warbirds would hit *Saber*'s weaker shields amidships and aft, and do even more damage to the ship. But pivoting the bow to face them wouldn't prevent damage, and *Saber* had already taken some hits from the enemy destroyer. He had a bad choice and worse choices.

"Two minutes to intercept."

CHAPTER 12

Rob's memory flashed back, startling him, remembering Ninja explaining how she worked. *"Firewalls aren't walls, you know. They're not solid. The idea is to have a flexible series of defenses so that something that gets past one gets stopped by the next."*

How could that help? He didn't have multiple layers of shields. He only had one set covering each part of—

Could that work? Why not try? "Lieutenant Cameron, cut main propulsion now." That would be a little earlier than the incoming warbirds expected, throwing off their approach a little. They'd have to focus on correcting for that on their intercepts.

"Cutting main propulsion," Cameron echoed, entering the command.

As the mighty propulsion units on *Saber*'s stern fell silent, Rob swung one finger through the air to illustrate his next orders to Cameron. "I want the pivot to put *Saber* bow on to the attack to start at the last possible moment, so we're just swinging our bow onto that vector as the aerospace craft intercept us."

"Uh . . . yes, sir," Lieutenant Cameron said, clearly puzzled. "Getting us stopped bow on at just that moment might be—"

"I don't want us to stop, Lieutenant Cameron," Rob said. "I want *Saber* to keep pivoting as we engage the warbirds."

"Sir?"

He knew everyone was watching him. Rob spoke with quiet confidence, trying to convince them of something he wasn't certain of himself. "None of our shields can stop the fire of all eight warbirds. But if we're pivoting while they hit us, we might be able to take most of the hits on the bow shields while the ship rotates to present our amidships shields to the later hits. If we can distribute the hits across more than one set of shields we might be able to avoid having them collapse."

"That's—" Lieutenant Cameron's eyes widened. "Yes, sir. I see. Setting maneuvering systems to initiate pivot maneuver at last moment possible and to allow the pivot to continue past bow-on aspect."

Ensign Reichert shook her head. "It wouldn't work against another warship on a firing run. The hits would come too fast for the pivot to make a difference. But at warbird engagement speeds . . . it's possible. We don't have time to run simulations to test it, though."

"Do you have a better suggestion?" Rob asked.

"No, sir, I do not. Thirty seconds to intercept. Pulse particle beams are opening fire."

Almost simultaneously with her announcement *Saber*'s thrusters fired, kicking her bow around and to the side to face the approach of the aerospace craft. In space, the warship would keep moving in the same direction at the same velocity until the main propulsion lit off again but could turn to face the greatest danger. The warbirds would expect that. *"War is based on deception,"* Mele had told him. *"That Sun Tzu guy said that, too. Let the enemy expect one thing and do another."*

Ninja had nodded in agreement. *"The easiest mark is someone who thinks they know exactly what's going to happen."*

With nothing else he could do in the final seconds as *Saber* swung around and the warbirds closed in, Rob hoped he'd get the chance to thank them both for their advice.

One of the warbirds on final approach blew up as a particle beam struck some of its armament.

The other seven bore in, weapons firing.

As the warbirds flashed past, *Saber* jerked from hits, the lights dimming as power was automatically diverted. Rob kept his eyes on his display, seeing another warbird come apart as it caught a volley of grapeshot head-on, and a third spin away after a particle beam sliced through it.

That left five opponents.

"Shields held except for spot failures," Chief Petty Officer Quinton reported. "We took a few hits through those spots."

"Number two pulse particle beam projector damaged," Ensign Reichert said, then paused very briefly before continuing. "Correction. It was destroyed. Initial casualty report, four dead, two wounded."

"They're coming back," Lieutenant Cameron said, grim. "Using full acceleration. They'll burn through their fuel fast at that rate."

"Fast enough they'll have to call off the attack?" Rob asked, feeling sick at the thought of the sailors *Saber* had lost.

"No, sir. Not that fast. Not unless we change something."

"Chief, can we get those shields back to full strength before they hit us again?"

"No, sir," Quinton said. "We're rebuilding shields as fast as we can."

With only a few minutes to think, Rob looked at the data from the engagement. *Saber*'s bow shields had taken about half the hits, the other hits walking down the amidships shields as the ship kept turning during the attack.

The weakened bow shields couldn't hold against five warbirds. Neither could the amidships shields. And he couldn't risk presenting the stern shields to the warbirds and possibly taking hits to his main propulsion.

"Let's see if we can fake them again," Rob said, surprised by how steady his voice was. "Same maneuver, but this time stop the pivot facing them, just as doctrine calls for."

"So maybe they'll expect us to keep pivoting and get thrown off?" Lieutenant Cameron said. "Yes, sir. Maneuver entered. Do you have any orders regarding main propulsion?"

"Chief Quinton, what's our fuel cell status?"

"Twenty-eight percent," the chief replied. "I am required to recommend breaking off action and refueling."

"Thank you. I don't think the enemy is going to let us do that," Rob said. "Lieutenant Cameron, keep main propulsion off to conserve fuel. That'll also simplify our fire control solution as much as possible. If we can take out three more of those birds we'll have a chance."

The warbirds had strained to come around in a faster arc than even a destroyer could manage, now "diving" down to an intercept, aiming to hit *Saber* again as quickly as possible. "Get us some hits, Ensign Reichert," Rob said.

"Yes, sir," she replied, her voice almost distracted as she focused on the incoming aerospace craft.

Saber came around again, thrusters firing, but this time other thrusters fired to halt her pivot just as the warbirds zoomed into their intercept. Bow straight on to the enemy attack, *Saber* rocked from several impacts, followed by the wail of an alarm.

"Forward shields have collapsed. We took five hits forward," Chief Quinton said. "Losing atmospheric pressure in the bow section."

"One dead, four wounded, estimated casualty count," Reichert said. "One aerospace craft destroyed. A second appears to have suffered serious damage, but is coming back around with the three other remaining enemy warbirds."

"Lieutenant Cameron," Rob said, "pivot *Saber* this time to take the attack amidships."

"Pivot to place amidships facing attack," Cameron repeated. "Maneuver entered."

"Captain," Quinton said, "our amidships shields will fail if four warbirds hit them. We'll take serious damage."

"We can't afford any more hits forward with the bow shields collapsed," Rob said. "And we can't afford to take serious damage aft on our main propulsion. I don't see where we have a choice."

"Yes, sir. Just advising you as my job requires, Captain."

Rob's eyes jerked to part of his display as another alert sounded.

"The damaged warbird came apart during their turn," Reichert said. "The force of his maneuvering thrusters was too much for the structural damage caused by our hit."

"What are our chances against three?" Rob asked Quinton.

The chief shrugged. "Better. Not as much serious damage. That's all I can say. Too many uncertainties."

"Understood. Let's pray the uncertainties fall in our favor."

The three remaining warbirds came in at full acceleration, their weapons hurling energy and projectiles at *Saber*'s midsection. *Saber* jolted again, the vibrations of the impacts carrying noise to Rob and the others on the bridge.

"Sir, number one grapeshot launcher fired!" Reichert said. "They must have gotten it online seconds before it needed to fire. We took out two of the remaining enemy aerospace craft. There's only one left."

"Amidships shields collapsed," Quinton reported. "Numbers one and two grapeshot launchers temporarily off-line due to hits sustained. Number one pulse particle projector damaged. Number three pulse particle projector off-line due to overheating. No estimated times to repair available. Estimated casualty count four more dead, seven wounded."

"There's only one left," Lieutenant Cameron said, smiling for just a moment before his elation faded. "Most of our shields are gone and we have no working weapons. One is all they need to finish us off."

"Yeah," Rob said, glaring at the image of that last warbird, already starting to come around again. Deception. That was the only weapon that *Saber* had left. "Intercept course for that warbird. Main propulsion at full. Go!"

"Sir? We don't have any working weapons," Ensign Reichert protested as a bewildered Lieutenant Cameron carried out the order.

"Would we charge to intercept that warbird without any working weapons?" Rob demanded. "Who in their right mind would do that? If we're moving to attack, we must have weapons, and that sole warbird can't handle us on its own if we have working weapons."

"That bird doesn't have the sensors to evaluate all the damage to us," Chief Quinton said. "But he can evade us."

"For how long, Chief? How's his estimated fuel state?"

Quinton rubbed his chin, thinking. "He's going to be deciding about now whether to keep fighting us here and run dry or head for home with just enough fuel to get back and docked."

Saber had come around, her hull pitted by damage, her bow section still open to space, but accelerating toward another meeting with the sole remaining warbird.

"One minute to intercept," Cameron said.

"Is this kind of action on any of the Earth Fleet checklists, Lieutenant?" Rob asked.

Cameron shook his head. "No, sir."

Ensign Reichert inhaled deeply. "Sir, we avenged *Claymore*. Even if this guy takes us out, we hurt them worse."

"Yes," Rob said. "But I'd still kind of like to get home again." He'd already checked the status of *Saber*'s escape pods. The idea of ordering abandon ship was almost too hard to think about, but if that warbird raked *Saber* in her current condition he might not have any choice.

Ninja had come to believe in the ancestor worship becoming common out here, far from Old Earth, crediting them with saving Rob's life three years before. He knew she would've been praying to them daily since *Saber* had left Glenlyon. His own beliefs were far less defined and certain, but at the moment he really hoped that Ninja was right and those ancestors were listening right now.

"Thirty seconds to intercept."

"Any repair status on those weapons?" Rob asked.

"No, sir," Quinton replied.

"Ten—He's breaking off!" Cameron cried.

Rob let out a breath he hadn't realized he was holding as the aerospace craft swung away under the push of its maneuvering thrusters on full, avoiding another engagement with *Saber*.

He slumped back in his seat as the warbird steadied out on a vector headed back toward the enemy invasion fleet. "Reduce main propulsion to one-third. Get us on a vector to assume station one thousand kilometers in higher orbit above that enemy formation. I need repair estimates on all weapons and time until shields can be restored. I want us ready for action again before that enemy destroyer realizes we took as much damage as we did." Rob paused, his elation at survival darkening. "And a final casualty count as soon as possible."

"Doc Austin knows what he's doing, Captain," Chief Quinton said. "If they can be saved, he'll do it."

"Thank you." But even Doc Austin couldn't help those already dead. Rob knew that. So did Chief Quinton.

Damn.

Sometimes victory tasted only a little less ugly than defeat.

Something had happened. Mele could tell that much. But she had no way of knowing what. The enemy had suddenly surged forward, not stopping despite their losses, and Mele had been forced to order another fallback. At least the militia was learning how to retreat in sections, one group covering another as they ran for the next set of defensive positions.

The food court, silent and deserted, briefly filled with soldiers racing through it without stopping, wending their ways between tables and chairs, the cleverer ones among them shoving over some of the chairs as they went to hinder whoever came behind them. The food court was too large, with too many ways into it, to offer any hope as a place to make any kind of stand except a last stand.

Behind them came the enemy, stumbling over the chairs, having to pause to take cover and orient themselves as militia snipers fired from the corridors down which their comrades had retreated.

Mele, judging the level of panic among the militia, had to abandon the idea of urging on laggards, instead racing ahead with strength she hadn't known she still had to get in front and stop the retreat. It took knocking down a few who tried to run past her, but with the help of Lieutenant Freeman, she got the militia into place behind the next set of cabinets, desks, and chairs piled across exits where the enemy would have to enter junctions before they could proceed farther into the facility.

"Corporal Gamba, how's it look?" Mele called.

"We've merged with the militia that were to the left of us," Gamba reported. "They lost their lieutenant. The remaining lieutenant . . . Captain, her armor is covered with blood and brains from someone she was fighting next to that caught a burst full on. She's like . . . robotic, you know. Not showing any feelings at all and going through the motions but liable to break down any second."

Mele sighed. "That sort of thing is hard for veterans to handle. She was probably a marketing manager or sales associate a couple of weeks ago. Try to get her to gradually cede authority to you. Give the orders for her and let the militia with you get used to your giving them. How's Yoshida?"

"Okay as long as his meds hold out. The wound isn't life-threatening, but it'll probably hurt like hell once he can feel it again."

Mele rubbed her faceplate, wishing the entire orbiting

facility hadn't lost atmosphere as a result of the fighting so far. The inability to scratch an itch was probably the worst part of being in sealed battle armor. "Lieutenant Freeman."

"Yeah, Captain." Freeman had been talking to some of his militia but came over at Mele's call.

"We lost one of the other lieutenants."

Freeman nodded slowly. "Danzig. I was talking to him when he . . . went off-line. Veren is okay, though."

"Veren's about to crack," Mele said.

"Oh." Freeman sounded suddenly even more tired.

"This is the next-to-last set of defensive positions before the final positions near the dock. You know these people better than I do. Can they still hold?"

"Yeah," Freeman said, his head coming up to look at her. "They can hold."

She wasn't nearly as confident as he was, but Mele didn't question his assessment.

And when the enemy came swarming forward along every available avenue of approach, the militia did hold. They stopped the first assault, and an hour later another.

But there were still too many ways for the enemy to advance through and too few defenders to cover them all. Mele saw the transient sensor readings that told her the defensive positions were about to be outflanked by invaders coming through two maintenance shafts. She gave the order to fall back just as another attack hit the force now effectively commanded by Corporal Gamba.

Mele wasn't sure how she got the militia's retreat stopped this time. Maybe it was because the enemy was so tired they couldn't pursue quickly even when Gamba's defensive position was overrun. Maybe it was because the militia was so worn-out they could no longer muster the strength for flight even in the throes of panic. Maybe it was the Marines offering a steady example. Whatever the reason, the militia fell into position at the last line of improvised barricades, not far behind them the hatches leading out onto the dock, and beyond them an open stretch before *Shark*.

"Corporal Gamba, give me your status," Mele called. No answer. "Corporal Gamba. Talk to me."

Someone else finally replied. "Captain, this is Private Yoshida. Uh . . . Gamba . . . I'm pretty sure . . ."

"Spit it out," Mele ordered.

"She's dead, Captain. During our fallback to here."

Damn. Damn. Damn. "How are you doing?"

"Still, uh, functional, Captain. Right arm is still no good, though."

"How's Lieutenant Veren?"

"I don't think she made it back here, either, Captain. All the militia keep asking me what to do. Am I in charge?"

"Yes, Private Yoshida, you're in charge," Mele said, anguished to have lost Cassie Gamba. "Do you understand? Those militia with you are looking to you. Be the leader they need. Can you do that?"

"Uh . . . yeah. Yes, Captain. I can do that. I think. But, Captain . . . they're almost beat. They've been doing good, but they don't have much left. I think."

"Hold on." Mele looked around for Lieutenant Freeman. "Freeman?"

"By . . . the hatch . . ." Freeman replied, his voice halting. "Main hatch."

"Have you been hit?"

"Yeah. I'm okay. I'll—"

"Stay at the hatch. Have your people got any portable sensors left? Stick them up to watch here and nearby areas." Maybe they could hold a little longer here. But Mele felt the currently unseen enemy presence in front looming and knew she had to plan now for the next, and last, phase of the defense.

"Private Yoshida. Listen up, Yoshi! If there are any portable sensors left with your group, have the militia stick them up in good spots to watch the area leading to the dock. Got that? Good. Now, I'm sending you an image from my display. See? When the militia with you fall back, *on my orders and not before*, take them to this area on the docks. There's a lot of heavy equipment there that'll provide cover.

We're already close to you. I'll bring my own group to the same spot."

"Shouldn't we—?" Yoshida paused, his voice wavering with stress. "Shouldn't we fall back to the ship, Captain?"

"Look at the layout of the dock," Mele said, putting force into her words. "There's a clean path from the air locks and cargo doors of the facility to the dock so they could move people and junk easily. There's no cover along that route. With the enemy still pushing us and close, they'd catch us partway to the *Shark* and cut us down."

"But—"

"*Listen*. We join up in this area, lots of heavy stuff to give us cover, and when they charge *Shark* we'll be able to hit them in the flank. They'll be the ones without cover. And we will plant ourselves among that heavy gear, and if the enemy tries to come after us there we will kill every single one of them."

Yoshida took a moment to reply, but when he did his voice was steadier. "Got it, Captain. I got it. Will do."

"You gonna hold until you have to fall back?" Mele pressed.

"Hell, yeah. I mean, yes, Captain."

"Is Private Lamar there?" Where was Lamar? Had Penny Lamar let her down? Had she misjudged Lamar that badly?

"Yes, Captain. Flat on her back and a little doped up, but she's got a weapon."

"Make sure you've got people assigned to carry her with you when you fall back. Assign those people now, and make sure they don't leave Lamar behind."

"Got it, Captain."

"All right. You've got your orders. You know what to do. Make me proud, Yoshi."

"Will do."

Thirty minutes later the enemy came at them again. Whoever was pushing them was pushing them hard, giving them barely enough time to rest enough to enable them to charge again. "Hold 'em!" Mele yelled into the circuit for all of the remaining militia as armored enemy soldiers stumbled forward.

Cursing at the lack of any more grenades, she dropped two attackers, but the militia soldier on her right lost part of his head to a hit. Mele tried to divide her attention between aiming and firing and keeping track of losses as green markers on her display went dark.

They threw back the first attack. Mele took a long look at how much of the facility they were still trying to hold, how many different approaches the enemy could make, and tried to judge the state of her battered and exhausted force.

Know yourself. Old, old advice. Mele didn't want to admit it, but these militia couldn't hold again. They were wavering on the verge of collapse. She either admitted that now or tried to hold again and watched her remaining force fall apart.

"We're pulling back," Mele said, trying to speak clearly and calmly. "You all have the position on your helmet displays. Out the hatches onto the dock, then left into the heavy gear located there. Do not run toward *Shark*. Out the hatches, then left. Lieutenant Freeman, are you still at the main hatch onto the dock?"

"Yes, Captain," Freeman said, his voice thin.

"Override the air lock controls so both the inner and outer hatches stay open. That'll get us out quicker. Can you make it to the last bastion?"

Absurdly, she realized that *the last bastion* sounded oddly romantic. *Captain Mele Darcy died defending the last bastion.* That wouldn't be a bad epitaph.

Except that she still had no intention of dying here.

"Start falling back," Mele said. "Everyone. Now. Maintain your discipline. Yoshi, make sure Lamar is with you." She shifted her circuit, hoping that despite the nearby enemy jamming she could still get through to the dock. "*Shark!* We're falling back out of the facility and heading to one side of the dock. None of our people will be coming your way. Anyone you see charging across the dock toward you is an enemy."

"Understood," *Shark* replied. "Captain Darcy, the enemy destroyer has been badly damaged and is almost out of fuel. And the enemy just expended what were probably their last aerospace craft attacking *Saber*. If we can get *Shark* clear, we've got this."

"Thanks for the update." Mele wondered who she was talking to over there. It didn't sound like Commander Derian. Probably the watch officer on the bridge or the . . . what did squids call it . . . the quarterdeck. Someone who couldn't help with the repairs but could help defend the ship until those repairs were done.

By the time she reached the air lock everyone else had already passed through. If the enemy had realized that the defenders had fallen back, they must still be advancing cautiously, having been hammered during pursuit before.

Outside on the dock she ran along the hatches, slapping the air lock overrides back into the off position so the outer hatches would close. Having to open those hatches again would slow down the enemy slightly and give Mele's people a little forewarning of the next attack.

As she ran to the left side of the dock, herding a few stragglers from the surviving militia ahead of her, Mele caught a glimpse of *Shark*. Some sort of barricade had been thrown together on the dock just outside an open hatch on the ship. *Shark* must have defenders behind that barricade, ready to make a last-ditch stand outside the ship if the enemy got that far.

It felt strangely peaceful out here, where fighting had not yet come, the lack of atmosphere causing heavy shadow wherever lights didn't directly play on something, few noises carrying as vibrations through the dock structure, the stars and the endless dark of space above both beautiful and unbearably cold and distant.

More tired than she'd thought possible, Mele staggered in among the heavy equipment on the left side of the dock, seeing her militia and those who had been with Yoshida sprawled about in postures of exhaustion. There were times that called for encouragement, times that called for persuasion. This wasn't one of those times. "*Get up*, you useless, pathetic excuses for men and women! Are you waiting for your mommies and daddies to show up and rock you to sleep? We are *not* done! There's a fight to be won, and we *will* win it even if I have to personally kick each one of you in the butt so hard that you'll wish you'd been shot! Get on your feet! Cover those hatches! You've got weapons! You've lost friends! *Fight!* I'm not giving up, and neither are you!"

She could almost feel the hate and anger radiating from the militia, but they got up and rested their weapons on convenient places on the equipment. "Yoshi! Where the hell are you?"

"On our left, nearest the ship," Yoshida called in reply. "I, uh, thought some of them might try to run to it from here so I sort of stuck myself in their way."

"Good job." Though, looking at her surviving militia slumping over their weapons, Mele wondered if any of them could run anywhere. Their own tiredness might have been the only thing that had prevented a panicked dash for the apparent safety of the ship. "Where's Lamar?"

"A little to my right. Even though she's lying down she's got a clean shot under some gear at anyone trying to run toward *Shark*."

"Hatch opening," Lieutenant Freeman gasped. "Two hatches."

Mele joined the others, standing behind a very thick, sturdy-feeling piece of loading equipment, her rifle leveled toward the hatches she could see cycling open. A group of enemy soldiers burst out of the hatches onto the dock and began their own exhausted run at *Shark*. Mele yelled "fire!" and what were left of the defenders opened up on the flank of the enemy. Taken by surprise and hit from an unexpected direction, several attackers fell at the first volley. Others turned and ran back inside. A few, too far forward, tried to keep on toward *Shark* and were cut down by the sailors defending the quarterdeck.

Mele waited for another charge, but nothing happened.

"What's going on?" one of the militia asked, sounding almost too tired to care.

"They must be regrouping," Mele said. "It's not over. Everyone stay sharp."

As more time crawled by, the lack of visible activity increasingly worried her. Why would the enemy commander, who had pushed them this far, suddenly let up the pressure with success in sight? Mele scrolled through the few portable sensors the militia had been able to post in the inside area leading to the dock and that hadn't already been spotted and destroyed by the enemy, trying to see what the enemy was doing despite the interference that nearly rendered the data feeds unreadable.

What was that? A bunch of enemy soldiers wrestling a big object toward a solid bulkhead facing the dock. Because of jamming, the image was grainy and static-riddled, breaking repeatedly into pixel fields, but Mele thought she recognized the object. Of course. The enemy would have brought something like that to ensure that *Shark* didn't get away. They'd hauled it with them all the way through the facility, and now its target was finally within reach. "Hey, *Shark*, what does this look like to you?" she asked, relaying the feed.

The reply took several moments. "We can't see enough to tell, Captain Darcy."

"To me it looks like a portable medium antiair weapon. Oh, yeah, there's the power section being brought up. *Shark*, you can't see it because they're behind a solid bulkhead, but they're setting up a particle beam to fire through that bulkhead and into you."

"Can't you stop them?"

"Negative," Mele said. "It'd be suicide to charge them with what I've got left. Can't you shoot first?"

"Anything we shoot will go on through the facility."

"It's already beat to hell, *Shark*, and there's nothing and nobody friendly left alive past that bulkhead."

Another pause, while she watched with growing nervousness as the power section was linked to the antiair weapon.

"Yeah," *Shark* finally said. "Yeah. We can't bring any weapons to bear until we pivot the hull a bit. Hold on. Keep your people where they are."

"No problem." Mele felt the vibration running through the dock as *Shark*'s thrusters fired on very low settings to slightly shift her hull without moving the ship away from the dock. "*Shark*, they felt that. I can see them working faster. They're getting ready to shoot."

This time the answer came in the form of a sudden blur of extremely fast-moving objects fired from *Shark* at the flat outer surface of the bulkhead the enemy weapon was sheltering behind. The bulkhead bent inward, dozens of large holes suddenly appearing in it. The image from Mele's sensor vanished as she stared at the result of warship grapeshot fired from close range. The shock of the grapeshot impacts could be felt through the structure, followed by an extremely rapid series of fading shocks as the same ball bearings slammed through other obstacles in their paths before finally being stopped somewhere deep in the facility.

An instant later light flared through the holes and the bulkhead ballooned outward as the damaged power supply for the heavy weapon let go all of its stored energy at once.

She heard a ragged gasp, the best cheer they could manage, from what was left of her defenders.

"Think that did it?" *Shark* called to Mele.

She nodded even though *Shark* couldn't see her. How many of the remaining enemy soldiers had been close enough to that destruction to be killed by it? Anyone not hit by the metal ball bearings or shrapnel from whatever they'd hit would have been caught in the power discharge. "Yeah, I'm sure that did it. Thanks, squids."

"You're welcome. Oo-rah, right? That's the Marine thing?"

"Yeah. Right. Oorah." Mele watched, waiting, but didn't spot any more enemy activity for the next twenty minutes.

Beside her, the remaining militia waited, slumped at their places.

"Captain Darcy." That was Commander Derian calling this time. She was sure of it. "We're going to go any moment now. Bring your people in."

Surprised, Mele looked out over the dock and over that long open area leading to *Shark*'s quarterdeck. She had no idea where the enemy soldiers were now, how many of them were probably covering that area with weapons too weak to threaten the destroyer's hull from this range but plenty strong enough to penetrate the protection her Marines and the militia wore. And the remaining militia wouldn't, couldn't, move fast. It had all the makings of a massacre. "Thanks, but we'd be targets in a shooting gallery trying to get to you. We're a lot safer staying holed up among this equipment."

"I promised to bring you off when *Shark* could get under way," Derian objected.

"And you're offering to do so," Mele said. "But it's my judgment that withdrawal to your ship would result in most of those of us left being killed or wounded. Sir, we can't run. I believe the enemy, to the extent they still are willing to attack, will lose that motivation once *Shark* gets clear. We'll sit here, nice and comfortable, until you get back."

"I want it clearly understood that we'll wait for you if you want to try to make the ship," Derian insisted.

"That is understood," Mele said. "But I'd rather live a little longer than try that run for your ship, sir."

"Very well. We'll be back for you, Captain Darcy. Us or *Saber*."

"Have fun attacking those enemy ships and give my best to Commander Geary." Mele braced herself before calling her troops. "*Shark* is pulling out. It's too dangerous for us to reach her. But that's fine. We're safe here. We'll wait until they come back."

Private Yoshida backed her up quickly. "All we have to do is sit and wait? I can do that, Captain."

"We'll be okay," Lieutenant Freeman agreed.

A few moments later Mele felt the dock trembling again, this time hard enough to shake her a bit. She looked over at the stars and saw the dark bulk of *Shark* eclipsing them as the destroyer moved away from the dock.

She gazed at the sight, smiling, never having realized how beautiful and graceful a warship could look as it moved. Mele called her surviving defenders again. "Congratulations, you apes. The space squids got their ride going, and we gave them the time they needed."

"So we wait now?" one of the militia called back, his voice too exhausted to carry emotion. "We're not giving up, are we?"

"Why the hell would we give up? We just won. Is there anybody left who can set me up to broadcast to the enemy troops?"

"Seamus," Lieutenant Freeman called. "You still with us? You do it."

It only took a few seconds before Mele's comm light glowed green. "Hey," she called. "Invading troops. This is Captain Mele Darcy, Glenlyon Marines, to the invading force aboard this facility. Are you ready to surrender?"

The reply that came was almost strangled by frustration. "You're the one who needs to surrender! Now! You're trapped! If you want any mercy, you'll surrender now!"

Mele heard someone laughing and realized she was the one doing it. "You got it wrong. You got it all wrong. We're not trapped. *You are*. Think about it. We've got two warships out there now. You've got one half-broke warship that's almost out of fuel. Your warbirds have been cut to pieces during the fighting in atmosphere and up here. What do you think is going to happen to the ships you came here on? And to any one of your shuttles that try to fly from this point on?

"It's simple," Mele continued. "You, and your entire invasion force on the planet, are about to be cut off. You can keep fighting until your ammo and power and rations give out, after which you'll get to find out what the people of Kosatka are going to do to the people like you who trashed their planet, or you can surrender now to me, a representative of Glenlyon. I might not be as unhappy as the people of Kosatka are. No promises, though, and the longer you wait, the unhappier I'll get."

"Damn you!"

"Let me know when you get to yes," Mele said. "You are the enemy commander, right?"

This time the voice sounded beaten. "Lieutenant Ostis. Senior surviving officer. You killed Captain Bostick when you destroyed our heavy weapon."

That explained the lack of enemy activity since then. Not only massively tired and suffering from terrible losses, but they'd lost their commander again, leaving leadership to a worn-out lieutenant who might have as little combat experience as the militia lieutenants Mele had worked with. "All right. You know the situation. I have no interest in wasting more lives, mine or yours. Sit there as long as you want and think about it. I'll wait for your surrender. As long as you refrain from attacking again, I won't attack you. But if you come after us one more time, we're going to hit back at you until every one of you is dead. Darcy, out."

Suddenly dizzy, Mele grabbed at the loading gear in front of her to keep her balance. "*Shark*, can you still hear me?"

"We hear you," Commander Derian replied. "You're one hell of a soldier, Captain Darcy."

"With all due respect, sir, I'm a *Marine*."

"Right. Sorry. You'll want to know about your people. We've got a Corporal Giddings aboard. I'm told he's stable."

"Thank you, sir. That's good news."

"Who's the surviving senior militia officer there?"

"Lieutenant Freeman, sir. He's hurt but still combat capable."

"Have him . . ." Derian paused. "Have him put together a consolidated casualty report when he can and any supply requirements you have. The militia took some heavy losses, didn't they?"

"Yes. They did good, Commander. They did real good," Mele said.

"Thank you. Do you have any messages for Commander Geary?"

Mele gazed upward at the stars. "Tell him we got the job done here. Finishing the rest of it is up to him."

CHAPTER 13

"Forward shields are at eighty percent, Captain. That's the best they'll be able to do until we can conduct major repairs. Amidships shields are at full."

Rob Geary nodded, his eyes on the display before his command seat on the bridge of *Saber*. "I'm seeing pulse particle beam projectors two and three online again as well as grapeshot launcher two."

"Yes, sir. Estimated time to repair grapeshot launcher one is another thirty minutes."

"*Shark* is under way," Lieutenant Cameron added.

"So I see." Rob called *Shark*, seeing the image of Commander Derian appear. Derian looked happier than Rob had seen him so far, but his words and movements still reflected accumulated tension wrapped tight inside him. "How are my Marines, Commander?" Rob asked.

Derian shook his head. "Still on the facility. I asked them to withdraw to my ship, but your Captain Darcy said it would be too risky, that she and the surviving militia were better off remaining in place until we could come back for them."

Rob tried not to let his disappointment and unhappiness at that news show. "That was Captain Darcy's judgment?"

"Yes, Commander," Derian said, looking as if waiting for a broadside from Rob. "I told her I'd wait. She said she'd lose too many people trying to reach my ship."

"Okay," Rob finally said, knowing it would be unfair to blame Derian for Mele's decision. "She's better at that particular problem than you and I are. Is *Shark* ready to hit that invasion fleet?"

"*Shark* is proceeding on a vector to do just that. I understand that you're concerned about attack runs through their formation? Because of the possibility of more surprises? I've had more time than I wanted to have to think about how to handle that," Derian said. "I recommend we approach slowly and take out the ships one by one from outside the formation. We'll work our way in like cracking open a nut. If that damaged destroyer of theirs stays in close to the passenger ship, we'll be able to eventually hit him together. If he decides to come out and fight, we can both hit him then."

Rob thought about the idea and didn't find any reason to object. "I concur. *Saber* will accompany *Shark* to hit the first two freighters."

They came in slowly, maintaining their own orbit of the planet below, closing on the invasion fleet. Rob wondered what sort of debates were raging among the captains of those ships. The freighters had no chance of outrunning the two destroyers. They were sitting ducks, and even if they scattered could be run down by the two warships before any could reach a jump point out of Kosatka Star System. The passenger ship could accelerate better than the freighters but would still be easy pickings once the outer "shell" of freighters in the formation had been peeled away. The obstacles posed by the freighters were, in fact, the primary protection the passenger ship had left. The enemy destroyer had rebuilt most of its shields, but there were no signs its thruster damage had been repaired, and it still had less than half its own weapons in working condition. *Saber* was battered as well, but when it came to shields and weaponry, *Shark* was at maximum strength. The next encounter with the enemy destroyer wouldn't be a long fight.

Derian took the initiative in calling for surrender. "Hostile shipping in orbit around this planet, you are to immediately surrender or face destruction. Each ship must drop its shields, its commanding officer must transmit his or her surrender, and all weapons must be powered down. Once you've surrendered you'll be directed to new orbital positions."

No answer. Rob took *Saber* toward one freighter while *Shark* targeted another.

This wasn't combat. It was more like target practice, Rob thought, as *Saber*'s weapons began hitting the freighter.

The freighter broke formation, its main propulsion pushing it away, thrusters firing to direct it down toward the planet.

"What's he trying?" Rob asked his bridge crew.

"Maybe trying to get far enough into atmosphere that we can't risk chasing him at high velocity?" Lieutenant Cameron suggested.

"That's his only chance," Chief Quinton agreed. "Make it a little difficult for us to chase him in the hopes we'll pick another target."

"He's getting down into atmosphere, and his main propulsion is still firing," Cameron said, puzzled. "Captain, he's exceeding safe speed."

"We must have hit his controls," Ensign Reichert suggested. "He can't stop accelerating, and he's too far into atmosphere to climb out in time."

The freighter's hull was already glowing as air friction created more and more heat. The ship's vector altered, the freighter sliding sideways as some of its thrusters failed and others kept firing, dipping deeper into atmosphere.

"Do you think they're already dead?" Cameron suggested.

The freighter traced a flaming path through the sky of the planet, pieces breaking free as parts of the structure failed, the death of the freighter and its crew making an oddly beautiful spectacle.

"That's one," Rob said, not feeling any particular joy,

just satisfaction that any supplies left on that freighter wouldn't go to help the invasion force on the surface. "Let's get another."

"*Shark*'s target is showing power core fluctuations," Chief Quinton reported. "Estimate overload or shutdown within the next few seconds."

The freighter being pummeled by *Shark* exploded moments later, the shock wave from its death rattling the remainder of the invasion fleet.

An urgent alert appeared on Rob's display. "The enemy destroyer is coming around," Lieutenant Cameron said. "His movements confirm he still has serious thruster damage. His main propulsion is lighting off . . . system is analyzing vector . . . Captain, he's running for the jump point for Kappa."

Was the enemy commander fleeing, abandoning the ships he was supposed to protect? Or had he been ordered to save his destroyer since it had no chance of survival otherwise? "Lieutenant Cameron—" Rob began.

"Captain," Chief Quinton interrupted, "we're low on fuel cells. If we try to chase that ship, we'll run dry by the time we catch him."

"He's lower on fuel than we are," Rob argued, frustrated.

"Yes, sir, but he just has to stay ahead of us. We'd have to accelerate long enough to catch him. Sir, *we can't do it*."

"Damn!" Rob hit his comm control with far more force than necessary. "*Shark*, *Saber* is too low on fuel to pursue and catch the enemy warship. Request you take him."

Derian shook his head, looking as unhappy as Rob. "We've only been able to do basic safety checks on our propulsion repairs. Ramping up to full power quickly on my main propulsion would be dangerous. Maintaining full power might be disastrous. I can't risk it."

"We have to let him go?"

"I'm afraid so. Hopefully, his masters will give him a warm welcome when he returns with news of this disaster he didn't prevent," Derian said.

Another alert sounded as the enemy destroyer kept accelerating away.

"Captain, shuttles are launching from the passenger ship," Reichert said. "Five . . . six total. And the surviving warbird is coming out, too."

Commander Derian had his eyes on his own display as he spoke to Rob. "*Saber*, you're in the best position to take those shuttles. If you would do me the favor of shooting them down, *Shark* will take care of that warbird for you."

"Agreed," Rob said.

Saber accelerated down toward the planet, angling under the survivors of the invasion fleet, as the shuttles dove down into atmosphere at the highest speed they could risk, the single remaining enemy warbird coming at *Saber*. "Don't engage him when he goes past," Rob said, knowing that a single aerospace craft couldn't knock down his ship's shields on a single pass even when those shields were weakened. And with *Shark* coming in fast, that warbird would only get a single pass at *Saber*. "All weapons concentrate on those shuttles."

"Maybe they were hoping we'd chase that destroyer so they'd be able to get safely down to the surface," Cameron suggested in a low voice, as depressed as the others at having to let the enemy warship escape.

"Maybe," Rob agreed.

"Or," Chief Quinton said, "maybe the real high brass transferred to that destroyer while it's been tucked in near that passenger ship, and they're sending their staffs down to get shot at to divert us from chasing the warship so the big bosses can get away."

That, Rob thought, sounded entirely too plausible.

Saber rocked twice as the warbird tore past, firing.

As the trailing shuttle came into maximum range, *Saber*'s working grapeshot launcher fired.

The warbird tried to whip around for another pass at *Saber* but went into an uncontrolled spin as a shot from *Shark* took out the thrusters on one side. The pilot ejected as the warbird spun away, beginning to break up under the stress of the uncontrolled maneuver.

The trailing shuttle exploded as some of *Saber*'s grapeshot tore into it.

Saber grazed the upper atmosphere of the planet, her particle beams shooting downward at the five remaining shuttles as they dove for the surface. The particle beams moved at nearly the speed of light, but in atmosphere the shuttles had to limit their velocity to avoid suffering the same fate as the freighter that had burned up. "Not quite sitting ducks," Ensign Reichert said, her focus on her display. "But close. Engaging farthest shuttle first."

Saber fired, spearing the shuttle leading the others down. Something critical hit, the shuttle's descent changed from a controlled series of evasive maneuvers during its dive to an erratic spin as it fell.

The pulse particle beams kept firing, occasionally missing as an evading shuttle made a lucky jog at just the right moment but taking out the second shuttle in line, then the third . . .

"Pulse particle beam projector beam two is overheating," Lieutenant Cameron warned. "Projector three is hot and heading for overheat."

"Got it," Reichert said, her gaze locked on her display.

A fourth shuttle twisted suddenly in flight and began falling.

"One to go," Rob said. "Can you nail it, Ensign Reichert?"

Instead of answering him, she fired again.

The last shuttle began a death spiral toward the planet below it.

Ensign Reichert sat back, grinning, a slight sheen of sweat on her face. "Nailed it, Captain."

"Well done," Rob said. His gaze went back to his display, where *Saber*'s visual sensors had zoomed in to show the falling shuttles.

They impacted the surface in a ragged series of crashes that left an irregular new constellation of craters in the plains outside the Kosatkan city of Ani.

"Thank you, *Saber*," Commander Derian said as he called in again. "That was probably the invasion force's high command fleeing for safety before we took out their flagship."

"One of my people suggested that the overall commanders of the operation may have fled on the destroyer and deliberately sacrificed the command staff to save themselves," Rob said.

Derian frowned. "I've met people who would do that. Maybe when we recover that warbird pilot they can sing a tune about that for us."

Only one more freighter died under fire from the destroyers before the others began surrendering, which seemed to confirm that whatever authority had held them in thrall had either fled or died.

"We've got a call from the passenger ship," Rob's comm watch announced.

The captain of the passenger ship didn't look military. He looked like a civilian who was extremely unhappy to be in the middle of a war. Rob wondered under what conditions that captain and his crew had been hired. "The last of the joint Apulu/Turan command staff have left this ship. I surrender it. Do not fire on us. Please. We'll comply with your demands."

"They're surrendering to us," Lieutenant Cameron pointed out. "Not to *Shark*."

"They probably expect *Shark* to be a lot angrier with them," Rob said. "We'll work out who gets what prizes later. For now, keep an eye on that enemy destroyer. I want to know if he turns."

"Sir, he can't," Chief Quinton said. "If he tries to alter vector that much, tries to slow down to come back at us, he'll be out of power in no time."

"Keep an eye on him anyway," Rob said, unable to believe that as far as the situation in space was concerned the fight was over. "Captain Darcy, this is *Saber*. How's your situation?"

Mele sounded as exhausted as he'd ever heard her, but

under that Rob could sense that she'd still fight if pushed. "We could use some beer. And we're a little low on ammo and other supplies. But there's no beer at all."

"I'll see what we can do about that," Rob said. "Kosatka should have some surviving shuttles hidden on the surface. They can bring up fresh troops to relieve you."

"Don't forget the beer. We're going to have some prisoners, too," Mele advised. "Is the invasion fleet a done deal?"

"Destroyed or surrendered," Rob said.

"I'll pass that on to my opponents."

"How are your people?" Rob asked.

Mele took a moment to answer. "I've still got Yoshida with me. Gamba and Buckland died. Giddings and Lamar were badly wounded."

"Damn . . . Giddings is all right on *Shark*."

"So I heard. Lamar should be okay, too."

"Mele . . ."

"Yeah."

They understood each other. There wasn't anything else to say.

Carmen huddled next to a blown-out window on the top floor of the Central Coordination Building, exposing just enough of herself to gaze out into the streets below as the sun began to rise. The occasional sound of a shot or an explosion echoed across the city. Both sides seemed to be running short of chaff rounds, but smoke from fires and the remnants of earlier chaff clouds drifted through those streets and among the buildings. Tinted red by dawn's early light, they looked like the clouds of fine dust that had often billowed among the cities of Mars, sifting through any available crack or crevice to eventually form a layer of reddish drift like old blood coating everything inside.

She'd hated that dust.

But the dawn created the illusion that it had followed her here, across the many light years from where Mars orbited about the star Sol. As if Mars itself had followed her here.

Fine. She'd beaten it once. She'd beat it again.

Carmen leveled her rifle, peering through the scope as she slowly traversed her view across the streets and buildings held by the invading forces. The scope itself was a thing of wonder, capable of not only magnifying the view but also automatically compensating for range and environmental factors like wind and air temperature. Even if Carmen hadn't gotten a lot of practice with the weapon in the last year, she'd still be able to hit far-off targets thanks to that scope.

Someone came into view as her scope swept slowly across a courtyard. A small group of soldiers in partial battle armor, their helmets off in such a "safe" spot. Another small group came to meet them, standing there while the men and women in the first group gestured about and spoke to a man standing in front of the second group.

Carmen knew a briefing when she saw one. Someone of higher rank getting a rundown on what was happening. Maybe a top commander who'd come down in one of the surviving enemy shuttles that had dropped in during the night.

She aimed as carefully as she could, the scope image helpfully shifting the aim point to compensate for everything that might send the bullet awry, waiting as a drift of red mist temporarily obscured her target, squeezing the trigger slowly. The buck of the weapon against her shoulder surprised her as the shot fired.

She kept her eye on the scope, waiting.

The high-ranking enemy officer fell sideways.

Two of those in the second group grabbed their fallen leader and carried him into the nearest building. Most of the others in the courtyard scattered, either running inside as well or looking about for the source of the shot.

But then they all started looking upward, pointing. Carmen lowered her weapon and gazed up into the sky turning from black to blue as dawn triumphed.

Something moved across the sky, something large, moving too fast, atmosphere heating it so it left a fiery trail. As

Carmen watched, pieces broke off, forming small bright streaks that accompanied the larger streak of fire.

The wreck of something, dying spectacularly in the atmosphere of this world. But what? That was too large to be a destroyer, wasn't it?

She tried to get a signal through the waves of jamming that filled the city, finally picking up part of the net. A freighter. The spaceship dying in fire was a freighter. Which meant it was an enemy.

A sudden chatter on the net, interrupted by agile jamming that broke it off. Carmen looked up again, seeing far off the blossom of an explosion like a new star suddenly appearing high in the morning sky. Another ship?

She focused her scope back on the enemy soldiers she'd seen earlier. They were still staring upward, and if she was any judge of body language they weren't happy with what they were seeing.

Carmen slid away from the window, careful not to expose herself to sight through it, searching for a landline she could link in to. She wouldn't let herself hope. Not yet.

"**H**ey, want to go somewhere private?"

Lochan looked in surprise at the woman standing in the doorway to his cabin on the *Oarai Miho*. The same one who had talked to him about backup plans and his previous experience against pirates. "That . . . depends."

She smiled. "We haven't really talked much. I'm Freya Morgan."

"Lochan Nakamura. What's your reason for being aboard?"

"I'm a trade negotiator."

He nodded, thinking something didn't fit in that description of her. "And what is it you want to negotiate with me?"

Freya smiled again and winked at him. "You know."

Lochan hesitated. But why the hell not? It wasn't like he and Brigit Kelly had any relationship yet. Certainly, they hadn't made commitments to each other. And with that pirate heading for an intercept with this ship, it seemed all too likely that he might not get another chance with any partner. Having spent far too many hours already sitting alone in this cabin watching the pirate grow steadily closer to the *Oarai Miho*, Lochan welcomed the chance for something else to do. Especially with someone like Freya Morgan. "Okay."

"Come on. I know a place."

He followed Freya through the passageway outside their cabins and through a smaller cross passage. At the end of that, Freya opened a sealed hatch about a meter in diameter. "In here. It'll be a little tight with both of us inside. I hope you won't mind."

He didn't think that'd be a problem. Lochan, still a little wary, let her go through first, then crouched to come through the hatch.

It was tight. She reached past him to pull the hatch shut. "Whew. Now we can talk."

"Talk?" Lochan wondered if he'd sounded as lame as he thought he just had.

"I'm sorry," Freya said, smiling apologetically. Her body pressed lightly against him in the small compartment but without any hint of passion. "Lochan, your cabin is probably bugged. I know mine is."

"Bugged? The captain has the cabins bugged?"

"No." Freya shook her head. "One of our fellow passengers. I don't know which one for certain. There might be more than one. Listen, I am sorry for misleading you, but I needed a way to get you here without anyone's suspecting I had any other motive."

Lochan's sense of humor came to his rescue. "I certainly didn't suspect it."

"I hope you understand—"

"Ever since I came down and out I've been meeting women younger than me who want to know me for reasons that have nothing to do with physical attraction," Lochan said dryly. "This is part of the pattern. Why exactly are we in here?"

"The pirates."

"You think we can hide in here when they board the ship?"

"Of course not. Even if the captain didn't rat us out, which I'm pretty certain she would, they'd check the passenger manifest and search the ship until they found us. No, I have an idea for dealing with that pirate ship," Freya said.

"An idea involving what?" Lochan asked.

"A bomb."

He paused, studying her again. "Exactly who are you?"

"I told you. Freya Morgan. Trade negotiator. For Catalan."

"Trade negotiator." Lochan waited a moment longer, but she said nothing else. "All right. Just what does a trade negotiator know about bombs?"

"A girl has to have a hobby," she explained in a low voice. "Lochan, I need backup on this. One person can't handle the physical aspects of it. It has to be someone I trust, and on this ship that's you."

"Why? You don't know me."

"No. But I know people who do know you, and I talked to them when you came aboard at Kosatka. They said if I needed help, you could be counted on."

"Thanks." Her reasons made sense to him, as did the need to do something. "If this plan could help stop the pirates, why aren't you asking the captain for help?"

Freya shook her head. "Because that'd be a bad idea. One, because so far the captain is playing the old game of going along with demands in the hopes of minimizing her losses, and two, because it's possible the captain has been paid off to not cause any trouble when the pirates showed up. Taking that kind of bribe can just be good business, you know. And three, this freighter is owned by a company that operates out of Hesta that is now effectively controlled by executives from Scatha."

"So they're supposedly neutral, and maybe still thinking of themselves that way, but to all intents and purposes they're the enemy because they know they're answering to bosses who work for Scatha. But what makes you think I can be trusted to help you with a bomb?" Lochan pressed.

"Self-interest," she replied. "I don't want to end up in the hands of those so-called pirates, and neither do you, right? More than that, though, I've done my research. I know your merit."

"So you think I'm the sort of guy to help you build a bomb." Lochan gazed at her, wondering what Freya Morgan was like and realizing that he'd spent too much time researching information about his mission and too little time learning more about his fellow passengers. "Why do *I* trust *you*?"

"Because I'm being honest with you on what I want to do and what I want you to help with. And, it's probably our only chance to avoid a sudden detour to a secret prison at Apulu or Scatha."

"Or Turan." Lochan looked at her again, wondering why parts of Freya reminded him of Mele Darcy and parts of Carmen Ochoa. But did the reasons for that matter as much as the fact that she was reminding him of women who had proven their right to be trusted? On top of that, Freya's arguments were solid. There wasn't any other option that Lochan knew of that offered any chance of escaping those pirates. "All right. I'm in."

Freya smiled. "Brigit told me I could count on you."

"Brigit? Brigit Kelly?" Lochan was abruptly glad that he hadn't made any effort to collect on Freya's implied promise that had lured him here. "You know her?"

"Let's say that she and I share some history and similar goals. And from what she told me while this ship was at Kosatka, I think you share those goals as well."

"I'm working for Kosatka," Lochan said, remembering that Brigit had suggested he might find a friend on the ship if he needed one. He suddenly understood that hadn't been about hooking up but a guarded reference to Freya Morgan if problems like a pirate showed up.

Freya shook her head again. "You're working for us all, aren't you?"

He considered those words before nodding in reply. "I guess I am."

"Good. I'll need to set some things up. When it's ready I'll stop by your cabin. We need to pretend that you and I are having a sudden and intense interest in playing reindeer games with each other. Trying to keep that quiet, sneaking about a little, will look totally natural to anyone who notices." Freya smiled again, ruefully. "I'm sorry, I know it's tight, but we should stay in here a little while longer. Just in case someone watched us. We want it to look like . . . what it looks like."

"I promise to be smiling when we leave."

She laughed. "You are a fine one. It's too bad you've got a thing with Brigit."

"I don't actually have a thing with Brigit yet," Lochan protested.

"Yeah, you do. You and Brigit just actually haven't figured it out yet."

Dinner that night didn't vary on the surface from the usual during the trip so far. Like most other freighters, the *Oarai Miho* tended to favor cheap, bulk food with long shelf life and simple preparation requirements. Like most such foods, the heat packs were labeled with colorful pictures and grand names such as Beef Teppanyaki Multi or Chicken Grande Ulti, and also like most such foods the contents bore little resemblance to the labels and tasted primarily like mush with slabs of cardboard mixed in. Usually, several of the twelve total passengers would eat in the mess/rec room, the others taking the food back to their cabins.

Lochan usually ate in the rec room to avoid having the off-putting smell of the food linger in his room, but he'd rarely interacted much with his fellow passengers, the majority of whom seemed equally uninterested in socializing. He didn't change that, though he stole some glances at Freya as she ate, noticing that she didn't look his way. Lochan did spot a couple of the other passengers giving him a look, followed by glances at Freya and a whispered conversation that provoked knowing smiles from the two.

The tall, thin man who was certain that piracy wasn't a thing, an actual pirate on intercept vector for this ship apparently not shaking his certainty in the least, spent his meal talking in a low voice to a shorter woman. They seemed to be in agreement on just about everything, though the bits of conversation that Lochan caught made it difficult for him to not jump in with some contrary opinions and actual facts.

When the freighter's first officer passed by, one of the passengers called out a question. "How long until that other ship reaches us?"

The first mate paused, shrugged, and gave the shortest possible answer. "Twenty-six hours."

Lochan kept his eyes on his unappetizing food to avoid looking toward Freya again. He had a feeling whatever she was planning would go down during the coming ship's "night," when the passengers and most of the crew were asleep.

Sure enough, late that evening he was roused from a light slumber by the door to his cabin opening. "Come on," Freya whispered. "I need you now."

The careful use of a phrase with a double meaning to confuse whoever had likely bugged his cabin made Lochan smile despite his nervousness. But even if the bug had vid capability, a smile would be natural enough, he thought.

This time they headed back toward where Lochan knew engineering lay, though he knew that only because he and the other passengers had been warned so many times not to ever go into that part of the ship. "How many are awake?" he whispered in Freya's ear.

She rolled her eyes contemptuously. "One's supposed to be awake on the bridge, but that one always sleeps. There's also supposed to be an engineering watch awake, but every time I checked they were asleep, too. In the crew compartment, not even bothering to stay in engineering while they sleep. They depend on the ship's systems to warn them if anything is going wrong and wake them with alerts."

"No one is awake at night? Is that . . . legal?"

"No," Freya replied in a matter-of-fact voice. "But, in addition to all of the other things humanity left behind at the Old Colonies and Old Earth, we also left the kind of people and organizations who enforce safety regulations on ships like this."

They reached a large, wide hatch with a smaller hatch set into it. Freya looked around the darkened, quiet passageway carefully before pointing to something above the hatch. "Security and safety camera. This one is broken and hasn't been repaired, which is handy for us."

"What if it had been working?"

"I'd have broken it. They just saved me the trouble of doing that." She opened the smaller hatch, going through and waiting for Lochan to follow before closing it.

He looked around the engineering section, which was also dimly lighted at this hour of the ship's day. Several equipment consoles and displays, another hatch labeled with a variety of warnings as well as the words *Power Core Access*, and a wide, short passage at the back.

Freya went straight to that passage. By the time Lochan caught up with her, she'd found a powered multiwheeled device with grabber arms and was using the handle controls to back it out and toward another wide hatch that was latched open.

Inside was a sort of storage shelf with rectangular objects bearing rounded sides and corners lined up along it, each one strapped in securely to some sort of heavy-duty mechanism. Each of the objects was over a meter in height and a little wider in diameter.

"What are those?" Lochan asked, as Freya unlatched the straps holding the last in line of the objects.

"Fuel cells," she said absentmindedly as she got the last one free of its holder.

"Fuel cells?" Lochan didn't think he'd sounded as calm as Freya had. "Aren't those really dangerous?"

She paused to look at him. "Yes and no. What do you know about fuel cells?"

"They're what's used to keep power cores going."

"Right. The fuel cells used by warships are bigger because of the differing power requirements, but they all work basically the same way. There's a lot of stuff in each of these that contains a lot of energy. The power core releases that energy in a controlled fashion. When one fuel cell is nearly expended, this feeder shelf loads in a new one. They've got all kinds of protection built into their construction to keep them from going unstable or releasing energy outside the power core, which is why the idiots running this ship haven't even bothered to keep that hatch locked as it should be to prevent unauthorized access to these fuel cells."

Lochan frowned at her. "And we're going to . . . ?"

"Use this heavy cargo lifter to haul this fuel cell to the freighter's lifeboat, load it aboard the lifeboat, and rig it to explode when the pirates recover the lifeboat."

"Oh." Lochan nodded, trying to think through the plan. "And why will the pirates bother recovering the lifeboat?"

"Because you and I will be aboard the lifeboat, trying to escape."

"Yeah. Okay. Freya, I see a problem with this plan."

She grinned. "We won't really be aboard it. They'll think we are. Lochan, we don't have much time to work with. I can't muscle this thing onto the lifter without your help. Trust me?"

"Sure." He moved close to the fuel cell rack, feeling worried at getting closer even though from what he knew of fuel cells if one went unstable now there wouldn't be any safe place on the whole ship. But humans had a natural aversion to getting close to really dangerous things even if those things seemed safe at the moment.

It took all his and Freya's strength combined to manhandle the fuel cell far enough out of the rack to fit into the lifter's grasp. Once that was done, Lochan took the lifter's handle and slowly, cautiously backed it through engineering.

While he was doing that, Freya went to a bank of cabinets and sealed shelves, selecting pieces of equipment that she stuffed into an expandable carryall. "Don't open the big hatch out of engineering yet," she warned. "There's an alarm on it."

Lochan waited as Freya went to the hatch panel and entered some commands to disable the alarm. Once satisfied, she touched a control and the big hatch slid back, making enough noise to cause Lochan to cringe.

They maneuvered the lifter out of engineering and a short distance down a different passageway to another hatch, this one labeled *Lifeboat—Emergency Access Only.* Once again Freya went to work. "I need to bypass another alarm," she explained. "I'm also diverting the video feed from that safety cam above the hatch. That one does work, which will be good for us later on. There. The alarm's off, and right now the camera is only showing a continuous loop of the empty corridor here."

This hatch resisted their efforts, but Lochan helped Freya throw the handle so it finally cracked open.

The lifeboat, big enough to carry the crew and a few others under tight conditions and keep them alive for a couple of weeks ("longer if they eat each other" Mele Darcy had once joked to Lochan), tightly filled the space beyond.

Freya opened the lifeboat's hatch, wide to allow rapid access, and helped Lochan maneuver the lifter in far enough to deposit the fuel cell in the center of the lifeboat. Once he'd backed out the lifter, Lochan found Freya frowning at the fuel cell. "What's the matter?"

"It's heavy enough it shouldn't shift when the lifeboat boosts away," Freya explained, "but I'd like to fasten it somehow just to be certain."

"No problem," Lochan said, happy to know something useful in this matter that Freya apparently didn't. He went to the emergency repair locker near the front of the lifeboat and opened it, immediately finding what he was looking for. "This'll do it."

Freya smiled at what he held. "Duct tape."

"Two rolls. Required as part of the emergency supplies on every shuttle, lifeboat, and escape pod," Lochan said. "A friend of mine told me that while we were, uh, killing time aboard a shuttle hoping to be rescued." He went to work wrapping duct tape around the fuel cell and fastening it to the frames of the nearest seats while Freya assembled the other items she'd taken from engineering.

"Is that a tool universal power pack?" Lochan asked.

"Yes," Freya answered, nodding toward the small, squarish object. "They can be found anywhere people use tools. And, unlike fuel cells, they're a lot easier to mess with. Someone who knows what they're doing, or someone who's an idiot, can rig them to explode."

Lochan saw her fastening the power pack to a place on the fuel cell where Freya had removed protective covers. "So that's the, uh, detonator?"

"Right," Freya said, working as she talked. "When it goes off here without any protection for this area it'll rupture some important things inside the fuel cell. I've already disabled other safety features that might still limit the failure of the fuel cell so it'll be certain to blow. And now I'm linking this receiver to the proximity alarm on the lifeboat. When the lifeboat comes in contact with another object, such as a ship owned by pirates, it should explode."

"Should?"

"It's always good to have backup, right?" Freya was laying out wires on the deck of the lifeboat, working as quickly as possible in the confined space. "Go on out. I'll be right behind you."

Lochan left the lifeboat, waiting outside the boat's hatch as Freya backed out, laying wire as she went, swinging the hatch closed most of the way before making some final touches and sealing it. "A nice, simple, manual backup. If the proximity alarm fails to set off the power pack, opening this hatch will cross some wires, complete a circuit, and make sure the job's done."

"Uh-huh," Lochan said, eyeing her in the dim light.

"Catalan certainly gives its trade negotiators interesting skill sets."

"You have to admit they came in handy." With Lochan's help, they carefully resealed the hatch to the lifeboat compartment, Freya examining it closely to ensure nothing looked amiss. "All right. I've gimmicked the video cam so I can feed it more signals later remotely. Let's get this lifter back to engineering, then get back to our cabins before anyone spots us."

The trip back felt more tense to Lochan than earlier as he worried about how much time it had taken to get this far. But they maneuvered the lifter back into place, Freya closed the latches on the now-empty fuel cell holder at the end of the rack to avoid making it obvious that one had been taken, and got the big hatch closed.

They were in the passageway where their cabins were, within a few meters of safety, when Lochan heard the scuff of a footstep from around the corner.

Before he could react, Freya pinned him against the nearest bulkhead and pressed her mouth against his.

Startled, Lochan kept his eyes open and saw a drowsy-looking crew member walk past. The crew member glanced at them, paused as if deciding whether to stop and watch for a while, then went onward.

"Sorry," Freya gasped in a whisper as she stood back from Lochan. "We had to make sure that guy thought we were out at this hour for fun and games."

"You don't have to apologize. It's been a while since I was kissed like that."

"I couldn't tell," Freya said with a wink. "Be prepared at any moment with your stuff ready to go. I'll come by, and we'll pretend to escape."

"How long?" Lochan asked.

"It's . . . sixteen hours until those pirates catch this ship. We'll make our escape when they're close, like we're panicking. All right?"

"All right. How are we going to launch it?"

"I rigged the flight controls so I can activate the launch

sequence remotely. See you in about fifteen hours, Lochan."

"Shouldn't we be seen plotting together before then?" Lochan asked. "So when this happens, the others can put two and two together and come up with the wrong sum?"

"Right. Good thinking. I'll see you at breakfast, then."

Lochan went back to his cabin and lay down but couldn't sleep. Finally, he got up and carefully packed his small travel bag. Just like someone planning on going somewhere soon.

CHAPTER 14

"All passengers are to go to their cabins and remain there until further notice."

Lochan listened to the announcement along with the others nervously waiting crowded together in the rec room. He gave Freya an obvious inquisitive look, and she returned an obvious nod. Everyone headed for their cabins, but after only a few minutes Lochan left his again after grabbing his bag.

He encountered Freya almost immediately. She gestured to one side and Lochan followed along a tight passageway to a different hatch than the one they'd used the first time, this one set near the deck.

The compartment on the other side was some sort of access, long and low. They could barely sit up in it. "What if this doesn't work?" Lochan asked in a whisper as Freya got the hatch closed and settled down near him.

"We get to see some parts of Scatha, or Apulu or Turan, that most people never see," Freya said, bringing out her pad. "All right, then. I need to link in to the freighter's systems and . . . done. What does this say? Am I reading it right?"

Lochan leaned close and squinted. "Twenty minutes to intercept. That pirate ship is close."

"As close as we want it to get. All right," Freya said again. "Here's the feed to the lifeboat video cam. I'm inserting this other image of you and me, with time marks making it look like this is happening right now. And . . . activate hatch alarm."

"I don't hear anything," Lochan said.

"It probably only sounds on the freighter's control deck. Now . . . this . . . and . . ."

Lochan felt a jolt run through the freighter as the protective cover for the lifeboat blew off, followed by another jolt as spring-loaded rams shoved the lifeboat away from the freighter. "So far, so good."

"Yeah. And now it's all on auto. Escape boost." Freya scrolled through commands on her pad. "Here's the freighter's exterior display again. There's the lifeboat boosting away as we make our escape."

"Where are we escaping to?" Lochan asked.

"The *Bruce Monroe*. They jumped into Tantalus from Kosatka a few days behind us, remember? They're following our track because they have to in order to get to the next jump point. We're trying to get to them so we can convince them to turn around and jump out before the pirates finish dealing with this ship and come after them." Freya's smile held a wicked edge. "I might have mentioned that someone could do that where someone else could hear me."

Lochan nodded, wondering why he felt fairly calm. "Could that have worked? I mean, as an alternative if we didn't want to use a bomb?"

"No way," Freya said, biting her lip as she stared at her pad. "I ran the math on my desk unit in my cabin, just to provide a little more misleading evidence. Even on the best trajectories available, we couldn't escape that way. The lifeboat isn't fast enough. But you and I are panicking, taking the only available means to escape. Most of those watching will assume we're two lovers on the lam, but there are others on this ship and the pirate who I'm sure will see other reasons for our wish to avoid being captured and questioned by those alleged pirates. They know who you are, a representative of Kosatka's government, and they'll see I came from Catalan, and they'll want to make sure we don't get away."

Lochan, slightly hunched over as he sat, couldn't help smiling despite his discomfort. "I'm a secret agent fleeing with an attractive fellow spy, eh? This is like one of those wish-fulfillment simulations."

She gave him a sidelong look, smiling. "Thanks for the compliment. What makes you think I'm a spy?"

"Nothing. You're just an average, everyday trade representative. I must have forgotten that while you were rigging that bomb." Lochan shivered. This compartment had some sort of insulation problem, rendering it uncomfortably cold as well as cramped.

"Listen," Freya cautioned. She kept the volume low, but Lochan could hear the captain's voice.

"Damned fools! Two of them! They've launched my lifeboat!" Lochan couldn't help flinching as the captain raged on the interstellar rescue frequency. "It's not my doing!"

The reply from the pirates was short and sharp. "Two of your passengers? Who?"

"Nakamura and Morgan. We've got vid of them at the lifeboat, and they're not anywhere aboard. Nakamura came on at Kosatka, and Morgan has been riding us since Catalan. I have nothing to do with this!"

"Maintain your current vector," the order came.

"The pirates are changing vector," Lochan said, watching the relay of the freighter's display.

"Yes. Let's see. The freighter's systems are showing it maneuvering to catch the lifeboat. Excellent."

"It looks like an easy move for them." Lochan shook his head. "You were right. We wouldn't have stood a chance if we'd tried to run for real."

"If this doesn't work," Freya replied, "we still won't stand a chance. Keep as quiet as you can. If we're found now it could ruin everything."

Lochan found that he couldn't look away from the relay of the freighter's display shown on Freya's pad. He could do nothing to change anything that was happening. Yet still he kept his eyes fixed to the display as if his attention were critically important to the outcome.

"They're getting close to catching that lifeboat," Lochan whispered.

Freya nodded, keeping her own gaze locked on her pad as she replied. "This freighter's systems are estimating five more minutes."

The pirate ship looked externally much like the *Oarai Miho*. Boxy, with main propulsion much smaller in proportion to the ship than would be the case on warships. Merchant freighters didn't waste money on using up more fuel cells than required, sticking to economical if slow rates of acceleration and deceleration. But Lochan could see what appeared to be an extra main propulsion unit added on the pirate vessel, allowing it to outaccelerate other freighters, and there were at least two extra bulges on the hull of the pirate craft that Lochan suspected concealed weapons. "I wonder if that really is the *Brian Smith*?"

"The one you said was taken at Vestri three years ago? It could be. You don't remember any distinctive features?"

"No. Not on the outside of the ship, anyway," Lochan said. "And it looks like they've done some work on the outside, so anything I remembered might be wrong. But it fits, doesn't it? Using a captured freighter as another privateer. That would help prevent anyone from tracing the sales record of the ship to see where it came from. And they've had plenty of time to add weapons and more propulsion to the *Brian Smith*."

"It's still not much to have us all so scared, is it?" Freya said. "A destroyer would take it apart in no time if anyone ever sent destroyers to patrol star systems like this and clean out pirates and privateers."

"In the valley of the blind, the one-eyed man is king," Lochan quoted. "With only us and the *Bruce Monroe* to worry about, and both freighters completely unarmed, that guy is the biggest dog in the neighborhood."

"So you're a philosopher, too, eh?" Freya asked. "Brigit's a lucky girl."

"Brigit and I haven't—"

"You will. Assuming our plan works and we don't both disappear into those secret prisons."

An alert appeared on the freighter's display, showing that the pirate *Brian Smith* was on final approach to the lifeboat, which following its automated flight pattern had stopped boosting away from the *Oarai Miho* and was now only coasting through space. "Grapnels," Lochan said. "Is that what that says? Is that something that lets a ship grab a lifeboat?"

"Apparently. Half a minute," Freya read off the display. "Keep your fingers crossed, and if you've anyone and anything to pray to, now's the time."

The seconds counted down. "Contact," Freya said, disappointed. "The proximity detonator signal failed."

"How long until we know if your manual backup—" Lochan began.

A brilliant, white flare of energy appeared where the lifeboat had been, engulfing a large part of the freighter. They heard nothing, of course, but Lochan's imagination supplied a vast boom to match the size of that explosion, a sound that felt so real it was almost as if he'd really heard it.

As the flare of light faded, several large, broken segments of what had once been the pirate *Brian Smith* could be seen tumbling away from where the burst of energy had torn apart most of the ship.

"Do you think we got them all?" Lochan asked.

Freya nodded, smiling once more. "Oh, yeah. See? They brought the lifeboat alongside their crew section. That was completely swallowed up by the energy released when the fuel cell let everything go at once. Scratch one pirate ship and one pirate crew, who've probably hurt a lot of people in the past." She entered commands rapidly, waiting. "And scratch everything on this pad that shows what I've been doing with it. But, since it's possible one of the freighter crew is the sort of hacker who can recover even triple-wiped and overwritten data . . ." She popped open the back of the pad, pulled out the memory coins, and held them up. "These are pretty hard to break."

"What are you going to do with them?"

Freya wriggled around enough to access some of the insulation and shoved the coins behind it. "That."

"Now what?" Lochan asked. "We have to come out of here sooner or later."

"Yeah. And the captain's going to be very unhappy with us," Freya said. "But they've got no evidence that we did anything."

"Those images of us at the lifeboat hatch—"

"Show us going there but don't show us opening it before the cam broke for reasons that won't be easily discovered." Freya grinned. "Don't you remember? We actually walked on past it, on our way to a private place where we could have one last deeply meaningful mutual physical experience before the pirates caught us."

"This has been one of the most passionate imaginary affairs I've ever had," Lochan said. "I hope it was good for you, too."

"You've satisfied my every desire, Lochan Nakamura," Freya said with a laugh. "I wanted to build a bomb and blow up that other ship, and we did." Her smile went away. "Don't forget. There's likely at least one enemy agent on this ship. All they've tried to do is spy on us so far. With the pirate ship out of the picture, they might try something more permanent before we reach Eire."

"I'll stay on guard," Lochan said.

There wasn't anyone in sight when they popped the hatch and struggled out, a bit stiff from the confinement inside. They were still working out the cramps as they walked when they encountered a member of the crew running along the passageway.

The sailor snarled at them. "In your cabins! What are

you doing out?" She ran on several steps, halted, and spun about to look at them again. "Who are you?"

"Freya Morgan," she answered as if unconcerned.

"Lochan Nakamura," he said.

"But you're . . . Don't move!" the crew member shouted at them. "No! Come with me! Right now!"

Word must have gotten around quickly about what had supposedly happened. Lochan saw people staring at him and Freya as if they were seeing ghosts. He tried to look puzzled as to what had happened, while also trying to spot any disappointment in the eyes of those watching at seeing him still alive, but if anyone aboard the *Oarai Miho* felt that particular emotion, they hid it very well.

The captain, on the other hand, didn't try to hide anything. When her gaze fell upon him it was so intense that Lochan felt physically threatened. The captain vented on them with an amount of rage that rivaled the output of the exploding fuel cell. The rage only multiplied as Freya and Lochan expressed confusion about what had happened.

But, as Freya had said, there wasn't any evidence that either she or Lochan had launched the lifeboat or caused the explosion. When the captain pressed her demands that they explain what they'd been doing when the lifeboat launched, Freya gave a lurid and graphic description of activity that Lochan wished he'd actually experienced. That apparent candor left the captain even less happy since it left no room for further questions.

She turned on Lochan with a new line of attack. "Why did the lifeboat explode like that?"

"It really exploded?" he asked, not giving away anything.

"Yes!"

"I don't know much about lifeboats," Lochan said, having long ago learned the importance of appearing to answer one question with a completely different piece of information.

"What made it explode?" the captain demanded.

"I'd guess the pirates must have done something to make

it explode," Lochan offered, which was true enough since they'd tripped the backup detonator system.

"That lifeboat was an expensive piece of equipment!"

"At least it looks like whatever caused the lifeboat to launch also took out the pirates," Freya interjected, as if trying to mollify the captain.

"*Shut up!* Both of you! You'll stay in your cabins every moment until we reach our next stop, then you'll be put off! If I catch either of you outside your cabins, or in each other's company again, I'll put you both in full body restraints and press charges for disobeying orders in an emergency situation! Get 'em out of my sight!"

As they were led to their cabins, past the shocked gazes of the other passengers who still had little idea what was going on, Freya blew Lochan a kiss. "See you at Eire!"

As he heard his cabin being locked from the outside, Lochan stretched out on the bunk, tired. He was still worried about what that mysterious agent aboard might do, but that was a possibility of trouble ahead. That didn't come close to matching what had, until a short time ago, seemed the certainty of being taken by those so-called pirates.

Sooner or later the crew of this ship would figure out a fuel cell was missing, but they shouldn't be able to pin that on Lochan and Freya, either. It was always possible that the captain would try to press charges despite the lack of physical evidence tying them to the missing fuel cell or the launch and explosion of the lifeboat, but Lochan didn't expect that. The captain would have to admit to violating a lot of important safety regulations if she tried to explain how two passengers could walk off with a fuel cell.

His safe trip to escape the fight at Kosatka had turned out to be a little more dangerous than anticipated. He wished he could tell Carmen about all this.

His elation vanished as Lochan thought about Kosatka again. The image of the invasion fleet approaching the planet, as it had been when the *Oarai Miho* entered jump space, haunted his memory. What was happening there? Was Carmen all right?

———

Carmen, once again looking out a high window in the Central Coordination Building, narrowed her eyes as she studied the enemy-held buildings facing her. The sun was setting, painting the higher portions of the tallest structures in pink and gold, like some fairy city. If fairies fought wars that wrecked the buildings their ingenuity could construct.

The enemy had launched one attack at midmorning, thrown back by defenders energized by the sight of invasion fleet shipping being blown apart in the space above the planet. Since then, the invaders had been quiet. Carmen didn't trust that but also didn't know what it portended.

She leveled her rifle, using the scope to magnify the images as Carmen slowly panned across what she could see. There was motion, but not the sort of movement that spoke of troops moving up for another attack. She'd seen that often enough to know how it felt, the slow, erratic increase in detections of movement, the buildup in enemy communications, the sense of unseen pressure getting ready to unleash toward her. This felt different.

Like . . . less pressure.

She'd found a landline link in this room and plugged into it for communications that were mostly free of jamming. Setting her scope to download what it was seeing, she sent out a report. "I don't know what's going on opposite the Central Coordination Building, north side. It feels like the enemy may be pulling back."

Hearing Loren Yeresh's voice respond was a pleasant surprise if also disorienting. Loren belonged to a different time, when this city had been a living thing instead of a war zone. "Carmen, we're getting similar reports, but nothing solid. If they're falling back to the north, you should be able to spot movement from their forces south of you through adjacent buildings as they try to join up with the others."

"I'll go look," Carmen said. "I might not be able to find

a working landline connection on that side, so I'll report as soon as I can."

"Sure. Be careful."

"What could happen?" Carmen unplugged her rifle from the landline and hastened through the deserted hallways toward the east side of the building. Many stretches of the hall were untouched by battle, creating the eerie illusion that nothing had really happened, that outside everything was normal, perhaps the very early close-to-dawn hours when this building was almost deserted and the lack of sound outside meant peaceful sleep instead of wary combatants for the moment lacking targets.

Some executive had occupied a nice corner office with big windows that faced west and north. The desk had been left in perfect condition, everything lined up neatly. Everything about the office, in fact, carried the mark of someone who demanded an almost sterile level of perfection.

Carmen reached out as she crawled toward the windows, shoving the perfectly aligned desk contents into a jumble.

A landline link sat in the floor next to the desk. She pulled out the link wire from her scope and plugged in her rifle. Symbols appeared on the scope when Carmen looked through it, confirming that the landline link was active.

Reaching the miraculously unbroken windows, she lay flat on her stomach and sighted through her rifle's scope, scanning the buildings across the way.

There. Something. Something else. There. Carmen waited, spotting more flickers of movement. "Are you guys copying this?"

"Yeah," Loren replied. "Getting some analysis done now. But our gut feeling is you're seeing movement to the north, like you thought you saw at the other location."

"Are they concentrating their forces?" Carmen asked, her eye to her scope as she continued to track her view across the windows of the facing building.

"We're trying to get someone in position to confirm, but we think they may be withdrawing everyone to the north."

"Withdrawing? You mean evacuating the city?"

"Maybe," Loren said, his voice cautious. "If they pulled out to the north, they could head for Ani and try to link up with the rebel forces there. That's their only chance. They're cut off here, isolated, without any way to get more food or ammunition. They can maintain power for a while using solar in places we can't hit, but not at a level necessary for combat operations."

Carmen squinted, zooming in more with her scope as the setting sun sent its rays directly into the windows of the building opposite. "Did you see that? Clear as day. A half dozen soldiers running north through the building."

"Yeah. Got it. I'll notify command."

"Are we going to let them go?" Carmen asked, feeling angry at the idea.

"Oh, hell, no. I've heard the combatant commanders talking. They've been hoping this would happen. When the enemy tries to retreat across Centrum under cover of darkness, they're going to find things a little difficult. Carmen, I need you there."

"Dominic is wounded. He's in the basement of this building."

Loren took a moment to reply. "I need you there."

"I need to keep an eye on Dominic!"

"If we take out the enemy forces in this city, Dominic will be safe. We need good tactical intelligence to take out the enemy. I need you at Centrum."

"Dammit, Loren, I'm a volunteer! You can't order me to go there!"

"I'm asking you to volunteer to go there."

Carmen lowered her face to the floor, gritting her teeth in anger. He was right. She knew he was. And she hated knowing that and knowing what she had to do. "Okay," she muttered.

"Thanks." Loren was smart enough to leave it at that.

Carmen unplugged her rifle and wriggled backward to ensure she wasn't seen from the buildings opposite her, finally getting onto her feet in the hall and running. She wanted desperately to stop by and see Dominic, but the sun was setting and the enemy was moving and there was no time to waste and she hated this war and the people who'd started it.

On the ground floor, strewn with the castoffs of battle and scarred by fighting, Carmen saw the remnants of Dominic's unit gathering. "What's going on?" one of the officers called as she ran by. "We got an alert to prepare for an advance."

"The invaders are withdrawing to the north to try to escape the city," she called in reply. "We're going to hit them as they try to cross Centrum."

The low cheer that answered her words sounded almost like the growls from a pack of wolves seeing their prey stumble.

She had to run a few blocks to the west to get past the edge of the area to the north held by the invaders, dropping to a walk occasionally to catch her breath. Going past the edge of the defender's perimeter on the southwest corner of the enemy enclave, she warned the soldiers there of the enemy withdrawal and turned north, heading for the area of the city known as Centrum.

Urban architects had been enjoying a golden age as humanity spread out to the stars and new cities rose on new planets. The ones who had laid out Lodz had made it almost two cities, divided by a broad rectangle of mass transit lines, parks, plazas, and pathways called Centrum. Centrum ran straight from the east to the west between the north and south parts of Lodz as if a huge bulldozer had cut a path over half a kilometer wide through the middle of the city. Some residents of Lodz loved Centrum, others hated it, but in a few years it had already become an icon of the city.

And now that open area was, paradoxically, a barrier to the enemy withdrawal to the north. In order to get out of Lodz and head for the region around Ani where they could find refuge, the invading troops would have to pass through Centrum. They were going to try at night, whose darkness offered far less cover than it once had but was still better than trying to cross that open space in daylight.

By the time Carmen got to the edge of Centrum the sun had nearly set, dark shadows stealing across the plazas and parks. An open-air amphitheater was being turned into a hastily fortified strong point as Carmen reached it. She went a little farther, finding the piece of public sculpture most people called the Torch, a hand rising from the ground and holding aloft a torch in what Carmen had been told was a mimicry of a famous monument somewhere on Old Earth. The narrow ledge running around the base of the Torch's "flame" offered Carmen an elevated view of the parts of Centrum east of her, which was where the invaders should try to cross.

She settled down, grateful for the chance to lie there, feeling guilty about leaving Domi. After a moment, Carmen picked up her rifle and began trying to find a link.

She locked in to the net surprisingly quickly. Enemy jamming was falling off as they abandoned equipment for which they could no longer supply power, and because with the loss of the invasion fleet in orbit and the destruction of their last shuttles and warbirds they no longer had means to jam broad areas from above.

Carmen knew what it was like to feel trapped, without enough resources and too many enemies all around. She wondered what morale was like in the enemy ranks.

"Carmen?"

She perked up as Loren Yeresh's voice came over her comm link. "Here. I'm in position."

"I see. That's a beautiful observation spot, Carmen. Headquarters is going to want the best feed you can give us of what's happening east of you."

"That's why I'm here," Carmen said, lowering her eye to the scope and beginning to study the ground to the east. "Have we been able to confirm the withdrawal has been ordered?"

"We've been able to confirm that enemy units are withdrawing, but it seems more like a mutual decision to run like hell than a coordinated operation under unified command," Loren said. "Their high command tried to make it down to the surface. They were aiming for somewhere around Ani."

"Tried? Did any of them get down?"

Loren laughed. "Oh, yeah, they all reached the surface. But they were going a lot faster than they should have been when they got there, courtesy of our warships in orbit. There are some new craters outside Ani where the enemy high command 'landed.'"

Carmen felt her lips draw back in a smile that had more snarl to it than anything else. "We've cut off the head of the dragon. The body can still do a lot of damage as it flails about."

"Let's see how much of the body we can take down tonight. Am I seeing something?"

"Yeah," Carmen said, zooming in her scope. "Scouts, I think, checking to see if there's a safe way across."

"The forces on the north side and to the east and west have been ordered to hold fire until the main body of the enemy starts across Centrum. We don't want them holing up in the buildings facing Centrum instead of trying to cross. Our forces to the south are going to start moving forward to push the invaders into Centrum."

"Good." Forces to the south. That would include the remnant of Domi's unit. She felt guilty relief that he wouldn't be among those attacking what must be an increasingly desperate enemy in the dark.

She kept catching glimpses of the scouts moving forward, encountering no opposition as the defending forces melted away before them to avoid warning the enemy of the trap that Centrum already was. "Loren, I'm seeing a big surge of movement on the south side of Centrum. It looks like they're starting across in strength."

Immediately after that gunfire and other sounds of battle erupted to the south, the sounds muffled and distorted by the buildings between the fighting and where Carmen was in Centrum. "More movement. The attacks to the south have spooked them, I think. They're coming across, Loren!"

He didn't answer.

The reply came in the form of a sudden explosion of fire from the eastern and western sides of Centrum facing the enemy withdrawal. Carmen saw the shadowy shapes of enemy soldiers break into runs, abandoning attempts to sneak through the darkness, stampeding north to where they thought cover from attack awaited.

Moments later the roar of battle sounded from the buildings to the north as the blocking force there opened up.

The enemy kept running forward. They knew they couldn't go back. She'd wondered if they had any chaff grenades left, but none popped, proving the enemy soldiers were out of concealment munitions and leaving them exposed.

Mortars whomped in the distance. Flares appeared overhead, illuminating with harsh light the figures of the enemy caught in the open, increasingly frantic groups of invaders rushing in different directions as fire flayed them from every side. Other mortar rounds fell among them and exploded, cutting down attackers as they surged to and fro among the sidewalks and stumps of ornamental trees and broken benches and scarred pieces of public art.

Carmen kept her scope moving to transmit as much of the situation as she could to those viewing the information back at headquarters. But every once in a while she paused to aim and fire at a figure who was clearly giving orders, clearly someone in authority. She felt no particular hate for the average enemy fighter, even a little regret when allowed time to think about having to kill them, but their officers, their leaders, were another matter. If they'd come from Mars, the officers had been drawn from the ranks of gang chiefs and associates, or jeds in the Thark and Warhoon mobs, or from executives and enforcers for oligarchs and dictators. Carmen had spent her youth fearing them and now pitied them not at all as they died.

Where had the others come from? The unemployed

masses of Old Earth and the Old Colonies? Men and women whose jobs and lives had become obsolete and unneeded? Or people with options, other ways to make it, who had chosen the one that had led them here to assist in trying to enslave the world of Kosatka?

They'd have to sort out the prisoners when this was done. For now, Carmen tracked the activity, aiming and firing whenever she saw a leader, watching others die as Kosatka's defenders hit them from every side and above.

They didn't break all at once. Carmen started seeing individuals and small groups who dropped to the ground and huddled there like small children hiding from monsters. Others dropped their weapons and stood still, arms raised in pleading.

From those small beginnings it spread, like a chemical reaction that raced through a solution. One moment the enemy was still striving to cross Centrum, pushing against the defenders, and the next the invaders were milling about, all direction lost, no longer fighting. A large group that Carmen could see held out a few moments longer. Perhaps they were former professional soldiers from an Old Colony or part of Old Earth. Or maybe places like Apulu were already developing that sort of professional military. But, whoever they were and wherever they'd come from, they could tell when further resistance would mean nothing but certain death. They, too, dropped their weapons and raised their hands to surrender.

Carmen watched Kosatka's forces moving into Centrum, collecting weapons and herding the prisoners into groups that were forced to sit with their hands on their heads. "Loren? Is it done here?"

"Yeah," he answered, sounding as tired as she felt. "No fighting registering anywhere around Centrum. If anybody got away into surrounding buildings, they're lying low, and we'll have to dig them out when daylight comes."

"What about Drava?"

"The same thing seems to be happening there. An attempt to withdraw toward Ani while we cut them to pieces.

Getting Ani back is still going to be a struggle, but we hurt these scum bad, Carmen."

She held her position a while longer, streaming video to headquarters, but eventually Loren told Carmen that was no longer needed. Getting down off the Torch was unexpectedly difficult, her muscles having stiffened considerably during the time spent lying on the ledge.

The last flares overhead were fading, being replaced in portions of Centrum by bright lighting as some of the public light poles were turned back on for the first time since the invaders had landed. Carmen walked slowly through lighted patches and back into darkened areas between them, her mind numb with weariness and spent emotion. But she jerked to awareness as she heard the low crack of an energy pulse weapon being fired. The fighting had stopped. Why the hell was someone firing a weapon?

She headed in the direction of the sound, hearing the crack of a second discharge.

Carmen finally spotted a group of Kosatka's forces standing, weapons in hand. A large number of disarmed prisoners were sitting on the ground near them, under guard.

A major was near the sitting prisoners. Two bodies sprawled not far from him. The major was in the act of pulling a third prisoner to his feet.

Carmen broke into a run, bringing her rifle up. "Hey! Halt!"

The major got the prisoner erect and stood back, leveling his pulse rifle toward the prisoner's head.

"Stop!" Carmen yelled, wondering why no one else was doing anything.

The major's finger was reaching for the trigger when Carmen rested the muzzle of her rifle against the side of his head. "I said *stop*."

"What?" Only the major's eyes moved, giving Carmen a sidelong look whose icy emptiness chilled her. "What the hell do you think you're doing?"

Carmen kept her rifle muzzle against his head. "What the hell do *you* think *you're* doing, sir?"

"Cleaning house. Eradicating vermin. Go away," the major said, his voice flat.

"No," Carmen said. "Lower your weapon."

"I'm ordering you to drop your weapon and get out of here. You're threatening a superior officer and disobeying orders in a war zone. I could have you shot."

Carmen shook her head. "I don't have to obey an illegal order or stand by and let you commit atrocities. Did I mention that I'm intelligence? This scope has been recording everything you're saying and doing. It's already been uploaded, Major. You can either turn yourself in or wait for someone to show up and arrest you."

The major hesitated, appearing uncertain.

Some of the other soldiers nearby finally moved, a lieutenant reaching to gently pry the major's weapon from his grasp.

The major stared about him wordlessly, then abruptly sat down, his head buried in his hands.

The lieutenant looked at Carmen, ashamed and confused. "We didn't know what to do. He said . . . and . . ."

"Lieutenant," Carmen interrupted, "you all knew what you should do."

"But they—"

"We're not them."

The lieutenant nodded, avoiding her gaze.

Carmen saw some officers running their way and stepped back. As an angry colonel took control of the situation, Carmen turned and walked off.

So easy. So very easy to stand back, to do nothing. It frightened her to see how quickly some of Kosatka's people had fallen into that.

By the time she made it back to the Central Coordination Building another dawn was beginning to paint the sky and Carmen's mind was a gray fog in which fatigue and shock swirled together. The building felt deserted as Carmen made her way to the basement, past the regions of darkness to the emergency medical station.

The room was empty except for two pallets that each held a body, sheets pulled up over their faces.

Trembling, Carmen raised each sheet enough to look on the face of the dead. Neither was Dominic. She staggered back into the hallway, shaking with relief but also confused and too tired to think.

"Hey," someone said. Carmen saw a couple of volunteers approaching. "Is there anybody in there?" the one who had already spoken added.

"Just . . . two dead," Carmen managed to answer.

"Two dead." The volunteers went in, crouching to get identity readings and enter the location of the bodies on their pads. "We're going to make sure they're picked up," the first told Carmen as they left the room. "Was one of them someone . . . ?"

"No," Carmen said. "Do you know where they went? Were taken? The wounded in here?"

"They should have been evacuated to hospitals in the city. Those are all up and working again on backup power."

"Thank you." Carmen leaned back against the hard, cold wall behind her, unable to stay on her feet.

"Are you okay? Do you need anything?"

"I just . . . have to rest." Carmen let her back slide down the wall until her bottom hit the floor. She had a vague sense of dropping to her side, her rifle cradled in her arms, before exhaustion overtook her and she finally slept.

L ochan had long since learned that for the most part the freighter *Oarai Miho*, like most freighters, confined the sounds and vibrations it generated to those of the life support systems. The gentle whisper of the fans circulating air, the soft gurgle of pumps moving liquids here and there, the low hum of a small robotic cleaner passing as it vacuumed up the dust that somehow appeared as if spontaneously generating out of the air. At odd and irregular intervals there'd be louder noises, scrapings and bangs and rattles, often accompanied by the distant echo of obscenities and curses as the crew worked on some piece of equipment.

But on rare occasions a series of mild jolts would mark the firing of thrusters pitching the ship around to face in a different direction, followed by a deeper, heavier vibration that rolled through the ship as the main propulsion fired to accelerate or slow down the *Oarai Miho*.

Lochan lay in his bunk, trying to figure out why that was happening now. If his memory was right, they were still a ways from the next jump point. And in any event, the freighter had been on a vector directly for that jump point, curving across the outer edges of Tantalus Star System from the point they'd arrived at from Kosatka and ending at the jump point for Eire. The *Oarai Miho* shouldn't have to maneuver at all before jumping out again.

He rolled up to a sitting position and tried activating the desk display. Since the lifeboat incident it sometimes wouldn't come on, obviously blocked on orders from the captain. Other times it did activate, perhaps reflecting a system reset that required someone in the crew to notice that Lochan's display was once again active and selectively shut it off again.

This was one of the lucky times. The display came to life, Lochan bringing up the image of the freighter and its path through space.

Everything looked the same. Why was the main propulsion lit off?

Had he felt thrusters firing before that? Had that been what woke him up? But in the image this freighter still seemed to be aligned with the same vector it had been using since arrival.

Lochan scratched his head, puzzled. Maybe if he asked for the projected course, he'd see some indication of why this ship's main propulsion was lit off.

The line extending outward from the *Oarai Miho*, indicating both her path through space and by its length her velocity, still pointed along the same curve. But the length was steadily shortening.

The freighter was braking velocity. Why? There wasn't anything around to explain that. Aside from the pieces of the former pirate ship that were still tumbling off into empty space, the only other human objects the display showed were this ship, and far off, back along the same vector, the freighter *Bruce Monroe*. The *Bruce Monroe*'s path exactly matched that of the *Oarai Miho* because the most efficient vector between the two jump points was the most efficient vector. Every ship followed the same one, and every maneuvering system would set the same vector with only tiny variations.

Lochan sat on his cabin's bench/bunk, staring perplexedly at the display as the freighter's main propulsion kept rumbling and the line marking the ship's velocity got shorter and shorter.

Eventually, it hit zero.

The main drive kept going, and the line began growing again.

In the opposite direction. The same vector, but reversed.

They were heading back toward the jump point for Kosatka.

And then, Lochan suspected, if this ship couldn't turn him and Freya over to the invasion fleet, it would jump for Hesta and deliver the two of them to Scatha there.

CHAPTER 15

Lochan leaned back, thinking. Had the captain decided on her own to return to Kosatka? That seemed unlikely given her earlier tirades about having to keep to schedule. More likely the captain had received new orders, perhaps from that agent Freya had warned about. There didn't appear to be any other plausible explanation for a freighter to break from its scheduled runs and head back to a place where a war was being fought.

From what he'd last seen, the invaders very likely controlled space around Kosatka. Even if the defenders had somehow triumphed, would they still have the means to intercept an "innocent" freighter passing through Kosatka on its way to Hesta? One way or another, Lochan figured that he and Freya were once more looking at trips to Scatha or Apulu whether they liked it or not.

He hadn't thought that he was that important. And certainly so far he hadn't had much success in getting help for Kosatka. But maybe Scatha, Apulu, and Turan knew something that Lochan didn't. Maybe their own information from other star systems was that aid for Kosatka was finally likely to come. Or maybe the empire builders were worried that their invasion of Kosatka might provoke a response if someone like Lochan was free to gather support.

Or, perhaps, this wasn't about him so much as it was about Freya Morgan. Kosatka was already fighting for its life and freedom. But Catalan, as far as Lochan knew, was as yet untouched by direct aggression. Making sure that Catalan remained isolated and weak might be a priority for Scatha, one well worth extra efforts to keep Freya from reaching Eire and other star systems.

Now what? What could he and Freya possibly do to get out of this mess? Lochan knew he wasn't anyone's idea of an action hero. Freya, on the other hand, clearly had some skills not usually found in trade negotiators. But they were stuck on this ship, in a star system without any permanent human presence. How could the two of them take control of this ship and maintain that control long enough to get to Eire?

There wasn't anything else that could change the course of the *Oarai Miho*. And there wasn't any way left to escape with the lifeboat having been blown to pieces.

Where would they escape to? The only other possible refuge was the *Bruce Monroe*, quite a few million kilometers away behind them.

Though that would change, Lochan realized as he stared morosely at his desk display. Instead of the distances between the two ships remaining fairly steady as both headed for the jump point for Eire, the two ships would now be getting steadily closer as the other ship kept heading for Eire and this one headed back for Kosatka.

Down the same vector, in opposite directions.

They wouldn't collide, of course. Lochan was no expert on ship maneuvers, but he knew that ships in space always kept some distance between them for safety. The *Oarai Miho* would ensure that its trajectory was a little off that of the *Bruce Monroe*. As little as the *Oarai Miho* could manage, of course, because any deviation from the most economical path between jump points would cost at least a little extra time and money. Also, of course, "little" in space would be at least a few hundred kilometers.

Too bad he and Freya couldn't jump ship and . . .

Could they?

Lochan frowned at his display, remembering a story that Carmen had told him that she'd been told by Mele Darcy about something that guy Rob Geary had done.

The *Oarai Miho*'s main propulsion cut off. The freighter was now settled on its vector back. Lochan did a quick check, hoping no one in the crew would notice what he was checking or guess why.

The *Oarai Miho* was projected to pass the *Bruce Monroe*, the closest the two ships would get, at a distance of two hundred kilometers, plus or minus fifty kilometers.

Not exactly walking distance.

But momentum and a long enough lead and jumping off in the right direction might add up to make it all feasible.

Maybe not all that smart, but feasible. And what other alternatives existed? This idea might work. Or he might know just enough to think up this plan and not know nearly enough to realize that it was impossible. If he was wrong, it'd mean a lonely death.

Freya Morgan might have more practical knowledge to judge the merits of the plan, but how could he talk to her about this? They were confined to their cabins, and Lochan wasn't foolish enough to think there was anyone else he could trust to pass notes between them. His choices came down to waiting for her to contact him, hoping she'd come up with something, or plan on his own and go find her when the time was right, regardless of risks.

Waiting for someone else to fix things usually meant nothing got fixed. Lochan had learned that the hard way before leaving Franklin.

His pad held some programs that could handle the calculations, ensuring that no one on the ship would spot them. He loaded in the data he had on the paths of the *Oarai Miho* and the *Bruce Monroe*, finishing just before his desk display went dead again.

He thought about two hundred kilometers of empty

space. About the infinite cold and infinite nothing he would have to dare to try this.

Lochan stared at his hands where they rested on the small desk, remembering his frustration at having to leave Kosatka to its fate as the invaders approached. Remembered wishing that he could do something more, could fight like Carmen could. That wasn't him. It never had been. Where someone like Carmen would instantly act or react, making the moves necessary to save their own life, Lochan knew that he'd hesitate and think and try to figure out the best thing to do. *"You shouldn't feel badly about that,"* Carmen had insisted more than once. *"There are things that call for acting without thinking, but there are also things where people need to think, then act. Too many of them act without thinking even then. We need people like you who think."*

He certainly had time to think now. But he had a suspicion that deep down inside he'd already made up his mind. The problem would be figuring out how to do it if Freya wasn't in a position to help.

But, as Carmen always said, he was pretty good at figuring out what to do if given the time.

Carmen had woken up in the afternoon, feeling as if her entire body was one big bruise. But her mind was clear enough to recall the conversation early that morning so she started walking to the nearest hospital in search of Domi.

Once there, she felt dirty and unkempt in the sterile corridors of the hospital, her fatigues and her body reeking of too many days without any opportunity to get clean, her hands and face still marked with dirt and smoke, her rifle a deadly contrast to the lifesaving devices around her.

But there were other soldiers in the hospital, some providing security in case stray enemy soldiers showed up, some visiting injured comrades, and some delivering new wounded. And far too many who'd already been wounded and received treatment.

"Captain Dominic Desjani," she asked the information desk, dreading what reply she might receive.

"Identification," the desk bot asked in reply.

Feeling her heart lift at what seemed like a positive response, Carmen tapped her lower arm with the ID chip emplaced in it against the bot sensor.

"Volunteer Officer Carmen Ochoa," the bot commented. "Registered next of kin. Access authorized. Floor five, section four, bay nine."

Domi was here. He was alive.

"Thanks," Carmen said. People still did that with bots, saying thanks to something that didn't even register the courtesy. She wasn't sure why they did that. But it didn't hurt.

She rode a crowded elevator up alongside a pair of worn-out doctors who seemed to be having trouble staying awake. "Can I get you guys anything?" Carmen asked. "Coffee?"

"Thanks, but we've got some waiting," one of the doctors replied with a quick look at Carmen. Her eyes lingered on the rifle. "We're not expecting any more trouble here, are we?"

"No," Carmen said. "I'm visiting my husband."

"Oh, good! Um, I mean . . ."

"I understand." Carmen nodded around her. "They didn't damage this place?"

"No," the other doctor said. "They probably wanted to be sure it was completely intact when they took over. Didn't work out that way, though."

The elevator stopped on the fourth floor, and the two doctors moved to get off. "Thank you," Carmen called after them.

"Just doing our jobs," the second doctor said, but he smiled at her as he left. "Thank *you*."

Carmen got off on the fifth floor and followed the signs, not wanting to bother pulling out her pad for personalized directions.

Bay nine had several occupants, all but one of whom were either asleep or sedated.

Dominic looked over as she came in. He grinned.

She stumbled to his bed, wiping away from her dirty face tears that had unexpectedly appeared. "Hi, Domi."

"Hi, Red." He reached up for her hand. "Good to see you safe. We got lucky."

"Sort of. You lost a few pounds."

"Yeah," Dominic said. "Nothing I can't live without. It might take a little while for them to set me up with a prosthetic. Sudden high demand for those, you know? And eventually they can try regrowing the part of my leg that's gone. I hear knees are still a little tricky."

She sat down on the side of the bed, gazing at him. "I seem to be more upset than you are."

"I'm probably still numb. And realizing how lucky I am." He looked at her in a way that made Carmen feel embarrassed. "Hey, Red. I'm going to have some time off. Convalescing, you know. Maybe we could find something to do."

"If you don't have half a leg, and there's no prosthetic," Carmen said, shaking her head, "you're going to be stuck in bed while you're convalescing."

His smile took on an unexpectedly wicked aspect. "Maybe we can think of ways to pass the time while I'm, um, stuck in bed."

She laughed. "Maybe."

Dominic's smile faded. "Seriously, though. What would you think of starting a family?"

"We're already . . . you mean have kids? Now?" Carmen waved around. "We're in a city that's half-wrecked, there are still the remnants of an invading army on the planet, you're lying there with half a leg gone, and you want to knock me up? That's what seems like a good idea to you? What have they got you on?"

"It's not meds talking, Red." Dominic looked away, upset. "I could have lost something more important than my leg, you know."

"If that's what's worrying you, we can have a bunch of your little guys frozen," Carmen said. "Available in case of need."

"That's not it. Really. Red, it could have been you. Or either one of us could have been killed. I've been talking to some of the others in here," Dominic added earnestly, gesturing to the other beds. "There's going to be a pause now, a break in big hostilities. Because we hurt them bad. They can't come back in strength tomorrow. But in another year or so, maybe a couple of years, they might come back."

"And you want me walking around nursing a baby when that happens?" Carmen asked.

"If it's ours," he said.

She looked down, sighing, not wanting to reject the idea out of hand but also worried for reasons that went back to her own childhood. "Domi, you're being romantic, thinking of something that doesn't just symbolize the future but is the future, and I'm being practical, seeing all the problems. I guess that's how men and women think of children. The men are all about the promise and the potential, and the women worry about what can go wrong and all the demands. Here I am, the person who gives speeches about not losing hope, and I'm afraid to risk something that's all about hope. Let me think about it. You might have second thoughts as well, you know."

"I might. Red, something tells me that Kosatka is going to need more Desjanis."

Carmen gave him a cross look. "And why are you certain they won't be Ochoas?"

"Good point. We haven't discussed that. How about if the girls are Desjanis and the boys Ochoas?"

"Turnabout? All right. But that doesn't mean I'm agreeing to starting anytime soon! Not yet."

"Fair enough." Dominic sagged back in bed as if exhausted by the brief conversation.

"Look at you, overstressing yourself," Carmen chided, fussing with his pillow. "Do you need anything? Stop talking strategy with your fellow wounded and get the rest you need."

He smiled. "Hey, you know what else I heard? The government is thinking about creating a royal family."

"A what? You mean, like a queen? For Kosatka?"

"Yeah. Because, what do we look to that makes us all Kosatka? There are political parties and stuff, but those divide, too. If there was a royal family that had no political power but served as symbols of Kosatka, they'd be something everyone could rally around. Can you imagine if the call to arms had come from Kosatka's prince or princess instead of First Minister Hofer?"

Carmen made a scoffing laugh. "That's crazy."

"Red, you've told me that one of the problems on Mars was that there wasn't anything to tie everyone together. It was lots of different groups with different agendas, and when that all fell apart no one knew what to turn to. Right?"

"Right," Carmen agreed reluctantly.

"Maybe it's not a bad idea. I mean," Dominic added, "as long as they don't have any real political power."

"Maybe. Where would we get a royal family from?"

"Import one from Old Earth, maybe. Or just pick someone who seems right. That's how all royal families started originally, right?"

"I suppose. But none of that will matter unless we get help," Carmen added. "We would've been in a hopeless situation if that ship from Glenlyon hadn't shown up and helped. A royal family might make a nice symbol, but what we need now is for Lochan to make it to Eire and convince others to finally offer some real assistance."

"Lochan's a lot tougher than he looks," Dominic said. "I mean, in ways that matter."

"He is," Carmen agreed, worrying about her friend and hoping he was safely almost to Eire by now. "I'm glad that you see that, too. How long are you going to be in here?"

"They're already talking about moving me out, but there's a shortage of undamaged beds at recovery facilities. I heard they're using hotel rooms."

Carmen smiled. "I got to stay at the Kosatka Grand Centrum for a while after I first got to Kosatka. That'd be a nice place to spend a few days. I'll see if I can talk to somebody.

It looks out over Centrum and . . . where . . . Domi . . ." Sudden tears threatened her again.

"I know," he said. "Red, I know." He clasped her hand.

They sat like that for a long time, not speaking, but together.

Lochan Nakamura had spent a day and a half waiting, as the combined speed of both freighters closed the distance between them. A day and a half spent waiting for periods when his display worked so he could check the situation and try to refine his plans. A day and a half hoping that Freya would somehow contact him.

Lochan knew he couldn't claim any special skills or experience when it came to figuring out intercepts in space. But the math was the sort of thing any computer could handle with ease, and at the velocities he was dealing with straight Newtonian physics was apparently good enough. The math had given him a time when it had to be done, a period of time it should take, and a time when they should arrive.

He was hazy on the rest. Maybe Freya could fill in the blanks.

The optimum time to do it would be early in the ship's day. Fortunately, the captain had dictated that Lochan, and he hoped Freya, only got one meal a day, which arrived about noon. If he did things right, he could escape his cabin, find Freya, and they'd be gone long before anyone noticed.

The time had come, well past midnight on the ship's clock. He either acted now or gave up, but nervousness threatened to paralyze him. Oddly enough, it wasn't the thought of Carmen's depending on him that got Lochan moving but the memory of Mele Darcy telling him to trust his own abilities and judgment.

Lochan knelt by the door to his cabin. He couldn't hear anything outside. The crew hadn't bothered posting a guard because where could Lochan go? He didn't think there'd be much risk of encountering anyone else at this time. Only the crew members standing watch on the control deck and in engineering should be awake. If even they were.

He'd once owned a company that, among other things, manufactured locks. The company had failed for reasons that had everything to do with Lochan's mistakes and little to do with the quality of the locks and other products. The lock on his door was similar enough to the cheapest designs he'd sold back then that he knew how to pop it. Locks on cabins were sort of a luxury item on freighters, so no one invested in top-of-the-line models. As long as it held the door shut, that was enough.

A thin slice of what was supposed to be meat, though Lochan wasn't sure what creature it might have come from, had been easy to palm at his last meal. Trying to keep the spork would have been noticed instantly, but who counted pieces of mystery meat? As soon as it had cooled and dried, pressed under Lochan's pad, the slice stiffened into a rigid blade, apparently as hard as iron, and the length of Lochan's thumb. It wouldn't have been good enough to defeat a decent lock in a well-set door, but it was plenty good enough to slide between door and jamb so that Lochan could unset the lock he was dealing with.

Outside, the passageway was silent, dark with the lights dimmed. It felt a little absurd to take his carryall along, but Lochan did, walking as silently and quickly as he could to Freya's cabin.

That lock was also easily defeated, though Lochan jerked with worry every time he thought he heard someone approaching.

To his surprise, Freya didn't get up when he opened the door. She lay still in her bunk. He approached her carefully, reaching out as far as he could to nudge her, not even wanting to whisper in case her cabin was still bugged.

She didn't react. He nudged her again, harder. Still nothing. If not for the sound of her breathing deeply, Lochan would have worried if Freya was all right.

He finally crouched over her bunk, using his pad to illuminate her face. Freya didn't react when he pried open one eyelid. Her pupil looked unusually large and shrank slowly under the light from his pad.

They'd drugged her. Maybe in her meal, judging Freya to be far more dangerous than he was. Before about three years ago, they would have been right.

He got Freya across his shoulders, moving awkwardly in the small cabin, used one hand to grab her bag as well as his, and shuffled out of the cabin. He needed one hand to hold her across his shoulders, so Lochan had to bend his knees and put down both bags to close the cabin door behind him. Picking up the two bags again, he headed for the place he had seen while moving around days before with Freya.

The hatch had a label, of course. *Personnel Air Lock.* He remembered coming in through it, seeing the lockers on one side holding survival suits. And another important item fastened on the other side, a strap-on maneuvering system to let someone in one of the survival suits direct their course through space.

Lochan paused, breathing heavily from his burden. He'd expected Freya to identify any alarm here, but she was still out cold. He examined the hatch carefully but didn't see any obvious signs of an alarm.

The lights in the passageway began glowing steadily brighter, warning that the ship's day was about to begin. With no alternative, Lochan crouched to set Freya down, then rose again to open the air lock's inner hatch.

Nothing obvious happened in the way of alarms or alerts. Lochan dragged Freya inside the air lock, grabbed both bags, and stepped inside again to close the hatch.

He sat in the dark for a few minutes, getting his breath back and waiting to hear any reaction, dreading the rapid thump of running feet headed for the air lock. But nothing happened. He did hear one set of footsteps clumping by but at the leisurely pace of someone who wasn't in a hurry.

Checking the time, he saw that he still had an hour left. Lochan used his pad to provide light again since he didn't want to fumble around in the dark and maybe activate an alarm, or the outer door to the air lock, while looking for a light control. The lockers did hold survival suits, and Lochan was able to figure out the suit-controls-for-dummies they all used, ensuring the air recyclers were working and the suits ready to go. Their outer shells seemed far too thin to trust against the emptiness of space, but the basic design was over a century old. Tough enough to hold up to the usual bumps and other hazards, cheap enough to be easily replaced if something important in the suit failed.

Lochan saw something else, an emergency medical kit. Maybe there was something in there that would help Freya. Digging around in it he found an item labeled "broad spectrum drug/poison neutralizer." That sounded useful.

Wishing he could ask Freya's permission before taking this risk, but knowing he had no choice, Lochan opened her mouth, lifted her tongue, and meted out several drops.

Sitting back again, Lochan waited.

It only took about a minute before Freya's breathing changed, growing quicker and shallower. Worried, he bent over her just as Freya's eyes opened.

Her stiffened hand stopped just short of his neck.

"You're lucky I have good enough reflexes to override them when I recognized you," she whispered. "What the hell is going on?"

"They drugged you," Lochan explained, moving a bit away from her. "I don't know when."

"Me neither. I was being careful about my meals. They could have sent gas into my air vent, though, to knock me out, then followed up with something to put me in a deep sleep." Freya sat up cautiously, looking around. "Is this the passenger air lock? What are we doing here?"

"We're escaping."

"Do you have time to explain this? Where are we escaping to? Are we at Eire?"

Lochan shook his head. "We're still at Tantalus. They reversed the ship to take us back to the jump point for Kosatka."

"Oh, hell. How long was I out? And how are we going to . . . ?" She frowned at him. "You've got a plan?"

"Yeah. Since we're coming back to the jump point for Kosatka using the most economical trajectory, and since that other freighter, the *Bruce Monroe*, is coming from that jump point using the most economical trajectory, the ships are going to pass fairly close to each other."

"Really?" Freya gave the air lock's outer hatch a worried look. "What does *fairly close* mean?"

"A few hundred kilometers. I mean, practically touching in terms of space, you know."

She stared at him. "A few hundred kilometers?"

"Two hundred, plus or minus fifty. We get into two of these suits," Lochan explained. "And there's a maneuvering unit over there so we can accelerate and slow down a bit. We jump along the right vector at the right time, and we'll meet up with the *Bruce Monroe*."

"Which will be going along a different vector at a very high speed compared to us," Freya said. "Have you ever seen a bug hit a windshield? This would be a lot worse than that."

"Maybe the *Bruce Monroe* will change course a bit to pick us up," Lochan said, worried by her reaction. "They came from Glenlyon. We should be able to trust them."

Freya lay down flat again, looking up at the top of the air lock. "This ship is taking us back to Kosatka. The reason for that is obvious. There's no other way off, is there?"

"I don't think so."

"So, short of killing the crew and all the other passengers and taking the ship to Eire ourselves, this is our only way to avoid being turned over to the bad guys."

Lochan stared at her. "I have to admit that the *killing everybody else on the ship* option hadn't occurred to me."

"It wouldn't be easy, and we'd have some trouble explaining doing that when we got to Eire," Freya admitted. "I never would have thought of jumping to the *Bruce Monroe*, though."

"Really?"

"Yeah. Because . . . it's really insane. You know that, right?"

"I know of a guy who led a bunch of people in a jump across space to another ship," Lochan argued.

"How far did he jump?"

"It was . . . something like . . . a hundred meters?"

"Which is a little less than two hundred kilometers!" Freya sat up again, rubbing her head. "Whatever they used on me gave me a headache. Is there any aspirin handy?"

"Yeah," Lochan said, depressed. "So we're not doing it?"

"Who said we're not doing it?" Freya popped the pain-killers before giving him a small smile. "A couple of hundred kilometers across open space to a ship on a different vector in suits designed for emergency use. What could possibly go wrong? It's crazy, but it's our only chance. And if the worst happens . . . it's liable to be a whole lot less painful than whatever would be waiting for us at Scatha or Apulu."

"We *are* doing it?"

"We're going to try. Amazing idea, if I didn't say so. Crazy enough to maybe work. When do we have to jump?"

Lochan checked the time. "Thirty-two minutes."

"Plenty of time. Let's make sure everything on those suits works, especially the comms, and see if we can figure out how to use that maneuvering unit. And Lochan . . . thank you. You've given us a chance."

As they got into the suits, leaving the hoods off to conserve the air recyclers as long as possible, Freya gave him a questioning look. "Why didn't they also drug you?"

"I guess they weren't worried about me," Lochan said with a shrug.

"They were wrong."

It felt good to hear that.

Freya found an alarm attached to the outer hatch and disabled it. "They might not even realize we've left," she told Lochan. "Like I said, this is crazy. No one who really understands space would think we could do this."

"Eight minutes to go," Lochan said, checking his pad. "I've got a bearing we're supposed to jump out on, and this pad should show where we need to go to meet the *Bruce Monroe* if that ship keeps going where it has been going."

"Good." Freya eyed the maneuvering unit. "Do you mind if I take that? I don't have much experience with that sort of thing, but—"

"Be my guest. You've got more experience than I do. We tie ourselves together?"

"Yeah. Use two . . . no use three lines. We've got plenty. Leave about three meters slack between us. No! We need to tie ourselves together to form a single mass for the maneuvering thrust to direct! If you're on the end of a tether, your mass will swing all over the place and we'll veer all over space."

"Tie ourselves together?" Lochan asked, feeling awkward again.

"Tie ourselves tightly together," Freya said, frowning down at the line in her hands. "The maneuvering unit fits on my back. I'll strap that on, then you'll have to go in front. Put your back to me. Come on! Press in. I know it's a little weird, but just think of it as that sort of kinky date you never really went on."

Lochan backed up until he was pressed against her front, the thinness of the survival suits separating them more apparent than ever, her head just behind his. Passing the line back and forth, they tied themselves together securely.

They shuffled to the outer door, pausing again to pull their hoods on and activate the seals. Lochan watched the simple display inside the helmet light up with a series of reassuringly green telltales. He shifted the comm circuit to the one he and Freya had agreed on. "Hello?"

"Hi," she called back. "You're loud and clear. How am I?"

"It sounds like you're right behind me," Lochan said.

"Good. Do you have your pad fastened to something so you won't lose it?"

Angry with himself for not thinking of that, Lochan pulled a tether from the survival suit's belt and clipped it to the pad. "Now I do."

"All right. I've got both of our bags strapped to my belt, so we shouldn't lose those. How's the time?"

"Two minutes."

"Let's open that hatch."

Lochan reached, touching the control to cycle the air lock. The external mics on his suit picked up the sound of atmosphere being pumped from the air lock, a sound that faded into nothing as the air grew thin, then turned to vacuum.

The outer hatch opened, endless empty space beyond, and Lochan felt a sudden surge of fear. Could he take that next step? Or would he be paralyzed with fright?

Freya's arms tightened about him from behind. "We can do this."

"Are you scared?" Lochan asked, his breath feeling short.

"Hell, yeah. You?"

"Yes."

"I'll jump if you do."

He couldn't help laughing, thinking of them tied together. Somehow knowing that she was also scared made it easier for him to admit to and deal with his own fears. "Deal."

The seconds were counting down. Keeping his eyes locked on his feet, Lochan shuffled forward until he was balanced on the edge of the air lock, standing over an infinity of emptiness, his hands gripping either side. Five. Four. Three. Two. One.

Closing his eyes tightly, Lochan jumped. His stomach lurched as they abruptly left the freighter's artificial gravity and suddenly became weightless.

Aside from the lack of weight, it didn't feel exactly like falling. There was nothing pulling at him, nothing rushing past to give a sense of motion. Lochan opened his eyes, seeing nothing ahead but endless nothing spangled with stars.

The stars were slowly rolling past, which was Lochan's only clue that he had pushed off unevenly and was rotating.

"Let me see the pad," Freya's voice urged.

He held it up, using one gloved hand to brush off some moisture on the screen that had almost immediately stiffened into ice crystals.

"All right," Freya said. "I can see the maneuvering system controls slaved to my suit. We need to . . . let's finish turning around, then I'll light off the unit along the right vector."

Lochan waited, trying to calm the panic that occasionally threatened, as the stars slid past until the dark bulk of the *Oarai Miho* appeared to block out part of space. He and Freya were sailing away from the ship under the force of Lochan's initial push off from the air lock, but otherwise, they were still moving along the same vector as the ship they'd left. Conservation of motion. He wondered what Isaac Newton would think if he could see that law of physics displayed so clearly out here far from the world that Newton had never left.

There wasn't any sign of trouble on the darkened exterior of the freighter. No indication that anyone had noticed the departure of two passengers who were supposedly locked safely and separately in their own cabins.

"Hang on," Freya cautioned him.

The only thing he could hang on to with one hand was the line across his body holding them together, his other hand extended holding the pad so that Freya could see the vector they needed to aim for.

He felt a jolt of acceleration, the illusion of some gravity suddenly returning as the maneuvering unit fired, hurling them away from the freighter and, hopefully, toward the *Bruce Monroe*.

The stars stopped sliding past, steadying before him and on all sides. Lochan stared about him, startled by the feeling of being accelerated, yet without any other clue that his senses could detect of actually moving. The only thing close enough to have provided that kind of reference was the *Oarai Miho* behind them, and he suspected the freighter was already becoming just one more spot in the darkness of space as Lochan and Freya accelerated away.

The acceleration, and the false feeling of some gravity, stopped as Freya shut off the maneuvering unit. Lochan's ears and stomach flip-flopped again before settling into a lower-key state of discontent.

"We should be on track, Lochan," she said.

"Now all we have to do is hang here?" he asked.

"We're moving pretty damned fast. But, yeah, it'll feel like that. I'm going to call the *Bruce Monroe* in about half an hour. By then the *Oarai Miho* will be far past any meaningful turnaround point to catch us again, and the *Bruce Monroe* will have time to prepare for changing their own vector to pick us up. We're actually going to travel a lot more than two hundred kilometers because we're on a vector to intercept the *Bruce Monroe* as it approaches, crossing the two hundred kilometers separation between the ships *and* leading the *Bruce Monroe* by enough to meet up with it."

"What if the *Bruce Monroe* doesn't maneuver to match vectors?" Lochan asked.

"We'll have two choices. Bug on the windshield or wave as we go by."

"I'm still scared," he admitted.

"Me, too. There's someone back on Catalan I'd like to see again. Have you got anyone besides Brigit?"

"I don't *have* Brigit. But . . . Carmen. She's a friend. Just got married."

"On Kosatka? I hope she's all right," Freya said.

"I hope you get back to Catalan. Is your whole family there?"

"Such as it is out here," Freya said. "My parents stayed back on Lagrange Three, orbiting Earth. I've got a brother who went far out so who knows if I'll ever hear from him again."

"Far out? You mean one of those corporate colonies that went out as far as they could?"

"That's right." Old upset and irritation entered her voice. "To get away from interference and unleash their full potential, they said. I told him that he was crazy, that out that far there'd be no one to make the corporation owning the colony follow through on their promises to people like my brother and his family. But I was told I didn't understand and effective corporate governance would ensure all agreements were honored. Why is it people who are so cynical about some things are so willing to idealize other things?"

"Beats me," Lochan said, grateful for the distraction posed by the conversation. "As a rule, I believe in people, but I only trust the ones who've shown me they're worth trusting."

"Yeah. Right." He felt her head moving behind him as Freya looked around. "It's big. So big. We're so small. But I think what we do matters. Do you?"

"Yeah, I think so, too," Lochan agreed.

"I thought you were like that. Do you want to work together once we get to Eire? Maybe two of us, representing two star systems, can get a lot more attention than each of us individually."

"Yes," Lochan said. "If we can, sure. If we both make it."

Her laugh surprised him. "Either we both survive this, or neither of us will, Lochan."

They didn't talk for a while after that. To his surprise, Lochan found himself drifting off to sleep. Weightless, suspended in nothing, no changes outside the suit, he felt cradled by infinity. Would this be how it would feel when the air recycler on the suit finally gave out? That wouldn't be so bad, would it?

But he did want to see Carmen again. And Brigit. And get the help that Kosatka needed.

The sound of Freya's broadcasting startled him to full wakefulness again.

"Freighter *Bruce Monroe*, freighter *Bruce Monroe*, please respond. This is a humanitarian emergency. Please respond."

"Will the *Oarai Miho* hear that?" Lochan asked when Freya paused.

"They will if they're listening," she said. "I had to use the emergency circuit that everyone is supposed to monitor full-time so I'd be sure the *Bruce Monroe* would hear us."

Freya had repeated her call twice more, while Lochan waited with a sinking sense of failure, when a response startled him.

"This is the *Bruce Monroe* replying to unknown caller on all-ships emergency frequency. Are you on the *Oarai Miho*? Your signal doesn't seem to be coming from there."

"We are two individuals in open space," Freya replied. "Survival suits and a maneuvering unit. We're on a converging vector with your ship's trajectory and need rescue."

The reply took a while.

"Two individuals in suits in open space," the voice from the *Bruce Monroe* repeated. "I need to know the circumstances that led to that."

"We were being forcibly taken to Hesta. Confined against our will," Freya said. "I am Freya Morgan, trade negotiator for Catalan. With me is Lochan Nakamura, special representative of Kosatka."

They were waiting for a new reply from the *Bruce Monroe* when another, all-too-familiar voice sounded on the circuit.

"Those two are criminals! This is the captain of the *Oarai Miho*. Those two are saboteurs and thieves, responsible for the destruction of valuable property and the theft of items from this ship! They are . . . in league with the pirates! Do not pick them up!"

Freya responded the moment the captain stopped. "*Bruce Monroe*, this is Freya Morgan. The captain of the *Oarai Miho* is lying. She is in league with the pirates and is under the control of Scatha. I promise you that the government of Catalan will compensate you for any expense involved in matching vectors and rescuing me and Lochan Nakamura."

Lochan's pad had no sensors, and the survival suits could only handle close-in situations, nothing far away. They couldn't tell what either ship was doing as the *Bruce Monroe* and the *Oarai Miho* began arguing directly with each other.

Was the *Bruce Monroe*'s signal getting stronger? It should be, since they should be getting closer, and the energy of the signal wouldn't be spreading out through space as much.

How much warning would they have if the *Bruce Monroe* didn't pick them up on its visual sensors, track them, and maneuver to match vectors closely enough to recover them? Would they have a moment of awareness of the freighter suddenly there close, then an impact that wouldn't do the ship any good and end their adventure forever? Or would there be a brief glimpse of a far-off object blocking a few stars as it raced past them, followed by a long wait for the end?

"Hey, Lochan," Freya said, her voice low.

"Yeah?"

"Thanks. We got this far. You know how to show a girl a fun time."

"You're welcome. I've had a great time, too. We should do this sort of thing again."

Her laugh sounded reassuringly normal, without any stress underlying it. "No, thank you."

The sound of the incoming transmission felt so loud that Lochan winced. "Citizen Morgan, Citizen Nakamura, this is the *Bruce Monroe*. We are matching vectors and rigging the emergency recovery net. Stand by. If you have any remaining power in your maneuvering unit, try to shift your vector up three degrees and eighty degrees to starward. Be advised there's a risk of physical injury during recovery under these circumstances."

"A risk of physical injury," Freya murmured, then laughed again.

Lochan felt the maneuvering unit's thrust push at them

once more as Freya tried to match the vector shift that the *Bruce Monroe* had asked for. "We could get hurt?" he asked her, before he started laughing as well.

For just a moment, he understood how Mele Darcy probably felt at times like this. *What the hell. Let's do this.*

CHAPTER 16

The recovery net had been braided from special artificial fibers with an immense amount of flexibility, able to absorb and distribute force with an efficiency no natural substance could match. But when they slammed into it Lochan still felt as if he'd suddenly fallen face-first onto a street from the roof of a building.

The fact that, by chance, he was on the bottom when they hit, with Freya on top, meant that he also felt as if someone else had fallen on him from the roof of a building.

Lochan's breathing was still ragged when the net was pulled in, compressing around him and Freya to form a comforting cocoon that didn't tighten enough to hurt. They were pulled inside one of the *Bruce Monroe*'s big cargo air locks, the large hatch sliding closed behind them.

He wasn't sure if the air inside his suit was really starting to get bad or if it was his overactive imagination feeding his fears. When the net was pulled away, and a figure without a helmet appeared before him to signal he could remove his hood, Lochan gasped with relief.

The line holding him and Freya tightly together was cut, allowing them to move, but Lochan lay there, hurting, as the crew member knelt by him. "Anything broken, space cowboy?"

"I don't know," Lochan said. "I don't think so."

"What about you, valkyrie?"

"I'll live," Freya said with a groan. She slapped Lochan on the arm. "Come on. We made it."

Lochan got to his feet with the help of the crew member, seeing two others waiting for him and Freya. One was a solemn-looking man who somehow looked like the captain of the *Bruce Monroe* without having to announce the fact. The other was a short woman with a disconcertingly intense gaze.

The captain spoke into a nearby comm panel. "We've got them. Get us back on vector for the Eire jump point. Don't worry about sparing the fuel cells."

Lochan could hear the reply. "Aye. Getting back on vector at best acceleration."

"What's that other doing?"

"The *Miho*? Looks like he's trying to come about. He won't come within a hundred thousand kilometers before we jump out of Tantalus, though, even if he pushes as hard as he can chasing us."

"They're short one fuel cell," Freya said, grimacing as she stretched her back. "That might limit their ability to accelerate again."

"A fuel cell? Is that what accounted for the pirate ship?" the short woman asked.

"Maybe. The answer depends on who you are?"

The woman smiled. "Let's go talk somewhere private. Is that all right with you, Captain?"

The captain of the *Bruce Monroe* shrugged. "You've already guaranteed costs for this diversion from our course. Do what you like. Those two will have to double up, though. We're full up on passengers already."

"We're not that kind of partner," Lochan said hastily.

"Work something out with the other passengers, or I'll work it out for you," the captain said as he left the cargo air lock.

The short woman led the way to a stateroom that while small still felt large and luxurious after the cabins on the freighter. "The captain is letting us use his stateroom for privacy so we can speak candidly with each other," she announced.

Freya dropped into one of the two chairs the stateroom boasted. "And just who are you that the captain is willing to lend you his stateroom?"

"Officially on this ship's passenger manifest I'm Alice Norton, librarian. But to you two, I'm Leigh Camagan, a member of the governing council of Glenlyon."

Lochan, who'd been sagging with weariness against one wall, jerked to alertness. "You've been sent out to get help for Glenlyon?"

"Get help, hire help, buy help." Leigh Camagan looked from one of them to the other. "And you two are from Catalan and Kosatka. I assume your missions are the same?"

Freya examined Leigh Camagan closely before finally nodding. "Officially, I'm a trade negotiator. But what I'm looking for is the sort of help Catalan realized it needs. We're already blockaded. Not officially, but that's just a formality at this point."

"You saw what's happening to Kosatka," Lochan said to Leigh Camagan. "But I guess your ship is helping? That destroyer?"

"Yes," Leigh said, smiling for a brief moment. "You got lucky because that ship is commanded by someone who might be able to save the day if anyone can. But we have to assume the worst, that Kosatka might fall."

"Leaving both Catalan and Glenlyon isolated deep inside space controlled by three star systems that want to start their own empires," Freya commented. "I take it you're arguing that we have the same mission *and* the same priorities?"

"Yes. We all need the same thing. Sufficient force to repel aggression against any of our homes. And allies who will stand with us to deter any further aggression. The three of us can either compete for forces and allies, or we can cooperate."

"Kosatka trusts Glenlyon," Lochan said. "You know that. Both because of the old debt, and now because Glenlyon's destroyer came to help again."

"But can Glenlyon and Kosatka trust Catalan?" Leigh asked.

"Yes," Lochan said immediately, drawing a surprised look from Camagan, who had apparently expected debate. "If Freya Morgan represents who they are, then we can count on them."

"How much do you know about her?" Leigh Camagan asked.

"I know that she risked her life to save mine, that her priorities are the same as mine, and that she can be trusted to stand by her friends."

Freya smiled. "I'd say the same of you, Lochan. Thank you. But I don't know you, Council Member Camagan."

"I've heard of her," Lochan said. "From my friend. Mele Darcy told me that Leigh Camagan was someone she knew she could count on. If Mele says Leigh Camagan is to be trusted, then I won't question that."

"So you're the go-between in this relationship?" Freya asked, smiling again. "We don't all know each other, but we each know enough it seems."

"All politics is personal," Leigh Camagan said. "For my part, Lochan Nakamura, anyone like you with Mele Darcy's approval, which is not easily won, has my trust. And clearly Darcy approves of your judgment, so I will accept it in the case of Catalan's representative. So, here we are. The representatives of three star systems. Can we work together?"

Freya eyed her closely again before replying. "This is about more than the current emergency, isn't it?"

"Yes. We need something there when the next emergency happens, something that lets free peoples live without the fear of constant attack or predation. If we work together, we might be able to lay the foundation for treaties that will bind star systems to help each other without binding their peoples otherwise."

"You're talking about some kind of alliance," Lochan said. "A long-term set of mutual security agreements."

"Yes. I suppose so," Leigh Camagan said. "Do you think we can sell that to Eire and other star systems? And do it in time to make a difference in the fate of our homes?"

"We can try," Lochan said. "Nothing about agreeing to work together binds us to accept the final product if we think it's bad for the interests of our homes."

Freya Morgan nodded. "All right. As long as it's understood that we'll work together on a final product, but I'm not bound to it if it comes out wrong for Catalan, I'm in. But there's something else we need to think about."

"What's that?" Leigh Camagan asked.

"Scatha and its friends not only had a privateer waiting in this star system for us, they had an agent on the *Oarai Miho* who nearly forestalled our mission," Freya said. She leaned forward, eyeing Lochan and Leigh. "How certain are you that there isn't an agent of our enemies aboard this ship? Perhaps waiting to act until other attempts to stop us fail?"

Lochan looked at Leigh Camagan, who shook her head, her expression bleak. "I can't be certain that there's no one aboard this ship working for our enemies," she said. "That's why my real identity has been kept secret and why our plans involving *Saber* weren't divulged to even me or the captain of the *Bruce Monroe*."

"So we're still on guard," Lochan said. "And still in danger, until we reach Eire."

"I'm not relaxing at Eire," Freya commented. "I have old friends there, but I might have some new enemies as well."

"I understand," Leigh said. "I'm not relaxing either."

"In that case," Lochan said, "I suggest we practice being allies starting now. We can watch out for each other, and watch for trouble. I'm not going to fail Kosatka or my friends."

"You're on," Freya said.

"Agreed," Leigh Camagan said. "Now let's figure out your sleeping arrangements since you two say you're not *that* close. It'd be easier to protect each other if you were."

"I couldn't do that to Brigit," Freya said.

"Brigit?"

"It's a long story," Lochan said. "I guess we'll have plenty of time to tell it while we're watching each other to make sure none of us gets poisoned, drugged, kidnapped, or knifed in the back."

Saber accelerated back toward the jump point for Jatayu at point zero eight light speed. Even though she'd taken on more fuel cells from Kosatka's badly battered orbital facility, Rob was still concerned about having enough reserves to get through Jatayu and to Glenlyon if *Saber* ran into any more trouble on the way. But he couldn't afford to waste any time getting home.

He'd also taken aboard "Lieutenant Commander Ivanova" from *Shark*, as well as two wounded Marines and Mele along with the other Marine who could still walk, and the remains of the two Marines who had given their all for Glenlyon and their fellow Marines.

First Minister Hofer, in a transmission sent from his world an hour and a half earlier, looked weary and not particularly jubilant. Given how badly Kosatka's cities and other infrastructure had been damaged during the fighting, Rob had no trouble understanding why Kosatka's people weren't celebrating in the streets. Plus, there were still enemy forces operating around the third city of Ani, promising more fighting on the planet.

"I'm attaching to this transmission," Hofer said, "a message for your government, Commander Geary. It's long past time we made a formal commitment to each other, though Glenlyon might be forgiven at this point for wondering when Kosatka will start coming to your aid. Nonetheless, we mean to do it when we can.

"You need not worry about the three badly injured crew members from *Saber* who were sent down to intensive care facilities on the planet's surface. They will be given the best care we can, taken care of afterward, and returned to Glenlyon along with the two captured freighters Kosatka is yielding to Glenlyon as thanks for its assistance. It may take a while to put together trustworthy crews for those ships, but Kosatka will get them to you."

Hofer paused, managing a smile. "We're still fighting. We hope you'll have the chance to visit Kosatka someday when we're not facing imminent attack. May your ancestors watch over you as you journey back to Glenlyon. Hofer, out."

Vicki Shen snorted as the transmission ended. "Two freighters? There were five ships captured, including the passenger ship that surrendered specifically to *Saber*, and they're giving us only two."

"Do they know the role you played in getting *Shark* operational in time to make a difference?" Rob asked her.

"Commander Derian said he'd keep telling people until someone acknowledged it," she replied.

"According to what Mele heard, Derian is catching a little heat from his government for placing Kosatka's militia on the orbital facility under her command."

"Some people are idiots," Vicki Shen said with a sigh. "I owe Mele Darcy, too. None of us on *Shark* thought that the militia could hold off the invaders long enough. But she did it."

"She'll never bring it up," Rob said. "Mele doesn't work that way."

"I'm going to keep thanking her anyway."

"I'm going back to visit the wounded. Want to come along?" They found Mele in the small compartment holding the bunks for the Marines. Two of those bunks were empty. Two others held Corporal Giddings and Private Lamar.

"Is Doc Austin taking good care of you?" Lieutenant Commander Shen asked.

"Yes, ma'am," Giddings replied. "Three hots and a cot, and nothing to do all day but lie in my rack."

"Living the dream," Lamar agreed.

"As soon as you're well enough, you'll both be out of those racks," Mele warned them.

"Is there going to be a space burial for Griff Buckland?" Private Lamar asked. "I'd like to be there."

"Buckland would want a space burial?" Rob said.

"Yes, sir. He's one of those star believers, that new thing spreading out from the Old Colonies."

Vicki Shen nodded. "They prefer burial in space. Not drifting, but launched on a trajectory toward the nearest star."

Rob gave her a surprised look. "That's taking cremation to an extreme."

"They say everything came from stars, including everything that made up them, so it should all go back to the stars when they die," Shen explained. "It makes sense, actually."

"No grave marker?"

Shen laughed. "Captain, it's a star! Can you imagine a greater grave marker?"

"When you put it that way, no," Rob said. "Do we have the right materials aboard for a burial service in accordance with Buckland's beliefs?"

"Yes, sir. One of the sailors we lost, Petty Officer Ibori, was also part of that belief system. We can do their burials together before we jump."

"Good," Rob said. "Are you okay, Captain Darcy?"

Mele nodded. "Been worse. Oh, I need you to confirm some battlefield promotions. Giddings to sergeant, and Lamar and Yoshida to corporal. Gamba posthumous to sergeant, and Buckland posthumous to corporal."

Rob saw the looks of surprise on the faces of Giddings and Lamar. "I won't have any trouble approving those promotions."

"And I'll have my after-action report to you this afternoon so you can see it and approve transmitting a copy to Kosatka's government," Mele continued. "I want Kosatka to know what those militia sacrificed and accomplished on that facility."

Commander Shen nodded to her. "Back on Earth a lot of places have old battles whose memory still serves as foundations for their sense of identity. Thermopylae, Hastings, the Alamo, Puebla, Sekigahara, Sinharat . . . that's just a few. Maybe you helped forge Kosatka's sense of self."

Mele Darcy shrugged, looking to Rob as if she was uncomfortable with the idea. "I just want what they did to be known and remembered. It's more important that Glenlyon remember what Gamba and Buckland and my other Marines accomplished."

"Weren't you there, too, Captain Darcy?" Shen asked dryly.

Mele shrugged again. "I demanded a lot of my people. So did the situation. What matters is that they rose to those demands. If you'll excuse me, I need to get to work on that report."

Vicki Shen shook her head at Rob as they walked onward to visit the wounded members of *Saber*'s crew. "How does Darcy think she's going to make general with that sort of attitude?"

Rob smiled at the sarcasm. "She really doesn't care about that."

"She got downsized by Franklin, right? Any idea why?"

"Ask her and she'll tell you. She made a lousy private." Rob smiled crookedly. "There're few things worse than a private who really ought to be a general or a general who really ought to be a private."

"What about you?" Shen asked. "Before you left Alfar?"

It was Rob's turn to shrug. "I got tired of beating my head against walls trying to accomplish things." They reached the bunks with the wounded sailors in them, and Rob smiled at them, genuinely happy that they'd survived their injuries. "How are you guys doing?"

They smiled back, and for a moment he could find satisfaction in knowing their losses could have been a lot worse. He hadn't done a perfect job, but Kosatka had been able to repel the invasion, *Claymore* had been partly avenged, and *Saber* would make it home.

The return trip proved to be devoid of excitement, which was fine with Rob. Jatayu didn't betray any sign that any other ships had visited since *Saber* and the *Bruce Mon-*

roe. The destroyer raced across the star system without any side trips, "straight" along the curved vector from the jump point from Kosatka to that for Glenlyon.

The urge to get home, to learn what might have happened in *Saber*'s absence and the fear that he might have misjudged the danger to his home, made jump space even more difficult to handle than usual for Rob. He sweated out the days, trying not to take out his nerves on his crew.

The last minutes before arrival seemed the longest.

"There's another light," Ensign Reichert commented. "Way off to the right."

"Is it way off?" Lieutenant Cameron asked.

"Hell if I know. I've tried tweaking our sensors, but they still don't show anything except the image of the light. It's like it's there, but nothing is generating it."

"Preparing to leave jump space," Cameron said.

Vicki Shen called from engineering. "The ship is at full combat readiness."

The infinite gray of jump space went away and the infinite dark filled with infinite stars of real space appeared around *Saber*.

No alerts sounded. As Rob's head cleared, he saw no indication of trouble at Glenlyon Star System.

"The communications we're picking up are routine," the comms watch reported.

Rob let out a sigh of relief. "Stand down from full combat readiness. Go to standard ship's routine."

His hand reached to send his action report to the government, pausing just above it before finally touching the control. They'd see the light showing *Saber*'s return and immediately after get his report.

He'd labored over the wording, trying to keep it dispassionate and professional, trying not to make it sound like his own actions had been particularly laudable, emphasizing the importance of what others such as Mele Darcy and Vicki Shen had done. Knowing that the higher the rank someone had, the more likely that they'd only read the short summary paragraphs at the beginning, Rob had done his best to put everything important in those.

> . . . after destroying the enemy warship at Jatayu, I made the decision based on intelligence discovered at Jatayu to continue onward to Kosatka instead of immediately returning to Glenlyon. Full responsibility for that decision rests with me. Once at Kosatka, we discovered an invasion under way. I made the decision to support Kosatka's sorely pressed defenders, judging that our mutual enemies could not have enough forces to simultaneously assault Kosatka and Glenlyon. After sustained combat, the enemy invasion force was crippled, with two more warships destroyed. In addition, four ships of the enemy invasion force were destroyed and five captured. Fighting was continuing on the ground near one city on Kosatka when we left, but the invasion force had sustained severe losses and no longer posed a threat to Kosatka's control of its primary world. The combined forces of Scatha, Apulu, and Turan have taken a major blow and lost many military assets. Balanced against that, *Saber* sustained damage and we lost a total of ten personnel from ship's crew and the embarked Marines. Responsibility for these losses is mine. I made the command decisions involved.
>
> The freighter *Bruce Monroe* was seen to jump safely for Tantalus en route to Eire.
>
> I must single out for praise the actions of Captain Mele Darcy, Glenlyon Marines, who led the defense of Kosatka's orbital facility against grave odds and ensured that Kosatka's warship *Shark* was not captured or destroyed by the enemy. Sergeant Cassie Gamba and Corporal Griff Buckland died in the engagement, while Sergeant Victor T. Giddings and Corporal Penny Lamar sustained serious injuries. Corporal Gary Yoshida received a less serious injury. All behaved in exemplary fashion and deserve the highest praise.

Lieutenant Commander Vicki Shen risked herself to join *Shark* and use her expertise to accelerate their propulsion repairs, thus saving *Shark*. The importance of her actions in contributing to victory over the invasion cannot be overstated. She has demonstrated exceptional command skills and personal courage.

The crew of *Saber* carried out their duties with perfect skill and professionalism, never flinching and rising to every challenge. Glenlyon can be justifiably proud of her fleet and the men and women who crew it.

"What do you think they'll do?" Vicki Shen asked him.

Rob spread his hands in the age-old gesture of uncertainty. "Maybe they'll give me a medal, then shoot me."

Mele Darcy nodded. "Or if they're really unhappy, they'll shoot you before they give you the medal."

"I don't want command of *Saber*," Shen said.

"Thanks," Rob said. "You might get it anyway."

"All the personal messages from the officers and crew to their families have been sent right after the official messages were done being transmitted."

"Good. Let me know if there's any trouble receiving the replies. I'm sure there are going to be a lot of happy people in Glenlyon today."

The reply to his official report came nearly half a day after the minimum time required for a message to go from *Saber* to Glenlyon's inhabited world and back again. Whatever it contained, Rob thought, at least they'd taken time to look at his report and discuss things instead of shooting off an immediate response.

He was a bit surprised to see the image of Council President Chisholm appear. Did that imply good or bad news? Chisholm gazed out of Rob's display as if she weren't a recording but someone watching him in real time. In the seconds before she began speaking, Rob unsuccessfully sought clues in Chisholm's eyes and expression for what this message would say.

"Commander Geary, welcome back," Chisholm began, making the *welcome back* sound both glad and accusing. "Needless to say, your return to Glenlyon is a very welcome event. The circumstances regarding your extended delay in returning led to considerable debate among the members of the defense subcommittee."

Chisholm paused as if thinking, but Rob was sure that she'd memorized this speech before beginning. "There was nearly unanimous agreement among the members of the defense subcommittee who are present at Glenlyon that you should be immediately relieved of command for both risking Glenlyon's sole remaining warship on a mission that required very generous interpretation of your orders and for risking Glenlyon itself by leaving it unprotected for so long."

Another pause. Rob waited, nerving himself for whatever came next.

"As I said," Chisholm continued, "the agreement was *nearly* unanimous. I did not agree, and as president, my vote counted for more than the others. My decision was not an easy one. I am worried about your taking it as a sign that adventurism will be rewarded, or at the very least that the government will turn a blind eye to such broad interpretations of the orders given to our military.

"But I'm not a fool. Your reasoning, that the forces arrayed against us could not simultaneously assault Kosatka with such strength and also attack Glenlyon, was sound. Your account of the events at Kosatka, supported by the records from *Saber*'s combat systems that you forwarded, and by the message from First Minister Hofer of Kosatka, show that *Saber*'s presence there, and your decision to act in conjunction with Kosatka's forces, made a decisive difference. I can't ignore that. The forces that would have subdued Kosatka would surely have regrouped and headed next for Glenlyon, vastly overmatching our own defenses. Instead, we now have a firm commitment from Kosatka to contribute forces to our defense if we should call for them.

"There may be a fine line between a hero and a fool,

between someone who accurately perceives what must be done despite the risks and someone who stretches their neck out until it is cut off. Perhaps," Chisholm said, "that line is simply the difference between winning and losing. Had you lost, had *Saber* been destroyed and your efforts to help Kosatka failed, then you, Commander, would be not just relieved of command but, if you had survived, also thrown into the worst prison that Glenlyon could build. But you won. Your decisions were validated by the results. Which means that the forces arrayed against both Glenlyon and Kosatka have been badly hurt, Kosatka is once again deeply in debt to Glenlyon, and other star systems wondering whether to support us will know that Glenlyon will risk everything it has to help its friends."

Chisholm finally smiled, a thin, hard expression. "That last may in the long term prove to be the most important result of all. We're going to need more friends. So, Commander Geary, you've saved Kosatka and your own neck. And there's no doubt that under your command *Saber*'s crew has a . . . fighting spirit . . . that wasn't seen from *Claymore*. Lieutenant Commander Shen's willingness to risk herself speaks well of her devotion to duty. And the actions of Captain Darcy have wiped out any resistance among the council to the idea of a Marine force for Glenlyon.

"That's the good news. Unfortunately, we have to agree with the assessment in the message to our government by the First Minister of Kosatka that simply defeating this attack will not eliminate the danger. Scatha, Apulu, and Turan remain untouched by the aggression they keep launching against others. And that, Commander Geary, is ultimately what decided it for me. Glenlyon is going to need you again. I'm certain of it. And this time I want to ensure that you are there rather than having to beg you to come back to service."

President Chisholm nodded slowly. "Welcome back," she repeated.

The message ended.

Rob was still sitting at his desk, gazing at where the message had been, when Vicki Shen knocked on the hatch.

"Sir?"

He looked over at her. "Bad news. You're not being given command of *Saber*."

She gave him a dumbfounded look, then smiled. "Darn."

Getting to Glenlyon's primary world and docking at the orbital facility seemed to take an eternity. Ninja had sent Rob a reply to his personal message, all smiles. "I knew you were okay," she said. "I knew I'd feel it if something happened to you, and it didn't. I can't wait to see you in person again."

He let most of the crew off the ship first, waiting and thanking them for the jobs they'd done as they rushed off to greet family members, loved ones, and friends, or for those unattached to simply head for the nearest bar before it got too busy.

Rob finally followed, walking off *Saber*'s quarterdeck and through the access tube to the facility and out into the entry hall, where sailors and families were mingling in a riot of almost feverish celebration.

Life was a truly amazing thing. Sometimes it was too easy to forget that. But not right now.

He saw Ninja, his heart feeling as if it stopped for a few seconds. She looked his way, smiling, and his heart started again. Somehow he was next to her and she was in his arms and they were kissing and Little Ninja ran up to wrap her arms around Rob's leg and the world that had felt askew for months was suddenly back just as it should be. He'd been briefly startled to see how much larger Ninja was. Despite counting the days and the weeks, it wasn't until he saw how much farther along her pregnancy was that the passage of time really hit, how long it had been that he'd been away from home.

She finally broke the kiss, smiling at him. "Hey, sailor. New in town?"

"And looking for a place to shack up tonight," Rob said, grinning.

"I know a place. Mele! Come here, girl!"

Rob stood a little back as Ninja embraced Mele. "Thanks for bringing him back, Mele."

"I did promise," Mele said.

"Hey, Little Ninja, look who's here!"

Little Ninja broke her lock on Rob's leg to race to Mele. "Aunt Mele! OORAH!"

Ninja rubbed her ear at the noise. "She's been practicing for when you got back."

"Oorah!" Mele agreed with a laugh as she picked up Rob's daughter. "How's my little Marine?"

Rob watched them. "Mele, at times like this I always feel a bit sad that you don't have a family or other loved ones to greet you."

"Who says I don't have a family?" Mele chided Rob. "Hey, Little Ninja, who am I?"

"Aunt Mele!"

"Are we family?"

"OORAH!"

"I stand corrected," Rob said. "How about coming for dinner tonight?"

Mele shook her head, putting down Little Ninja. "I imagine you and Ninja have a few things to catch up on. How about tomorrow? Tonight I'm going to meet my guys at the bar so we can drink farewells to our missing friends. That's one tradition I'm going to set in stone."

Ninja nodded, her expression serious. "Make one round on us. And thank you again."

Mele smiled and nodded in return. "Thank your guy there. He came through for me, speaking of traditions. The fleet's always there for the Marines, right?"

"Right," Rob said, "and the Marines are always there for the fleet."

"Be careful tonight," Ninja added. "I hear that the new security chief here is pretty tough on rowdy parties in bars."

"Now you made it a dare," Mele pretended to complain.

"See you around." Raising her voice so it filled the room, she called out, "Marines! Muster in the Planet View Bar at Eighteen Hundred! Farewell to absent friends!"

"Eighteen hundred, Planet View Bar!" the reply thundered back from various places.

Rob and Ninja walked back toward their home, Rob carrying their daughter.

"How long will you be here?" Ninja asked in a low voice.

"Awhile," Rob said. "There's plenty of damage to be repaired on *Saber*. The number one pulse particle beam projector will need to be completely replaced. And . . . we're going to need some replacement crew."

"That won't be a problem," Ninja advised him. "Most of the survivors from the *Claymore* will be beating down your door to get a job on *Saber*."

"I don't think we're going to be leaving Glenlyon again. Not anytime soon," Rob said. "If that destroyer made it back to Apulu, they'll know Glenlyon played a role in their defeat at Kosatka."

"And they'll come here to get revenge."

"They took some losses," Rob said. "It'll take them a while to hit us again. If Leigh Camagan can get us some extra help before then, things might not be that bad."

"Did I mention that in his message to the government that guy Hofer from Kosatka attached copies of a bunch of encrypted files they'd captured from the guys who invaded them? And that the government has asked a certain specialist to see if she can break them?"

"Have you had any luck so far?" Rob asked, curious but also worried about what the answer might be.

"A bit." Ninja jogged her head upward, toward space. "They are planning to hit us again, and I think there are some data in there on how many warships they'll have left after the fight at Kosatka. We may not have all that much time."

"I'm surprised you're not more worried about that."

"I'm great at hiding my feelings. Remember how long it took you to figure out I was interested in you? But as long as you're here, we'll handle whatever comes next when it comes. And I hear you made some new friends out there."

"I guess. Kosatka finally committed to a formal defense agreement with us."

Ninja gave him an inquisitive look. "Did I also hear you met Salomon out there? From Alfar?"

"You knew Salomon?"

"Met her a couple of times at, um, disciplinary proceedings before I got kicked out of the fleet. Tough but fair. How's she doing?"

Rob looked away from Ninja, his thoughts in turmoil. "She's dead. Died fighting the invasion. Along with . . . I lost some more people, Ninja."

Little Ninja squirmed wordlessly in his arms, sensing his distress. Ninja's voice went soft and low. "I know."

"So did Mele. I wish I could handle it as well as she does."

"Mele feels it as badly as you do. She just doesn't show it the same way."

"I don't want to do this."

Ninja stopped walking, holding him. "Hey. If you don't do this, who's going to save us next time?"

"Ninja . . ."

"I *know*."

"What if Little Ninja does decide to become a Marine? What if our son decides to join Glenlyon's fleet?"

She laughed. "It's not like there's this long tradition in our families of military service, Rob. But if they do, there are worse ways to make a living, right?"

"But—"

"Hey. That's tomorrow. So is whatever else Scatha and its ugly friends are planning. Tonight, you're back. Can we have one night? Welcome home, sailor."

Ron smiled at her, trying not to think about what might happen next, about what Scatha might do when they learned from that destroyer that Glenlyon had frustrated their designs at Kosatka. A vast shadow loomed over tomorrow.

Rob's comm pad chimed. He looked down at it, seeing a short text message from Mele Darcy. TELL NINJA I'VE GOT YOUR BACK, SPACE SQUID.

He tapped a quick reply. SHE KNOWS. SAME HERE.

Plus Ninja by his side, the officers and crew of *Saber*, the people like Commander Derian, whom he'd supported in the fighting at Kosatka, whatever Leigh Camagan managed to accomplish . . .

He couldn't do it alone, but he wasn't alone. And now neither was Glenlyon.

Read on for an exciting excerpt from
the next book in The Genesis Fleet series

TRIUMPHANT

by Jack Campbell

Available May 2019 from Ace

The city of Ani, dead before it had been officially born, felt ghostlier than usual this night under the slowly shifting light of Kosatka's primary moon. Carmen Ochoa eased carefully among the deserted buildings constructed to house families and businesses that hadn't appeared before the foreign invaders who called themselves "rebels" infested the area.

She paused before entering an area scarred by war, the wide street half-blocked by the front portion of a tall structure that had collapsed when artillery fire tore into it. The rubble provided perfect cover for ambushers, while also forcing anyone traveling this way to divert their path into the open for a short space. Carmen knelt down in the shadow of an intact building, using the scope of her high-powered rifle to study the path ahead. Given time, the multispectral sensors in that scope could identify just about any threat.

The silent, empty city where unseen dangers lurked in the night reminded Carmen of a book she'd once read, a story set on a world called Barsoom that held many ancient, abandoned cities. It'd been a shock to realize that Barsoom was supposed to be Mars, Carmen's childhood home. The romantic, crumbling glory of Barsoom's lost cities had nothing in common with the squalid and ugly slums of Mars that Carmen had known, except perhaps for the fact that both contained endless threats to the life and freedom of anyone who lived there, and perhaps also that both were places where dreams of a brighter future had long since died.

Someone was trying to turn the recently settled world of Kosatka into such a place. Carmen wasn't going to allow that.

The invaders had been pushed out of the other two cities that Kosatka boasted, though both Lodz and Drava had taken a lot of damage as the price of that victory. The human cost had also been painful. But as long as the invaders continued to maintain a toehold on this world around and in Ani, the risk of the next attack succeeding remained too high, and no one knew if the star systems that had attacked Kosatka would return anytime soon with another invasion fleet. The more that could be learned about the military resources of Scatha, Apulu, and Turan Star Systems, and the more the area controlled by the remaining invaders could be shrunk and their numbers reduced, the better chance Kosatka would have.

Which was why she was here tonight, slinking through the shadows of an empty city, rather than back in Lodz with her new husband Dominic.

Satisfied that no dangers awaited, Carmen moved cautiously forward once more. The remaining invaders had lost a lot of equipment, especially the sort of sensors that could have spotted infiltrators such as her, and the sort of mines and automated defenses that could have threatened her. But Carmen kept her progress slow and careful as she flitted through empty buildings whose ground-floor doors and windows had been blown out or forced open during past fighting. She passed like a ghost through what would have been the large lobby of an apartment building, around the edges of what could have become a corner office or small shop, stepping over drifts of dirt on the floors in which weeds were striving to take root, past the empty maws of inner doorways and unfinished ventilation ducts. In the darkness those openings gaped with a deeper gloom that seemed somehow sinister, as if enemies lurked within, watching and waiting. But her sensors detected nothing, so Carmen kept moving.

Her first warning that she'd finally reached an enemy perimeter came when her scope alerted her to energy use and body heat ahead. Sentries, their gear battered enough that it could no longer offer the concealment it once had. The concealment that Carmen's outfit still had and kept them from detecting her.

Carmen waited, watching through her scope, long enough to spot the nearest sentries when they moved. Their camo clothing matched itself to the buildings and wreckage, but movement still showed against the otherwise deserted surroundings.

Finally, she slid warily through the nearest buildings and into a small park, the trees and bushes planted there nearly four years ago grown into a stunted and tangled mass. As Carmen had expected, the invaders had counted on anyone entering that to make enough noise to be heard, but she'd learned how to move slowly and cautiously enough to pass through such obstacles. She kept her eyes open and her scope active, spotting a single trip wire in time to avoid stumbling into it, and stepping carefully past it.

Finally, Carmen reached a position where she could lie next to a tree, gazing toward a building where several individuals were visible as shadows through the shattered windows. She focused on them, zooming in, but the features remained vague and the lips too ill defined for the scope to be able to read the words they spoke. There were enough other invaders present to make any attempt to get closer far too dangerous. The signal pickup on her scope remained quiet, showing that these invaders weren't using any electronic communications that didn't depend on fiber-optic landlines.

That left little chance of any intelligence collection. But she'd already pinpointed this enemy-held area. One more task and she could call in a strike. Carmen watched, patient and remorseless, until she could be sure which of the figures was in charge by the way the others acted.

Finally, she aimed her rifle up toward the satellites orbiting the planet, all controlled by Kosatka's own government, and used the high-gain transmitter in her scope to send a tight burst signal that identified the invaders' location, as well as a requested time for the strike.

Then she had to wait a little longer, the night quiet about her, occasional movements of enemy soldiers visible, the group inside the building still talking, the timer on her scope counting down. As the numbers dwindled to less than a minute, Carmen zoomed in on the leader she'd identified, aimed with infinite care, and then fired, the noise of the shot shattering the calm of the night.

Her target jolted away and fell as the high-powered bullet slammed into them, the others around their leader scattering and diving for cover.

Carmen was already moving, no longer trying to remain silent, moving fast to put distance between herself and the invaders, hearing alerts sounding behind her, a few shots tearing through the bushes around her. As she had wanted, the invaders had all taken cover, lying low, their attention fixed on the buildings around them.

The strike came down.

It had been dropped by *Shark*, Kosatka's remaining destroyer. Streamlined, solid metal projectiles, released from low orbit on precise trajectories, falling for hundreds of kilometers, gaining energy as they fell. Carmen saw multiple sudden shadows spring to life in front of her as the projectiles drew bright lines of light through the night sky behind her, a display beautiful to anyone far enough away but terrifying to those at the aim points. The invaders, belatedly realizing the strike was inbound, might be springing to their feet to flee, or might be cowering helplessly on the ground.

It didn't matter what they were doing, because anything they did was too late now. Carmen felt her lips pulling back in a snarl of anticipation as she ran, her breath rushing between her teeth.

The ground beneath Carmen shook as the projectiles slammed to the surface, releasing their accumulated energy, tearing apart anything they struck, cratering the soil, blowing apart buildings. In a moment of insane fury, a small portion of the dead city of Ani ceased to exist.

Carmen dropped to the ground as pieces of debris whipped past above her. A large piece of wreckage rocked the ground as it plummeted down a few meters to one side. She stared at it, feeling her heart pound in belated reaction to how close death had come that time. The roar of destruction blanketed all other sounds, momentarily deafening Carmen as she scrambled back to her feet and ran once more.

As the multiple roars of the impacting projectiles faded, Carmen heard the rumble of buildings collapsing and felt the rush of air and dust at her back.

Part of Ani was gone, but so were the invaders who'd sheltered there. A little more of Kosatka was free.

Carmen didn't linger near the site of the strike, moving a few kilometers through the dark and once-more-silent city before risking sending out a full report, her scope relaying the data and video it had recorded.

Eventually, she reached the building where the unit she was with had holed up. Outwardly, it looked as deserted and dead as the rest of the city. But sentries with weapons at the ready greeted Carmen in the outer rooms. A large inner room, shielded from the outside, held twenty men and women as well as their equipment. Inside, most wore only T-shirts and trousers, their camo, personal weapons, and body armor (if they had any), placed on the floor beside where they sat or lay on the floor. Officially, those twenty and the five sentries on watch outside made up the Third Company of the Second Regiment of the First Brigade of Kosatka's planetary militia. The unit had been one hundred strong before the invaders landed, made up mostly of people who'd come to Kosatka to start new lives in a wide variety of occupations but had found themselves forced to defend their new homes. Some of those hundred had been called back for critical jobs, others for family emergencies, others wounded. The rest had died. Those remaining wore the weary, fatalistic expressions of men and women who were going to see their job through but didn't expect to be there when victory finally came. If it ever did.

Carmen received nods of recognition as she entered, feeling a small rush of pleasure at being accepted as one of them. She'd spent a long time feeling alone. Carmen felt herself finally relaxing, exchanging greetings with her comrades, peeling off her camo, and gratefully accepting a cup of coffee.

"Kosatka is short on a lot of things, but they make sure we always have coffee," Captain Devish said as he crouched down beside her. "It's lousy coffee, but it's here."

"There's no more coffee in Drava or Lodz," Carmen told him. "What's left on the planet is being sent to the fighters here around Ani."

"I hope the planet gets more shipments in before it all runs out. You did a good job, Carmen."

"Thanks," she said. "What's the assessment?"

"No signs of life. The strike wiped out that invader strongpoint." Captain Devish, among the few professional soldiers in the unit, had come to Kosatka from Brahma, one of the Old Colonies. When asked, he always gave his reason for emigrating as "I was bored." He certainly wasn't bored now.

"Good." Carmen took a drink of the hot and bitter coffee, feeling exhausted. "Did my report make it through?"

"Yeah. Clean upload." Devish gave her a searching glance. "I heard you worked for Earth government once."

"Yeah. After I got off Mars." She didn't try to hide her origins anymore. People could accept her or reject her. Carmen no longer cared. "I worked in Albuquerque."

"Albuquerque? What was that like?"

"Better than Mars."

Devish grinned. "What'd you do?"

"I was in the Conflict Resolution Office," Carmen said.

"Working to find legal and peaceful resolutions for conflicts and disputes on Earth and all settled worlds."

"You're kidding." Devish shook his head. "How effective was that?"

"It worked when people believed in it. When they stopped believing, stopped caring, it didn't work. I came out here to try to make people believe in that kind of thing again. Because what's happening to Kosatka shouldn't be happening anywhere." Carmen touched her rifle. "That's why I'm using this now. But someday we need to get back to depending on laws for our protection."

"That'd be nice," Devish said, not quite hiding his skepticism that such a day would ever come. "Anyway, you can relax. We've been ordered to stay under cover through daylight today, so there won't be any more action until nightfall."

Finishing the coffee, Carmen went into a side room for some privacy and uplinked to Kosatka's planetary net using landline relays to keep anyone from being able to tell where her signal was coming from. Fiber cables run to the roofs of other buildings linked them to antennas communicating to the satellites above.

This room, like most rooms in Ani, lacked furniture, so she sat on the floor, settling down with her back against the wall behind her. Carmen set her comm pad down long enough to comb her hands through her hair and rub her face so she wouldn't look like someone who'd just spent the night crawling through a dead city. Fixing a smile on her face, Carmen tapped a link.

After a long moment, the image of Dominic Desjani appeared. His face still bore signs of the strain of the injuries that kept him mostly confined to bed. "Hey, Red," he said, smiling. Red, the common slur aimed at those from Mars, had somehow become an affectionate nickname by Dominic for her, one she loved hearing from him. "How are you?"

"Working late," Carmen said. "Sorry."

"I never knew collecting intelligence was so stressful."

"Yeah, well, fieldwork. You know." She didn't want to

lie to him, but she also didn't want to admit to all of the risks she was running. "How's the leg?"

"The one that's missing? Still gone." Dominic gestured vaguely. "I'm told maybe another month before I get a prosthetic. There's a big backup manufacturing them for all the wounded, and I'm sort of low on the priority scale."

"What about regeneration? Weren't they looking at a regrow for you?" Carmen asked.

"Still looking." Dominic smiled. "I can wait. There are others who need stuff grown back worse than I do."

"As long as you're okay," Carmen said.

"What have you actually been doing, Red?"

She sighed. "Collecting intelligence."

"That covers a lot of different ground. You look pretty worn out."

"I'm doing my part, Domi."

He stayed silent, unhappy, his eyes on her.

"I'm going to be back in Lodz in a few days," Carmen added, trying to change the subject. "What do you want to do?"

Dominic shook his head, still gloomy. "Maybe have some more honeymoon."

"That'd be nice. Domi, I'm sorry. You know who I am. You knew what you were getting when you asked me to marry you. I'm a Red."

"You came from Mars. But you're not like those gangsters fighting for the invaders." Dominic looked away. "You are a fighter. I knew that, yeah. Maybe someday you'll tell me everything you did on Mars. Everything you did to get off that hellhole of a planet."

"You don't want to know, Domi." Carmen forced another smile. "What matters is that I made it here and found you. Hey, estimates are that the invaders are down to a couple of thousand in the areas of Ani they still occupy and the land just outside the city. They're short on everything, and they lost another senior leader tonight. They could crack at any time."

He nodded, not seeming happy at the news. "How'd you hear about them losing a leader?"

Stupid. Why had she said that? "Uh . . ."

"That's what I thought. Red—"

"Don't. Or I'll bring up the subject of you leaving your police job to become an officer in the militia."

Dominic eyed her, then smiled. "We're two of a kind, huh? Well motivated. Not too smart."

"Maybe too smart for our own good," Carmen admitted.

"Somebody has to do it. Any estimates on when the next invasion force will show up?"

"No. We have no idea what Scatha, Apulu, and Turan might have left."

"We know what we have left." Dominic pointed outward. "One warship, *Shark*. And a planetary militia that's low on supplies, weapons, and people."

Carmen nodded. "Lochan went for help, remember? And we're formally allied with Glenlyon now. Kosatka's not alone anymore."

"It still feels pretty alone," Dominic said. He laughed, the sound more bitter than humorous. "I was told that if another invasion fleet jumps into the star system, I'll be jumped up the priority list for a smart prosthetic so I'll be combat capable again. Nice of them, huh?"

"Yeah. Nice." Carmen had to look away this time, remembering seeing Dominic wounded, his lower leg gone, awaiting evacuation. For a moment her sight of the empty room about her was overlaid by her memories of the dimly lit basement where she'd found Dominic during the battle for Lodz, the stench of blood in the air, tired medics doing all they could, Domi himself sedated, her guts churning with fear that he might not make it. It took a major effort to wrench her thoughts away from that, to compose herself enough to smile at him once more. "I'll see you in a couple of days."

After the call ended she sat on the floor, gazing out at the vacant room, wondering what would happen and how long she and Dominic might have left together. *Please don't let us down, Lochan.*